Praise for the novels of

ERICA SPINDLER

"Spindler's latest moves fast and takes no prisoners. An intriguing look into the twisted mind of someone for whom murder is simply a business."
—*Publishers Weekly* on *Cause for Alarm*

"If you enjoy the suspense of the classic 'woman in jeopardy' mystery, *See Jane Die* makes perfect beach reading."
—*Cleveland Plain Dealer*

"Creepy and compelling, *In Silence* is a real page-turner."
—*New Orleans Times-Picayune*

"Fans of Erica Spindler know that, in her hands, even an old idea gets a new spin. That's what makes *In Silence* her best to date."
—*Globe and Mail*

"A classic confrontation between good and evil."
—*Publishers Weekly* on *Dead Run*

"Solid characters, a great setting and a really good plot."
—*Globe and Mail* on *Dead Run*

All Fall Down is "shocking, emotional, an engrossing read."
—*New York Times* bestselling author Stella Cameron

"A compelling tale of kinky sex and murder."
—*Publishers Weekly* on *Shocking Pink*

Shocking Pink is "one of the best, most frightening novels of the year."
—*Painted Rock Reviews*

Dear Reader,

If you've read the novel's back cover or first page, you know that *Killer Takes All* is set in my beautiful New Orleans. When I wrote this story, Hurricane Katrina was only a "worst-case scenario" people talked about. No longer. Many of the places I've depicted in this novel—and others I've written—are changed now. Some are gone, the colorful people who flavored those places with them.

Those of you who have read my stories before know that with each book, I offer a giveaway—or as we say here in The Big Easy, "lagniappe" (a little something extra!). This year I wanted to do something special for you—and the city I love. For every sales receipt you send me* before August 1, 2006, from the purchase of one of my paperback novels, I'll donate 5 percent of the sales price (excluding taxes) on that book toward rebuilding New Orleans. In addition, I'll send you a personalized thank-you and a specially designed commemorative magnet.

In closing, I hope you'll look for *Copycat*, out in hardcover June, 2006. Be sure to check www.ericaspindler.com for the really fun giveaway I'm offering with it!

Until next time, best wishes,

Erica Spindler

Please send receipts to:
P.O. Box 8556
Mandeville, LA 70470-8556

*Offer good in U.S. and Canada only and only while supplies last. Original receipts must be received by August 1, 2006. No used books sales accepted. Magnets will be mailed after September 1, 2006. Please allow four to six weeks from this date for delivery of magnet. MIRA Books is not connected or affiliated with this promotion.

ERICA
SPINDLER

KILLER TAKES ALL

MIRA®

ISBN 0-7783-2305-6

KILLER TAKES ALL

Copyright © 2005 by Erica Spindler.

www.MIRABooks.com

Printed in U.S.A.

AUTHOR'S NOTE

Thanks to all who helped in the completion of
Killer Takes All, giving generously and enthusiastically of
their time and expertise. I'd especially like to acknowledge:

Michele Kraus, owner of Gamer's Conclave, for making
sense of the world of role-playing games. Your patience with
this novice was astounding; thank you!

Judy Midgley, CRS Coldwell Banker Realty, Carmel-by-
the-Sea, California, for taking an entire day to show me
properties from Carmel-by-the-Sea to Monterey. It was as fun
as it was informative! Thanks, Judy!

Warren "Pete" Poitras, Detective Sergeant, City of Carmel-by-
the-Sea Police Department, for the time, tour and insights;
all were highly appreciated.

Thanks also to Frank Minyard, M.D., Orleans Parish
Coroner; Colonel Mary Baldwin Kennedy, Director of
Communications, Orleans Parish Criminal Sheriff's Office;
NOPD Captain Roy Shakelford; Jason Blitz, Munchen Motors
and John Lord, Jr., Arms Merchant, LLC.

In addition, thanks to those who make every day a good
day: my agent Evan Marshall, my editor Dianne Moggy and
the entire MIRA crew, my assistants Rajean Schulze and
Kari Williams. And last but always first, my family and my
God.

Also by ERICA SPINDLER

CHAPTER
1

Monday, February 28, 2005
1:30 a.m.
New Orleans, Louisiana

Stacy Killian opened her eyes, fully awake. The sound that had awakened her came again.

Pop. Pop.

Gunshots.

She sat up and, in one fluid movement, swung her legs over the side of the bed and went for the Glock .40 that waited in the drawer of her nightstand. Ten years of police work had conditioned her to react to that particular sound without hesitation.

Stacy checked the gun's magazine, crossed to the window and inched aside the drape. The moon illuminated the deserted yard. Several spindly trees, dilapidated swing set, dog pen minus Caesar, her neighbor Cassie's Labrador retriever puppy.

No sound. No movement.

Padding silently on bare feet, Stacy made her way out of the bedroom, into the adjoining study, weapon out. She rented one half of a hundred-year-old shotgun double, a style of home made popular in the era before air-conditioning.

Stacy swung left, then right, taking in every detail: the stacks of research books for the paper she was writing on Shelley's "Mont Blanc," her open laptop computer, the half-drunk bottle of cheap red wine. The shadows. Their depth, stillness.

As she expected, each room in the house proved a repeat of the last. The sound that had awakened her had not come from inside her apartment.

She reached the front door, eased it open and stepped out onto the front porch. The sagging wood creaked beneath her feet, the only sound on the otherwise deserted street. She shivered as the wet, chilly night enveloped her.

The neighborhood appeared to be asleep. Few lights shone from windows or porches. Stacy scanned the street. She noted several unfamiliar vehicles, which wasn't unusual for an area inhabited mostly by university students. All the vehicles appeared empty.

Stacy stood in the shadow of her front door, listening to the silence. Suddenly, from nearby, came the sound of a trash barrel toppling over. Laughter followed. Kids, she realized. Practicing the urban equivalent of cow tipping.

She frowned. Could that have been the sound that awakened her? Altered by sleep and instincts she no longer trusted?

A year ago such a thought wouldn't have crossed her mind. But a year ago she'd been a cop, a homicide detective with the Dallas P.D. She'd yet to endure the betrayal that had not only stripped her of her confidence but had galvanized her to act on her growing dissatisfaction with her life and job.

Stacy gripped the Glock firmly. She was already freezing her ass off, she might as well take this thing to its conclusion. She slipped into her muddy gardening clogs that were perched on a rack by the door. She made her way across the porch and down the steps to her side yard. Circling around to the back-yard, she acknowledged that nothing appeared out of order.

Her hands shook. She fought the panic wanting to rise up in her. The fear that she had lost it, and gone totally around the bend.

This had happened before. Twice. The first time just after she moved in. She'd awakened to what she thought were shots fired and had roused all her neighbors within earshot.

And those times, like now, she'd uncovered nothing but a silent, sleeping street. The false alarm had not ingratiated her to her new neighbors. Most had been understandably pissed off.

But not Cassie. Instead, the other woman had invited her in for hot chocolate.

Stacy shifted her gaze to Cassie's side of the double, to the light that shone from one of the rear windows.

She stared at the lit window, head filling with the memory

of the sound that had awakened her. The shots had been too loud to have come from anywhere but right next door.

Why hadn't she realized that right away?

Overcome with a feeling of dread, she ran for Cassie's porch stairs. She reached them, stumbled and righted herself, a dozen different reassurances racing through her head: the sound had been a figment of her subconscious; seriously sleep deprived, she was imagining things; Cassie was in a deep, peaceful sleep.

She reached her friend's door and pounded on it. She waited, then pounded again. "Cassie!" she called. "It's Stacy. Open up!"

When the other woman didn't respond, she grabbed the knob and twisted.

The door opened.

Gripping the Glock with both hands, she nudged the door open with her foot and stepped inside. Absolute quiet greeted her.

She called out again, hearing the hopeful note in her voice. The quiver of fear.

Even as she told herself her mind was playing tricks on her, she saw that it wasn't.

Cassie lay facedown on the living room floor, half on and half off the oval rag rug. A large, dark stain haloed her body. Blood, Stacy acknowledged. A lot of blood.

Stacy began to tremble. Swallowing hard, she worked to quell the reaction. To step outside herself. Think like a cop.

She crossed to her friend. She squatted beside her, feeling

herself slipping into professional mode. Separating herself from what had happened, who it had happened to.

She checked Cassie's wrist for a pulse. When she found none, she moved her gaze over the body. It looked as if Cassie had been shot twice, once between the shoulder blades, the other in the back of the head. What was left of her blond, curly bob was matted with blood. She was fully dressed: denims, cloud-blue T-shirt, Birkenstocks. Stacy recognized the shirt; it was one of Cassie's favorites. From memory she knew the front read: Dream. Love. Live.

Tears choked her; Stacy fought them. Crying wouldn't help her friend. But keeping her cool just might help catch her killer.

A sound came from the back of the apartment.

Beth.

Or the killer.

Stacy firmed her grip on the Glock, though her hands shook. Heart thumping, she stood and, as quietly as possible, inched deeper into the apartment.

She found Beth in the doorway to the second bedroom. Unlike the other woman, Beth lay on her back, her eyes open, vacant. She wore pink cotton pajamas, patterned with gray-and-white kittens.

She'd also been shot. Twice in the chest.

Quickly, careful not to disturb any evidence, Stacy checked the woman's pulse. As with Cassie, she found none.

She straightened, then swung in the direction from which the sound had come.

Whining, she realized. A snuffling at the bathroom door. *Caesar*.

She made for the bathroom, softly calling the dog's name. He responded with a yip and she carefully eased the door open. The Lab lunged at her feet, gratefully whining.

As she scooped the squirming puppy up, she saw that he had messed on the floor. How long had he been locked up? she wondered. Had Cassie done it? Or her killer? And why? Cassie crated the dog at night and when she wasn't home.

Puppy tucked under her arm, Stacy made a quick but thorough search of the apartment to ensure the shooter was gone, though her gut told her he was.

She would guess he got out in the few minutes it had taken her to make her way from her own bedroom to the front porch. She hadn't heard a car door slam or an engine start, which could mean he'd escaped on foot—or nothing at all.

She needed to call 911, but was loath to hand the investigation over before she absorbed all she could of the crime scene. She glanced at her watch. A 911 homicide call would yield an immediate cruiser if one was in the area. Three minutes or less from the time dispatch received the call, she guessed, turning back to the scene. If not, she could be looking at fifteen minutes.

Judging by what she saw, Stacy felt certain Cassie had been killed first, Beth second. Beth had probably heard the first two shots and gotten out of bed to see what was happening. She wouldn't have immediately recognized the sound as a gun discharging. And even if she had suspected gunshots, she would have convinced herself otherwise.

That explained the phone, untouched, on the nightstand by the bed. Stacy crossed to it and, using the edge of her pajama top, picked up the receiver. The dial tone buzzed reassuringly in her ear.

Stacy ran through the possibilities. The place didn't appear to have been robbed. The door had been unlocked, not broken into. Cassie had invited the killer inside. He—or she—was a friend or an acquaintance. Someone she had been expecting. Or someone she knew. Perhaps the killer had asked her to lock up the dog?

Tucking her questions away for later, she dialed 911. "Double homicide," she said to the operator, voice shaking. "1174 City Park Avenue." And then, cuddling Caesar to her chest, Stacy sat on the floor and cried.

CHAPTER
2

Monday, February 28, 2005
1:50 a.m.

Detective Spencer Malone drew his 1977, cherry-red, mint-condition Chevy Camaro to a stop in front of the City Park neighborhood double. His older brother John had bought the car new. It had been his baby, his pride and joy until he'd gotten married and had babies to tote to and from daycare and birthday parties.

Now the Camaro was Spencer's pride and joy.

Spencer shifted into Park and peered through the windshield at the double. The first officers had secured the scene; yellow crime-scene tape stretched across the slightly sagging front porch. One of the officers stood just beyond, signing in those who arrived, noting the time of their entrance.

Spencer narrowed his eyes, recognizing the officer as a third-year rookie and one of his staunchest accusers.

Connelly. The prick.

Spencer took in a deep breath, working to control his temper, the short fuse that had gotten him in too many brawls to count. The hot head that had held him back professionally, that had contributed to the ease with which everyone had bought into the accusations that had almost ended his career.

Hot tempered *and* a major league fuckup. An ugly combination.

He shook the thoughts off. This scene was his. He was lead man. He wasn't going to screw it up.

Spencer opened the car door and climbed out just as Detective Tony Sciame wheeled to a stop in front of the double. In the New Orleans Police Force, detectives didn't have set partners, per se, they worked a rotation. When a case came in, whoever was next in line got it. That detective chose another to assist, and the factors involved in that choice were availability, experience and friendship.

Most of the guys tended to find someone they clicked with, a kind of symbiotic "partnership." For a number of reasons, he and Tony worked well together, filling in the other's blanks, so to speak.

Spencer had a hell of a lot more blanks to fill than Tony did.

A thirty-year veteran of the force, twenty-five of it in Homicide, Tony was an old-timer. Happily married for thirty-two years—and a pound overweight for each of those years—he had four kids, one grown and on his own, one still at home, and two at Louisiana State University in Baton Rouge, one mortgage and a scruffy dog named Frodo.

Although their partnership was new, they'd already been likened to Mutt and Jeff, Frick and Frack, and Laurel and Hardy. Spencer preferred a Gibson and Glover comparison—with him being the good-looking, renegade Mel Gibson character—but their fellow officers weren't going for it.

"Yo, Slick," Tony said.

"Pasta Man."

Spencer liked to rag Tony about his pasta gut; his partner returned the favor by addressing him as Slick, Junior or Hotshot. Never mind that Spencer, at thirty-one and a nine-year veteran of the force, was neither rookie nor kid, he was new both to rank of detective and to Homicide, which in the culture of the NOPD made him a mark for ribbing.

The other man laughed and patted his middle. "You're just jealous."

"Whatever you need to tell yourself." Spencer motioned to the crime-scene van. "Techs beat us to the scene."

"Eager-beaver assholes."

They fell into step together. Tony squinted up at the starless sky. "I'm getting too old for this shit. Call caught me and Betty in the middle of busting our youngest for staying out past curfew."

"Poor Carly."

"My ass. That girl's a menace. Four kids and the last one is hell on wheels. See this?" He indicated the nearly bald top of his head. "They've all contributed, but Carly… Just wait, you'll see."

Spencer laughed. "I grew up with six siblings. I know what kids are like. That's why I'm not having any."

"Whatever *you* need to tell yourself. By the way, what was her name?"

"Whose?"

"Tonight's date."

Truth was, he'd been out with his brothers Percy and Patrick. They'd had a couple of beers and a burger at Shannon's Tavern. The closest he'd gotten to scoring was sinking the eight ball in the corner pocket to defeat Patrick, the family pool shark.

But Tony didn't want to hear that. The Malone brothers were legends in the NOPD. Handsome, hard-partying hot-heads with reputations as lady-killers.

"I don't kiss and tell, partner."

They reached Connelly. Spencer met his eyes and it all came rushing back. He'd been working the Fifth District Detective Investigative Unit, in charge of a kitty of informant money. Fifteen hundred bucks, not that much in today's world. But enough to be raked over the coals when it turned up missing. Suspended without pay, charged, then indicted.

Charges had been dropped, his name cleared. Turned out Lieutenant Moran, his immediate superior and the one who had placed the kitty in his care, had set him up. Because he "trusted him." Because he believed "he was up to the responsibility" even though he'd only worked DIU six months.

More like, Moran believed Spencer was a patsy.

If it hadn't been for his family refusing to accept his guilt, the bastard would have gotten away with it. If Spencer had been found guilty, not only would he have been kicked off the force, he would have done jail time.

As it was, he'd lost a year and a half of his life.

Thinking about it still chapped his ass. Remembering how many of his brothers in arms had turned against him—including this little weasel—infuriated him. Up until then, he had thought of the NOPD as his extended family, his fellow officers as his brothers and sisters.

And until then, life had been one big party. *Laissez les bon temps rouler,* New Orleans-style.

Lieutenant Moran had changed all that. The man had made his life a living hell; he'd destroyed Spencer's illusions about the force and about being a cop.

The parties weren't as much fun now. He saw the consequences of his actions.

To keep Spencer from suing, the department had reinstated him with back pay and bumped him up to ISD.

Investigative Support Division. His dream job.

In the late nineties the department had decentralized, taking detective units, such as Homicide and Vice, out of headquarters and positioning them in the eight district stations throughout the city. They bundled them into a multitask Detective Investigative Unit. The detectives in DIU didn't specialize; they handled everything from burglary to vice to rubber-stamp homicides.

However, for the top homicide detectives—the ones with the most experience and training, the cream of the crop—

they'd created ISD. Located in headquarters, they handled cold-case homicides—ones unsolved after a year—and all the juicy stuff as well: sex crimes, serial murders, child abductions.

Some touted decentralization a huge success. Some called it an embarrassing failure—especially in terms of homicide. In the end, one thing was certain, it saved the department money.

Spencer had accepted the department's obvious bribe because he was a cop. More than a job, it was *who* he was. He'd never considered being anything else. How could he have? Police work was in his blood. His father, uncle and aunt were all cops. So were several cousins and all but two of his siblings. His brother Quentin had left the force after sixteen years to study law. Even so, he hadn't strayed far from the family business. A prosecutor with the Orleans Parish D.A., he helped convict the guys the other Malones busted.

"Hello, Connelly," Spencer said tightly. "Here I am, back from the dead. Surprised?"

The other officer shifted his gaze. "I don't know what you mean, Detective."

"My ass." He leaned toward the other man. "You going to have a problem working with me?"

The officer took a step backward. "No problem. No, sir."

"Good thing. Because I'm here to stay."

"Yes, sir."

"What've we got?"

"Double homicide." The rookie's voice shook slightly. "Both female. UNO students." He glanced at his notes. "Cassie Finch and Beth Wagner. Neighbor there called it in. Name's Stacy Killian."

Spencer glanced in the direction he indicated. A young woman, cradling a sleeping puppy in her arms, stood on the porch. Tall, blond and, from what he could see, attractive. It looked as if she was wearing pajamas under her denim jacket. "What's her story?"

"Thought she heard gunshots and went to investigate."

"Now, there was an intelligent move." Spencer shook his head in disgust. "Civilians."

They started toward the porch. Tony angled him a glance. "Way to set the record, Slick. Stupid little prick."

Tony had never succumbed to the Malone bashing that had become the favorite pastime of many in the NOPD. He'd stood by Spencer and the entire Malone clan's belief in Spencer's innocence. That hadn't always been easy, Spencer knew, particularly when the "evidence" had begun to stack up.

There were some who still didn't buy Spencer's innocence—or Lieutenant Moran's guilt. Despite the department's reinstatement or Moran's confession and suicide. They figured the Malone family had "fixed" it somehow, used their considerable influence within the department to make it all go away.

It pissed him off. Spencer hated that he had been involved, albeit innocently, in the sullying of his family's reputation, hated the speculative glances, the whispers.

"It'll get better," Tony murmured, as if reading his mind. "Cops' memories aren't that good. Lead poisoning, in my humble opinion."

"You think?" Spencer grinned at him as they climbed the steps. "I was leaning toward excessive exposure to blue dye."

They crossed the porch. He was aware of the neighbor's gaze on him; he didn't meet it. There would be time later for her distress and questions. Now was not it.

They entered the double. The techs were at work. Spencer skimmed his gaze over the scene, experiencing a small rush of excitement.

He had wanted Homicide for as long as he could remember. As a kid, he'd listened to his dad and Uncle Sammy discuss cases. And later, had watched his brothers John and Quentin with awe. When the department had decentralized, he'd wanted ISD.

ISD was the big time. Top of the heap.

He'd been too much of a screwup to earn the appointment. But here he was. Payoff for his cooperation and goodwill.

He hadn't been proud enough to turn it down.

Spencer returned his attention to the scene before him. Typical college student's apartment, Spencer saw. Junky, third- and fourth-hand furniture, overflowing ashtrays and about two dozen diet Coke cans littered the room. An all-chick place, Spencer thought. If a guy lived here, the cans would be Miller Lite. Or maybe south Louisiana's own Abita Beer.

The first victim lay facedown on the floor, the back of her head partially blown off. The coroner's investigator had already bagged her hands.

Spencer shifted his gaze to a young detective he recognized as being from the Sixth District. He couldn't remember his name.

Tony did. "Yo, Bernie. You the one who dragged us out tonight?"

"Sorry about that. This is no rubber stamp, figured the sooner you guys got involved the better."

The young detective looked nervous. He was new to DIU, probably hadn't handled anything but gangbanger shootings.

"My partner, Spencer Malone."

Something flickered in his eyes. Spencer figured the other cop had heard of him. "Bernie St. Claude."

They shook hands. Ray Hollister, the Orleans Parish coroner's investigator, glanced up. "I see the gang's all here."

"The midnight riders," Tony said. "Lucky us. You worked with Malone yet, Ray?"

"Not this Malone." The officer nodded in his direction. "Welcome to the late-night homicide club."

"Glad to be here."

That brought a groan from a couple of the techs.

Tony shot Spencer a grin. "The scary thing is, he means it. Back way off on the enthusiasm, Slick. People will talk."

"Kiss my ass," Spencer said good-naturedly, then returned his attention to the coroner's representative. "What do you have so far?"

"Looks pretty straightforward right now. Shot twice. If the first bullet didn't kill her, the second sure as hell did."

"But why was she shot?" Spencer wondered aloud.

"That's your job, kid. Not mine."

"Sexual assault?" Tony asked.

"I'm thinking no, but autopsy will tell the tale."

Tony nodded. "We're going to take a look at the other victim."

"Have a ball."

Spencer didn't move; he stared at the fanlike spray of blood on the wall adjacent to the victim. Turning to his partner, he said, "The shooter was sitting."

"How do you figure?"

"Check it out." Spencer circled around the body, crossing to the wall. "Blood splatter sprays up, then out."

"I'll be damned."

Hollister weighed in. "Wounds are consistent with that theory."

Excited, Spencer glanced around. His gaze settled on a desk and chair. "Shooter was there," he said, crossing to the chair. Not wanting to disturb possible evidence, he squatted beside it. He visualized the event: shooter sitting, the victim turning her back on him, then: *Bang. Bang.*

What had they been doing? Why had he wanted her dead?

He shifted his gaze again, to the dusty desktop. It bore a subtle outline, about the size and shape of a laptop computer. "Take a look, Tony. I'm thinking there was a computer here." The desk's location supported the theory: the adjacent wall sported both an electrical outlet and a phone jack.

Tony nodded. "Could be. Might've been books, notebooks or newspaper."

"Maybe. Whatever it was, it's gone now. And, it appears, quite recently." He fitted on a pair of latex gloves and ran a finger across the rectangular space. Finding it dust free, he motioned the photographer over and instructed him to get a shot of the desk, its top and chair.

"Let's make sure they dust that area well."

Spencer knew his partner meant dust for prints and nodded. "Done."

He and Tony moved on. They found the second victim. She had also been shot. The scenario, however, was totally different. She had been tagged twice in the chest and lay on her back, straddling the bedroom doorway. The front of her pj's were bloody, a ring of red circled her body.

Spencer crossed to her, checked her pulse, then glanced back at Tony. "She was in bed, heard the shots and got up to see what was going on."

Tony blinked and shifted his gaze from the vic to Spencer, his expression strange. "Carly has those same pajamas. She wears 'em all the time."

A meaningless coincidence, but one that touched too close to home. "Let's nail this bastard."

Tony nodded and then finished examining the body.

"Robbery wasn't a motive," Tony said. "Neither was sexual assault. No sign of a break-in."

Spencer frowned. "Then why?"

"Maybe Ms. Killian can help."

"You or me?"

"You're the one who has a way with the ladies." Tony smiled. "Go for it."

CHAPTER
3

Monday, February 28, 2005
2:20 a.m.

Stacy shivered and adjusted Caesar against her chest. The pup, barely old enough to have been weaned, whimpered a protest. She should have crated him, Stacy thought. Her arms ached; any moment he would awaken and want to play.

But she hadn't been able to let go. She still couldn't.

She rubbed her cheek against his soft, silky head. Between the time she'd made the call and the first officers arrived, she had returned to her apartment, stashed her Glock and grabbed a coat. She carried a permit for the gun but knew from experience that an armed civilian at the scene of a homicide would be at worst suspect, at best a distraction.

She'd never been on this side of the process before   the

helpless bystander, loved one of the deceased— though she had come terrifyingly close last year. Her sister Jane had narrowly escaped a murderer's grasp. In those moments, when Stacy had thought she'd lost her, she'd decided she'd had enough. Of the badge. What went along with it. The blood. The cruelty and death.

It had become clear to Stacy that she yearned for a normal life, a healthy relationship. Eventually, a family of her own. And that it wasn't going to happen while she was in the job. Police work had marked her in a way that made "normal" and "healthy" impossible. As if she wore an invisible *S*. One that stood for *shit*. The worst life had to offer. The ugliest, man's inhumanity to man.

She had acknowledged that nobody could change her life but her.

Now, here she was again. Death had followed her.

Only this time, it had found Cassie. And Beth.

Sudden anger surged through her. Where the hell were the detectives? Why were they moving so slowly? At this rate the killer would be in Mississippi before these two finished processing the scene.

"Stacy Killian?"

She turned. The younger of the two detectives stood behind her. He flashed his shield. "Detective Malone. I understand you called this in?"

"I did."

"Are you all right? Do you need to sit down?"

"No, I'm okay."

He motioned to Caesar. "Cute pup. Lab?"

She nodded. "But he's not…he was…Cassie's." She hated the way her voice thickened and fought to steady it. "Look, could we just get on with this?"

His eyebrows lifted slightly, as if surprised by her brusque response. He probably thought her cold and uncaring. He couldn't know how far from the truth that assessment was—she cared so much, she could hardly breathe.

He took out his notebook, a pocket-size spiral bound identical to the kind she had used. "Why don't you tell me exactly what happened."

"I was sleeping. Thought I heard gunshots and went to check on my friends."

Something flickered across his face and was gone. "You live here?" He indicated her unit.

"Yes."

"Alone?"

"I'm not sure that's important, but yes, I live alone."

"How long?"

"I moved in the first week of January."

"And before that?"

"Dallas. I moved to New Orleans to attend graduate school at UNO."

"How well did you know the victims?"

Victims. She winced at the label. "Cassie and I were good friends. Beth just moved in a week or so ago. Cassie's original roommate dropped out of school, went home."

"You categorize the two of you as good friends? You only knew each other a matter of what, a couple months?"

"We shouldn't have been, I suppose. But we just…clicked."

He looked unconvinced. "You say you were awakened by gunshots and went to check on your friends? What made you so certain? Couldn't the sound have been firecrackers? A car back- firing?"

"I knew they were gunshots, Detective." She looked away, then back at him. "I was a cop for ten years. In Dallas."

Again, his eyebrows lifted slightly; obviously the information had altered his original opinion of her.

"What happened next?"

She explained about heading out front, circling the property and seeing Cassie's light on. "That's when I realized the sound…it had come from next door."

The other detective emerged from the doorway behind him. Detective Malone followed her gaze and turned. She used the opportunity to study the two men. The aging cop partnered with the hotshot novice, a duo depicted in any number of Hollywood films.

In her experience, she'd found the fictionalized coupling much more effective than its real life inspiration. Too often, the older of the two was a burnout or a coaster, the younger a swaggerer.

The man crossed to them. "Detective Sciame," he said.

At the sound of the other man's voice, Caesar opened his eyes and wagged his tail. She set the puppy down and held out a hand. "Stacy Killian."

"Ms. Killian here is a former cop."

Detective Sciame turned his gaze back to her, warm brown

eyes friendly. And intelligent. He may be a coaster, she decided, but he was a smart one.

"That so?" he said, shaking her hand.

"Detective First Grade. Homicide, Dallas PD. Call me Stacy."

"Tony. What are you doing in our beautiful city?"

"Graduate school at UNO. English lit."

He nodded. "Had enough of the job, huh? Thought about leaving myself, a number of times. Got retirement in sight now, no sense making a change."

"Why grad school?" Malone asked.

"Why not?"

He frowned. "English lit seems a world away from law enforcement."

"Exactly."

Tony motioned to Cassie's half of the double. "You take a good look at the scene?"

"I did."

"What are your thoughts?"

"Cassie was killed first. Beth when she got up to investigate. Robbery was not a motive. Neither was sexual assault, though the pathologist will make the final determination. I'm thinking the killer was either a friend or acquaintance of Cassie's. She let him in, locked up Caesar."

"You were a friend of hers." This came from Malone.

"True. But I didn't kill her."

"So you say. First to the scene—"

"Is always a suspect. Standard operating procedure, I know."

Tony nodded. "You carry a gun, Stacy?"

She wasn't surprised the man asked the question. She was grateful, actually. It gave her confidence this might get solved.

"A Glock .40."

"Same bad boy we carry. You got a permit?"

"Of course. Would you like to see both?"

He said he would and she scooped up the puppy and headed inside. They followed. She didn't protest. Again, standard operating procedure. Because she was first to the scene, she was—if only momentarily—a suspect. No detective worth his or her salt would allow a possible suspect to disappear into their home to retrieve a gun. Or anything else, for that matter. Nine times out of ten, said suspect would disappear out the back door. Or come back out the front, gun blazing.

After leaving Caesar in her bedroom, she produced the gun and permit. Both detectives inspected them. Obviously, the Glock hadn't been fired recently and Tony handed it back.

"Cassie have a boyfriend?"

"No."

"Any enemies?"

"Not that I know of."

"Was she into the bar scene?"

Stacy shook her head. "RPGs and school. That's it."

Malone frowned. "RPGs?"

"Role-playing games. Her favorites were Dungeons & Dragons and Vampire: the Masquerade, though she played others."

"Pardon my ignorance," Tony said, "are these board games? Video games?"

"Neither. Each game has set characters and a scenario, decided upon by the game master. The participants role-play the characters."

Tony scratched his head. "It's a live-action game?"

"Not really." She smiled. "I don't play, but the way Cassie explained it, RPGs are played with the imagination. The player is like an actor in a role, following an unfolding script, without costumes, special effects or sets. The games can be played real-time or by e-mail."

"Why don't you play?" Detective Malone said.

Stacy paused. "Cassie invited me to join her group, but her description of play didn't appeal. Danger at every turn, living by your wits. I had no desire to role-play that, I lived it. Every day I spent on the force."

"Know any of her fellow gamers?"

"Not really."

Detective Malone cocked an eyebrow. "Not really. What does that mean?"

"She introduced me to several of them. I see them around the University Center sometimes. They occasionally play at Café Noir."

Tony stepped in. "Café Noir?"

"A coffeehouse on Esplanade. Cassie spent a lot of time there. We both did. Studying."

"When did you last see Ms. Finch?"

"Friday afternoon…out at scho—"

The hair on the back of her neck prickled. It came flooding back, their last meeting. Cassie had been excited, she'd met someone who played a game called White Rabbit. This person had promised to hook her up with what she'd called a Supreme White Rabbit. Arrange a private meeting with him.

"Ms. Killian? Have you remembered something?"

She filled them in, but they appeared unimpressed.

"A Supreme White Rabbit?" Tony asked. "What in God's name is that?"

"Like I said, I don't play. But as I understand it, in RPGs there's something called the game master. In D & D that person's the Dungeon Master, who basically controls the game."

"And in this new scenario, that person's called the White Rabbit," Tony said.

"Exactly." She pressed on. "The thought of her meeting this guy struck me wrong. Cassie was really trusting. Too trusting. I reminded her that this person was a stranger and urged her to select a public place for their meeting."

"What was her response to your warning?"

What do you think, some game geek's going to get pissed off and shoot me?

"She laughed," Stacy said. "Told me to lighten up."

"So the meeting took place?"

"I don't know."

"She give you a name?"

"No. But I didn't ask."

"The person who promised the introduction, where'd she meet him?"

"She didn't say and, again, I didn't ask." Stacy heard the frustration in her own voice. "I'm thinking it was a guy, though I'm not even certain of that."

"Anything else?"

"I have a feeling about this."

"Women's intuition?" Malone asked.

She narrowed her eyes, irritated. "The instinct of a seasoned detective."

She saw the older man's mouth twitch, as if with amusement.

"What about her roommate?" Tony asked. "Beth? She play those games?"

"No."

"Did your friend have a computer?" Malone asked.

She swung her gaze to him. "A laptop. Why?"

He didn't answer. "She play these games on her computer?"

"Sometimes, I think. Mostly she played real time, with her game group."

"So they *can* be played online."

"I think so." She shifted her gaze between the two. "Why?"

"Thank you, Ms. Killian. You've been helpful."

"Wait." She caught the older detective's arm. "Her computer's gone, isn't it?"

"I'm sorry, Stacy," Tony murmured, sounding like he meant it. "We can't say any more."

She would have done the same; it pissed her off, anyway. "I suggest you check out this White Rabbit game. Ask around, see who's playing. What the game involves."

"We will, Ms. Killian." Malone closed his notebook. "Thank you for your help."

She opened her mouth to say more, to ask if they would update her on their progress, then shut it without speaking. Because she knew they wouldn't. Even if they agreed to, it would be an empty platitude.

She didn't have the right to the information, she acknowledged, watching the two walk away. She was a civilian. Not even family of the deceased. They weren't required to give her anything but courtesy.

For the first time since leaving the force, she understood the ramifications of what she had done. Of what she was.

A civilian. Outside the blue circle.

Alone.

Stacy Killian wasn't a cop anymore.

CHAPTER
4

Spencer and Tony entered police headquarters. Located in City Hall, at 1300 Perdido Street, the mirrored glass building housed not only the NOPD but the mayor's office, the New Orleans Fire Department and city council, among others. The Public Integrity Division, the NOPD's version of Internal Affairs, was housed outside headquarters, as was the crime lab.

They signed in and took the elevator to ISD. When the doors whooshed open, Tony headed for the box of breakfast pastries, Spencer for his messages.

"Hey, Dora," he said to the receptionist. Though a civilian employed by the city, she wore a uniform. Her extra-large, top-heavy frame strained at the confines of the blue fabric, revealing glimpses of hot pink lace. "Any messages?"

The woman handed Spencer the yellow message slips, sliding her gaze over him appraisingly.

He ignored the look. "Captain in?"

"Ready and waiting, stud."

He cocked an eyebrow at her and she cackled. "You white boys have no sense of humor."

"No sense of style, either," offered Rupert, another detective, sidling past them.

"That's right," Dora said. "Rupert here knows fine threads."

Spencer glanced at the other man, taking in his sleek Italian suit, colorful tie and bright white shirt, then down at himself. Jeans, chambray shirt and tweedy jacket. "What?"

She groaned. "You're working ISD now, top of the heap, baby. You need to be dressin' the part."

"Yo, Slick. Ready?"

Spencer turned and grinned at his partner. "Can't. In the middle of a free fashion consultation."

Tony returned the grin. "Lecture, you mean."

"Don't even go there." Dora wagged her finger at the older man. "You're hopeless. A fashion disaster."

"What? Me?" He held his hands out. His gut protruded over the waist of his Sansabelt trousers, the fabric shiny from age, and strained the buttons of his short-sleeved plaid shirt.

The woman made a sound of disgust as she handed Tony his messages. Turning to Spencer, she said, "You just come see Miss Dora, baby. I'll fix you right up."

"I'll keep that in mind."

"You do that, sugar pie," she called after him. "Ladies go for a man with style."

"She's right, sugar pie," Tony teased. "Take it from me."

Spencer laughed. "You'd know this how? The way the ladies stay away in droves?"

"Exactly." They turned the corner, heading for the open door of their captain's office.

Spencer tapped on the casing. "Captain O'Shay? Got a minute?"

Captain Patti O'Shay looked up, waved them in. "'Morning, Detectives. It's been a busy one already, I hear."

"We got a double," Tony said, lowering himself into one of the chairs across from her.

Patti O'Shay, a trim, no-nonsense woman, was one of only three female captains in the NOPD. She was smart, tough but fair. She'd worked her ass off to get where she was, twice as hard as any man, overcoming doubt, chauvinism and the good old boy network. She'd been bumped up to ISD this past year and some predicted she'd make deputy chief one day.

She also happened to be Spencer's mother's sister.

It was hard for Spencer to reconcile this woman with the one who had called him "Boo" growing up. The one who'd slipped him cookies when his mother hadn't been looking. She was his godmother, a special relationship for Catholics. And one she took seriously.

However, she had made it clear his first day under her command that here she was his boss. Period.

She turned her miss-nothing gaze on him. "Think DIU jumped the gun by calling us in?"

He straightened, cleared his throat. "No way, Captain. This was no rubber stamp."

She shifted her gaze to Tony. "Detective Sciame?"

"I agree. Better to get it now, before the trail's cold."

Spencer took over. "Both vics were shot."

"Names?"

"Cassie Finch and Beth Wagner. UNO students."

"Wagner just moved in a week ago," Tony offered. "Poor kid, talk about some bad fuckin' luck."

The woman didn't seem to notice the language, but Spencer winced.

"Robbery doesn't appear to have been the motive," Spencer offered, "although her laptop is missing. Neither does rape."

"What, then?"

Tony stretched his legs out in front of him. "Crystal ball's not working this morning, Captain."

"Clever," she said, her tone leaving no doubt she found it to be anything but. "How about a theory, then? Or is that asking a bit much after only a couple doughnuts?"

Spencer jumped in. "Looks like Finch was killed first. We figure she knew her killer, let him in. Probably killed Wagner because she was there. Of course, it's speculation so far."

"Leads?"

"A few. We're going to pay a visit to the university, the places both women hung out. Talk to their friends, professors. Boyfriends, if any."

"Good. Anything else?"

"Canvas of the neighborhood's complete," Spencer continued. "With the exception of the woman who phoned it in, nobody heard a thing."

"Her story checks out?"

"Seems legit. She's a former cop. Dallas PD Homicide."

She frowned slightly. "That so?"

"I'm going to run her through the computer. Call the Dallas PD."

"Do that."

"Coroner notified the next of kin?"

"Done."

She reached for her phone, signaling their meeting was over. "I don't like double homicides in my jurisdiction. I like them even less when they're unsolved. Understood?"

They agreed they did, stood and started toward the door. The captain stopped Spencer before he reached it. "Detective Malone?"

He looked back.

"Watch that temper of yours."

He flashed her a smile. "Under control, Aunt Patti. Altar boy's honor."

As he walked away, he heard her laugh. Probably because she remembered what a total failure he had been as an altar boy.

CHAPTER
5

Monday, February 28, 2005
10:30 a.m.

Spencer stepped into Café Noir. The scent of coffee and baking cookies hit him hard. It'd been a long time since breakfast—a sausage biscuit from a drive-thru window just as the sun cracked the horizon.

He just didn't get the whole coffeehouse thing. Three bucks for a cup of fancy coffee with a foreign-sounding name? And what was with the whole tall, grande, super-grande thing? What was wrong with small, medium and large? Or even extra large? Who did they think they were fooling?

He'd made the mistake of ordering an americano once. Thought it would be a good, old-fashioned cup of American coffee. It had proved to be anything but.

Shots of espresso and water. Tasted like burned piss.

He decided to save his money and wait until he got back to HQ for a cup. Glancing around, he saw that from what he knew of coffeehouses, this one was pretty typical. Deep, earthy colors, groupings of comfy, oversize furniture interspersed with tables for conversing or studying. The building, located on a triangular sliver of land called neutral ground in New Orleans, even sported a big old fireplace.

For all the good it would be, he thought. This was New Orleans, after all. Hot and humid, twenty-four/seven, nine months out of twelve.

Spencer crossed to the counter and asked the girl at the cash register for the owner or manager. The girl, who looked to be college-age, smiled and pointed at a tall, willowy blonde restocking the buffet. "The owner. Billie Bellini."

He thanked her and crossed to the woman. "Billie Bellini?" he asked.

She turned and looked up at him. She was gorgeous. One of those flawlessly beautiful women who could—and probably did—have their pick of men. The kind of woman one didn't expect to see managing a coffeehouse.

He'd be a liar or a eunuch to say he was immune, though he could honestly claim she wasn't his type. Too damn high maintenance for a regular Joe like him.

A smile touched the corners of her full lips. "Yes?" she said.

"Detective Spencer Malone. NOPD," he said as he flashed his badge.

One perfectly arched eyebrow lifted. "Detective? How can I help you?"

"You know a woman named Cassie Finch?"

"I do. She's one of the regulars."

"A regular. What exactly does that mean?"

"That she spends a lot of time in here. Everybody knows her." Her smooth brow wrinkled. "Why?"

He ignored her question and asked another of his own. "How about Beth Wagner?"

"Cassie's roommate? Not really. She was in once. Cassie introduced us."

"What about Stacy Killian?"

"Also a regular. They're friends. But I suspect you already know that."

Spencer dropped his gaze. The fourth finger of her left hand sported a major rock and a diamond studded gold band. That didn't surprise him.

"When did you last see Ms. Finch?"

Concern leaped into her eyes. "What is this in reference to?" she asked. "Is Cassie okay?"

"Cassie Finch is dead, Ms. Bellini. She was murdered."

She brought a hand to her mouth, which had pulled into a perfectly formed O. "There must be some mistake."

"I'm sorry."

"Excuse me, I—" She fumbled behind her for a chair, then sank onto it. For long moments, she sat motionless, struggling, he suspected, to compose herself.

When she finally looked back up at him, it was without tears. "She was in yesterday afternoon."

"For how long?"

"A couple of hours. From about three to five."

"Was she alone?"

"Yes."

"She talk to anyone?"

The woman clasped her hands tightly in her lap. "Yes. All the usual suspects."

"Pardon?"

"Sorry." She cleared her throat. "Other regulars. The usual crew was in."

"Was Stacy Killian in yesterday?"

Again, her expression tightened with alarm. "No. Is Stacy... is she all right?"

"As far as I know, she's fine." He paused. "It would help us immensely if I could get the names of the people Cassie hung out with. The regulars."

"Of course."

"Did she have any enemies?"

"No. I can't imagine she did, anyway."

"Altercations with anyone?"

"No." Her voice shook. "I can't believe this is happening."

"I understand she was into fantasy role-playing games." He paused; when she didn't disagree, he went on. "She always have her laptop with her?"

"Always."

"Never saw her without it?"

"Never."

He nodded. "I'd like to speak with your employees, Ms. Bellini."

"Of course. Nick and Josie are coming in at two and five, respectively. That's Paula. Shall I call her over?" He nodded and retrieved a business card from his jacket pocket. He handed it to her. "If you think of anything else, call me."

It turned out Paula knew even less than her boss had, but Spencer gave her a business card as well.

He stepped out of the coffeehouse and into the cool, bright morning. Channel 6's meteorologist had predicted the mercury would top seventy today, and judging by the warmth already, she'd been right.

Loosening his tie, he started for his car, which was parked at the curb.

"Detective Malone, wait!"

He stopped, turned. Stacy Killian slammed her car door and hurried toward him. "Hello, Ms. Killian."

She motioned to the coffeehouse. "Did you get everything you needed here?"

"For the moment. How can I help you?"

"I was wondering, have you looked into White Rabbit yet?"

"Not yet."

"May I ask what's taking so long?"

He looked at his watch, then back at her. "By my calculations, this investigation is only eight hours old."

"And the probability of it being solved lessens with each passing hour."

"Why'd you leave the Dallas force, Ms. Killian?"

"Excuse me?"

He noticed the way she subtly stiffened. "It was a simple question. Why'd you leave?"

"I needed a change."

"That the only reason?"

"I don't see what that has to do with anything, Detective."

He narrowed his eyes. "I just wondered since you seem pretty anxious to do my job."

Color flooded her cheeks. "Cassie was my friend. I don't want her killer to get away."

"Neither do I. Back off and let me do my job."

He started past her; she caught his arm. "White Rabbit is the best lead you have."

"Says you. I'm not convinced."

"Cassie had met someone who promised to introduce her to the game. They had planned to meet."

"Could be a coincidence. We meet people all the time, Ms. Killian. They come and go in our lives, strangers who cross our paths on a daily basis, making deliveries, speaking to us in the checkout line, offering to pick up something we've dropped. But they don't kill us."

"Most of the time they don't," she corrected. "Her computer was gone, wasn't it? Why do you think that is?"

"Her killer took it as a trophy. Or decided he needed one. Or it's at the repair shop."

"Some games are played online. Maybe White Rabbit is one of them?"

He shook off her hand. "You're stretching, Ms. Killian. And you know it."

"I was a detective for ten years—"

"But you're not now," he said, cutting her off. "You're a civilian. Don't get in my way. Don't interfere with this investigation. I won't ask you so nicely next time."

CHAPTER
6

Monday, February 28, 2005
11:10 a.m.

Stacy strode into Café Noir, fuming. *Stupid, arrogant, swaggerer.* In her experience, bad cops fell into three categories. Top of the list sat the dishonest cop. No explanation necessary. Next came the coaster. Cops who were content to do the minimum for whatever reason. Then came the swaggerers. For this group, the job was all about how it made them look. They endangered their partners by showing off; they jeopardized cases by refusing to see anything but their own glory.

Or by refusing to follow a hunch that was somebody else's.

Sure, that's all it was. A hunch. Based on a coincidence and a gut feeling.

Over the years she had learned to trust her hunches. And

she wasn't going to allow some cocky, still-wet-behind-the-ears gun jockey to blow this case. She would not sit back and do nothing while Cassie's killer went free.

Stacy drew a deep breath, working to calm herself, shifting her thoughts from the past meeting to the one ahead.

Billie. She would be crushed.

Her friend stood at the counter. Six feet tall, blond and beautiful, she turned heads everywhere she went. Stacy had discovered her to be exceptionally smart—and exceptionally funny as well, in a dry, acerbic way.

Billie looked up, met Stacy's eyes. She had been crying.

Stacy closed the distance between them and held out a hand. "I'm devastated, too."

Billie clasped her hand tightly. "The police were here. I can't believe it."

"Me, neither."

"They asked me about you, Stacy. Why—"

"I'm the one who found her. And Beth. I called it in."

"Oh, Stacy...how horrible."

Tears flooded Stacy's eyes. "Tell me about it."

Billie waved her employee over. "Paula, I'll be in my office. Call me if you need me."

The young woman looked from one to the other, eyes watery, face pale. No doubt Malone had questioned her as well. "Go ahead," she said, voice thick, shaky. "Don't worry, I've got the bar."

Billie ushered Stacy through the stockroom to her office. When they reached it, she partially shut the door. "How are you holding up?"

"Just dandy." Stacy heard the edge in her voice but knew it would be pointless to try to soften it. She hurt. She itched to take her anger and despair out on someone.

Cassie had been one of the sweetest people she had ever met. Her death wasn't only a senseless loss, how she'd died was an affront to life.

Stacy faced Billie. "I could have saved her."

"What? You couldn't—"

"I was right next door. I have a gun, I'm a former cop. Why didn't I know?"

"Because," Billie said gently, "you're *not* a psychic."

Stacy fisted her fingers, knowing Billie was right but finding more comfort in blame than helplessness. "She told me about this White Rabbit. I had a feeling about it. I warned her to be careful."

Billie cleared off the small office's single chair. "Sit. Back up. Tell me everything."

Stacy recounted the story. Billie listened, eyes growing wet. When she finished, Stacy saw her friend struggle to compose herself and speak. When she did, her voice quivered.

"It's just too awful. It's— Who would do this? Why? Cassie is...she—"

Was.

Past tense now.

Billie choked the words back. It hurt too much, Stacy knew, to say them aloud. She took over. "This game, White Rabbit, you ever heard of it?"

Billie shook her head.

"You're certain?"

"Absolutely."

"Cassie was really excited," Stacy continued. "She said this person agreed to set up a meeting between her and an expert at the game."

"When?"

"I don't know. I was rushing to class and thought we would see each other——" Her voice cracked; she couldn't finish.

Later. She had thought they would see each other later.

This time Billie stepped in. "And you think she met with this person and that he might have had something to do with her death?"

"It's possible. Cassie was so trusting. It would have been totally like her to invite a stranger into her house."

Billie nodded. "The whole White Rabbit thing could have been a ruse. This person, whoever he is, might have known she was a gamer and used the lure of a new game scenario to get into her house."

"But why?" Stacy stood and began to pace, too agitated to stay still. "The way it looked to me, Cassie was killed first. Beth simply because she was there. It didn't look as if they'd been robbed or raped."

She paused, glanced back at Billie. "The police asked if she had a computer."

"They asked me about it, too."

"What else did they ask you?"

"Who Cassie hung out with. About her game group. If she had any enemies. Run-ins with anybody."

Standard stuff.

"Did they ask about White Rabbit?"

"No."

Stacy brought the heels of her hands to her eyes. Her head throbbed. "I'm thinking they asked about the computer because they didn't see one."

"She took it everywhere with her. I asked her once if she slept with it." Billie's eyes filled. "She laughed. Said she did."

"Exactly. Which means her killer took it. The question is, why?"

"Because he didn't want the police to see something on it?" Billie offered. "Something that would lead them to him. Or her."

"That's my theory. Which leads me back to this person she was meeting with."

"What are you going to do?"

"Ask around about it. Talk to Cassie's gamer friends. See if they know anything about this White Rabbit. Find out if it's played on the computer or real time. Maybe she told them about this White Rabbit person."

"I'll ask around, too. A lot of gamers come in here, somebody's bound to know something."

Stacy caught her friend's hand. "Be careful, Billie. You get any negative vibes, call me or Detective Malone right away. We're trying to expose someone who's killed two people already, two that we know of. Believe me, he won't hesitate to do it again to protect himself."

CHAPTER
7

Tuesday, March 1, 2005
9:00 a.m.

The University of New Orleans sat squarely on 195 acres of prime Lake Pontchartrain-fronted property. Established in 1956 on a former U.S. navy air station, UNO catered mostly to those living in the metro region of Louisiana's largest city.

The campus couldn't compare to the state's flagship school, Louisiana State University in Baton Rouge, or to the ivy-covered prestige of uptown New Orleans' Tulane University, but it had managed to secure itself a solid reputation of quality for a medium-size university. The schools of Maritime Engineering, Hotel and Restaurant Management and of all things, Film, were particularly highly rated.

Stacy parked in the student lot closest to the University

Center. The UC was the hub of social activity on campus, particularly since most of the students lived off campus and commuted. If a student wasn't in class or at the library studying, they were shooting the breeze in the UC.

It was there, Stacy was certain, she would run across Cassie's friends.

She entered the building, found a table and dumped her backpack before scanning the cavernous room. She hadn't expected a crowd this early, and she didn't get one. Numbers would begin to swell after the first classes of the day concluded, reaching maximum capacity at midday, when students stopped for a bite of lunch.

She bought a cup of coffee and a muffin and carried them back to her table. She sat, unpacked Mary Shelley's *Frankenstein,* the novel she was reading for her class on Later Romantics, but didn't open it.

Instead, she sweetened her coffee and took a sip, thoughts scrolling forward to her goal for the day. Make contact with Cassie's friends. Question them about White Rabbit and the night of Cassie's death. Get something solid to move forward on.

She had spoken with Cassie's mother the night before. She'd called to express her condolences and to make arrangements for Caesar. The woman had been in shock and her responses to Stacy's questions had been robotic. She'd told Stacy that as soon as the coroner's office released Cassie's body, she planned to take her home to Picayune, Mississippi, for burial. She'd asked Stacy if she would help arrange a memorial service. She thought it would be best to hold it at the Newman Religious Center on campus.

Stacy had agreed. Cassie had had a lot of friends; they would want the opportunity to say goodbye.

And the police would want an opportunity to see who attended the service.

Killers, particularly thrill killers, were known to attend their victims' funerals. They also had a proclivity for visiting their victims' graves or revisiting the scene of their crime. Through those activities they relived the sick thrill they had derived from the act.

Had Cassie and Beth's murders been thrill kills? Stacy didn't think so. Neither shooting had the ritualistic aspects of most thrill kills, but that didn't exclude the possibility. She'd found that for every rule, there was an exception—especially when it came to human behavior.

Stacy caught sight of two members of Cassie's game group. Ella and Magda, she remembered. They were laughing as they made their way from the concession line to a table, their expressions carefree.

They hadn't heard yet.

She stood and crossed to their table. They looked up and smiled, recognizing her. "Hey, Stacy. What's up?"

"May I sit down? I need to ask you something."

At her expression, their smiles slipped. They motioned to one of the empty chairs and she sank onto it. She decided to ask about the game first. Once she told them about Cassie, the chance of getting a coherent answer was slim.

"Have either of you heard of a game scenario called White Rabbit?"

The two women exchanged glances. Ella spoke up first. "You're not a gamer, Stacy. Why so interested?"

"So you have heard of it." When they didn't respond, she added, "It's really important. It has to do with Cassie."

"Cassie?" The woman frowned and looked at her watch. "I expected her to be here already. She e-mailed us both Sunday night. Said to be here by nine this morning, she had a surprise."

A surprise.

White Rabbit.

Stacy leaned toward them. "What time did she e-mail?"

Both women thought a moment; Ella answered first. "Around 8:00 p.m. for me. Magda?"

"The same, I guess."

"Have you heard of the game?"

They glanced at each other again, then nodded. "Neither of us has played, though," Magda offered.

Ella jumped in. "White Rabbit is...sort of radical. It's totally underground. Passed from gamer to gamer. To learn the game, you have to know someone who plays. As a group, they're really clannish."

"And secretive," Magda added.

"What about the Internet? Surely you can find information about it there?"

"Information," Ella murmured, "sure. But a player's bible, not that I've seen. You, Mag?" She looked at the other woman, who shook her head.

No wonder Cassie had been so excited. What a coup.

"Is it played online? Or real time?"

"Both, I guess. Like most." Ella frowned slightly. "Real time is Cassie's favorite. We all like getting together as a group to game."

"It's more social that way," Magda offered. "Playing on the computer is for the folks who can't find a group to play with or who don't have the time to devote to real play."

Ella jumped in. "Or are in it simply for the thrill of it."

"Which is?"

"Outmaneuvering and outwitting their opponents."

"Did Cassie mention meeting someone who played?"

"Not to me." Ella looked at Magda. "You?"

The other girl shook her head once more.

"What else can you tell me about it?"

"Not much." Ella looked at her watch again. "It's weird that Cassie hasn't shown up." She looked at her friend. "Check your cell pho—"

Just then another of their group, Amy, called their names. They turned to see her making her way toward them. Judging by the girl's face, she had heard about Cassie. Stacy braced herself for the scene to come.

"Y'all, oh my God!" she said when she reached the table. "I just heard the most horrible thing! Cassie's...I can't... she's—" She brought a shaking hand to her mouth, eyes filling with tears.

"What?" Magda asked. "What's wrong with Cassie?"

Amy began to cry. "She's...dead."

Ella launched to her feet, sending her chair skidding backward. People at the surrounding tables looked their way. "That can't be true, I just talked to her!"

"Me, too!" Magda cried. "How——"

"The police came by the dorm this morning. They want to talk to you guys, too."

"The police?" Magda said, looking panicked. "I don't understand."

Amy sank onto a chair, dissolving once again into tears.

"Cassie was murdered," Stacy said quietly. "Sunday night."

Magda simply stared. Ella rounded on her, face pinched with anger and grief. "You're lying! Who would hurt Cassie?"

"That's what I'm trying to find out."

For a moment the three were silent. They stared blankly at her. Then understanding crept into Ella's expression. "That's why you were asking all those questions about White Rabbit. You think——"

"The game?" Amy asked, through tears.

"I saw Cassie Friday," Stacy explained. "She said she met someone who played. He was going to introduce her to a Supreme White Rabbit. Did she say anything to you about it, Amy?"

"Uh-uh. I talked to her Sunday night. She said she was going to have a surprise for us this morning. She sounded really happy."

"We got an e-mail saying the same thing," Magda offered.

"Anything else?"

"She had to go. Said someone was at the door."

Stacy's heart beat faster. *Someone. Her killer?* "She give you a name?"

"No."

"Did she indicate whether this person was a man or a woman?"

Amy shook her head, looking miserable.

"What time was this?"

"Like I told the police, I don't remember exactly, but I'm thinking it was around nine-thirty."

At nine-thirty Stacy had been deep into her research paper. Her sister Jane had called; they'd chatted for about twenty minutes about the baby, the amazing little Apple Annie. Stacy hadn't heard or seen anything.

"Are you certain she didn't say anything else? Anything at all?"

"No. Now I wish…if only I'd—" Amy's words broke on a sob.

Ella turned to Stacy, face red. "How do you know so much?"

Stacy explained about waking to what she thought were gunshots and going to investigate. "I found her. And Beth."

"You used to be a cop, right?"

"I used to be, yes."

"And now you're playing cop? Reliving your glory days?"

The accusation in the other woman's words took her by surprise. "Hardly. To the police Cassie's just another victim. She was much more than that to me. I intend to make certain whoever did this doesn't get away with it."

"Her murder had nothing to do with role-playing games!"

"How do you know?"

"Everybody's always pointing fingers at us." Ella's voice shook. "Like role-playing games turn kids into zombies or killing machines. It's stupid. You'd do better to talk to that freak Bobby Gautreaux."

Stacy frowned. "Do I know him?"

"Probably not." Magda was hugging herself and rocking back and forth. "He and Cassie dated last year. She broke up with him. He didn't take it well."

Ella looked at Magda. "Didn't take it well? At first he threatened to kill himself. Then he threatened to kill her!"

"But that was last year," Amy whispered. "Surely, that threat was made in the heat of the moment."

"Don't you remember what she told us a couple weeks ago?" Ella asked. "She thought he'd been following her."

Amy's eyes widened. "Oh, my God, I'd forgotten."

"Me, too," Magda admitted. "What do we do now?"

They turned to her, three young women whose lives had just taken an irrevocable turn. One precipitated by a dose of very ugly realism.

"What do you think?" Magda asked, voice shaking.

That this changed everything. "You have to call the police and tell them exactly what you told me. Do it right away."

"But Bobby really loved her," Amy said. "He wouldn't hurt her. He cried when she ended it. He—"

Stacy cut her off as gently as possible. "Believe it or not, as many murderers are motivated by love as by hate. Maybe more. Statistically, more men kill than women, and in cases of domestic violence, women are almost always the victim. In addition, more men stalk their previous partners and have restraining orders filed against them."

"You think Bobby's been stalking her? But why wait a year before—" She choked on the words, obviously unable to bring herself to say them.

But they hung heavily in the air.

Before killing her.

"Some of these guys are mindless brutes who strike immediately. Others think it through, lying in wait for the right moment. They refuse to let go of their fury. If he was stalking her, Bobby Gautreaux would fall into the latter category."

"I feel sick," Magda moaned, dropping her head into her hands.

Amy leaned close and gently rubbed her friend's back. "It's going to be okay."

But of course it wasn't. And they all knew it.

"Where can I find this Bobby Gautreaux?" Stacy asked.

"He's an engineering student," Ella offered.

"I think he lived in one of the dorms," Amy said. "At least he did last year."

"Are you certain he's still a UNO student?" Stacy asked.

"I've seen him around campus this year," Amy said. "Just the other day, in fact. Here, in the UC."

Stacy stood and started packing up her things. "Call Detective Malone. Tell him what you told me."

"What are you going to do?" Magda asked.

"I'm going to see if I can find Bobby Gautreaux. I want to ask him a few questions before the police do."

"About White Rabbit?" Ella asked, an edge in her voice.

"Among other things." Stacy hefted her backpack to her shoulder.

Ella followed her to her feet. "Drop the gaming angle. It's a dead end."

She found it odd that one of Cassie's supposedly good friends seemed more concerned about gaming's reputation than catching her friend's killer. Stacy met the other woman's gaze directly. "It may be. But Cassie's dead. And I'm not dropping anything until we know who killed her."

Ella's defiance seemed to melt. She sank to her chair, expression defeated.

Stacy gazed at her a moment, then turned to go. Magda stopped her. Stacy looked back.

"Don't leave it up to the police, okay? We'll help you in any way we can. We loved her."

CHAPTER
8

Tuesday, March 1, 2005
10:30 a.m.

Being a university that catered to commuters, UNO had only three residence facilities, and one of those exclusively housed students with families. Since Bobby Gautreaux hailed from Monroe, Stacy figured he lived in one of the residences for single students, either Bienville Hall or Privateer Place.

She also figured she'd get nowhere in an attempt to wheedle an address out of the registrar's office, but she might do some good at the engineering department.

She quickly formulated a plan and assembled the pieces she needed to carry it out, then made her way to the engineering building, located on the opposite side of the campus from the UC.

Every department had its own secretary. That person knew her department inside and out, and was familiar with every student major, knew each faculty member, complete with their peculiarities. They also tended, within their respective domains, to be more powerful than God.

Stacy had also learned that if they liked you, they would move heaven and earth to help you solve a problem. But if they didn't, if you crossed them, you were screwed.

The woman in charge of the engineering department fiefdom, Stacy saw, had a face as round as the moon and a big broad smile.

One of the motherly ones. Good.

"Hi," she smiled, and crossed to the woman's desk. "I'm Stacy Killian, a grad student from the English department."

The woman returned her smile. "How can I help you?"

"I'm looking for Bobby Gautreaux."

The woman frowned slightly. "I haven't seen Bobby today."

"He doesn't have an engineering class on Tuesdays?"

"I believe he does. Let me check." She swung toward her computer terminal, accessed the student records, then typed in Bobby's name.

"Let's see. He did have a class earlier, though I didn't see him. Maybe I can help you?"

"I'm a family friend from Monroe. I was there this past weekend, visiting my folks. Bobby's mom asked if I would bring this to him." She held up the card she'd just purchased at the bookstore, now marked "Bobby" on the envelope.

The woman smiled and held out a hand. "I'll be happy to give it to him."

Stacy held back. "I promised I'd give it directly to him. She was pretty insistent about that. He lives in Bienville Hall, doesn't he?"

Stacy saw a wariness creep into the secretary's expression. "I'm sure I don't know."

"Could you check?" Stacy leaned closer, lowering her voice. "There's money in it. A hundred dollars. If I leave it and something happens...I'd never forgive myself."

The woman pursed her lips. "I certainly can't take the responsibility for cash."

"That's just the way I feel," Stacy agreed. "The sooner I hand it to Bobby, the better."

The woman hesitated a moment more, gazing at her, seeming to size her up. After a moment, she nodded. "Let's see if I have that information."

She returned her attention to the computer screen, tapped in some information, then turned back to Stacy. "It is Bienville Hall. Room 210."

"Room 210," Stacy repeated, smiling. "Thanks. You've been a lot of help."

Bienville Hall, a graceless but utilitarian high-rise dormitory built in 1969, was located directly across the commons from the engineering department.

She entered the building. The days of lockdown, single-gender dorms had gone the way of the dinosaur, and none of the students she passed paid any attention to her.

She took the stairs to the second floor, then made her way to room 210. When no one responded to her first knock, she knocked again.

Still no response. She glanced around her, saw she was alone in the hall, then nonchalantly reached out and tried the door.

It swung open.

She stepped inside, quietly closing the door behind her. What she was doing was illegal, though less of an offense now that she was no longer the law. Bizarre but true.

Stacy moved her gaze quickly over the small, pin-neat room. Interesting, she decided. Single guys were not known for their tidiness. What other norms did Bobby Gautreaux defy?

She crossed to the desk. Three neat piles graced its top. She thumbed through each, then eased open the desk drawer. She poked through its contents.

Finding nothing that looked incriminating, she shut the drawer, her attention going to a photo tacked to the corkboard above the desk. Of Cassie. Wearing a bikini, smiling at the camera.

He'd drawn a bull's-eye over her face.

Excited, she shifted her gaze. There were several other snapshots of the woman, one he'd adorned with devil's horns and a pointed tail, another with *Burn in hell, Bitch*.

He was either innocent—or incredibly stupid. If he had killed her, he had to know the police were going to come calling. Leaving those photos on the bulletin board assured him a lot of heat.

"What the hell?"

She turned. The young man in the doorway looked like he'd had a very bad night. He could be a poster child for Alcoholics Anonymous.

Or a walking, talking mug shot.

"The door was open."

"Bullshit. Get out."

"Bobby, right?"

His hair was wet; he had a towel looped over his shoulders. He moved his gaze over her. "Who wants to know?"

"A friend."

"Not of mine."

"I'm a friend of Cassie's."

Something ugly crossed his face. He folded his arms across his chest. "Big friggin' deal. I haven't talked to Cassie in ages. Get the fuck out."

Stacy closed the distance between them. She tilted her head back to meet his eyes. "Funny, I got the impression from her that the two of you had spoken quite recently."

"Then she's not only a bitch. But a liar, too."

Stacy bristled, offended. She swept her gaze over him. He had dark, curly hair and dark brown eyes, a gift from his French Acadian ancestors. If not for his surliness, he would have been quite handsome.

"She said you might know something about the game White Rabbit."

His expression altered subtly. "What about White Rabbit?"

"You know the game, right?"

"Yeah, I know it."

"Ever played it?"

He hesitated. "No."

"You don't sound so sure."

"You sound like a cop."

She narrowed her eyes, deciding there was little to like about the young man. He was a punk, through and through. She'd dealt with them daily in her years on the Dallas force.

Busting toads like him had been the best part of the job. She wished she had a badge now; she'd like to see him pee his pants.

Imagining just that, a smile touched her mouth. "Like I said, I'm just a friend. Doing a little research. Tell me about White Rabbit."

"What do you want to know?"

"About the game. What it's like. How you play. Things like that."

He curled his lip. She supposed it was his sleazy version of a smile. "It's not an ordinary game. It's dark. And it's violent."

He paused, his expression seeming to come alive. "Think Dr. Seuss meets Lara Croft, Tomb Raider. Wonderland is the setting. It's crazy. A bizarre world."

Sounded like a big barrel of laughs. "You say it's darker. What does that mean?"

"You're not a gamer, are you?"

"No."

"Then fuck you."

He turned away; she caught his arm. "Humor me, Bobby."

He looked from her hand on his arm to her eyes. The expression in them must have convinced him she meant business. "White Rabbit is a game of survival of the fittest. The smartest, most capable. Last man standing takes all."

"Takes all?"

"Kill or be killed, doll. Game's not over until only one character is left alive."

"How do you know so much about the game when you've never played it?"

He shook off her hand. "I've got connections."

"You know someone who plays?"

"Maybe."

"Cute. Do you or don't you?"

"I know the big man. The Supreme White Rabbit."

Bingo. "Who is he?"

"The game inventor himself. A dude named Leonardo Noble."

"Leonardo Noble," she repeated, searching her memory for recognition.

"He lives in New Orleans. Heard him talk at CoastCon. He's pretty cool but kind of manic. You want to know about the game, go to him."

She took a step back. "I will. Thanks for your help, Bobby."

"Don't mention it. Always happy to help a friend of Cassie's."

She found something about his smile almost reptilian. She moved around him to get to the door.

"Have you heard?" he called as she stepped through it. "Cassie went and got herself killed."

Stacy stopped in the doorway and turned slowly to face him. "What did you say?"

"Somebody whacked Cassie. That dyke girlfriend of hers, Ella, called me up, hysterical. Accused me of doing it."

"Did you?"

"Screw you."

Stacy shook her head, amazed at his attitude. "Are you really that stupid? You're going to cop an attitude? Don't you get it? You're the front-runner right now. I suggest you lose the 'tude, my friend, because the police don't need an excuse."

Two minutes later, she stepped out into the gray, breezy day. Coming toward her were Detective Malone and his partner. "Hello, boys," she said cheerfully.

Malone scowled as he recognized her. "What are you doing here?"

"Just stopped by to see a friend of a friend. That's not against the law, is it?"

Tony muffled a chuckle; Malone's scowl deepened. "Interfering in an investigation is."

"Did someone say I was?"

"It's just a warning."

"Received and noted." She smiled and started off, feeling both men's gazes on her back. She stopped and glanced over her shoulder at them. "Check the bulletin board over the desk," she called. "I think you'll find it interesting."

CHAPTER
9

Tuesday, March 1, 2005
1:40 p.m.

Spencer's lunch, a hot roast beef po'boy from Mother's Restaurant, grew cold on the desk in front of him. At first Bobby Gautreaux had been defiant. He'd tossed a shitload of bad attitude their way—until they pointed out the bull's-eye photograph. Then the defiance had become trepidation, which had transformed into pasty-faced terror when they'd announced they were taking him in for further questioning.

On the strength of Cassie Finch's friends' statements and the incriminating photographs, they'd requested a search warrant for Gautreaux's dorm room and car. Unlike in some states, Louisiana police were required to officially charge a suspect to hold him. With the exception of drug cases, which had to be expedited in twenty-four hours, they then had thirty days to submit their case to the D.A.'s office.

Unless the search yielded something stronger, they'd be forced to release him.

"Yo, Slick." Tony ambled over, then settled his large frame into the chair in front of the desk.

"Pasta Man. How's the kid doing?"

"Not well. Pacing. Looking like he's going to puke."

"He ask for a lawyer?"

"Called daddy. Daddy's getting one." He eyed the sandwich. "You going to eat that?"

"You didn't get lunch?"

He made a face. "Rabbit food. A salad with fat-free dressing."

"Betty's got you on another diet."

"For my own good, she says. She can't understand why I'm not losing weight."

Spencer cocked an eyebrow. Judging by the powdered sugar on the front of his partner's shirt, he'd hit the doughnuts again this morning. "I'm thinking it could be the Krispy Kremes. I could call her and—"

"Do and die, Junior."

Spencer laughed, suddenly starving. He pulled his sandwich closer and made a great show of taking a large bite. Gravy and mayonnaise oozed out the sides of the French bread.

"You're a nasty little prick, you know that?"

He wiped his mouth with the paper napkin. "Yeah, I know. But never say *little* and *prick* in the same sentence, it's just not cool. At least when you're talking to a guy."

Tony laughed loudly. A couple of the other guys glanced their way. "What do you think about Gautreaux?"

"Besides the fact that he's a spoiled punk?"

"Yeah, besides that."

Spencer hesitated. "He's a good suspect."

"I'm hearing a 'but' in your voice."

"It's too easy."

"Easy's good, pal. It's a gift. Take it with a 'Thank you, God' and a smile."

Spencer moved aside the sandwich to access the file folder beneath it. Inside were the toxicology and autopsy reports on Cassie Finch and Beth Wagner. Notes from the scene. Photographs. Names of family, friends and acquaintances.

Spencer motioned to the folder. "Autopsy confirmed the bullet killed her. No sign of sexual assault or other body trauma. Nails were clean. She never saw it coming. Pathologist set the TOD at 11:45 p.m."

"Toxicology?"

"No alcohol or drugs."

"Stomach contents?"

Spencer flipped open the file. "Nothing significant."

Tony leaned back in the chair; the frame creaked. "Trace?"

Spencer knew he referred to trace evidence. "Some fiber and hair. Lab's got it now."

"The shooter deliberately offed her," Tony said. "It fits with Gautreaux."

"But why would he openly stalk and threaten her, kill her, then leave such damning evidence tacked to his bulletin board?"

"Because he's stupid." Tony leaned toward him. "Most of 'em are. If they weren't, we'd be in a world of hurt."

"She let him in. It was late. Why would she do that if she was as frightened of him as her friends have claimed?"

"Maybe she was stupid, too." Tony glanced away, then back. "You'll learn, Slick. Mostly, the bad guys are stupid brutes and the victims are naive, trusting fools. And that's what gets 'em whacked. Sad but true."

"And Gautreaux took the computer because he sent her love letters or angry threats."

"You got it, my friend. In Homicide, what you see is likely what you're gonna get. We keep the pressure on Gautreaux and hope the lab results give us a direct link between him and the victim."

"Open and shut," Spencer said, reaching for his po'boy. "Just the way we like it."

CHAPTER
10

Wednesday, March 2, 2005
11:00 a.m.

Stacy pulled up in front of 3135 Esplanade Avenue, home of Leonardo Noble. Using the information she'd gotten from Bobby Gautreaux, she'd done an Internet search on Mr. Noble. She'd learned that he was, indeed, the man who had invented the game White Rabbit. And just as Gautreaux had claimed, he lived in New Orleans.

Only a matter of blocks from Café Noir.

Stacy shifted into Park, cut the engine and glanced toward the house once more. Esplanade Avenue was one of New Orleans' grand old boulevards, wide and shaded by giant live oak trees. The city, she had learned, was located eight feet *below* sea level, and this street, like many others in New Orleans, had once upon a time been a waterway, filled in to create a road. Why explorers had thought a swamp would be a good choice for a settlement eluded her.

But of course, the swamp had become New Orleans.

This end of Esplanade Avenue, close to City Park and the Fairgrounds, was called the Bayou St. John neighborhood. Although historically significant and beautiful, it was a transitional neighborhood because a meticulously restored mansion might sit next to one in disrepair, or to a school, restaurant or other commercial endeavor. The other end of the boulevard dead-ended at the Mississippi River, at the outermost edge of the French Quarter.

In between lay a wasteland—home to poverty, despair and crime.

Her online search had yielded some interesting information about the man who called himself a modern-day Leonardo da Vinci. He'd only lived in New Orleans two years. Before that, the inventor had called southern California home.

Stacy recalled the man's image. California had fit in a way the very traditional New Orleans didn't. His appearance was unconventional—equal parts California surfer, mad scientist and *GQ* entrepreneur. Not really handsome, with his wild and wavy blond hair and wire-rimmed glasses, but striking nonetheless.

Stacy mentally reviewed the series of articles she'd found on the man and his game. He had attended the University of California at Berkeley in the early eighties. It was there that he and a friend had created White Rabbit. Since then he'd created a number of other pop culture icons: ad campaigns, video games and even a bestselling novel that had become a hit movie.

She'd learned that White Rabbit had been inspired by Lewis Carroll's fantasy novel, *Alice's Adventures in Wonderland*. Not a particularly original idea: a number of other artists had been inspired by Carroll's creation, including the rock group Jefferson Airplane in their 1967 hit "White Rabbit."

Stacy drew in a deep breath and pulled her thoughts together. She had decided to pursue the White Rabbit angle. She hoped Bobby Gautreaux was the one, but hope didn't cut it. She knew how cops worked. By now, Malone and his partner would have focused all their energy and attention on Gautreaux. Why spend valuable time pursuing other, vague leads with such a good suspect in hand? He was the easy choice. The logical one. Many cases were solved because the one who looked most guilty was.

Most cases.

Not all.

Cops had lots of cases; they always hoped for a quick solve. But she wasn't a cop anymore. She had one case.

The murder of her friend.

Stacy opened the car door. If Bobby Gautreaux fell through, she planned to have another trail for the dynamic duo to follow, bread crumbs and all.

Stacy climbed out of the car. The Noble residence was a jewel. Greek Revival. Beautifully restored. Its grounds— which included a guest house—encompassed a full block.

Three massive live oak trees graced the front yard, their sprawling branches draped in Spanish moss.

She crossed to the wrought-iron front gate. As she passed under the oak's branches, she saw that they were beginning to bud. She'd heard that spring in New Orleans was something to behold and she was looking forward to judging that for herself.

Stacy climbed the stairs to the front gallery. She didn't have a badge. There was no reason the Nobles should even speak with her, let alone reveal information that might lead to a killer.

She had no badge; she meant to create the illusion that she did.

She rang the bell, slipping into detective mode. It was a matter of stance and bearing. Expression. Tone of voice.

And the flash of imaginary police identification.

A moment later a domestic opened the door. Stacy smiled coolly and flipped open her ID, then snapped it shut. "Is Mr. Noble home?"

As she had expected, a look of surprise crossed the woman's face, followed by one of curiosity. She nodded and stepped aside so Stacy could enter. "One moment, please," she said, closing the door behind them.

While Stacy waited, she studied the home's interior. A huge, curved staircase rose from the foyer to the second floor. To her left lay a double parlor, to her right a formal dining room. Dead ahead, the foyer opened to a wide hallway, which most probably led to the kitchen.

Fitting her original impression of Leonardo Noble being

both surfer dude and mad scientist, the interior was a mish-mash of the comfortable and the formal, the modern and classic. The art, too, was bizarrely eclectic. A large Blue Dog painting, by Louisiana artist George Rodrigue, graced the stairwell; next to it, a traditional landscape. In the dining room hung an antique portrait of a child, one of those hideous representations of a child as a miniature adult.

"The portrait came with the house," a woman said from the top of the stairs. Stacy looked up. The woman, of obvious mixed Asian descent, was gorgeous. One of those cool, self-possessed beauties Stacy admired and despised—both for the same reason.

Stacy watched as she descended the stairs. The woman crossed to her and extended her hand. "It's quite awful, isn't it?"

"Pardon?"

"The portrait. I can hardly bear to look at it, but for some obscure reason Leo's grown attached." She smiled then, the curving of her lips more practiced than warm. "I'm Kay Noble."

The wife. "Stacy Killian," she said. "Thank you for seeing me."

"Mrs. Maitlin said you're a police officer?"

"I'm investigating a murder." *That much was true.*

The woman's eyes widened slightly. "How can I help you?"

"I was hoping to speak with Mr. Noble. Is he available?"

"I'm sorry, he's not. However, I'm his business manager. Perhaps I can be of some assistance?"

"A woman was murdered several nights ago. She was heavily into fantasy role-playing games. The night she died she was meeting someone to play your husband's game."

"My ex-husband," she corrected. "Leo's the creator of a number of RPGs. Which one?"

"The game that refuses to die, I'll bet."

Stacy turned. Leonardo Noble stood in the doorway to the parlor. The first thing she noted was his height—he was considerably taller than he had appeared in his press photo. The boyish grin made him look younger than the forty-five she'd read his age to be.

"Which one would that be?" she asked.

"White Rabbit, of course." He bounded across the foyer and stuck out his hand. "I'm Leonardo."

She took it. "Stacy Killian."

"*Detective* Stacy Killian," Kay added. "She's investigating a murder."

"A murder?" His eyebrows shot up. "Here's an unexpected twist to the day."

Stacy took his hand. "A woman named Cassie Finch was killed this past Sunday night. She was an avid fan of role-playing games. The Friday before her death, she told a friend she had met someone who played the game White Rabbit, and he had arranged a meeting between her and a Supreme White Rabbit."

Leo Noble spread his hands. "I still don't understand what this has to do with me."

She took a small spiral notebook from her jacket pocket,

the same type of notebook she had carried as a detective. "Another gamer described *you* as the Supreme White Rabbit."

He laughed, then apologized. "Of course, there's nothing about this situation that's funny. It's the comment...a Supreme White Rabbit. Really."

"As the game's creator, aren't you?"

"Some say so. They hold me up as some sort of mystical being. A god of sorts."

"Is that the way you view yourself?" she asked.

He laughed again. "Certainly not."

Kay stepped in. "That's why we call it the game that refuses to die. The fans are obsessed."

Stacy moved her gaze between the unlikely pair. "Why?" she asked.

"Don't know." Leonardo shook his head. "If I did, I'd re-create the magic." He leaned toward her, all boyish enthusiasm. "Because it is, you know. Magic. Touching people in a way that's so personal. And so intense."

"You never published the game. Why?"

He glanced at his ex-wife. "I'm not the sole creator of White Rabbit. My best friend and I created it back in 1982, while we were grad students at Berkeley. D & D was at the height of its popularity. Dick and I were both gamers, but we grew bored with D & D."

"So you decided to create your own scenario."

"Exactly. It caught on and quickly spread by word of mouth from Berkeley to other universities."

"It became clear to them," Kay offered quietly, "that they had done something special. That they had a viable commercial success at their fingertips."

"His name?" Stacy asked.

Leonardo took over once more. "Dick Danson."

She made a note of the name as the man continued. "We formed a business partnership, intending to publish White Rabbit and other projects we had in the works. We had a falling out before we could."

"A falling out?" Stacy repeated. "Over what?"

The man looked uncomfortable; he and his ex-wife exchanged a glance. "Let's just say, I discovered Dick wasn't the person I thought he was."

"They dissolved the partnership," Kay said. "Agreed not to publish anything they worked on together."

"That must have been difficult," Stacy said.

"Not as difficult as you might think. I had lots of opportunities. Lots of ideas. So did he. And White Rabbit was already out there, so we figured we weren't losing that much."

"Two White Rabbits," she murmured.

"Pardon?"

"You and your former partner. As co-creators, you could both go by the title of Supreme White Rabbit."

"That would be true. Except that he's dead."

"Dead?" she repeated. "When?"

He thought a moment. "About three years ago. Because it was before we moved here. He drove off a cliff along the Monterey coast."

She was silent a moment. "Do you play the game, Mr. Noble?"

"No. I gave up role-playing games years ago."

"May I ask why?"

"Lost interest. Grew out of them. Like anything done to excess, after a while the endeavor loses its thrill."

"So you went looking for a different thrill."

He sent her a big, goofy smile. "Something like that."

"Are you in contact with any local players?"

"None."

"Have any contacted you?"

He hesitated slightly. "No."

"You don't seem certain of that."

"He is." Kay glanced pointedly at her watch; Stacy saw the sparkle of diamonds. "I'm sorry to cut this short," she said, standing, "but Leo's going to be late for a meeting."

"Of course." Stacy got to her feet, tucking her notebook into her pocket as she did.

They walked her to the front door. She stopped and turned back after she had stepped through it. "One last question, Mr. Noble. Some of the articles I read suggested a link between role-playing games and violent behavior. Do you believe that?"

Something passed across both their faces. The man's smile didn't waver, yet it suddenly looked forced.

"Guns don't kill people, Detective Killian. People kill people. That's what I believe."

His answer seemed practiced; no doubt he had been asked that question many times before.

She wondered when he had begun to doubt his answer.

Stacy thanked the pair and made her way to her vehicle.

When she reached it, she glanced back. The couple had disappeared into the house. Odd, she decided. She found something about them very odd.

She gazed at the closed door a moment, reviewing their conversation, assessing her thoughts about it.

She didn't think they had been lying. But she was certain they hadn't been telling the whole truth. Stacy unlocked her car, opened the door and slid behind the wheel. But why?

That's what she meant to find out.

CHAPTER
11

Thursday, March 3, 2005
11:00 a.m.

Spencer stood at the back of the Newman Religious Center's chapel and watched Cassie Finch and Beth Wagner's friends file out. Located on the UNO campus, the multidenominational chapel, like every other building on site, looked grimly utilitarian.

The chapel had proved too small to accommodate the many who had come to pay their last respects to Cassie and Beth. It had been filled to overflowing.

Spencer shook off crushing fatigue. He had made the mistake of meeting some friends at Shannon's the night before. One thing had led to another and he'd closed the place at 2:00 a.m.

He was paying the price today. Big time.

He forced himself to focus on the rows of faces. Stacy Killian, expression stony, accompanied by Billie Bellini. The members of Cassie's game group, all of whom he had spoken with, Beth's friends and family as well. Bobby Gautreaux.

He found that interesting. Very interesting.

The kid had acted remorseless a couple of days ago; now he presented the picture of despair.

Despairing over the fate of his own ass, no doubt.

The search of his car and dorm room hadn't turned up a direct link—yet. The crime-lab guys were working their way through the hundreds of prints and trace lifted from the scene. He wasn't giving up on Gautreaux. The kid was the best they had so far.

From across the room he caught the eye of Mike Benson, one of his fellow detectives. Spencer nodded slightly at Benson and pushed away from the wall. He followed the students out into the bright, cool day.

Tony had been stationed out front during the service. Police photographers with telephoto lenses had been planted, capturing the faces of all the mourners on film, a record they would cross-reference against any suspects.

Spencer moved his gaze over the group. If not Gautreaux, was the real killer here? Watching? Secretly excited? Reliving Cassie's death? Or was he amused? Laughing at them, congratulating himself on his cleverness?

He didn't have a sense either way. No one stood out. No one looked like they didn't belong.

Frustration licked at him. A feeling of inadequacy. Ineptitude.

Damn it, he didn't belong in charge of this. He felt like he was drowning.

Stacy separated herself from friends and crossed to him. He nodded at her, slipping into the good ol' boy role that fit him so well. "'Morning, former-cop Killian."

"Save the charm for somebody else, Malone. I'm beyond it."

"That so, Ms. Killian? Down here we call it manners."

"In Texas we call it bullshit. I know why you're here, Detective. I know what you're looking for. Anybody stand out?"

"No. But I didn't know all her friends. Anyone jump out at you?"

"No." She made a sound of frustration. "Except for Gautreaux."

He followed her glance. The young man stood just outside the circle of friends. The man beside him, Spencer knew, was his lawyer. It seemed to Spencer the kid was working damn hard to look devastated.

"That his lawyer with him?" she asked.

"Yup."

"I thought maybe the little weasel would be in jail."

"We don't have enough to charge him. But we're still looking."

"You got a search warrant?"

"Yes. We're still waiting on print and trace reports from the lab."

Part of her had hoped for better: the weapon or some other incontrovertible evidence. She glanced at the young man, then back at Spencer. She was angry, he saw. "He's not sorry," she said. "He's acting all broken up, but he's not. That pisses me off."

He touched her arm lightly. "We're not going to give up, Stacy. I promise you."

"You really expect me to be reassured by that?" She looked away, then back. "You know what I told the bereaved friends and family of every victim I ever worked? That I wouldn't give up. I promised. But it was bullshit. Because there was always another case. Another victim."

She leaned toward him, voice tight with emotion, eyes bright with unshed tears. "This time I'm *not* giving up."

She turned and walked away. He watched her go, reluctant admiration pulling at him. She was a hard-ass, no doubt about it. Determined to a fault. Pushy. Cocky in a way few women were, down here, anyway.

And smart. He'd give her that.

Spencer narrowed his eyes slightly. Maybe too damn smart for her own good.

Tony ambled over. He followed the direction of Spencer's gaze. "The prickly Ms. Killian give you anything?"

"Besides a headache? No." He looked at his partner. "How about you? Anybody jump out?"

"Nope. But that doesn't mean the bastard wasn't here."

Spencer nodded, turning his attention back to Stacy. She stood with Cassie's mother and sister. As he watched, she clasped the older woman's hand, leaned close. She said something to her, expression almost fierce.

He swung back toward his partner. "I suggest we keep an eye on Stacy Killian."

"You think she knows something she's not telling?"

About Cassie's murder, he didn't. But he did believe she had the ability and determination to uncover information they needed. And in a way that might attract attention. The wrong kind. "I think she's too smart for her own good."

"That's not necessarily a bad thing. She just might solve this thing for us."

"Or get herself killed." He met the older man's eyes once more. "I want to follow up the White Rabbit angle."

"What changed your mind?"

Killian. Her brains.

And her balls.

But he wasn't about to tell Tony that; he'd hear never-ending shit about it.

Instead, he shrugged. "Nowhere else to go. Might as well."

CHAPTER
12

Thursday, March 3, 2005
3:50 p.m.

"This is it," Spencer said, indicating the Esplanade Avenue mansion Leonardo Noble called home. "Pull over."

Tony did, whistling long and low. "It appears there's big money in fun and games."

Spencer grunted a response, eyes on the Noble residence. He'd done a search and discovered that Leonardo Noble, White Rabbit's creator, did indeed live in New Orleans. He'd also learned the man had no priors, no outstandings, not so much as an unpaid parking ticket.

That didn't mean he wasn't guilty as hell. Only that if he was, he was smart enough to get away with it.

They crossed to the wrought-iron gate and let themselves

through. No dogs barked. No alarms went off. He glanced at the house; not a burglar bar on even one window.

Obviously Noble felt safe. Risky in a marginal neighborhood like this one, especially with such obvious wealth.

They rang the bell and a woman in a black dress and crisp white apron answered. They introduced themselves and asked to see Leonardo Noble. In a matter of moments, a forty-something-looking man with an athletic build and a head of wild, wavy hair hurried out to greet them.

He held out a hand. "Leonardo Noble. How can I help you?"

Spencer shook his hand. "Detective Malone. My partner, Detective Sciame. NOPD."

He looked at them expectantly, eyebrows raised in question.

"We're investigating the murder of a UNO coed."

"I don't know what else I can tell you."

"You haven't told me anything yet, Mr. Noble."

The man laughed. "I'm sorry, I already spoke with your associate. Detective Killian. Stacy Killian."

It took a second for the man's words to register and a split second more for Spencer's temper to flare. "I'm sorry to tell you this, Mr. Noble. But you've been duped, there is no Stacy Killian at the NOPD."

The man stared at them, expression confused. "But I spoke with her. Yesterday."

"Did she show you her——"

"Leo," a woman said from behind them, "what's going on?"

Spencer turned. A beautiful, dark-haired woman crossed to stand beside Leonardo Noble.

"Kay, Detectives Malone and Sciame. My business manager, Kay Noble."

She shook both their hands, smiling warmly. "His ex-wife as well, Detectives."

Spencer returned her smile. "That would explain the name."

"Yes, I suppose so."

The inventor cleared his throat. "They say the woman who was here the other day wasn't a police officer at all."

She frowned. "I don't understand."

"Did she show you a badge, ma'am?"

"Not me, our housekeeper. I'll get her. Excuse me a moment."

Spencer experienced a moment of pity for the housekeeper. Kay Noble didn't look like the type of woman who tolerated mistakes.

Moments later, she returned with the woman, who looked upset. "Tell the officers what you told me, Valerie."

The housekeeper—sixtyish with iron-gray hair swept up into a flattering French twist—clasped her hands in front of her. "The woman flashed a badge...or what I thought was a badge. She asked to speak with Mr. Noble."

"You didn't take a good look at her identification?"

"No. I—" The woman cut her eyes toward her employer. "She looked like the police and sounded like..." Her words trailed off; she cleared her throat. "I'm very sorry this happened. I promise it won't again."

Before Kay Noble could comment, Spencer stepped in. "Let me assure you, I don't believe any harm's been done. She was a friend of the deceased and is also an ex-cop. Not NOPD."

"It's no wonder you were fooled," Tony added, "she's got the whole cop schtick down pat."

The housekeeper looked relieved; Kay Noble furious. Leonardo surprised them all by laughing loudly.

"I hardly find this funny, Leo," Kay snapped.

"Of course it is, love," he said. "It's all funny."

Color flooded her face. "But she could have been anybody. What if Alice—"

"Nothing happened. Like the officer said, no harm done." He gave her a quick hug, then turned to Spencer. "So, Detectives, how can I help you?"

A half hour later, Spencer and Tony thanked Leonardo Noble and headed for their car. The inventor had answered all their questions. He hadn't known Cassie Finch. Had never been to either UNO or Café Noir. Nor did he know, or was he in contact with, any local White Rabbit players. He explained that he and a friend had invented the game, that they'd never published it and that his co-inventor was dead.

The two detectives didn't speak until they had settled inside, safety belts fastened, motor idling. "What do you think?" Spencer asked.

"Babe one, Slick zero."

"Kiss my ass, Pasta Man."

Tony laughed. "I'll pass. Frankly, I'm not into that."

"I was talking about Noble, by the way. What did you think?"

"He's a little different. And that thing about working with his ex-wife. No way I could work with mine."

"You and Betty have been married forever."

"Yeah, but if we weren't, she'd drive me crazy."

"You think he's on the up-and-up?"

"Struck me that way, but hard to tell without the element of surprise."

"Killian," Spencer muttered. "She's in my way."

"What're you going to do about it, hotshot?"

Spencer narrowed his eyes. "Café Noir is just up the street. Let's see if the meddling Ms. Killian is there."

CHAPTER
13

Thursday, March 3, 2005
4:40 p.m.

Stacy looked up to see Detectives Malone and Sciame heading across the coffeehouse toward her. Malone looked *really* pissed.

He had found out about her visit with Leonardo Noble.

Sorry, fellas. Free country.

"Hello, Detectives," she said as they neared her table. "Coffee break? Or social call?"

"Impersonating a police officer is a crime, Ms. Killian," Spencer began.

"I know that." She smiled sweetly and shut her laptop. "And what does that have to do with me?"

"Don't bullshit me. We talked to Noble."

"Leonardo Noble?"

"Of course, Leonardo Noble. Creator of the game White Rabbit and considered by fans to be *the* Supreme White Rabbit."

"Glad to see you've been paying attention."

Behind Spencer, Tony cleared his throat. She saw he struggled not to laugh. She decided she liked Tony Sciame. A sense of humor was a good thing in the job.

"Still," she continued, "I don't understand what this has to do with me?"

"You told him you were a NOPD detective."

"No," she corrected, "he *assumed* I was. His housekeeper, actually."

"Which was exactly what you wanted."

She didn't deny it. "Last time I checked, that wasn't against the law. Unless law here in Louisiana is a lot different than in Texas."

"I could haul you in and charge you with obstruction."

"But you won't. Look..." She stood so she could stand nose to nose with him. "You could take me in, keep me for a few hours, give me a hard time. But at the end of the day you wouldn't arrest me because it wouldn't stick."

"She's got a point, Slick," Tony said. He shifted his focus to her. "Here's the deal, Stacy. Can't have you questioning potential suspects before we do. We need to get 'em cold, so we can gauge their reactions to our questions. You know this, you were a cop. You know we can't have you leading a witness. Putting thoughts in their heads that weren't there before. It taints their testimony. I'd define that as obstruction."

"I can help," she said. "And you know it."

"You don't have a badge. You're out of it. Sorry."

She wouldn't be dissuaded. Not until she felt certain the investigation was on solid footing. But she wasn't about to let them know that. "Consider me a source, then. Like a snitch."

Tony nodded, expression pleased. "Good. You get a lead, you pass it to us. I have absolutely no problem with that. You, Slick?"

Stacy cut her eyes to the younger detective. *He wasn't falling for her submissive routine. Smarter than the average bear, after all.*

"No problem with that," he said, not looking at his partner.

"Glad that's settled." The older cop rubbed his hands together. "So, what do they have here that's good?"

"I'm particularly fond of the cappuccinos, but it's all good."

"I think I'll try one of those frozen thingies that all the teenagers are drinking. Want anything?"

Spencer shook his head, still not taking his gaze from Stacy.

"What?" she asked as Tony walked away.

"Why are you doing this?"

"I told you why. At the memorial service."

"It's not smart, Stacy. Involving yourself in this investigation. You're not a cop anymore. You were first to the scene. You very well may have been the last person to see Cassie Finch alive."

"Surely not the last. That would make me a murderer. And you and I both know I'm not."

"I know no such thing."

She made a sound of frustration. "Give me a break, Malone."

"I have, Stacy. But the game's over." He leaned slightly toward her. "The fact is, I'm the law and you're not. This is the last time I'll ask nicely. Stay out of my way."

Stacy watched him walk away, joining his partner just as he took his first sip of the frozen coffee-and-chocolate concoction he'd ordered. She smiled to herself.

May the best investigator win, fellas.

CHAPTER
14

Friday, March 4, 2005
10:30 p.m.

The Earl K. Long Library stood at the center of the UNO campus, facing the quad. Two hundred thousand square feet and four floors, like most buildings at the university, the library had been built in the 1960s.

Stacy sat at a table on the fourth floor. The fourth housed the Multimedia Center, which included microfilm and microfiche, video and audio collections. She'd been researching RPGs since she'd left her afternoon class. Tired and hungry, she sported a splitting headache.

She was loath to go home, anyway. The information she'd

uncovered about role-playing games, and White Rabbit in particular, was fascinating.

And disturbing. Article after article linked role-playing games to suicides, death pacts and even murder. Claims from gamers' parents of dramatic behavior transformation in their children, of obsession with playing so intense they feared for their children's mental health. A number of parent groups had formed in the attempt to alert others to the dangers of role-playing games and to force manufacturers to label the games with warnings.

The circumstantial evidence against the games had proved so impressive that several politicians had gotten involved in the fray, although to date nothing had come of it.

In all fairness, a number of other researchers discounted such findings, calling them unproved and alarmist. But they, too, acknowledged that in the wrong hands the material could be a powerful tool.

It wasn't the game that was dangerous, but the obsession with the game.

A variation on Leo Noble's "Guns don't kill people, people kill people" schtick.

Stacy brought a hand to her temple and absently rubbed, longing for a cup of strong coffee or a chocolate chip cookie. Each—or both—would knock out her headache. She glanced at her watch. The library closed at eleven; she might as well stick it out until then.

She returned her attention to the material in front of her. The most written-about game was Dungeons & Dragons. It had been first on the market and had remained the most popular. But even though White Rabbit sat way outside the main-stream, Stacy had found several references to the game. One parent group labeled it "unholy," another "deplorably violent."

A movement from the corner of her eye caught her attention. Someone leaving, she supposed, noting the library was almost deserted. A straggler like herself. The other students had retired their pursuit of knowledge—or grades, for they were at times mutually exclusive—and headed home for TV or out for drinks with friends.

At eleven campus security would begin clearing the building, starting on the fourth floor and working their way to the first.

She had closed the library many times already in her short tenure as a grad student.

Her thoughts drifted to Spencer Malone. Their confrontation. She was lucky he hadn't hauled her in. In the same position, she probably would have. Just on principle.

What was it about Detective Malone that caused her to lash out?

Something about him reminded her of Mac.

At thoughts of her former DPD partner and lover, her chest grew tight. With hurt? Or was it longing? Not for him, for the man she loved hadn't even existed. But for what she thought they'd had. Love. Companionship. Commitment.

She sucked in a sharp breath. That part of her life was over. She had survived Mac's betrayal; it had been the catalyst that forced her to take hold of her life. Change it. She was stronger for it.

She didn't need a man, or love, to make her happy.

Doggedly, she returned to her research. Various studies provided a picture of the typical gamer: a higher-than-average IQ, creative with a vivid imagination. Otherwise, gamers crossed all social, economic and racial borders. The games, it seemed, were outlets for fantasy. They offered excitement and an opportunity for players to experience things they could never hope to in real life.

A sound came from the stacks behind her. Stacy lifted her head and turned in that direction. The sound came again, like a pent-up breath expelled.

"Hello," she called. "Anybody there?"

Silence answered. The hair on the back of her neck prickled. She'd been a cop long enough to sense when something wasn't right. Call it a cop's sixth sense or heightened instinct for self-preservation, it rarely let her down.

Adrenaline pumping, Stacy got slowly to her feet, automatically reaching for her weapon.

No shoulder holster. No weapon.

Not a cop anymore.

Stacy's gaze landed on her ballpoint pen, a lethal weapon when used accurately and without hesitation. And most effective when the blow was delivered to the base of the skull, the jugular or an eye. She picked it up and curled her right hand around it.

"Anyone there?" she called again, forcefully.

She heard the rumble of the elevator, on its way to the fourth floor. Campus security, she realized. Clearing the building. Good. Backup, in case she needed it.

She started toward the stacks, heart pounding, pen ready. A sound came from the opposite direction. She whirled. The lights went off. The stairwell door flew open and light spilled out as a figure darted through.

Before she could shout for him to stop, she was grabbed from behind and dragged against a broad chest. With one arm he held her tightly against him, arms pinned. With the other, he covered her mouth and immobilized her head.

A man, she determined, tabling her terror. Tall. Several inches taller than she, which would put him at better than six feet. One who knew what he was doing; the angle he held her head made breaking her neck relatively easy. He had size and strength on his side; struggling would be both futile and a waste of precious energy.

Stacy tightened her fingers on the pen, waiting for the right moment. Knowing it would come. He had used the element of surprise to trap her; she would return the favor.

"Stay out of it," he whispered, voice thick, muffled by design, she was certain. He pressed his mouth closer, then speared his tongue in and out of her ear. Bile rose in her throat, threatening to gag her.

"Or I won't," he finished. "Understand?"

She did. He was threatening to rape her.

The bastard would regret that threat.

Her moment came. Reassured by what he no doubt thought her immobilizing fear, he shifted. He intended to shove her, she realized. Then run. As the realization registered, she reacted. Shifting her own weight, then spinning around, she grasped hold of him with her left hand and plunged the ballpoint into his stomach with her right. She felt his blood on her fingers.

He howled in pain and stumbled backward. She did, too, falling into a cart of books. The cart tipped, the books crashed to the floor.

A flashlight beam sliced through the dark. "Who's there?"

"Here!" she called, fighting to right herself. "Help!"

Her attacker got to his feet and ran. He reached the stairwell door a moment before the campus cop found her.

"Miss, are you all ri—"

"The stairs," she managed to say, pointing. "He ran that way."

The man didn't waste time on words. He darted in that direction, radio out, calling for backup.

Stacy stood, legs wobbly. She heard the cop's feet pounding on the stairs, though she doubted he would catch the man. Even wounded, he'd had too great a head start.

The lights came on. Stacy blinked at the sudden change. As her eyes adjusted, she saw the books and toppled cart, the trail of blood leading to the stairwell.

A woman rushed toward her, expression alarmed. "Are you all— My God, you're bleeding!"

Stacy looked down at herself. Her shirt and right hand were bloody. "It's his blood. I stabbed him with my ballpoint."

The woman went white. Afraid she might faint, Stacy led her to a chair. "Put your head between your knees. It'll help."

When the woman did as she instructed, she added, "Now breathe. Deeply, through your nose."

After several moments, the woman lifted her head. "I feel so silly. You're the one who should be—"

"Never mind that. Are you okay now?"

"Yes, you—" she breathed deeply several times "—you were really lucky."

"Lucky?" she repeated.

"You could have been raped. Those other girls—"

"Weren't so lucky."

Stacy turned. The campus cop who had come to her aid was back. He was young, she saw. Probably twenty-five. "You didn't catch him, did you?"

He looked frustrated. "No. I'm sorry." His motioned to her hand and bloodstained shirt. "Are you hurt?"

"She stabbed him with her pen," the librarian supplied.

The campus cop looked at her, his expression a combination of admiration and disbelief. "You did?"

"I was a cop for ten years," she said. "I know how to defend myself."

"It's a good thing you do," he said. "There've been three rapes on campus this year, all during the fall term. We thought maybe he'd moved on."

Stacy had heard about the rapes, had been warned by her adviser to be careful. Especially at night. She didn't believe the man who'd attacked her was this rapist. If his intention had been rape, why the warning "To stay out of it"? Why had he been prepared to let her go? He would have dragged her to the floor, tried to get at her clothing.

No. It didn't add up.

Stacy told him so.

"The MO's the same. He's attacked women alone at night on campus. All three have occurred between 10:00 and 11:00 p.m. The first right here in the library."

"This wasn't that guy. His intention wasn't rape." She relayed the sequence of events. How he whispered in her ear to stay out of it. "He was about to let me go. That's when I made my move."

"Are you certain of what you heard?"

"Yes. Absolutely."

The cop didn't look convinced. "That fits the rapist's MO as well. He whispered into each one of his victims' ears."

Stacy frowned. "Then why let me go with a warning?"

The cop and librarian exchanged glances. "You're upset. Understandably. You've had a shock—"

"And I'm not thinking clearly?" she finished for him. "I worked Homicide for ten years. I've been through shit a lot more shocking than this. I'm not mistaken about what I heard."

The young officer's face reddened; he took a step back from her. She supposed using the S word had put him off, but damn it, she'd been making a point.

"Yes, ma'am," he said coolly. "I've got to call the NOPD. Get someone over here to collect evidence. Tell your story to them."

"Ask for Detective Spencer Malone," she said. "ISD. Tell him it's about the Finch case."

CHAPTER
15

Saturday, March 5, 2005
12:30 a.m.

Spencer greeted the officer standing sentinel at the door of the UNO library. He was an old-timer. "How's it going?"

The other man shrugged. "Okay. Wish spring'd get here. It's still too damn cold for these old bones."

Only a New Orleanian would gripe about nighttime temperatures in the sixties.

The man held out a clipboard; Spencer signed in. "Upstairs?"

"Yeah. On four."

Spencer found the elevator. He had been asleep when he'd gotten the call. At first he thought he'd misunderstood the dispatcher. Nobody was dead. An attempted rape. But the victim claimed it had something to do with the Finch murder.

His investigation.

So he'd dragged his butt out of bed and headed what seemed like halfway across the world to the UNO campus.

The elevator reached four; he stepped off and followed the sound of voices. The group came into view. He stopped. *Killian.* Her back was to him, but he recognized her, anyway. Not just by her glorious blond hair, but something about the way she held herself. Erectly. With a kind of confidence that had been earned.

To her left stood a couple of the campus cops and John Russell, from DIU, Third District.

Spencer closed the distance between them. "Trouble follows you, doesn't it, Ms. Killian?"

The three men looked his way. She turned. He saw that her shirt was bloodstained.

"It's starting to seem so," she said.

"Do you need medical attention?"

"No. But he might."

He wasn't surprised she'd gotten the best of him. He motioned toward the library table nearest her. They crossed to it, then sat.

He took the spiral notebook from his pocket. "Tell me what happened."

Russell wandered over. "Attempted rape," he began. "Same MO as three earlier, unsolved—"

Spencer held up a hand. "I'd like to hear Ms. Killian's version of events first."

"Thank you," she said. "It wasn't an attempted rape."

"Go on."

"I was working late."

He glanced at the material on the table, scanning titles. "Research?"

"Yes."

"On role-playing games?"

She lifted her chin slightly. "Yes. The library was deserted, or seemed to be. I heard someone, behind the stacks. I called out. Got no answer and went to investigate."

She paused. Smoothed her hands over her thighs, her only outward sign of nerves. "When I reached the stacks, the lights went off. The stairwell door flew open and someone darted through. I started to go after him. That's when I was grabbed from behind."

"So there were two people besides you here?"

Her expression registered something akin to surprise. He'd only repeated her words in a different way; clearly she hadn't put the two together.

She nodded. He looked at the other officers. "Any of the other victims report more than one attacker at the scene?"

"No," the youngest of the university officers replied.

Spencer returned his gaze to hers. "He grabbed you from behind?"

"Yes. And held me in a way that indicated he knew what he was doing."

"Show me."

She nodded, stood and motioned to the campus cop. "Do you mind?" He said no, and she demonstrated. A moment later, she released him and returned to her seat.

"He was several inches taller than me. And quite strong."

"So how did you get away?"

"Drove a ballpoint pen into his belly."

"We've got the pen," Russell offered. "Bagged and tagged."

"And how does this relate to the Finch and Wagner murders?"

She made a sound of frustration. "He told me to stay out of it. Or else he wouldn't. Then he poked his tongue in and out of my ear. And asked me if I understood."

"Sounds like a direct threat of rape," Russell said.

"He was warning me to keep my nose out of the investigation." She jumped to her feet. "Don't you see? I've stepped on somebody's toes. Gotten too close."

"Whose toes?"

"I don't know!"

"We've alerted the infirmary to watch for a student who comes in with a puncture wound to be treated."

Stacy made a sound of disbelief. "With at least two dozen doc-in-the-box clinics in the metro area, you think he'll go to the infirmary?"

"Maybe," the cop said defensively. "If he's a student."

"I'd say, that's a mighty big 'if,' Officer." Stacy looked at Spencer. "Can I go now?"

"Sure. I'll give you a ride."

"I've got my car, thanks."

He skimmed his gaze over her. If she was pulled over for some reason, the cop would take one look at her and haul her in for questioning.

Bloodstained shirts had that effect on police officers.

"I think, considering your present condition, I'll follow."

It looked as if she was going to protest. She didn't. "Fine."

Spencer followed her across town, angling his Camaro into the space by a fire hydrant. He flipped down his visor, revealing his NOPD identification and climbed out of the car.

Crime-scene tape still stretched across the Finch side of the double. He made a note to take it down before he left. The scene should have been cleared for cleanup days ago. He was surprised Stacy hadn't busted him on it.

Stacy slammed her car door. "I can take it from here."

"What? Not even a thank you?"

She folded her arms across her chest. "For what? Seeing me home? Or thinking I'm full of shit?"

"I didn't say that."

"You didn't have to. Your expression shouted it."

He arched an eyebrow. "Shouted?"

"Forget it."

She spun on her heel and started for her front steps. He caught her arm, stopping her. "What's your problem?"

"Right now, you."

"You're pretty when you're mad."

"But not when I'm not?"

"Stop putting words in my mouth."

"Believe me, I couldn't. I don't know Bubba-speak."

He gazed at her a moment, torn between frustration and amusement. Amusement won; he laughed and released her arm. "You have any coffee up there?"

"Are you making a pass at me?"

"I wouldn't dare, Killian. Just figured I'd give your theory another chance."

"And why's that?"

"Because it might have merit." He grinned. "Stranger things have happened."

"Not that. The other. Why wouldn't you dare make a pass at me?"

"Simple. You'd kick my ass."

She stared at him a moment, then sent him a killer smile. "You're right, I would."

"We agree on something." He brought a hand to his heart. "It's a miracle."

"Don't push it, Malone. Come on."

They climbed the stairs, then crossed the porch to the front door. She unlocked it, stepped inside and flipped on a light. He followed her in and to the kitchen, located at the back of the apartment.

She opened her refrigerator, peered inside, then glanced back at him. "Coffee's not going to do the trick tonight. Not for me." She held out a bottle of beer. "How about you?"

He took it, twisted off the cap. "Thanks."

She followed suit, then took a swallow of the beverage. "I needed that."

"Big night."

"Big year."

He had called the DPD and now he knew a little about her past. She was a ten-year veteran of the DPD. Highly regarded within the force. Resigned suddenly after cracking a big case that had involved her sister, Jane. The captain he'd spoken with had indicated some personal reasons for her resignation but hadn't provided details. Spencer hadn't pushed.

"Want to talk about it?"

"Nope." She took another swallow.

"Why'd you leave the force?"

"Like I told your partner, I needed a change."

He rolled the bottle between his palms. "It have anything to do with your sister?"

Jane Westbrook. Stacy's half sister and only sibling. An artist of some renown. The target of a murderous plot. One that had damn near been successful.

"You checked out my story."

"Of course."

"The answer to your question is no. Leaving the force was about me."

He brought the bottle to his lips and drank, never taking his gaze from hers.

She frowned. "What?"

"You ever hear the old saying, you can take the cop out of the job, but you can't take the job out of the cop?"

"Yeah, I've heard it. I don't put much stock in old sayings."

"Maybe you should."

She checked her watch. "It's getting late."

"That it is." He took another swallow of the beer, ignoring her not-so-subtle hint that he should go. Taking his time, he finished his beer. Set the bottle carefully on the table, then stood.

She folded her arms across her chest, annoyed. "I thought you wanted to hear my story one more time?"

"I lied." He grabbed his leather jacket. "Thanks for the brew."

She made a sound. Of outraged disbelief, Spencer guessed. He fought a smile, crossed to the door, then looked back at her. "Two things, Killian. First, clearly you have no idea what a 'Bubba' is."

A smile tugged at her mouth. "And second?"

"You might not be so full of shit after all."

CHAPTER
16

Saturday, March 5, 2005
11:00 a.m.

Stacy worked to focus on the text in front of her. John Keats's "Ode to Psyche." She had chosen to study the Romantics because the sensibility was so foreign to today's—and so far from the brutal reality she'd been a part of for the past ten years.

Today, however, the poem of beauty and spiritual love seemed overwrought and just plain silly.

She felt battered and punchy, though she wasn't sure why. Beyond a couple of bruises, the man hadn't hurt her. Truth be told, save for the adrenaline rush, she hadn't even been frightened. She'd never felt the situation out of her control.

So why the shakes now?

Stay out of it. Or I won't.

A warning. She had made someone very uncomfortable.

But whom? Bobby Gautreaux? It didn't seem likely, because the police had already pinpointed him. Someone else she had spoken with about White Rabbit? Yes. But who?

The cops wouldn't be any help. They were convinced her attacker was the same man who had raped those other coeds—that he had escalated his attacks.

She didn't blame them; the MO of the encounter was nearly identical to that of the raped coeds. She reviewed what they'd told her about the campus rapist. A big man, he targeted women alone on campus at night, grabbed them from behind. They had nicknamed him Romeo because of the sweet nothings he murmured in his victims' ears. Things like "I love you," "We'll be together forever," and most damning, "Stay with me."

You might not be so full of shit after all.

Did Malone believe her? Or was he simply tossing her a bone to shut her up?

I wouldn't make a pass at you, Killian. You'd kick my ass.

The comment bothered her. Was she that intimidating? That much of a hard-ass? Somewhere along the line had she lost the ability to be approachable?

"Ball-buster Killian," her DPD colleagues had called her. It appeared she was moving up in the world   she was an ass-kicker now. What next? Gut-crusher?

"Hello, Detective Killian."

Stacy looked up. Leonardo Noble was headed across Café Noir for her table, in one hand a plate with a scone, in the other a cup of coffee. "I'm not a detective," she said as he reached her. "But I suspect you already know that."

Without asking if he could join her, he set his cup and plate on the table, pulled out a chair and sat. "But you are," he said. "Homicide. Ten years with the Dallas force. Distinguished a number of times, including this past fall. You resigned in January to pursue a graduate degree in English literature."

"All true," she said. "You have a point?"

He ignored her question and took a leisurely sip of his coffee. "If not for you, your sister would be dead and her killer free. Her husband would no doubt be rotting in prison right now, and you'd be—"

She cut him off. She didn't need to be reminded of where she would be. Or how close Jane had come to dying. "Enough with the dossier, Mr. Noble. I lived it. Once was enough."

He sampled the scone, made a sound of pleasure, then returned his attention to her. "It's incredible how much you can learn about someone these days with little more than a few keystrokes."

"Now you know all about me. Bully for you."

"Not all." He leaned forward, eyes alight with interest. "Why, after all those years as a cop, did you resign? From what I read, seemed like you were born to do the job."

Ever hear the old saying, You can take the cop out of the job, but you can't take the job out of the cop?

"You shouldn't believe everything you read. Besides, that would be my business, not yours." She made a sound of irritation. "Look, I'm sorry you got the wrong idea the other day. I didn't mean to—"

"Bullshit. Of course you did. You deliberately misled me. And let's be honest, Ms. Killian, you're not sorry. Not one damn bit."

"All right." She folded her arms across her chest. "I'm not. I needed information, and I did what was necessary to get it. Satisfied?"

"Nope. I want something from you." He took another bite of the scone, waiting for her reaction. When she didn't give him one, he went on. "I wasn't completely honest with you the other day."

That she didn't expect. Surprised, she sat forward. "Your answer to my question about the potential of the game leading to violent behavior?"

"How did you know?"

"Like you said, I was a cop for ten years. I interrogated suspects on a daily basis."

He inclined his head, as if with admiration. "You are good." He paused. "What I said, about people killing people, I didn't lie about that. I believe it. But even the most innocent thing in the wrong hands—"

He let the words, their meaning, hang between them a moment, then reached into his jacket pocket. He drew out two postcards and handed them to her.

The first was a pen-and-ink illustration, the image a dark, disturbing representation of Lewis Carroll's Alice chasing the White Rabbit. Stacy turned the card over. She read the one word scrawled across the back.

Soon.

She shifted her attention to the second card. Unlike the first, it was a dime-store variety postcard depicting the French Quarter.

It read: *Ready to play?*

She returned her gaze to Leonardo Noble's. "Why are you showing me these?"

Instead of answering, he said, "I received the first one about a month ago. The second last week. And this one yesterday."

He handed her a third card. Another pen-and-ink illustration, she saw. This one depicted what appeared to be a mouse, drowning in a pool or puddle. She flipped the card over.

Ready or not, game in play.

Stacy thought of the anonymous notes her sister had received. How the police, including her, had considered them more crank than threat. Until the end. Then they had realized them a serious threat indeed.

"White Rabbit is different from other role-playing games," the man murmured. "In those, there's a game master, a sort of referee who controls the game. He creates obstacles for the players, hidden doors, monsters and the like. The best game masters are completely neutral."

"And in White Rabbit?" she asked.

"The White Rabbit is the game master. But his position is far from neutral. He beckons the players to follow him, down the rabbit hole, into his world. Once there, he lies. Plays favorites. He's a trickster and a deceiver. And only the most cunning player can best him."

"The White Rabbit has a big advantage."

"Always."

"I would think playing a stacked deck wouldn't be much fun."

"We wanted to turn the game on its edge. Upend the players. It worked."

"I was told your game is the most violent. That it's a winner-take-all scenario."

"Killer takes all," he corrected. "He pits the players against one another. Last man standing faces him." He leaned toward her. "And once the game's in play, it doesn't end until all the players are dead but one."

Killer takes all. Unease slid up her spine. "Can the characters stand together to take him out?"

He looked surprised, as if no one had ever suggested such a thing. "That's not the way it's played."

She repeated her original question. "Why are you showing me these?"

"I want to find out who sent them and why. I want you to determine if I should be afraid. I'm offering you a job, Ms. Killian."

She stared at him a moment, momentarily nonplussed. Then she smiled, understanding. She had scammed him; he was returning the favor. "This is when you say 'Gotcha,' Mr. Noble."

But he didn't. When she realized he was serious, she shook her head. "Call the police. Or hire a private investigator. Bodyguard work isn't my line."

"But investigation *is* your line." He held up a hand as if

anticipating her protest. "I haven't been overtly threatened, what can the police do? Absolutely nothing. And if what I fear is true, a private dick is going to be way out of his depth."

She narrowed her eyes, admitting to herself that she was intrigued. "And what exactly is it you fear, Mr. Noble?"

"That someone's begun playing the game for real, Ms. Killian. And judging by these cards, I'm in the game, like it or not."

He laid one of his business cards on the table and stood. "Maybe your friend was in the game, too. Maybe she was the first of the White Rabbit's victims. Think about it. Then call me."

Stacy watched him walk away, mind racing with the things he had told her, the things she had learned about the game. They turned to the man who had attacked her the night before.

He had warned her to "stay out of it." Stay out of what? she wondered. The investigation? Or the game?

It's not the game that's dangerous, but obsession with the game.

Stacy stopped on that. What if someone *had* become so obsessed with the game, they'd begun to play for real? Begun to confuse fantasy and reality?

Could Cassie have gotten unwittingly pulled into that game?

A powerful tool in the wrong hands.

So many things in life were. Power. Guns. Money. Almost anything.

She considered the scenario Leonardo had painted: some wacko playing a fantasy role-playing game for real. A game in which the only way to win was to kill off the other characters, then face the White Rabbit himself—face the one controlling the game, the ultimate trickster.

A real-life White Rabbit.

The connection between Cassie and the scenario Leonardo Noble painted was flimsy at best, but she couldn't help but wonder if the two were related.

Stranger things had happened.

Last year in Dallas.

Billie sauntered over with a plate of samples. Chocolate chip muffins, Stacy saw. Rich, dark chocolate. Billie's sample plate and the timing of its appearance was a running joke among the regulars. If there was trouble brewing or juicy dish to be had, the sample plate came out. Billie seemed to innately know the right moment—and the right pastry—to share.

Billie smiled the enigmatic smile that had helped her snare four husbands, including her present spouse, ninety-year-old millionaire Rocky St. Martin. "Muffin?"

Stacy helped herself to a piece of the pastry, knowing full well the treat wasn't free. Billie expected payment—in the form of information.

Sure enough, Billie set the plate on the table, pulled out a chair and sat. "Who was he and what did he want?"

"Leonardo Noble. He wanted to hire me."

Billie arched a perfectly shaped eyebrow and nudged the plate of muffin pieces closer to Stacy.

Stacy laughed, took another and slid the plate back toward the other woman. "It has to do with Cassie. Sort of."

"I thought so. Explain."

"Remember what I told you about Cassie having set up a meeting with a White Rabbit?" The other woman nodded. "That man, Leonardo Noble, is the inventor of the game."

Stacy saw interest flare in her eyes. "Go on."

"Since we talked last, I've found out more about the game. That it's dark and violent. That the White Rabbit and the last player alive play to the death."

"Charming."

Stacy explained about the postcards the man had received, about his theory that someone had begun playing the game for real. "I know it sounds out there, but—"

"But it could happen," Billie filled in for her. She leaned toward Stacy. "Studies have shown that in people for whom the line between fantasy and reality is blurred, fantasy role-playing games can be a dangerous tool. Throw a game like White Rabbit or Dungeons & Dragons into the mix, games in which the emotional and psychological involvement is intense...it can prove explosive."

"How," Stacy asked, "did you know that?"

"In a former life, I was a clinical psychologist."

She should be surprised, she supposed. Or suspect the woman of being a pathological liar or con artist. After all, in the relatively short time she'd known Billie, the woman had mentioned four marriages, a stint as both a flight attendant and runway model. Now this. She wasn't that old.

But Billie always had facts or authentic-sounding anecdotes to back up her claims.

Stacy shook her head, thoughts returning to Leonardo Noble and the events of the past days. "I've stepped on someone's toes."

She said it almost to herself, and Billie's brow wrinkled in question. Quickly, Stacy told her about the night before. About being attacked, the words the man had murmured against her ear, that campus security believed he was the same man who had raped three coeds earlier in the school year.

"I didn't mistake what I heard," Stacy said.

For a long moment her friend said nothing, then she nodded. "I know you didn't. You were a cop, those are the kinds of mistakes you wouldn't make."

Billie stood, taking the sample plate with her. She gazed down at Stacy. "I suggest you be very careful, my friend. I have no desire to go to your memorial service."

Stacy watched her go, thoughts turning to what the woman had said. A blurred line between fantasy and reality. Could Cassie have unwittingly become involved with a madman who'd begun a role-playing game for real? Had she stepped on *his* toes, called attention to herself?

Damn it. She knew what she had to do. Stacy opened her cell phone and punched in Leonardo Noble's cell number.

"I'll take the job," she said when he answered. "When do you want me to start?"

CHAPTER
17

Sunday, March 6, 2005
8:00 a.m.

Leonardo suggested the meeting time and Stacy picked the place—Café Noir.

Sunday mornings before ten tended to be quiet at the coffeehouse. Apparently, the regular clientele either worshipped early or enjoyed sleeping late.

"You're here early," Stacy said to Billie as she reached the counter.

"So are you." Billie swept her gaze over Stacy. "You're taking the job, aren't you? The one that game inventor offered you?"

"Leonardo Noble. Yes."

Her friend rang her sale up without inquiring what she

wanted. She didn't have to; Billie knew if she wanted anything other than her usual cappuccino with an extra shot of espresso, she would say so.

Stacy handed her a twenty; Billie made her change, then crossed to the espresso machine. She drew the shots and frothed the milk without speaking.

Stacy frowned. "What?" she asked.

"I'm not sure I like this."

"Tough."

"Are you certain he's even for real?"

"Meaning?"

"Seems to me, someone who invents games might like to play them."

She had considered that. That Billie had as well, surprised her. "You're one smart cookie, you know that?"

"And here I thought I was just another pretty face."

Stacy laughed. When a woman looked the way Billie did, she was rarely appreciated for her brains. Hell, she was guilty of it. Upon meeting Billie, she had categorized her as a brainless blonde. She knew better now.

"I'm pretty good at finding things out," she said. "You need a mole, call me."

Billie Bellini, super spy. "You'd look damn good in a trench coat."

"You bet your ass, I would." She smiled. "And don't forget it."

She wouldn't, Stacy acknowledged as she walked away from the espresso bar. No doubt Billie could easily uncover information others couldn't pry free with a crowbar.

As long as the sources were male.

Stacy chose a table in back and sat. As she took her first sip of the hot drink, Leonardo Noble arrived. Alone. She'd thought he might bring Kay.

He scanned the room for her, smiling when he found her. He indicated he meant to get a coffee, then pointed to her in question. She lifted her cup, indicating she was already hooked up.

Espresso. The staff of life.

She watched as he ordered. He said something to Billie, who laughed. Was he for real? she wondered. Were the bizarre cards he'd received authentic? Or had he manufactured them?

Until she spent more time with him, she was reserving judgment on everything, including his honesty.

He approached the table, his usual energetic step replaced by a sleepy shuffle. He looked bleary-eyed. His hair was even wilder than usual.

"Not a morning person, I see," she said.

"A night person," he countered. "I only need a couple hours of sleep in a twenty-four-hour period."

Stacy arched an eyebrow. "That's not how it looks to me."

He smiled, the first sign of life coming into his eyes. "Trust me."

"Said the spider to the fly."

He took a sip of his coffee. She noted that he'd gotten the super grande size. From the mountain of froth, she figured it was a cappuccino.

"So that's what that look was about," he said. "Distrust."

"What look?" She took a swallow of her own coffee.

"The one when I was ordering. I had the distinct impression you were dissecting me."

"Your motives, yes. Goes with the territory." She met his gaze, hers unflinching. "No one is beyond suspicion, Mr. Noble. Including you."

Obviously unfazed, he laughed. "Which is exactly why I want to hire you. And call me Leo or the deal's off."

She laughed, too. "All right, Leo. Tell me more about your household."

He looked at her over the top of his coffee cup. "What do you want to know?"

"Everything. For example, your office is there?"

"Yes. Kay's also."

"Any other employees?"

"Housekeeper. Mrs. Maitlin. Troy, my driver and all-around guy Friday. Barry takes care of the grounds and pool. Oh, and my daughter's tutor, Clark Dunbar."

This was the first she'd heard of a daughter, which Stacy found odd. At her expression, he went on, "Kay and I have one child. Alice. She's sixteen. Or, as she's fond of saying, almost seventeen."

"Does she live with you? Or Kay?"

"With both of us."

"Both of you?"

"Kay lives in my guest house." One corner of his mouth lifted in a sort of lopsided—and winning—smile. "I see by your expression that you find our arrangement strange."

"I'm not here to pass judgment on your personal life."

As if he took her at her word, he moved on. "Alice is the light of my life. Until recently, she—" He bit the thought back. "She's gifted. Intellectually."

"I suppose that makes sense. I hear you're a modern day Leonardo da Vinci."

He grinned. "I see I'm not the only one who knows how to do an Internet search. But Alice really is a genius. She makes both Kay and I look average."

Stacy digested that. She wondered at the burden of that kind of intellect. How it must color every aspect of the teenager's life, from intellectual pursuits to relationships. "Has she ever gone to regular school?"

"Never. We've always provided her with private tutors."

"And it works well?"

"Yes. Until—" He laced his fingers, for the first time looking uneasy. "Until recently. She's been agitating to go to university. She's become defiant. I'm afraid she dishes poor Clark a lot of attitude."

Sounded like typical teenage angst.

"University?" she said. "Like Tulane or Harvard?"

"Yes, intellectually she's ready. She has been for some time. But emotionally...she's young. Immature. The truth is, we've sheltered her. Too much, I fear." He cleared his throat. "Plus, the divorce has been difficult on her. More difficult than either of us anticipated."

Stacy couldn't imagine navigating university life at sixteen. "I'm sorry."

He shrugged. "Oil and water, that's me and Kay. But we love each other. And we love Alice. So we settled on this arrangement."

"For Alice?"

"For all of us, but Alice most of all." He smiled then, a kind of loopy, boy-next-door grin. "Now you know all about our dysfunctional little troupe. Still willing to join up?"

She searched his expression, once again wondering if he was for real. How did a man achieve what he had without being ruthless? Without both withholding and exploiting information?

She leaned toward him, all business. "Here's the deal, Leo. Anonymous letters like the ones you've received are almost always sent by someone within the circle of the recipient."

"My circle? I don't—"

She cut him off. "Yes, your circle. They're sent in an effort to terrorize."

"And what's the point if they're not close enough to witness that terror. Right?"

Smart man. "Right. The more frightened you are, the better."

He narrowed his eyes slightly. She noticed they were a light hazel. "So screw 'em. I'm not scared, they give up. Like the school bully who doesn't get the reaction he's looking for."

"Maybe. If your note writer is typical of others of his ilk. They send notes and letters because they like to watch. They don't want to get too close."

"At heart they're yellow."

"Yes. Too afraid to fully confront their anger or hatred with a direct confrontation. So they're a minimal threat."

"That's the typical. What's the atypical?"

She looked away, thinking of her sister, Jane. Her terrorizer had been as atypical as they come. He'd had every step carefully planned, each bringing him closer to killing her. She returned her gaze to his. "Sometimes the letters or calls are simply foreplay for the main event." At his blank expression, she leaned slightly forward. "They get close enough to touch, Leo."

He sat silently a moment, as if digesting that. For the first time he looked shaken. "I'm so grateful you agreed to help—"

Stacy held up a hand, stopping him. "First things first. I'm not accepting this job to help you. I'm doing it for Cassie, on the off chance her murder and your postcards are related. Second, you understand that I'm in graduate school. My studies come first. They have to. Do you have a problem with either of those conditions?"

"Absolutely not. Where do we begin?"

"*I* begin by integrating into the household. Getting to know everyone. Earning their trust."

"You think he's there."

"He or she," she corrected. "It's a possibility. A strong one."

He nodded slowly. "If you want to earn everyone's trust, we have to create a nonthreatening reason for you to be hanging around."

"Any ideas?"

"Technical expertise. For a new novel. Starring a homicide detective with a major urban force."

"Works for me." She smiled slightly. "Are you really writing a novel?"

"Among other things, yes."

"I expect you want your ex-wife and daughter informed of the real reason I'm around."

"Kay, yes. Alice, no. I don't want to frighten her."

"Fine." Stacy finished her coffee. "When do I start?"

He smiled. "Now's good for me. How about you?"

Being a proactive kind of person, Stacy agreed. Leo jumped to his feet, eager to get home. As she followed him out of the coffee shop, she glanced at Billie to find the the woman watching her.

Something in her friend's expression caused her steps to falter.

Leo glanced back. "Stacy? Something wrong?"

She shook off the sensation and smiled. "Nothing. Lead the way."

CHAPTER
18

Tuesday, March 8, 2005
1:00 p.m.

After two days hanging around the Noble mansion, Stacy had a clear understanding of why Leo had used the word *troupe* to describe the mansion's inhabitants—life in the house was like a three-ring circus, with people coming and going, all day long. Personal trainers, manicurists, delivery people, lawyers, business associates.

She had advised Leo to treat her the same as he would any new employee. She'd learned that meant a sort of sink-or-swim introduction to the household. He had given her an office that adjoined his, and she had spent a lot of the time wandering around, trying to look busy. As she ran across people, she'd introduced herself.

People's responses to her had varied from cool, to curious, to friendly. In the three days she'd met everyone but Alice, which she found most interesting.

Especially since she had met the girl's tutor, Clark Dunbar. He was quiet, in the way some intellectuals were, but seemed to her to always be watching and listening. Like a cat who's seen but not heard.

Mrs. Maitlin avoided her. When their paths did cross, she acted jumpy. She looked everywhere but directly at Stacy. Even though Stacy had apologized for tricking the woman and claimed Leo had asked her to play the part, she suspected the woman knew she was here for a reason other than technical expertise. She only hoped she kept her suspicions to herself.

Troy, Leo's driver and guy Friday had been the friendliest of the lot—but also the nosiest. She wondered at his questions—was he simply curious or did he have darker motivations?

Barry had proved the quietest. As groundskeeper and pool man, he had plenty of opportunity to chat with people coming or going, but he never did. Instead, he kept to himself—although he seemed to see everything that went on.

Stacy glanced at her watch and collected her things. She'd attended her 8:00 a.m. class but needed to get back out to UNO to make her two-thirty medieval lit.

"Hello."

Stacy turned. A teenage girl stood in the doorway to Leo's office. She was small and slender, with her mother's coloring and exotic features but her father's wild, wavy hair.

Alice. Finally.

"Hi," she said, smiling at the girl. "I'm Stacy."

The girl looked bored. "I know. You're the cop."

"Former cop," Stacy corrected. "I'm helping your dad with technical stuff."

Alice arched an eyebrow and sauntered into the office. "Stuff," she repeated. "Now *that's* technical."

This was no ordinary sixteen-year-old. She would do well to remember that. "I'm his technical adviser," she corrected. "On all things associated with law enforcement."

"And crime?"

"Yes, of course."

"A crime expert. Interesting."

Stacy ignored the gibe. "Some think so."

"Dad's been all over me to stop down here and introduce myself. You know who I am, right?"

"Alice Noble. Named for the most famous Alice."

"The White Rabbit's Alice."

"That's an odd way to put it. I would have said Lewis Carroll's character."

"But you're not me."

The girl crossed to the bookshelves that lined the walls. She picked up a framed photo of her and her parents. She gazed at it a moment, then glanced back at Stacy. "I'm smarter than them both," she said. "Did Dad tell you that?"

"Yes. He's very proud of you."

"Only .4 percent of people have an IQ of 140 and above.

Mine's 170. Only one in seven hundred thousand have an IQ that high."

Her father wasn't the only one who was proud. "You're a very bright young woman."

"Yes, I am." She frowned. "I thought we should talk. Set the ground rules."

Intrigued, Stacy set down her book bag and thought of her class, conscious of time passing. "Shoot."

"I don't care why you're working for Dad. Just stay out of my way."

"Have I done something to offend you?"

"Not at all. Dad has all sorts of hangers-on, and I'm not interested in getting to know any of them."

"Hangers-on?"

She narrowed her eyes slightly. "Dad's rich. And charismatic. People flock to him. Some are starstruck. Some are sincere. The rest are merely leeches."

Stacy folded her arms across her chest, intrigued. "What about me? I accepted a job from him, does that constitute flocking?"

"It's not about you." The girl lifted a shoulder. "He hooks up with someone new, is all excited about them, then it's over. I've learned not to get attached."

Interesting. Seemed there had been a number of severed relationships in the Noble troupe. Could one of them be carrying a grudge?

"Sounds like you've been here before."

"I have. Sorry."

"No apologies necessary. I'll do my best to stay out of your way."

The first thing approaching a smile touched the girl's mouth. It softened her face. "I appreciate that."

She left the office, having to duck by her tutor on the way out. Clark Dunbar. Forty-something. Long, thin face. Bookish. Good looking in a professional way.

He watched her go, then turned back to Stacy. "What was that all about?"

Stacy smiled. "She was setting ground rules. Putting me in my place."

"I was afraid of that. Teenagers can be trying."

"Especially ones who are so bright."

He leaned against the doorjamb, his tall, lanky frame seeming to fill it. She noticed how startlingly blue his eyes were and wondered if they were colored contacts. "Even the most wonderful gift can sometimes be a burden."

She had never thought of it quite that way, but it was true. "You've had experience with gifted kids?"

"I'm a glutton for punishment."

"More like Clark Dunbar, super tutor."

He laughed. "I always wondered what my parents were thinking, naming me after the mild-mannered stiff who never got the girl."

"What's your middle name? Any help there?"

He hesitated. "None, I'm afraid. It's Randolf."

She laughed and waved him in. She sat on the edge of her desk; he in the big chair in front of it. "Have you always been a private tutor?"

"Always been an educator," he corrected. "Better pay and better hours in this. Better class of student."

"That surprises me. Where did you teach?"

"Several universities."

She arched her eyebrows. "And you prefer this?"

"It sounds hokey, but it's a privilege to work with a mind like Alice's. And a thrill."

"But if you taught university, surely many of your students—"

"Not like Alice. Her mind—" he paused, as if searching for the right description "—awes me."

Stacy didn't know what to say. She supposed someone as ordinary as herself couldn't comprehend such an intellect.

He leaned slightly forward, expression almost mischievous. "Truth is, I'm a bit of a hippie throwback. I like the freedom private tutoring gives me. We set our own classes and times. Nothing is rote."

"Sometimes the expected is a good thing."

He nodded and leaned back in his seat. "You're speaking of your own experiences now. A former homicide detective turned technical adviser? There's a story in that, I'll bet."

"Just a badass turned softie."

"Got tired of the blood and guts?"

"Something like that." She glanced at her watch and stood. "I hate to cut this short, but—"

"You have a class," he said. "And so do I." He smiled, something about his expression wistful. "Perhaps we can discuss the Romantics sometime."

As they parted, she had the distinct feeling he wanted something more from her than a discussion of literature.

But what?

CHAPTER
19

Tuesday, March 8, 2005
9:30 p.m.

Stacy sat at a table on the second floor of the UNO library, surrounded by books. One of them an edition of *Alice in Wonderland*. She'd read the story——a mere 224 pages then begun picking through a half-dozen critical essays on the author and his most famous work.

She had discovered that Lewis Carroll was considered by some to be the Leonardo da Vinci of his time. She found that interesting, as her new boss called himself a modern-day da Vinci. She tucked that away, and returned her attention to sifting through the things she had learned about the nineteenth-century author. Although simply a tale he'd made up to amuse a young girl during a park outing and only written down later, the story had become a classic.

Not just a classic, but one that had been analyzed damn near to death. According to the essays, *Alice in Wonderland* was far from a childish fantasy about a girl who tumbles down a rabbit hole and into a bizarre world, and was rife with themes of death, abandonment, the nature of justice, loneliness, nature and nurture.

So much for a lighthearted romp.

Stacy wondered if critics and academics made up these things to justify their own existence. She frowned at her thoughts. Ones like that wouldn't sit well with her professors.

She had already managed to get herself on Professor Grant's shit list. She'd been late for class and he'd been pissed. To top it off, she hadn't been prepared, a fact the man had quickly ascertained and pounced on.

He had made it clear that the department expected better from their grad students.

Stacy tossed down her pen and rubbed the bridge of her nose, tired, hungry and disappointed in herself. Grad school was her chance to change her life. If she blew it, what would she do? Go back to police work?

No. Never.

But she had to nail the bastard who killed Cassie. Her friend deserved that from her. If it cost her brownie points—or grade points—so be it.

She returned her attention to the essay in front of her. *The underlying notion of a world where the sane was insane and the rules of—*

The print blurred. Her eyes burned. She fought the tears, the urge to cry. She hadn't since that first night, when she found the bodies. And she wouldn't. She was tougher than that.

She suddenly became aware of how quiet the library was. A prickle of déjà vu tickling the back of her neck, she closed her fingers around her ballpoint.

Stacy waited. Listened. As if in a replay of the previous Thursday night, a sound came from behind her. A footfall, a rustling.

She leaped to her feet and spun around, pen out.

Malone. Grinning at her like Carroll's damned Cheshire Cat.

He lifted his hands in surrender. He held a copy of Cliff's Notes on *Alice in Wonderland*.

Just great, the two of them were thinking alike. Now she would cry.

Spencer motioned to the ballpoint. "Whoa. Back down. I'm unarmed."

"You startled me," she said, annoyed.

"Sorry."

He didn't look sorry at all. She tossed the pen on the table. "What're you doing creeping around the library?"

He arched his eyebrows at her word choice. "Same as you, it seems."

"God help me."

He laughed, pulled out a chair, swung it around and straddled it, facing her. "I like you, too."

She felt herself flush. "But I never said I liked you, Malone."

Before he could respond, her stomach growled. He smiled. "Hungry?"

She pressed a hand to her middle. "And tired with a killer headache."

"Low blood sugar, no doubt." He reached into his windbreaker pocket and pulled out a Snickers bar. He held it out. "You need to take better care of yourself."

She accepted the candy. Opening it, she took a bite and made a sound of pleasure. "Thanks for your concern, Malone, but I'm doing just fine."

She took another bite. The effect of the sugar on her headache was nearly immediate. "You always carry Snickers bars in your pocket?"

"Always," he said solemnly. "Payola for snitches."

"Or to coax information out of hungry, headachy women."

He leaned forward. "Rumor has it you're spending a lot of time with Leo Noble. Mind telling me why?"

"Who are you following?" she countered. "Me? Or Leo?"

"So why has Noble hired a former homicide detective? Protection? From whom?"

She didn't deny she was working for the man. It wouldn't do any good, anyway; Malone knew the truth. "Technical advice. He's writing a novel."

"Bullshit."

She changed the subject, glancing at the book Malone was holding. "I'm impressed. It looks like you're doing your homework. Even if it is Research Lite."

One corner of his mouth lifted in a smirk. "Don't be too impressed. I haven't read it yet."

"Above your head?"

"Biting the hand that fed you isn't nice. And there's chocolate on your teeth."

"Where?" She ran her tongue over her teeth.

"Do that again." He rested his chin on his fist. "It's turning me on."

She laughed despite herself. "You want something from me—" she held a hand up to hold off the smart-ass answer she felt certain was coming "—what is it?"

"How does the game White Rabbit relate to the story of *Alice in Wonderland?*"

Stacy thought of the cards Leo had received. "Simply, Noble used Carroll's story as inspiration for his game. The White Rabbit controls play. The characters from the story are the game characters, though it's all been morphed into something violent and disturbing."

He motioned to the material on the table in front of her. "If it's so simple, why all this?"

He had her there. Damn it. "From other gamers, I've learned White Rabbit's a renegade scenario. Outside the gaming mainstream. Its enthusiasts are more cultish than other gamers. More secretive. It seems that's part of the game's allure."

"What about its structure?"

"More violent, to be sure." She paused, thinking of what she had learned. "The major difference in structure is in the role of game master. Most game masters are absolutely impartial. White Rabbit's is not. He's a character, playing to win. The objective for all the players," she finished, "is kill or be killed."

"Or to survive by any means, depending on your perspective."

She opened her mouth to reply; his cell phone rang, cutting her off.

"Malone."

She watched his face as he listened, noted the slight tightening of his mouth. The way his eyebrows drew together in a scowl.

The call was business.

"Got it," he said. "Be right there."

He had to go, she knew. Somewhere, somebody was dead. Murdered.

He reholstered the phone, met her eyes. "Sorry," he said. "Duty calls."

She nodded. "Go."

He did, without a backward glance. Everything about his posture and stride shouted purpose, determination.

She watched him. For ten years she had gotten calls like that. She had hated them. Dreaded them. They had always come at the worst times.

Then why did she feel this biting sense of loss now? This feeling of being on the outside looking in?

She turned to collect her things. And saw Bobby Gautreaux, striding toward the stairs. She called his name, loudly enough, she knew, to be heard.

He didn't slow or look back. She shot to her feet, called his name again. Loudly. He started to run. She took off after him; hitting the stairs in seconds.

He was already gone.

She ran down the steps, anyway, earning a scowl from the

librarian. A student worker, Stacy ascertained, crossing to her. "Did you see a dark-haired guy with an orange backpack just now? He was running."

The young woman skimmed her gaze over Stacy, expression openly hostile. "I see a lot of dark-haired guys."

Stacy narrowed her eyes. "The library's not that busy. He was running. You want to change your answer?"

The coed hesitated, then motioned to the main entrance doors. "He went that way."

Stacy thanked her, then headed back upstairs. She wouldn't accomplish anything by going after him. First, she doubted she would find him. Second, what would it prove if she did? If he had been spying on her, he wouldn't admit it.

But if he had been, why?

She reached the second floor, crossed to her table and began to collect her things, freezing as a thought occurred to her. Bobby was a big guy. Taller than she was. Not as tall as she'd guessed her attacker of the other night to have been, but considering the circumstances, she could have been wrong.

Maybe Bobby Gautreaux hadn't been spying on her at all. Maybe his intentions had been darker.

She would have to be very careful.

CHAPTER
20

Tuesday, March 8, 2005
11:15 p.m.

Spencer stood on the sidewalk in front of the dilapidated fourplex, waiting for Tony. The other man had arrived just behind him, but had yet to emerge from his vehicle. He was on his cell phone; his conversation appeared to be a heated one. No doubt the infamous teenager Carly, Spencer thought. Back for round twelve.

He turned his attention to the street, the rows of homes, most of them multifamily units. On a desirability scale, this Bywater neighborhood ranked no better than a three, though he supposed that depended on one's perspective. Some would die to live here, others would kill themselves first.

One corner of his mouth lifted in a grim smile. And some, simply, would have death thrust upon them.

He shifted his gaze to the fourplex. The first officers had cordoned off the area and yellow crime-scene tape was draped across the front porch. In its youth, the structure had been a nice middle-class home, roomy enough for a big family. Sometime during its life, as the area had slid into disrepair and disfavor, it'd been divided into a multifamily residence, its handsome facade replaced with that awful tar-paper siding popular after World War II.

Spencer turned at the sound of a car door slamming. Tony had finished his conversation; though by his thunderous expression Spencer suspected it was far from over.

"Have I told you I hate teenagers?" he said as he reached Spencer.

"Repeatedly." They fell into step together. "Thanks for coming."

"Any excuse to get out of the house these days."

"Carly's not that bad," Spencer said, grinning. "You're just old, Pasta Man."

Tony glowered at him. "Don't mess with me, Slick. Not now. The kid's pushed me to the breaking point."

"Cop goes postal. Sounds ugly. Very ugly." Spencer lifted the crime-scene tape for Tony, then ducked under himself. A scrawny dog stood at the neighbor's chain-link fence, watching them. He hadn't barked the entire time, a fact Spencer found odd.

They crossed to the first officer, a woman his brother Percy had dated. It hadn't ended well. "Hello, Tina."

"Spencer Malone. I see you've moved up in the world."

"Livin' large in the Big Easy."

"How's that no-good brother of yours?"

"Which one? I've got several who answer to that description."

"That you do. Present company included."

"No denials from me, Officer DeAngelo." He smiled. "What've we got?"

"Upper-right unit. Victim in the bathtub. Fully dressed. Rosie Allen's her name. Lived alone. Tenant directly below called it in. Water dripping from the ceiling. She tried to rouse the woman, couldn't and called us."

"Why'd you call us and not DIU?"

"This one had ISD written all over it. Killer left us a calling card."

Spencer frowned. "The neighbor hear anything? See anything that seemed suspicious?"

"No."

"What about the other neighbors?"

"Nothing."

"Crime-scene guys called?"

"On their way. Coroner's rep as well."

"Touch anything?"

"Checked her pulse and turned off the water. Moved the shower curtain. That's it."

Spencer nodded; he and Tony started up the walk. When he reached the unit's open door, he stopped and turned. "I'll tell Percy you asked about him."

"If you want to die. No problem."

Chuckling, he and Tony climbed the stairs, which emptied into the unit's living room. It had been converted into a workroom, complete with two sewing tables fitted with sewing machines, both commercial-quality machines, from the look of them. Baskets heaped with clothing sat along one wall, along another, racks of hanging garments, one entirely costumes. The kind that got big applause at the gay fashion show during Carnival. Lots of sparkle. Overdone to the extreme. Against the far wall sat an old couch. In front of it a battered coffee table. A stack of paperback novels sat on its top, one upside down, propped open. Beside it a pretty china teacup and saucer. Old-fashioned-looking. Feminine.

Spencer crossed to the table. The cup was empty save for the dregs of the beverage. A half-eaten cookie perched on the saucer.

He shifted his attention to the books. Romances. A few mysteries. Even a western. He didn't recognize any of the titles.

"No TV," Tony said disbelievingly. "Everybody has a television."

"Maybe it's in the bedroom."

"Maybe."

From behind them came the sound of the techs arriving. Like a herd of cattle tromping up the wooden stairs. Not waiting to greet their colleagues, Spencer motioned Tony toward the bathroom. They'd been the first to arrive; they'd earned the right to be first to examine the scene.

The unit had one bathroom, located at the back of the apartment, between the bedroom and the kitchen. An inch of water stood on the black-and-white checked tile floor. Nothing looked out of place—save for the slippered feet and bony legs sticking out of the end of the claw-footed tub.

Spencer skimmed his gaze over the room. A virgin scene told tales, in a whisper, drowned out by too many warm bodies. Not always. But sometimes...if they were lucky.

Spencer stepped into the room. And he felt it, a kind of presence. A kind of echo of the act that made his skin crawl.

He swept his gaze over the room, hardly big enough for the tub, nestled against the far wall. The vinyl curtain, mounted on a circular rod, had been pushed to the backside of the tub.

They crossed to the tub. Tony muttered something about his shoes being ruined. Spencer didn't acknowledge him. He couldn't take his eyes from the woman.

She stared up at him from her watery grave, her eyes a faded blue. Had they faded with age? he wondered. Or death? Her hair circled her head like gray sea grass, weightless. Her mouth was open.

She wore a chenille robe, the same color as her eyes. A white cotton gown underneath. The pink fuzzy slippers perched on her feet were dry.

Those eyes, her unseeing gaze, called to him. Seemed to beg him to listen.

Spencer leaned closer. *Tell me. I'm listening.*

She'd been ready for bed. Reading. Enjoying a cup of tea and a cookie. Judging by the condition of the bathroom and the dry slippers, she hadn't fought her attacker.

Her hands, hovering helplessly below the water's surface, looked clean.

"This is a strange one," Tony said. "Where's that calling card?"

"Good question. Let's check—"

"Smile, boys, you're on *Candid Camera*."

They turned. The camera's flash popped, and the tech-squad photographer grinned at them. Employed by the NOPD but not sworn officers, some of the tech guys were downright bizarre, Ernie Delaroux among them. Spencer had heard rumors that the man kept a personal album of photos from every scene he'd shot—his own little book of horrors.

"Screw off, Ernie."

The man only laughed and splashed noisily into the room, like a five-year-old through a puddle.

Chasing away the whispers, Spencer thought. Before he'd had the chance to make them out.

"Loopy bastard," Tony muttered, making room for the man to get his shots.

"I heard that," he called, sounding almost gleeful.

"Hello, boys."

The greeting came from Ray Hollister. "Hello, Ray. Welcome to the party."

"A dubious honor." He squinted at the floor. "This is going to ruin my shoes. I liked these shoes."

"My thoughts exactly," Tony said.

The Orleans Parish coroner employed six pathologists. Those six, also called coroner's investigators, visited the scene of every death in the parish. At the scene with them was a driver, also employed by the Coroner's Office, whose duty it was to secure and load the body—and to photograph the scene. Not only did the Coroner's Office want their own photographic record, but the dual records often proved invaluable in court.

It was imperative that the photos be taken before the body was disturbed.

Ray waited while the two men snapped their shots. "What happened here?" he asked.

"We were hoping you'd tell us."

"Sometimes there's a rabbit in my hat, sometimes there's not."

Spencer nodded. Any cop worth his salt knew that's the way it worked. Some cases closed so easily and quickly, it was as if by magic. Others presented one brick wall after another—no matter how skilled or conscientious the crime-scene team.

The nature of the beast.

"Victim appears to have drowned," Spencer said. "Position of legs and feet indicate a homicide, but there's no sign of a struggle. Weird."

"I've seen weirder, Detective Malone." Both photographers finished and went on to capture the rest of the scene on film. Ray fitted on gloves and crossed to the tub. "Evidence is going to be a bitch, because of the water."

"Tell us something we don't know."

"I'll try, Detectives. Give me a few minutes."

Spencer and Tony made their way to the front room. The fingerprint techs were already at work. Spencer and Tony circled around them and into the bedroom. Bed neatly turned back. Dirty clothes in a hamper. Untouched glass of water on the bedside table; a small white pill waiting beside it.

Nothing out of order. Not a single sign of anything amiss.

Like a stage set, Spencer thought. A moment frozen in time. It gave him the creeps.

They thumbed through the closets and drawers, then headed for the small kitchen. It was in good order like the rest of the apartment. A tin of butter cookies sat on the counter. A box of tea beside it. Sleepytime, Spencer saw.

"Love those cookies," Tony said. "Wife refuses to buy 'em anymore. Too much fat, she says."

Spencer looked at his partner. "She's a smart lady, Pasta Man. You should listen to her."

"Kiss mine, Slick."

"Thanks, but I'll pass. Big hairy butts aren't my thing."

Tony chuckled. "So what do you think? What happened to Rosie?"

"She was ready for bed. Robe, slippers, bed turned back."

Tony nodded and took over. "She's sitting on the couch, having a cup of tea and a cookie, reading a few pages before turning in."

"The doorbell rings. She answers and bam! Goodbye, Rosie."

"Knew the guy, I'm thinking. That's why she opens the door in her robe, lets the guy in. That's why there's no struggle."

"But wouldn't she have resisted when she realized the situation was going south? It still doesn't work for me."

"He incapacitates her, my friend."

"How?"

"Maybe Ray can tell us that."

When they reached the bathroom, they saw Ray already had the victim's hands bagged.

"Hands look clean," the man said, not looking at them. "No blood, no bruising. Nothing appears broken. I suspect we'll find water in her lungs."

"No sign of a blow to the head, anything like that?"

"Nope."

"Can you give me anything, Ray?"

He looked over his shoulder at them. "Got yourself a real mystery, boys. Take a look at this."

He pushed the shower curtain away from the back wall. Spencer sucked in a sharp breath. Tony whistled.

The calling card. A message scrawled on the tile wall behind the curtain, in what appeared to be lipstick. A god-awful shade of orange.

Poor Little Mouse. Drowned in a pool of tears.

CHAPTER
21

Wednesday, March 9, 2005
2:00 a.m.

The ringing phone dragged Stacy from sleep. She opened her eyes, disoriented. *Dispatch.* She blinked, fighting to shake off the fog. *Somebody's dead. Got to—*

The device screamed again and she snatched up the receiver, answering as she had on the job.

"Killian here."

"Got a question."

Malone, she realized, fog clearing. Not dispatch. New Orleans, not Dallas. She shifted her gaze to the bedside clock.

2:05.

A.M.

"It'd better be a good one."

"In *Alice in Wonderland,* does a mouse drown? In a pool of tears?"

Stacy sat up, instantly, fully awake. She recalled the pen-and-ink drawing Leo had received, of the creature in a pool of what had looked like blood.

She pushed the hair out of her face. "Why?"

"I've got a homicide. Killer left us a message. Poor little mouse, drowned in—"

"A pool of tears," she finished for him.

"Is it in the story?"

"Not exactly," she said, glancing at the clock once more, calculating how long it would take her to dress and get to Leo's. "But yes."

"Not exactly," he repeated. "What does that mean?"

"That it's close enough for there to be a connection. Read the Cliff's Notes, you'll understand."

"You know something about this, Killian. What is it?"

Great, now he gets perceptive. "It's the middle of the night, Malone. Mind if I get back to my beauty sleep?"

"I'm going to want to talk to your boss."

"Free country. Talk to you when the sun's up." She hung up before he could argue, then punched in Leo's office number. The man claimed he never slept; she would put that claim to the test.

He answered on the second ring.

"Something's happened," she said. "I'm on my way over."

"You're headed over? Now?"

"No time to explain. I want to beat Malone and his partner."

"*Detective* Malone?"

"Trust me, okay?" She scrambled out of bed and started toward the bathroom. "And get some coffee on."

CHAPTER
22

Wednesday, March 9, 2005
2:55 a.m.

Fifteen minutes later, Stacy braked in front of Leo's. She'd thrown on a pair of jeans and a light sweatshirt, taking the time for nothing else but pulling her hair back into a ponytail.

She climbed out of the car and hurried up the walk. The house was dark, save for the gas porch lights. Leo sat on the top step waiting for her.

He stood as she reached him. "There's been another murder," she said without preamble. "It appears to be related to *Alice in Wonderland.* And to one of the cards you received."

He paled. "Which one?"

She quickly explained about Spencer's call, sharing all she

knew. "I fully expect him to show up here. I thought we should talk first."

He nodded. "Let's go inside."

Leo led her to the kitchen. As she had requested, he had coffee waiting. He waited as she lightened and sweetened it.

Obviously a man who understood the powerful pull of caffeine.

"What does this mean?" he asked after she had taken a sip.

"There may be a connection between this murder and you."

"The game. The White Rabbit."

"I said there *may* be. You have to show the police the cards."

"Did you tell Malone—"

"About the cards? No. I thought you should."

"When will they come?"

"Any minute is my guess. Though they may wait until morning. Depends on what else they have and their sense of urgency."

As if on cue, the doorbell rang. Leo looked at her; she indicated he should answer and that she would wait in the kitchen.

Moments later he returned with the two detectives.

"Thought you'd be here," Spencer said when he saw her.

She smiled slightly. "Ditto."

"Coffee?" Leo asked.

The men both refused, though Tony reluctantly.

Spencer began. "Obviously, Ms. Killian filled you in."

"Yes." Leo glanced at her, then back at Malone. "But before we go on, there's something you need to know."

"What a surprise," Spencer said, looking at her.

Stacy ignored his sarcasm. Leo continued. "In the past

month, I've received three cards from someone claiming to be the White Rabbit. One depicts a mouse, drowned in a pool of tears. The cards are signed the *White Rabbit*."

Spencer frowned. "From the game?"

"Yes." Leo quickly explained about the role of the White Rabbit in his game and his fear that someone had begun to play the part for real. "I've gotten plenty of crank mail over the years," he finished, "but these…something about them unnerved me."

"That's why he hired me," Stacy said. "To find out who sent them. And if that person was dangerous."

"I'd like to see the cards."

"I'll get them."

"I'll go with you," Tony said, falling in step with the other man.

Stacy watched them go, then turned to Malone. "What?"

"Going into the private dick business?"

"Just helping a friend."

"Noble?"

"Cassie. And Beth."

"You think the cards are from their killer."

It wasn't a question; she answered, anyway. "They could be."

"Or not."

Leo and Tony returned then. Tony handed Spencer the cards, exchanging a telling glance with his partner. By his expression, Stacy knew he believed they were onto something.

Spencer studied the three cards. He lifted his gaze to Leo's. "Why didn't you call us about these?"

"And say what? I wasn't overtly threatened. Nobody was dead."

"Somebody's dead now," Spencer said. "Drowned in a pool of tears." He took out a photo and handed it to Leo. "Her name was Rosie Allen. Know her?"

Leo stared at it, shook his head and handed it back.

"What's going on?"

They turned. Kay stood in the doorway, looking fresher than she should for the hour.

"There's been a murder," Leo answered. "A woman named Rosie Allen."

Kay frowned. "I don't understand. What does this Rosie have to do with us?"

Spencer stepped in. "She was murdered in a manner similar to a card your ex-husband received."

"The mouse in a pool of tears," Leo said.

Spencer held out the photo. "Ever seen this woman before?"

The woman stared at the picture, her face going white. "It's the sewing lady," she whispered.

"You know her?"

"No...yes." She brought a hand to her mouth. Stacy saw that it trembled. "She did some...mending and...alterations for us."

Spencer and Tony exchanged glances. Stacy knew what the look meant: this was no coincidence. It was a connection.

Leo crossed to the kitchen table, pulled out a chair and sank onto it. "What we feared, Kay. It's true. Someone's playing the game for real."

The detectives ignored that. "When did you last see Rosie Allen?"

Kay looked blankly at Spencer. He repeated the question. Before she answered, she followed Leo's lead and sat down. "Just the other day. A suit of mine needed alterations."

"And she fitted you?"

"Yes."

"But you didn't know her name?"

"Mrs. Maitlin...she takes care of such things."

Tony frowned. "Such things."

"Taking care of the help. Arranging appointments. Paying for their services."

"I'll need to question her. And the rest of the household staff."

"Of course. The staff arrives at eight. Will that be soon enough?"

Both detectives checked their watches, then nodded. Having been there herself, she recognized their thought processes. It was five-thirty now. They'd go home for a quick shower, then meet somewhere to grab some grub. That would put them back here just as the staff was arriving for the day.

After telling Leo she would call him later, Stacy followed the two detectives out, hurrying to catch up. She missed Tony, but stopped Malone as he unlocked his car door.

"Spencer!" she called.

He turned, waited. She reached him. "The murder tonight, any similarities to Cassie's?"

"Nothing that I saw," Spencer answered.

She fought disappointment. And frustration. "You'd tell me if there was, right?"

"You'll be the first to know when there's an arrest."

"Nice evasion."

"Damn decent, if you ask me. Don't think I owe you more than that."

"I'll make a deal with you, Malone. Mutual cooperation. I'll share anything I get with you, if you do the same with me."

"And why would I want to do that, Killian? You're not a cop. I am."

"It'd be the smart thing to do. I'm determined. I'm working for Noble. I could help you."

"The connection between Noble and Cassie is paper thin. If you don't see that—"

"Believe me, I do. But it's the only connection I've got, so I'm going with it." She held out her right hand. "Mutual cooperation?"

He gazed at her outstretched hand a moment, then shook his head. "Nice try. But NOPD doesn't make deals like that."

"Their loss. And yours."

He climbed in his car and drove off. She watched him go, then crossed to her own car. She unlocked it and slipped inside. He'd be back. He was arrogant but not stupid.

The name of the game was solving the case. He needed her to do that.

He just didn't realize it. Yet.

CHAPTER
23

Wednesday, March 9, 2005
10:40 a.m.

"It took you two long enough to make it in this morning," Captain O'Shay snapped, simultaneously plucking a tissue from the box on her desk.

"Couldn't be helped, Captain," Spencer said. "Interviewed a half dozen of the vic's acquaintances since eight this morning."

"Where are we?"

"Woman dead in the bathtub. One Rosie Allen. Ran an alteration business out of her home. Looks like she was drowned. Coroner's report should be back this afternoon."

"No sign of struggle," Tony jumped in. "No defensive injuries, hands were clean. We're figuring her killer subdued her, maybe with a stun gun."

Spencer took over. "She's ready for bed, in her robe and pj's. Opens the door, anyway."

The captain sneezed, then blew her nose. "She knew the person at the door."

"That's what we figure. But this is where the story gets interesting. Killer left us a nice little message. Poor Little Mouse, drowned in a pool of tears."

"Written on the bathroom wall behind the tub," Tony said. "Orange lipstick."

"The lipstick?" Captain O'Shay asked.

"Atrocious, old-lady orange." Tony made a face.

The captain looked irritated. "Status of?"

"Missing. Taken either as a trophy or to cover his ass."

"You're certain it was hers?"

Tony leaned forward. "Affirmative, Captain. Acquaintances all confirmed orange was her shade."

Spencer took over, filling in his superior on Allen's connection to Noble, the cards Noble had received and Spencer's theory that a fanatic had begun to play the game for real.

When he finished, she stared at him, eyes glassy. "You don't look so good, Captain," he said.

"Damn allergies," she said. "Everything's in bloom."

"Including your nose." Tony grinned. "If you don't mind me saying so."

She snatched a second tissue from the box. "Not at all. If you don't mind working Traffic."

"Backing down, Captain. I'm too old and too fat for that detail."

A hint of a smile touched her mouth. "This game, tell me about it."

"Ever heard of Dungeons & Dragons? It got a lot of media attention a few years ago."

She nodded. "Worked a case back in '85, involved a couple kids heavily into D & D. They were romantically involved and killed themselves in a suicide pact. Media had a field day with it. Claimed 'research' about the game brainwashing the kids. Leading them to murder and suicide.

"It all came to little more than hype. The girl had been diagnosed as clinically depressed and the parents had threatened to break the couple up. The whole gaming angle complicated things, made it tough to do our jobs."

Typical media. "This game's darker than D & D. From what I gather, the most violent of the lot. Based on the book *Alice in Wonderland.*"

She muttered something about nothing being sacred as she blew her nose again.

"This game's scenario is kill or be killed. The White Rabbit's the ultimate assassin."

"Now come to life," Captain O'Shay said, moving her gaze between her two detectives.

"That's Noble's theory," Spencer agreed.

"For God's sake, keep it from the media." The captain grimaced. "That's all we need, a repeat of the '85 circus."

"The Nobles claim they didn't even know the vic's name," Tony said. "The mister didn't even recognize her from a photo."

"Just one of the countless many who serve," Spencer said dryly. "According to the ex-Mrs. Noble, the woman dealt mostly with the housekeeper, Mrs. Maitlin."

"You spoke with her?"

"Yup. Didn't have much to bring to the party." He checked his notes. "Hardly knew her. Found her through an ad. The woman agreed to come to the house for fittings, which isn't customary. The housekeeper described her as a mousy woman. Her words."

Patti O'Shay frowned. "Interesting."

"We thought so," Tony offered. "Checking the National Crime Information Center for priors. On Maitlin. The rest of the household as well."

"None of them recalled seeing her. They could be lying, of course."

"Anything else?"

"Good news. Got a break in the Finch and Wagner murders. A fingerprint match from the scene."

"Gautreaux?"

"Bingo. Also got a strand of her hair from his jacket. And a strand of hair consistent with his from her T-shirt. Not enough to charge him, because of their past relationship, but—"

"Enough to get a court-ordered DNA swab. If the hair proves to be his, he's ours." She pressed a tissue to her nose. "Call Judge—"

"Already done. Should have it within the hour."

"Good work, Detectives. Keep me informed."

Her phone rang; she reached for it, signaling their meeting

had ended. Spencer and Tony stood and headed for the door. There, Spencer stopped and turned back toward his aunt, waiting for her to finish the call.

She hung up and looked at him in question. The dark circles under her eyes concerned him. He told her so.

She smiled wanly. "No need to be. Hard to sleep when you can't breathe. It's taking its toll."

"You certain that's all that's going on?"

"Absolutely." She straightened, her expression becoming all business. "I heard something I didn't like this morning."

Spencer stiffened slightly. "From?"

"From isn't the pertinent question here. *What* would be more appropriate."

"I'll bite. What did you hear?"

"That you were partying at Shannon's until closing. The night before an important stakeout."

He felt his temper rise and worked to hold it in check. "I was off duty."

"Yeah, you were off duty. But three hours later you were on duty." She rose to look him directly in the eye. "On *my* time. Hung-over."

"I did my job," he countered defensively.

"Use your head, Spencer. Think about what made you vulnerable to Lieutenant Moran."

He wanted to argue. He was angry. Pissed at whoever had gone running to her.

But mostly at himself.

Palms on her desk, she leaned toward him. "You're not

going to screw up under my command. I'll transfer you first. Understand?"

Back to DIU. Or worse. She had the power. No doubt she was under the microscope, being pressured by the same folks who had appeased him by assigning him to ISD.

They wanted him out. They'd figured he wouldn't last.

That's why they'd offered him this juicy plum. Got the department off the legal string—and it cost them nothing.

He straightened. Furious. Feeling betrayed by those he had trusted. "Understood, Captain. Don't worry about me, my eyes are open now."

CHAPTER
24

Thursday, March 10, 2005
11:45 a.m.

On her first trip to the French Quarter, Stacy had learned that finding a parking spot on the street was damn near impossible. She had cruised the network of narrow one-way streets, only to give up after thirty minutes and pull into one of the Quarter's exorbitantly priced lots.

Today she didn't even bother trying to look for a spot. She turned into the first lot she came upon, took a ticket and handed the attendant her keys.

New Orleans still amazed her. She felt like a stranger in a strange land. Dallas was relatively young; locals were proud when they could trace their roots back to 1922. New Orleans, on the other hand, was a historic city. One that boasted rich social traditions based on one's lineage, beautifully crumbling architecture and hundred-year-old cockroaches. Or so she had been told.

And New Orleans was a city that reveled in its own excesses. Big meals. Raucous laughter. Too much drink. All perfectly acceptable in the city whose motto—Let The Good Times Roll—was more than a Department of Tourism tagline.

It was a way of life.

And nowhere was that attitude more apparent than in the French Quarter. Strip clubs and bars, restaurant upon restaurant, souvenir and antique shops, music clubs, hotels and residences all coexisted in the seventy-eight-square-block area that made up this, the original settlement of New Orleans.

In addition, the Quarter boasted dozens of poster shops and art galleries. Not big art, not the high-end pieces that carried price tags in the tens of thousands, but small, commercial art for the masses.

The reason for her visit today.

She intended to hunt down possible sources of Leo's postcards. One was obviously mass-produced and probably sold at better than a hundred outlets in the Quarter alone. The other two, she suspected, were unique.

Stacy stood on the sidewalk, at the corner of Decatur and St. Peter Streets. All manner of people streamed by her, from men in business suits to a cross-dresser wearing fishnet stockings and a red leather miniskirt.

Stacy figured the cards were a limited edition by a local artist and sold at a limited number of shops. Leo had given her the card depicting the White Rabbit leading Alice down the rabbit hole. Spencer had taken the other as evidence. If it had been her case, she would have confiscated both.

Lucky for her it wasn't.

She started up the block, walking until she reached the corner of Royal Street and a poster shop called Picture This. She stepped inside.

The clerk, a kid with a mop of wild, curly hair, stood at the counter, talking on a cell phone. When he saw her, he ended his call and crossed to her. "Can I help you find something?"

"Hi." She smiled. "This card was sent to a friend, and I was trying to find one like it."

He glanced at the card and shook his head. "We don't have it."

"Do you have any that are similar?"

"Nope."

She held it out again. "Any idea where I might look?"

Another customer entered the shop. He looked her way, then back at Stacy. "Nope. Sorry."

The next half-dozen shops proved near carbon copies of the first. Stacy cut over to the opposite side of Royal, heading back toward Canal Street. A poster shop called Reflections sat on the closest corner. She ducked inside, she saw immediately that the shop's merchandise was more varied than the last stores she had visited, and ran more toward unique and one-of-a-kind items.

"Can I help you?" a man asked from the doorway to the back room. She saw that he had been eating his lunch.

"I hope so." Stacy sent him a winning smile as she crossed the shop. "I'm wondering if you carry these?" She showed him the card.

"Sorry."

She couldn't quite hide her disappointment. "I was afraid you were going to stay that."

"May I?" He held a hand out. She gave him the card. He studied the illustration, eyebrows drawn together in a slight frown. "Interesting imagery. Where'd you get this?"

"Several were sent to a friend. I'm a big fan of *Alice in Wonderland* and thought I'd buy a box, if they weren't too expensive."

He rubbed a corner between his index finger and thumb. "No one carries these by the box, I'm afraid."

"Excuse me?"

"This is an original, not a print. " He held it up to the light, squinting. "Pen and ink." He ran his thumb along the card's ruffled edge. "Good paper—one hundred percent rag. Acid-free. The artist knows what he, or she, is doing."

"Do you recognize the artist?"

"I might."

"Might?"

"I've never seen this image before, but the artist's hand reminds me of a local artist. Pogo."

"Pogo?" she repeated. "You're serious?"

He shrugged. "I didn't name him. He creates images like these. Disturbing. In pen and ink. He's had a few shows, gotten good reviews. But never took off."

"Do you know where I might find him?"

"Sorry." He handed the card back. "But the curator over at Gallery 124 might. If memory serves, 124 hosted Pogo's last show. On the corner of Royal and Conti."

Stacy smiled and started backing toward the shop's entrance. "Thanks so much for your help and time. I really appreciate it."

"You won't get them cheap," he called after her. "I could show you something similar——"

"Thanks," she said again, over her shoulder. "But I have my heart set on these."

She stepped out onto the French Quarter sidewalk and headed toward Conti. Gallery 124 was just where the man had said it would be.

Stacy checked traffic, then darted across the street. As she entered the gallery, the bell above the door jingled. The too-cold air-conditioning spilled over her. Followed by the realization that she wasn't as smart as she thought she was.

Malone had beat her there.

He stood at the back of the gallery, obviously waiting to speak with the curator, a woman in a dangerously short skirt and a brilliantly colored gypsy blouse. Her short hair was bleached almost white and worn in a spiky boy cut.

The word that came to mind was hip. With a capital H. Stacy had seen dozens just like her attending Jane's openings over the years.

Malone looked her way. Their gazes met. And he smiled. Or rather, smirked. *Cocky bastard.*

She closed the distance between them. "Well, wonders never cease," she said. "Detective Spencer Malone, in an art gallery. It just doesn't seem like your style."

"Really? I'm a big fan of art. In fact, I own several good pieces."

"On black velvet?"

He laughed. "I heard about an artist I'm certain I'm going to be interested in. A guy named Pogo."

She glanced toward the spiky-haired girl, then back at him. "How'd you beat me here?"

"Better investigative skills."

"My ass. You cheated."

Before he could respond, the woman finished with her customer and started toward them, cool smile fixed in place. "Good afternoon. How can I help you?"

Spencer showed her his ID. "Detective Malone, NOPD. I need to ask you a few questions."

Her expression registered surprise, then unease. Stacy stepped in before the woman could respond. "I'm in a bit of a rush. Should I come back another time?"

"Excuse me? You're not together? I assumed—"

"That's quite okay." Stacy turned to Spencer, smiling apologetically. "Do you mind? I'm on my lunch break."

He arched one dark eyebrow, clearly amused. "Please. Take your time."

"Thanks, Detective. You're the best." She swung back to the salesperson. "I understand you represent an artist named Pogo."

"Pogo? We did, but we haven't in better than a year."

"No. I'm so disappointed. I had my heart set on one of his pieces."

The woman perked up, no doubt calculating if she could somehow make the sale, anyway. "One of his prints?"

"A drawing. Pen and ink. Imagery based on *Alice in Wonderland*. Very dark. Powerful. I saw one and absolutely fell in love with it."

"Sounds like Pogo's work. When he was producing."

"When he was producing?"

"Pogo's his own worst enemy. Gifted but unreliable."

"Are you familiar with his 'Alice' series?"

"No. They must be new." She paused, as if weighing her options. "I could call him? Have him bring his portfolio by?"

"So he's local?"

"Yes. Lives right here in the Quarter. If I'm able to reach him, I bet he could be here in ten minutes."

Stacy glanced at her watch, working to look torn.

"He lives really close," the woman added quickly. "Barracks near Dauphine."

"I don't know. I wanted something that would be a good investment…but if he's unreliable…" As the woman opened her mouth, no doubt to assure her that her earlier statement wasn't quite accurate, Stacy shook her head. "I'll think about it. Do you have a card?"

She did. Stacy thanked her and strolled past Spencer, waggling her fingers at him. "Thank you, Detective."

She exited the gallery, stepped out of the doorway and

waited. Exactly two and a half minutes later, Spencer emerged from the shop.

He ambled over to her. "Sneaky, Killian. Brilliant performance."

"Thanks. Was she pissed when you asked about Pogo?"

"Confused, mostly. I got his address from her, but I'd like to see you play this out. Tag along."

She laughed. "You've surprised me, Detective. And I don't surprise easily."

"I'll take that as a compliment. Strut your stuff, Killian."

"Barracks and Dauphine, you familiar with the area?"

He nodded and they fell into step together. After a block, she angled a glance him. "So, how'd you pinpoint Gallery 124 so quickly?"

"My sister Shauna studied art. I showed her the card, she didn't recognize it but directed me to Bill Tokar, the head of the New Orleans Arts Council. He suggested Gallery 124."

"And the rest is history."

"Is that grudging respect I hear in your voice?"

"Absolutely not." She smiled. "Is Shauna your only sibling?"

"Nope. One of six."

She stopped. Looked at him. "You have six *siblings?*"

He laughed at her disbelief. "I'm from a good Irish Catholic family."

"The Lord said, be fruitful and multiply."

"So did the pope. And my mother takes the pope's directives very seriously." They fell back into an easy stroll. "What about you?" he asked.

"Just me and Jane. What's it like? Being part of such a big family?"

"Crazy. Sometimes irritating. Always loud." He paused. "But really great."

The affection in his tone made her ache to see her sister. To hold her new niece.

They reached the cross streets. The area was a shabby mix of retail and residential space. The eighteenth-century buildings stood side-by-side in various states of disrepair. All part of the Quarter's charm.

"Okay." She slid him an amused glance. "Bet you a cup of coffee I'll have Mr. Pogo's address in ten minutes."

"That's a no-brainer, Killian. Make it five and you're on."

She took the bet and scanned the street. Small grocery with lunch counter. Seedy bar. Souvenir shop.

She pointed toward the grocery. "You wait. Don't want to scare the straights."

"Funny." Smirking, he looked at his wrist. "Clock's ticking."

Stacy headed into the grocery, stopping just inside the door. It appeared to be a mom-and-pop family business. A sixtyish-looking man stood behind the lunch counter, a like-aged woman at the cash register. *Whom to approach?* Aware of the minutes ticking past, she decided on the woman.

Stacy crossed to her. "Hi." She infused her voice with what she hoped was the right combination of sincerity and friendliness. "I hope you can help me."

The woman returned her smile. "I'll try." She had the raspy voice of a lifetime smoker.

"I'm looking for an artist who lives right around here. Pogo."

The woman's expression altered in a way that suggested there was no love lost between the two.

She held the card out. "I bought this card from him last year and I'd like to buy some more. I tried his phone, but it's out of order."

"Probably disconnected."

"What's that, Edith?"

That came from the man. Stacy glanced over her shoulder at him. "This lady's looking for Pogo. She wants to buy some of his art."

"You paying him cash?" he asked.

"Sure," she said. "If I can ever find him."

The man nodded at his wife; she scribbled the address on the back of a register receipt. "Next door," she said. "Fourth floor."

Stacy thanked the pair and headed back out to Spencer. He looked at his watch. "Four and a half minutes. You have the address?"

She held up the scrap of paper.

He checked it against the one he had gotten from the gallery curator and nodded. "I would have chosen the bar. *Unreliable* and *drink* go together."

"Yeah, but everybody has to eat. Plus, bartender's going to be more suspicious and less likely to be forthcoming. Nature of the business."

"Coffee's on me. Wait here, I'll check him out."

"Excuse me? I don't think so."

"Police business, Stacy. It's been fun, but—"

"But nothing. You're not going in there without me."

"Yes, I am."

He started toward the neighboring building. She went after him, stopping him with a hand to his arm. "This is bullshit and you know it."

He inclined his head. "Maybe. But my captain would have my ass if I questioned a suspect while in the presence of a civilian."

"You'll scare him away. I'll keep up the charade, pretend to be an art buyer. He'll talk to me."

"The minute he sees the card, he'll know the gig's up. I'm not about to put you in harm's way."

"You're assuming he's guilty of something. Maybe he was commissioned to do the drawings and has no idea what their purpose was."

"Forget it, Killian. Don't you have a class or something?"

"You are the most irritating, pigheaded creature that I've ever had the misfortune of…"

Her words trailed off as she became aware of a commotion in front of the grocery store.

The man from inside, she saw. He stood with a long-haired, bearded man, motioning her way.

No, she realized. Not her way. At her.

Pogo.

The man looked from her to Spencer. She saw the moment he realized they were the law. "Spencer, quick—"

Too late, the artist bolted in the opposite direction. Spencer swore and took off after him, Stacy on his heels.

Pogo obviously knew the area well. He darted down side streets and cut through alleys. He was fast, too. A small guy, thin and wiry. Within minutes, Stacy lost sight of both men.

She stopped, panting. She was out of shape, she acknowledged, bending at the waist, resting her hands on her knees. Damn. She needed to start working out.

When she caught her breath, she headed back to the grocery. She saw that sometime during his chase, Spencer had called for backup. Two cruisers sat double-parked in front of the artist's building. One of the cops was questioning the grocer and his wife. The others were nowhere to be seen.

Fanning the area for Pogo, no doubt. Questioning the artist's neighbors.

She ducked behind the rack of postcards outside a souvenir shop. She didn't want the grocer to spot her and send the cop her way. Spencer wouldn't appreciate her part in today's debacle being in anyone's official report.

Tony pulled up, angled his car into the fire lane and climbed out. She thought about calling to him, then decided against it. She would let Malone call the shots.

Spencer returned. He was sweating. And looked pissed off.

Pogo had gotten away.

Damn it.

He crossed to Tony's side. They exchanged words, then he turned, scanning the area. For her, Stacy knew. She stepped out from behind the rack. He caught sight of her, and she signaled for him to call her, then turned and walked away.

CHAPTER
25

Thursday, March 10, 2005
2:00 p.m.

They had a search warrant within the hour. Spencer handed it to the landlord, who in turn unlocked the artist's apartment door. "Thanks," Spencer told him. "Hang around, okay?"

"Sure." The man shifted from one foot to the other. "What'd Walter get himself into?"

"Walter?"

"Walter Pogolapoulos. Everybody calls him Pogo."

Weird. But it made sense.

"So what'd he do?"

"Sorry, we can't discuss an ongoing investigation."

"Of course. I understand." He nodded his head vigorously. "I'll be right here if you need anything."

They entered the apartment. Tony grinned at him. "Ongoing investigation, indeed. Thought the guy was going to wet his pants at that."

"Everybody's got to have a hobby."

"Good work, by the way," Tony said.

"Haven't you heard? He got away."

"He'll be back."

He'd better be. They'd have him now, if he had been upstairs waiting for the artist when he arrived home, instead of out front playing games with Stacy, arguing like some damn rookie instead of doing his job correctly.

"Was that Killian I saw downstairs?"

"I don't want to hear that name."

Tony leaned toward him, "Killian," he murmured three times, then laughed.

Spencer made a great show of flicking him off, then turned to the task at hand. Pogo's was a typical, old New Orleans apartment. Sixteen-foot ceilings, windows with the original glass, cypress moldings that didn't exist in new construction, even for the wealthy.

The apartment also sported cracked plaster walls and ceilings. Peeling paint, probably chockful of lead. Bathroom and kitchen fixtures from the fifties—no doubt the last time the place had been updated. The musty smell of damp walls; the sound of cockroaches scurrying inside those walls.

Pogo's living room smelled of turpentine. And no wonder, art dominated every room. Drawings and paintings in every stage of completion were tacked or taped to walls, laid across tables and propped up in corners. Art supplies littered the apartment. Brushes and paint. Pencils, pens, pastels. Other tools as well, ones Spencer couldn't name.

Interesting, Spencer thought, looking over the room again. No family photos or curios, no evidence of life outside himself and his art.

Damn lonely, he would think.

"Over here, Slick," Tony called.

He crossed to where the other man stood, a drafting table in the corner. He followed the direction of the other man's gaze.

Spread across the top of the table were a half-dozen "Alice" death scenes, in various stages of completion. The most complete depicted the playing card characters, the Five and Seven of Spades, torn in half. Another appeared to be the March Hare slumped over a table, blood leaking from his head and pooling on the table.

Spencer met Tony's gaze. "Holy shit."

"Looks like we hit the jackpot, my friend."

Spencer grabbed a tissue, using it to keep from contaminating the evidence as he thumbed through them. The Queen of Hearts, impaled on a fork. The Cheshire Cat, its bloody head floating above its body. And finally, Alice, hanging by the neck, face a bloated distortion. At the bottom of a stack, some rough sketches for the cards Leo had already received.

"If this isn't our guy," Tony said, "he knows who is."

And he should have had him. He'd blown it.

"I want to know everything about Walter Pogolapoulos,

ASAP." Spencer motioned to one of the uniforms. "Call in the techs," he said. "I want a full search of the apartment. Access to the man's bank and phone records. Cell, too. I want to know who he's been talking to. Canvass the neighborhood. Let's find out who his friends are and where he hangs out."

"Want a broadcast?" Tony asked, referring to a bulletin put out on all police channel radios.

"You bet your ass I do. Mr. Pogo's not going to slip through my fingers again."

CHAPTER
26

Thursday, March 10, 2005
5:40 p.m.

Stacy pulled up in front of her apartment. She'd left the French Quarter to race out to the university. She'd made her class, though late and unprepared. The professor had been annoyed by the former and furious when he'd discovered the latter.

He'd chastened her in front of the entire class and again after, in his office. They expected better of their grad students, he'd told her. She had better get it together.

She hadn't made excuses. Hadn't brought up Cassie's death or the fact that she had discovered the body. Truth was, *she* expected better of herself.

Stacy shut off the engine and climbed out of the car,

acknowledging being mentally and emotionally exhausted. Maybe she should let this whole thing go. Tell Leo she'd had enough; the police were legitimately involved now. Malone had proved himself more capable than she had given him credit for. Hell, he'd beat her to Pogo.

But what about finding Cassie's killer? She couldn't let go until she knew for certain Malone was on the right track.

A movement on the front porch caught her eye. Alice Noble, she saw. Sitting on her front step.

Curiouser and curiouser.

"Hello, Alice."

The girl stood, arms wrapped protectively around her middle. "Hello."

Stacy reached the steps. She smiled at the young woman. "What's up?"

"I was waiting for you."

"I see that. I hope you weren't waiting too long."

"A couple hours." She hiked up her chin. "No big deal."

"Come on up. These books are heavy." Stacy climbed the three stairs to the porch, crossed to the door and dropped her backpack. "Want something to drink?"

"I want you to tell me the truth."

"The truth," she repeated. "About what?"

"You're not helping dad write a book."

Stacy wouldn't lie. It felt wrong. And Alice Noble was too old and too smart for glib reassurances.

"You were at the house last night. Late. With a couple men. Police, is my guess."

"You need to talk to your parents about this. Not me."

She looked suddenly upset. "Are Mom and Dad in some sort of trouble? Are they in danger?" When Stacy didn't reply, she fisted her fingers. "Why won't you tell me what's going on?"

Stacy held a hand out. "It's not my place, Alice. I'm not your parent. Go to them. Please."

"You don't understand! They won't tell me." Her tone turned adult—and bitter. "They treat me like I'm a baby. Like I'm six instead of sixteen. I can drive a car, but they're afraid to trust me with real life."

"It's not a matter of trust," Stacy said softly.

"Of course it is." She met Stacy's gaze evenly. "Somebody died, didn't they?"

Stacy stilled. "Why do you say that?"

"That's the only time people call in the middle of the night. Right? With bad news that can't wait." Alice grabbed her hand, squeezing it with a force that surprised Stacy. "If those men were the police, what does it mean? Was someone murdered? Kidnapped? What does it have to do with my family?"

"Alice," Stacy said softly, "did you eavesdrop on our conversation last night?"

She didn't reply. The lack of response told her that she had—hearing only enough to terrify her.

"Please tell me," Alice whispered. "Dad and Mom don't have to know you did."

Stacy hesitated. On the one hand, Alice was a teenager, too old to be kept in the dark the way a young child would be. And certainly too intelligent. She seemed more than capable of handling this; in Stacy's opinion, she should be included for her own well-being. The monster you know is less terrifying than the one you don't.

On the other hand, Stacy wasn't her parent. Or anyone else's, for that matter.

"You drove here?" Stacy asked.

"Walked." Her mouth twisted into a bitter-looking grimace. "Remember, I have my own car, but I have to ask permission to use it. And it practically takes an act of God to get permission."

"Look, I'm on your side in this. But I don't have the right to tell you. I won't go against your parents' wishes."

"Whatever."

She turned to go; Stacy caught her arm. "Wait. I'll drive you home. If your dad's there, I'll speak with him and try to convince him to tell you. Okay?"

"For all the good it'll do."

Stacy left the backpack, then the two stood and crossed to Stacy's car. They climbed in, buckled their safety belts, and Stacy started the car. They drove in silence, the girl slumped in her seat, the picture of adolescent misery.

Stacy parked in front of the mansion; they both climbed out. Alice didn't wait for Stacy, simply darted for the house, disappearing through the front door as Stacy reached the porch.

She followed the girl into the house. Leo stood at the bottom of the staircase, looking up. On the second floor, a door slammed.

He looked at Stacy, perplexed. "I thought she was upstairs."

"She was at my apartment."

"Your apartment?" His eyebrows shot up. "I don't understand."

"Can we talk?"

"Sure."

He led her to his study, closed the door behind them and waited.

"When I got home, I found Alice on my doorstep. She said she'd been there a couple hours."

"A couple hours? Good God, why—"

"She's scared, Leo. She knows something's going on. That I'm not a technical adviser. She wanted me to tell her the truth."

"You didn't, did you?"

"Of course not. She's your daughter, and you asked me not to."

"I don't want her frightened."

"She already is. She saw Malone and Sciame here last night. She heard at least a portion of what was discussed."

He paled. "She should have been asleep. In the guest house."

"Well, she wasn't. She guessed, correctly, that they were police. She even suspected it had to do with a murder."

"But how?" He pushed away from the desk, face creased with worry.

Stacy lifted her shoulders. "She's a bright girl, she put two and two together. As she said, people only call in the middle of the night when somebody's died."

A reluctant smile pulled at the corners of his mouth. "She never ceases to amaze me."

"She's afraid you and Kay are in danger. You need to reassure her. She's sixteen, Leo. Think back. What were you like at sixteen?"

He ran a hand across his face. "You don't know Alice. She's high-strung. The gifted often are. She needs more guidance than most kids her age."

"You're the parent, of course. But in my experience, the known is much less frightening than the unknown."

He was quiet a moment, then nodded. "Kay and I will discuss it."

"Good." She checked her watch. "I'm beat. If you don't mind, I'm heading home."

"Go ahead." He stopped her when she reached the door. "Stacy?"

She looked back at him in question.

"Thank you."

The gratitude in his expression made her smile. She exited the office. As she passed through the foyer, she saw Alice hovering at the top of the stairs. Their eyes met, but before Stacy could call goodbye, Kay appeared behind the girl.

Obviously, the older woman hadn't seen Stacy. Judging by the way Alice turned quickly away, Stacy sensed the teenager didn't want her to. Stacy hesitated a moment more, then left the mansion.

Within minutes, she was on her way home. Hungry, she stopped at the Taco Bell and picked up an enchilada bowl. As she waited for her food, she thought about Spencer and wondered if he had caught up with Pogo. She glanced at her cell phone, confirming that it was on and that she hadn't missed a call.

Stacy parked in front of her place, shut off the engine and headed inside. She dropped the bag of fast food in the kitchen, checked her recorder for messages—and saw that she had none—then crossed to the bathroom.

Pajamas, she decided. She would take a long hot shower, put on her pj's and eat in front of the TV. If Spencer hadn't called her by ten o'clock, she would call him.

She reached into the shower and turned on the hot water. While it heated, she undressed. Steam billowed from behind the curtain, and she inched it aside to add cold water. She frowned. A thread of pink water mixed with the clear and swirled down the drain.

She pushed the curtain back. A sound flew to her throat. Part surprise. Part horror.

A cat's head. Suspended from the ceiling above the tub with nylon fishing line. A tabby, the creature's mouth stretched into a bizarre snarl.

It appeared to be smiling at her.

She turned away, struggling to calm herself. She breathed deeply through her nose. *Divorce yourself from it, Killian. It's a scene. Like the dozens, hundreds, of others you've worked.*

Do the job.

She grabbed her robe from the hook on the back of the bathroom door, slipped into it, then retrieved her gun from the nightstand. She began a systematic search of the apartment, from the bedroom forward.

In the kitchen she discovered how the perp had entered: he'd broken a pane of glass in the kitchen door, reached inside and unlocked the dead bolt. Looked like he'd cut himself doing it, a sloppy mistake.

But good for the home team.

The rest of her search revealed nothing unexpected. Nothing appeared to have been taken or disturbed. No sign of the rest of the cat, poor thing. Clearly, the perp's intention had been to frighten her.

She returned to the bathroom. Swallowing hard, she studied the creature, the way it had been suspended from the ceiling. Nothing fancy, but it had taken a bit of both ingenuity and skill. She lifted her gaze. A cup hook screwed into the ceiling. Nylon fishing line attached to the hook and the cat's head.

Stacy ran her gaze along the lines—there were two—the end of each fitted with a fish hook. The hooks attached to the animal's ears.

She lowered her eyes to the tub floor. A plastic bag had been taped to the tub directly under the cat's head. The resealable kind, used for food storage.

She saw that there was something in the bag. A note. Or note-card-sized envelope.

Stacy stared at the bloodied bag, pulse pounding in her head. She forced herself to breathe. To think clearly.

Leave it. Call Spencer.

Even as the thought registered, she turned and headed for

the kitchen. To the sink and the rubber gloves she stored underneath. She bent, retrieved the package and drew out a pair.

She fitted them on and returned to the bathroom. Bending, she carefully freed the bag, unzipped it and eased the notecard out.

It said, simply: *Welcome to the game.* It was signed the White Rabbit.

CHAPTER
27

Thursday, March 10, 2005
8:15 p.m.

Spencer sped through the Metairie Road, City Park Avenue and I-10 intersection, making the turn onto City Park, cherry lights bouncing crazily off the underpass walls. Stacy's first call had come in while he and Tony had been in with the captain. The second one while he was on his way home. He'd made a U-turn, heading back toward central city, before he had even ended the call.

Spencer tightened his grip on the wheel, weaving around vehicles that didn't get out of his way fast enough. Stacy had said little besides "Get over here, ASAP." But he'd heard the strain in her voice the hint of a quiver—and had reacted without question.

He'd decided to make the call solo. Assess what had happened and who was needed. Give Tony a chance to eat the meal waiting for him at home. Spencer had learned the hard way that coming between the Pasta Man and his food wasn't pretty.

He reached Stacy's double. She sat on her porch step, waiting. He parked in the fire zone, climbed out of his vehicle and headed up to meet her.

As he neared, he saw her Glock was resting across her knees.

He stopped before her. She lifted her face. "Sorry to call you out like this. I remember what it was like."

"No problem." He searched her expression, concerned. "Are you all right?"

She nodded and stood. "Tony coming?"

"Nope. Thought I'd give him a chance to eat dinner. Pasta Man's like a grizzly if you get in between him and his next meal. What've you got?"

She crossed to the door, opened it for him. "See for yourself."

Her voice lacked inflection. Whether with shock or the effort to keep her emotions at bay, he didn't know.

He followed her inside. She led him from the front of the double to the back, to the single bathroom.

He saw the creature immediately. He stopped short, no doubt about what he was looking at.

The Cheshire Cat, its bloody head floating above its body.

Pogo's sketch brought to life.

"How did he get in?" he asked, tone sounding gruff to his own ears.

"Kitchen door. Broke one of the panes of glass, reached inside and unlocked the door. Cut himself, left some blood."

"You touch anything?"

"Just that." She indicated the bloody plastic bag and note card on the floor. Beside them were a pair of bright yellow Playtex gloves. The kind he had seen his mother use when washing dishes.

As if she read his mind, she said, "So I didn't contaminate anything. If you're worried, they were new."

"I wasn't worried."

She frowned as if with thought. "I was heating the water for a shower. I just reached in…without looking. In the process some evidence might have been washed away."

He glanced sideways. Saw the khaki capris she had been wearing earlier, the white short-sleeved sweater. A lacy bra in a delicate lavender color.

He looked quickly away, feeling like a Peeping Tom.

"Sorry," she muttered, crossing to the garments and scooping them up. "I wasn't thinking. I threw on a robe and…"

Her words trailed off. He shook his head. "You don't need to apologize. This is your home, I shouldn't have looked."

She laughed then, one perfectly timed, infectious laugh. "You're an investigator. Seems to me, that's your job."

It broke the awkwardness of the moment. He chuckled. "You have a point. I'll remember that."

He fitted on a pair of gloves, crossed to the note card and picked it up. The message was as simple as it was chilling.

Welcome to the game.

It was signed the White Rabbit.

Spencer looked at her. She met his gaze, hers unflinching. Steady. "I asked too many questions," she said. "Stepped on somebody's toes. I'm in the game now."

He wished he could reassure her otherwise. He couldn't.

"The Cheshire Cat," she continued. "A character with long claws and lots of teeth. In the story the queen tries to behead it, but it disappears before she can." She pressed her lips together a moment, as if using the time to regain emotional control. "This one wasn't so lucky."

"The cat fades in and out throughout the story," Spencer said, thinking of the Cliff's Notes he had read the night before. "Further evidence of a world in which reality has been distorted."

"Am I the cat?" she asked. "Is that what this means? That I'm the cat, and he means for me to die this way?"

Spencer frowned. "You're not going to die, Stacy."

"You can't guarantee that." Her eyebrows drew together. "You can't tell me I won't. It's the nature of the beast."

The beast.

Man with the will to murder.

He crossed to the tub, examined the creature, then fanned out until, finally, he had taken in the entire apartment. He took his time, making notes as he went. After dumping the clothes in a hamper, Stacy silently shadowed him. Giving him space, letting him come to his own conclusions.

Spencer checked his watch. Tony should be good and full by now. He needed to get the evidence collection team over. The prints techs. If they were lucky, the bastard had left a print to go along with the blood on the broken window.

"Go ahead," she said. "Make your calls." She smiled slightly at his expression. "I don't read minds, unfortunately. It's the obvious next step in the process."

He opened his cell, punched in Tony's number first. While he spoke to his none-too-happy partner, he was aware of Stacy grabbing a jacket and heading out to the front porch.

He finished his calls and followed her outside. She stood at the edge of the porch, near the stairs. She looked cold. He glanced up at the cloudless dark sky, thinking that the temperature had dipped into the fifties. He hunched deeper into his jacket and crossed to stand beside her.

"They're on their way," he said.

"Good."

"Are you okay?" he asked for the second time that night.

She rubbed her arms. "I'm cold."

For a reason that had nothing to do with temperature, he suspected. He wished he could draw her against his chest, comfort and warm her.

He wouldn't cross that line.

Even if he could, she wouldn't let him.

"We have to talk. Quickly. Before the others get here."

She turned. Met his eyes in question.

"Pogo's the one," he said. "We found sketches for the cards Leo received. And for others."

Her gaze sharpened with interest. Became intent. He sensed her analytical mind kicking in, digesting the facts, categorizing, organizing.

"Tell me about the others," she said.

"The March Hare. The two playing cards, the Five and Seven of Spades. The Queen of Hearts and Alice. All dead. Their deaths gruesome."

"And the Cheshire Cat? Was he there?"

He paused, then nodded. "Decapitated, the head floating above its body."

She pursed her lips. "If the Allen murder is the first in a series, then the people the cards represent will be victims."

"Yes."

"Including me."

"We don't know that, Stacy. Leo received the first cards, yet he wasn't the intended victim."

She agreed, though she didn't look convinced. The team arrived then. Tony first. The crime-scene van immediately behind. Spencer started toward his partner; she caught his arm, stopping him.

"Why'd you tell me that?"

"You're in the game now, Stacy. You needed to know."

CHAPTER
28

Thursday, March 10, 2005
11:30 p.m.

Stacy surveyed her apartment, moving from room to room. The crime-scene techs had just finished. Spencer had followed them out. He hadn't said goodbye.

She swallowed hard. She had known what to expect, of course. The black powder left by the fingerprint techs, the freshly vacuumed floor—done to pick up any trace evidence—the general sense of chaos.

She hadn't expected the way it had made her feel. Stripped bare. Violated. She found herself on the other side of the process, once again. And again, it sucked.

Stacy reached the bathroom door. She saw that they had taken her shower curtain, and she curved her arms around her middle. Something about that naked tub hit her hard. She knew what the tub floor looked like. Streaked red, the color deepening with the deoxidization process.

Police collected evidence of a crime.

They didn't clean up after it.

She crossed to the tub, adjusted the showerhead and turned on the water. It jettisoned out of the head, mixing with the blood, turning it pink.

Washing it away.

She watched it swirl down the drain.

"I'm sorry, Stacy."

She looked over her shoulder. Spencer hadn't left. He stood in the doorway, his gaze intent. "For what?"

"The mess. The late hour. That a half dozen strangers just tromped through your house. That some wacko broke in and left you that gruesome gift."

"None of it is your fault."

"But I can still be sorry."

Tears pricked her eyes, and she turned quickly back to the tub. She flipped off the shower, then mopped up the water that had sprayed on the floor. She glanced over her shoulder at him. He hadn't moved.

"You can go," she said. "I'm fine."

"You have a friend you can stay with tonight?"

"No need for that."

"The door—"

"I'll nail a board over it. It'll be good for tonight." She

smiled grimly at his concern. "Besides, I've got my old friend Mr. Glock to protect me."

"You always been such a hard-ass, Killian?"

"Pretty much." Stacy wrung out the towel and laid it across the edge of the tub. "It made me popular around the DPD. Ball-buster Killian, they called me."

He didn't smile at her attempt at humor. She made a sound of exasperation. "He's not coming back, Malone. He may intend for me to die, but not tonight."

"Invincible, are you?"

"No. But I'm figuring this guy out. It's a game. He's engaging me in a battle of wits. And will. His cat to my mouse. If he'd wanted a quick kill, he would have orchestrated it that way."

"If you won't go, I'm staying."

"You're not."

"I am."

A part of her was touched by his concern for her. Warmed by it.

But the sensation reminded her of Mac. Her partner and friend. Her lover.

Liar. Betrayer.

He'd broken her heart. And worse.

And the way he'd hurt her.

She steeled herself against the memory and crossed to stand in front of him. She met his eyes. "What are you thinking here? That I'm going to fall apart and need a big strong man? You thinking you're going to get lucky?" She cocked up her chin. "I'll save you the rude reality check, Malone. You're not."

As she stepped around him, he caught her arm, stopping her. "Nice try. But I'm staying."

She opened her mouth to argue; he cut her off. "The couch will be fine. No sex required, expected or, frankly, desired."

Her cheeks heated. She knew he could see the color in them.

"I can't force you to let me stay, but sleeping in the car will be damn uncomfortable, so I'm asking for mercy. What's it going to be, Killian?"

She folded her arms across her chest. He would do it, too. The man was more pigheaded than she was, for heaven's sake. She'd done surveillance detail, and spending the night in a car ranked up there with cold showers and stepping in shit with bare feet.

"Fine," she said. "I'll show you the guest bedroom."

She found an extra blanket, a never-been-used toothbrush and travel-size tube of Crest.

"A toothbrush, too," he said when she handed him the things. "I'm overwhelmed."

"I didn't want you to stink up the place."

"You're all heart."

"Just so you know, I'm going to lock my bedroom door."

He removed his shoulder holster and began unbuttoning his shirt. "Have at it, sweetheart. I hope you and Mr. Glock have a great night."

"Arrogant," she muttered. "Pigheaded, stubborn, know-it—"

She bit the words back as she realized they all described her. As she shut her bedroom door behind her, she heard him laugh.

CHAPTER
29

Friday, March 11, 2005
2:10 a.m.

Spencer opened his eyes, instantly awake. He went for his weapon, tucked under the mattress, curled his fingers around its grip and listened.

It came again. The sound that had awakened him.

Stacy, he realized. Crying.

The sound was thick, as if she was trying to muffle it. No doubt, she perceived tears as a sign of weakness. She would hate it that he had heard her. She would be embarrassed if he checked on her.

Spencer closed his eyes and tried to block the sound out. He couldn't. Small, hopeless-sounding, her grief tore at him.

Both were so foreign to the woman she wanted him to think she was.

He couldn't simply wait for her crying to stop. *That* was foreign to the man he was.

He stood, stepped into his jeans and fastened them. Taking a deep breath, he went to her bedroom. He stood outside the door a moment, then tapped on it. "Stacy," he called, "are you all right?"

"Go away," she called, voice thick. "I'm fine."

She wasn't. Clearly. He hesitated, then tapped again. "I have a pretty good shoulder. Best in the Malone clan."

She made a strangled sound, one that sounded part laugh, part sob. "I don't need you."

"I'm sure you don't."

"Then go back to sleep. Or better yet, go home."

He grabbed the doorknob and twisted. The door eased open.

She hadn't locked it, after all.

"I'm coming in. Please don't shoot me."

As he stepped into the dark bedroom, the light came on.

Stacy was sitting up in bed, blond hair a wild tangle, eyes red and puffy from crying. She gripped the Glock with both hands, the weapon aimed at his chest.

He stared at it a moment, feeling like a cat burglar caught in the act. Or a deer in the headlights of a truck. A big one, traveling too damn fast for comfort.

He raised his hands over his head, fighting a smile. *Pissing her off would be a bad idea.*

"The chest, Stacy? You couldn't aim for a leg or something?"

She inched the barrel directly south. "Better?"

His nuts ran for cover. "That's equipment I'd rather die for than do without, sweetheart. Do you mind?"

She grinned and lowered the Glock. "Are you hungry?"

"I'm always hungry. It's genetic."

"Good. Meet me in the kitchen in five?"

"Sounds good." He started through the door, then stopped. "Why are you being nice to me?"

"You made me forget," she answered simply.

He left her bedroom, mulling over what she had said. The turn of events. She had surprised him. The invitation. Her honest answer to his question.

Stacy Killian was one complicated, high-maintenance woman. The kind he made a practice of steering clear of.

So what the hell was he doing meeting her for a midnight pajama party?

She joined him in the kitchen. "What do you like to eat?"

"Everything. Except beets, liver and brussels sprouts."

She laughed, crossed to the fridge. "Don't have to worry about those, not with me." She peered inside. "Enchilada bowl. Leftover Peking duck. Though I'd give it the sniff test first. Tuna. Eggs."

He peered over her shoulder, made a face. "Pickings are slim, Killian."

"I was a cop, remember. Cops always eat out."

It was true. His refrigerator was emptier than hers.

"How about cereal?" she asked.

"That depends, what've you got?"

"Cheerios or Raisin Bran."

"The O's are good, definitely. Whole milk or skim?"

"Two percent."

"That'll do."

She took the carton of milk from the fridge and closed the door. He saw her check the date on the carton before she set it on the counter. She took two bowls from one cabinet and two boxes of cereal from another.

They filled their bowls—she took the bran, no surprise there—and carried them to the small café table by the window.

They ate in silence. He wanted to give her time. A little space. A chance to become comfortable with him. And to decide if forgetting was enough, or if she needed someone to talk to.

She hadn't asked him to the kitchen because she was hungry. Or because she was worried that he was.

She had needed company. Another's support, even if that support only came in the form of a cereal buddy.

One of his sisters, Mary, third oldest of the Malone brood, was like that. Tough as nails, stubborn as a mule, too prideful for her own good. When she had gone through a divorce a couple of years ago, she had tried to keep it all in, handle everything—including her hurt—by herself.

She had finally confided in Spencer. Because he had first allowed her the space, and then the opportunity to do so. And maybe, too, because he had made so many mistakes in his own life, she figured he would be less judgmental of hers.

"Want to talk about it?" he asked finally as her spoon scraped the bottom of her bowl.

She didn't ask about what; she knew. She stared into her bowl, as if preparing her answer.

"I didn't want to do this," she said after a moment, looking at him. "Not anymore."

"Breakfast cereal with near strangers?"

A ghost of a smile touched her mouth. "Are you ever totally serious?"

"As infrequently as possible."

"I'm thinking that would be a nice way to be."

He thought of Lieutenant Moran. "Trust me, it has drawbacks." He inched aside his bowl. "So, you left police work behind, moved to New Orleans to study Literature and start a new life?"

"Something like that," she said with a trace of bitterness. "But it wasn't the police work I wanted to leave behind. It was the ugliness of the job. The absolute disregard for life." She let out a long, weary-sounding breath. "And here I am, smack dab in the middle of it again."

"By your own doing."

"Cassie's murder was not my doing."

"But putting yourself into the investigation was. Signing on with Noble was. Stepping through each door that opened was."

She looked as if she wanted to argue. He reached across the table and caught her hand, curving his fingers around hers. "I'm not criticizing you. Far from it. You're doing what comes natural. You were a cop for ten years. We both know that law enforcement isn't a job, it's a way of life. It's not what you are, it's who you are."

He had discovered just how true those words were when he was falsely accused, suspended and facing a lifetime without police work.

"I don't want to be that person, not anymore."

"Then let it go, Stacy. Get out of it. Go back to Texas."

She made a sound of frustration and stood. She carried her bowl to the sink, then turned to face him once more. "What about Cassie? I can't just…leave."

"What about her? You hardly knew her."

"That's not true!"

"It is, Stacy. You were friends for less than two months."

"She didn't deserve to die. She was young. And good. And—"

"And the morgue is filled with young, good people who shouldn't be dead, but are."

"But they're strangers to me! And Cassie…Cassie was the person I wished I was!" She fell silent a moment; he saw her struggle for control. "And someone killed her. The same ugliness that I wanted to escape…followed me."

Understanding, he stood and crossed to her. He caught her hands. "You think the ugliness found you? Followed you? And she died because of it?"

"I didn't say that." Eyes bright with tears, she shook her head and moved to free her hands from his.

He tightened his grip. "Cassie's death doesn't have anything to do with what you've involved yourself in. There's nothing similar about her death and the White Rabbit killings."

She knew he had a good point; he saw it in her expression. "What about her computer?"

"What about it?"

"She stumbled onto something that put her in harm's way. It had to do with White Rabbit."

"You believe," he countered. "The facts don't support that belief." He leaned toward her. "The most obvious is most often the one 'whodunit.' You know that."

"Gautreaux."

"Yeah, Gautreaux. We have physical evidence linking him to the murders."

"What?" she asked, eyes narrowing. "What do you have?"

"A print—"

"His or hers?"

"His. Retrieved from her apartment. And some trace."

She nodded, skepticism becoming excitement. "What kind of trace?"

"Hair. Hers. On his clothing. Because of their past relationship, neither is strong enough to prove he did it."

"Bullshit. No way there should be a print of his in her place. They didn't break up amicably. The guy stalked and threatened her, no way she just let him in for a nice little chat. Plus, they broke up last year. Doesn't he wash his clothes?"

"Jacket," he corrected. "Denim. Doesn't look like it's ever seen a washing machine."

She swore and stood. "I hate defense lawyers. They can twist the facts—"

"Hold on, there's more. We found a hair consistent with his on her T-shirt. We got the order for the swab, results are due next week. If we're lucky—"

"DNA will tie him to the scene. Nasty little prick."

Spencer turned her earlier question back on her. "So why'd he take her computer?"

"To cover his ass. Maybe he sent her hate mail, maybe he knows she saved it. So when he kills her, he takes away the evidence. Or he takes it as a trophy. Or because it was the thing he perceived she loved most. Certainly more than him."

Spencer smiled. "By George, I think she's got it."

She frowned suddenly. "When did you swab him?"

"Three days ago."

"And you really think he hasn't skipped?"

"I'm not a complete rookie, you know. We've got a GPS tracking device on his car. He takes one step too close to the state line and we grab him."

He caught her hands in his, holding them gently. "Go home to Texas, Stacy. We've got Cassie's killer. She doesn't need your help anymore."

Her hands trembled; he felt her indecision, the conflict raging inside her.

She wanted to.

She couldn't bring herself to let go.

Spencer tightened his fingers on hers. "Go. Visit your sister. Stay until we find this crazy White Rabbit character and get him behind bars."

She shook her head. "School doesn't work that way. Can't

just come and go. Besides, I only have a little over a month to go in this semester."

He frowned. "We both know a month is a long time. A lot can happen in a month."

He knew she understood what he was saying. That death could find her in the blink of an eye.

And that this one scared him.

"He'll follow me," she said softly. "He knows all about me now."

"You're just guessing. You don't know that for certain—"

"But I do, Malone. He's playing the game. So am I. And the game doesn't end until there's only one man standing."

He stroked the back of her hands with his thumbs. "Then go somewhere he won't think to look for you. Someplace you've no connection to."

"And how do we know he won't wait me out? For years, the rest of my life, even. I have family, a life outside this. I'm not going to go into hiding."

"But we're going to catch him. Long before years pass."

"You hope."

She moved to slip her hands from his; he tightened his fingers on hers. "I *will* catch him, Stacy. I promise you that."

CHAPTER
30

Friday, March 11, 2005
9:20 a.m.

Stacy awakened to the sound of the toilet flushing. Spencer. Moaning, she rolled onto her side to see the clock. She stared at the numbers a moment, struggling to think.

Today was Friday. Malone's shift probably started around 7:30 a.m., standard for most P.D.'s detective units.

She flopped onto her back. What did she have today? *Professor Schultze's class. Introduction to Graduate Studies in English. About as exciting as watching grass grow.*

She might as well head back to Texas. She was probably going to be booted out of grad school.

Stacy stared at the ceiling. A long crack ran diagonally across it, nearly from corner to corner. Should she? Tuck tail and run back to Dallas?

And do what? She'd given up her job. Sold her house. She could move in with Jane and Ian for a couple of weeks, then what? And to what end?

She believed what she had told Spencer, that the White Rabbit would follow her. That he not only knew her identity, but that he knew *her*. She based that belief on nothing but her gut—and what she had been told about the game.

Who was the White Rabbit? Why was he playing the game? Most murders were motivated by love or hate, by greed, by a desire for revenge or jealousy.

The serial killer, on the other hand, was a different animal. He usually preyed on strangers; he killed to fulfill some sick need within himself.

Who were they dealing with? And why had she been included in his game?

For a specific reason, she was certain. One other than the fact that she had poked her nose into what he considered his private business. She interested him. He wanted to play with her.

Hide and seek. Cat and mouse.

She frowned and sat up, her head filling with the image of the beheaded cat. Its obscene grin.

Was she the cat? Stacy brought a hand to her throat. Did he mean for her to die in that gruesome way?

If the Allen murder set the pattern for more to come, the answer to that question was yes.

They needed to get into his head, Stacy acknowledged. Figure out what made him tick.

There was only one way to do that: play the game.

She scrambled out of bed and slipped into her robe before heading to the kitchen. She found Spencer, his back to her, making coffee.

She gazed at him a moment, remembering her tears of the night before, wondering what he thought of her now. If he would be able to take her seriously.

Like a dope, she had revealed how badly the White Rabbit's visit had shaken her. How upset she was.

She'd revealed that she was a big fake. Hard as nails Stacy Killian was like one of those Tootsie Roll Pops—hard shell, soft, chewy center.

Once a guy knew the center could be chewed, that's what they did. Chewed you up and spit you out. Or swallowed you, bite by bite. Goodbye respect. Goodbye self-esteem.

She had been down this road before. It didn't lead anywhere she wanted to go.

Though Malone seemed different. He could be funny. And kind. Certainly not the Bubba she had first pegged him to be.

Which meant exactly nothing. Cops were off-limits, period.

As if sensing her presence, he looked over his shoulder and smiled. "Morning. I was going to let you sleep a bit more."

"I have a class." She returned his smile. "But thanks."

"You're welcome." The coffeemaker sputtered as it finished

brewing and he turned back to it. She saw that he'd found the mugs already; she watched as he filled two.

He held one out for her. She crossed to him, took it and went about adding milk and sweetener. That done, she took a sip, then looked at him over the rim of her mug. "It occurred to me that we're going about this the wrong way."

"Going about what the wrong way? Our romance?"

For a moment she couldn't breathe. She shook it off and crossed to a chair and sat. "Get a grip, Romeo. Catching the White Rabbit."

"Last I checked, you were a civilian and I was the detective. There is no 'we' in that scenario."

She ignored that. "It seems to me, if we played the game, we'd have a better handle on what we're up against. And who we're up against."

"Get into this Rabbit's head."

"Exactly. If the killer really is someone who's begun playing the game for real, what better way to predict his moves?"

He gazed at her a moment, then nodded. "I'm in. So's Tony."

"Good. I'll talk to Leo about setting it up. After all, who better to help understand the White Rabbit than the man who created him?"

He nodded again, drained his mug and set it on the counter. He started for the doorway, stopping and looking back at her when he reached it. "Call me when you have the details. And Stacy?"

"Hmm?"

"If you don't get that door fixed, I'm sleeping over again to-night. That's a promise."

She watched him go, a smile tugging at the corners of her mouth. *She had to admit, a part of her would like to test that promise.*

CHAPTER
31

Friday, March 11, 2005
10:30 a.m.

"'Morning, Mrs. Maitlin," Stacy said as the woman opened the door of the Noble mansion. "How are you today?"

The woman frowned slightly. "Mr. Leo isn't up yet. But Mrs. Noble is in the kitchen."

Which didn't answer her question. But did reveal the difference in the way the housekeeper felt about her employers. Stacy thanked her and started for the kitchen. The Nobles' was a big, old-fashioned country kitchen, with a brick floor and exposed beam ceiling. Kay sat at the large butcher-block-style table, reading the newspaper and sipping orange juice. Sunlight fell across her, accenting the inky highlights in her dark hair.

She looked up when Stacy entered the kitchen and smiled.

"'Morning, Stacy. I thought Friday mornings you were at school."

The woman had a mind like a steel trap.

"I overslept," Stacy fibbed, crossing to their coffeemaker, a newfangled, high-tech machine that ground the beans and brewed one perfect serving at a time—from a single shot to a full eight-ounce cup.

She coveted the machine. She figured she'd have to sell her soul to afford to buy one.

"Overslept?" Kay repeated, sounding disapproving. "Something you and Leo have in common."

"Why do I have the feeling I'm being dissed here?"

They both turned. Leo stood in the doorway, bleary-eyed, his hair standing on end. Obviously, he had just rolled out of bed and into a T-shirt and pair of rumpled khakis.

The mad scientist returns, Stacy thought, turning back to the pot to hide her grin. She pressed the appropriate buttons and the machine whirred to life, grinding, brewing and dispensing a perfect double shot.

The smell filled the air.

"Leo," Stacy said. "There's something I need to—"

"Coffee," he croaked, coming up behind her.

Kay made a sound of disgust. "For God's sake, you're like Pavlov's dog."

He wasn't the only one. Stacy handed him the cup, then brewed herself another. When she reached the table, he was slouched in a chair, slurping the beverage. He'd managed to make a mess—sugar on the table, dribbled cream, used spoon. Like a small tornado—or Dennis the Menace—he came into a room and stirred things up.

Stacy sat. "Leo, there's something we need—"

"Not yet," he said, holding up a hand. "One more sip."

"You should sleep at night," Kay said. "Then we wouldn't have to go through this every morning."

"I'm best at night."

"That's just an excuse to get your own way."

She glanced at her watch, then at Stacy. "The man would be a pauper if not for me. The rest of the world doesn't operate on Leo time."

"Quite true." Leo leaned over and kissed his ex-wife's cheek. "I owe everything to you."

The woman's expression softened. She laid a hand against his cheek and looked affectionately at him. "You drive me crazy, you know that?"

"Yeah." He grinned. "That's why you divorced me."

As if on cue, they turned their full attention on her. She blinked, slightly embarrassed, as if she had just witnessed an intimate moment meant for only them.

Stacy collected her thoughts. "As of yesterday," she began, "I'm in the game." She quickly described the cat, how she had found it and the note she had been left.

Welcome to the game.

"My God." Leo stood and crossed to the counter, visibly upset. There, he stopped, as if uncertain what to do next.

"I don't understand," Kay murmured. "Why is this happening?"

"You tell me."

She looked startled. "Excuse me?"

"It seems to me both of you might have a better idea why this is happening than I would. I'm a late addition."

Leo spread his hands. "Someone's obsessed with the game."

"Or with you," Stacy countered. "Because of the game."

"But why?" he asked. "It doesn't make sense."

"The very nature of obsession defies logic."

Mrs. Maitlin appeared at the kitchen doorway. "Excuse me, Mr. Noble, those detectives from the other day are here. They say they need to speak with you."

"Send them back, Valerie."

He looked at Stacy in question. She saw what she thought was fear in his eyes. She shook her head. "As far as I know, nobody's dead."

Mrs. Maitlin showed them in. After a round of greetings, Spencer began. "We identified the artist who created the cards you received. A local guy named Walter Pogolapoulos, Pogo for short. Do you know him?"

They looked at each other, then shook their heads.

"Heard the name before?"

Again, they indicated they hadn't.

Tony showed them a picture. "Ever seen him? Hanging around the neighborhood? At the mall, in the park? Anything like that?"

"No," Leo said, sounding frustrated. "Kay?"

She stared at the photo, then hugged herself. "No."

"You're certain?"

"Yes. Is he the one who…killed that woman?"

"We don't know," Tony said, sliding the photo back into his pocket. "He could be. Or he simply could have been hired to create the drawings."

"We've yet to question him," Spencer said. "But we will."

Leo looked confused. "If you've identified him, why haven't you questioned—"

"He got wind of us and disappeared."

"But don't worry," Tony added. "We'll get him."

The couple didn't look convinced. Stacy couldn't blame them.

"Have you received another card?" Spencer asked.

"No." Leo frowned. "Do you expect us to?"

Spencer was silent a long moment. Stacy knew he was deciding what he should say and what he should keep to himself.

He began. "We found sketches of the cards you received as well as several others, in various stages of completion."

"Others?" the man repeated.

Stacy stepped in, though she knew doing so might earn her Spencer's ire. "One of the cards depicted the Cheshire Cat, its bloody head floating above its body."

"Dear God." Kay clasped her hands together.

"If the Allen murder set the pattern, the chances are good that I'm the Cheshire Cat."

Spencer sent her an irritated glance, then continued. "In addition to the Cheshire Cat, we found cards depicting the deaths of the Five and Seven of Spades, the March Hare, the Queen of Hearts and Alice."

"Alice," Kay repeated weakly. "You don't think that's our—"

"Of course it's not our Alice," Leo exclaimed, voice gruff. "What a thought, Kay!"

Spencer and Tony exchanged glances. "Is it so far from the realm of possibility, Mr. Noble?"

They all knew it wasn't. Leo frowned. "Let's just say, I refuse to accept it as a possibility. I have no clue what any of this is about."

Kay turned to her husband, obviously upset. "How can you take that blindly optimistic approach? It very well could be our Alice. For all we know, I could be the Queen of Hearts!"

The room fell silent. Stacy studied the others. Malone and his partner were already thinking ahead, to the next bullet on their agenda. Leo and Kay, on the other hand, were scrambling to figure out how much danger they were in.

"I don't like this," Kay said, breaking the silence. "Maybe I should take Alice and go somewhere. Call it a holiday, a mother and daughter excurs—"

"I'm not going anywhere."

They all turned. Alice stood in the doorway, ramrod straight, hands balled into fists. "I mean it. I'm not."

Leo took a step toward her, hand out. "Alice, sweetheart, now's not the time to discuss this. Go to your room and—"

"It is the time! I'm not a baby, Dad. When are you going to get that?"

"Go to your room!"

She held her ground. "No."

Leo's mouth dropped, as if he couldn't even imagine such defiance coming from his daughter's lips.

"I know something's going on." She turned to Stacy. "You're not a technical consultant. You're interested in Dad's game, White Rabbit.

"And you two—" she indicated Malone and Sciame "—are cops. You were here the other night and again now. Why?"

Kay and Leo exchanged glances. Kay nodded and Leo turned back to his daughter. "The police are asking our help in tracking down a killer. He claims to be the White Rabbit."

"That's why they were here the other night," Alice said. "Because someone had been murdered."

"Yes."

She moved her gaze between the adults, as if deciding whether they were being truthful. "But why take me away?"

Kay took a step toward her. "Because your father...he might...he's—"

"In danger?" The words seem to catch in the girl's throat. She suddenly looked younger than her sixteen years. And as vulnerable as any child.

Leo crossed to her and hugged her. "We don't know that for certain, pumpkin. But we're not taking any chances."

She seemed to digest that. "Am I in danger?"

Spencer stepped in. "At this moment, we don't have a strong reason to believe so."

The girl was silent. When she spoke, the vulnerability was gone. "If I'm not in danger, why send me away? Seems to me, Dad's the one who should consider running."

"We don't want to expose you to danger," Kay said. "If some crazy person has targeted your—"

"I'm not leaving Dad."

Leo sighed. Kay looked frustrated. Stacy felt for them. She turned to Spencer. "Do you think it's safe for Alice here?"

He frowned, then nodded. "For the moment, yes. That could change."

Stacy looked at the teenager. "If it did, would you go then?"

"Maybe," she said. "We could talk about it."

She sounded like an adult. Had the intellect to reason like one. But she wasn't an adult. She was a child. And one who didn't live in the real world. Because of her intellect. And because of her wealth.

Alice squared her shoulders and looked directly at Spencer. "I want to help. What can I do?"

Leo pressed a kiss to the top of her head. "Pumpkin, I'm sure the detectives appreciate your offer, but you're—"

Stacy cut him off. The teenager knew enough to be afraid. Helping might ease those fears.

"Detective Malone and I have an idea," she said. "It's something you might be able to help with, Alice."

The girl turned eagerly toward her. Stacy ignored the Nobles' shocked expressions. "We figure we need to get into this guy's head. He claims to be a White Rabbit, so—"

"You want to play the game," Alice said. "Of course. What better way to anticipate his moves?"

CHAPTER
32

Saturday, March 12, 2005
2:00 p.m.

Leo had been reluctant to play; said he'd left gaming behind years before. Kay had flatly refused. White Rabbit belonged to a time of their lives she would rather not relive.

Stacy had attempted to overcome Leo's reluctance by explaining that Alice was absolutely right when she'd ascertained that they planned to use the game as a way to understand who they were up against. Getting into the head of a killer was a technique as old as crime and investigation, but perfected by the FBI in the 1980s.

The feds had dubbed the technique "profiling," the investigators who specialized in the technique "profilers." It was about as sexy as police work got. Lots of media coverage. Respect and awe from both the public and law enforcement. Some damn spectacular success stats.

Even so, in the end it'd been Alice who'd convinced her father. She'd begged him. She would set up the game. All he'd have to do was show up. It'd be fun.

So here she was. Alice met them at the door. She wore a bright patchwork vest—similar to the rabbit's in Carroll's story.

"Hurry," the girl said. "We're late. So very, very late."

Stacy began to correct her—she was actually right on time—then realized that Alice was already in character.

"Follow me…follow me…"

She turned and hurried inside, leading them to the kitchen. It looked like a snack truck had exploded in the room. The center island was covered with bags and bowls of every snack food possible. A small cooler sat in the midst of the chips, pork rinds and M&M's candies.

Stacy crossed to it and saw it was loaded with soda pops and coffee drinks.

The front doorbell rang and Alice hurried to answer, muttering about the time.

In the next moment, Alice scurried back into the room, shadowed by Spencer, Tony and Leo. All the while, Alice tapped her foot impatiently, muttering under her breath and repeatedly checking her pocket watch.

"Alice isn't being rude," Leo explained. "She's IC. In character."

"Exactly," Alice said, grinning at her father. "And right now I'm OOC, out of character."

"What's with the junk food?" Tony asked, wandering to the island.

"It's a gamer thing. Energy drinks, pork rinds, chips, the nastier the better."

"My kind of game," he said, reaching for the basket of barbecue cracklings.

"Energy drinks?" Stacy asked. "Mountain Dew?"

"Lots of caffeine. At Dad's insistence, we also have Starbucks Double Shots."

They did, indeed. Stacy helped herself to a can, popped the top and poured the coffee beverage over a cup of ice. When they had all helped themselves to a refreshment, they sat.

"Since you're all newbies," Alice began, "I figured we'd play a really basic version."

Leo cleared his throat. "Newbie? Excuse me?"

She laughed. "Except for Dad, of course." She continued, "There are a number of different scenarios, even a one-on-one, between a player's character of choice and the White Rabbit.

"The basic story goes like this. The White Rabbit has taken control of Wonderland. Once a place where time had been turned on end, a place of maddening but benign beauty, he has turned it into a place of death. And of evil. Nature turned inside out. Using dark magic, he controls the creatures who reside in Wonderland. Alice and her band of heroes must destroy the White Rabbit, not only saving Wonderland and its king and queen—but the world above as well. For the White Rabbit is dangerously close to adapting his dark magic to our world."

Leo stepped in. "Like any good book or film, the best RPGs

have a narrative, its heroes a grand mission. The stakes are high, the clock ticking."

"Jeez," Tony said around a mouthful of cracklings, "and here I thought I was going to get to kick some fantasy creep's ass."

Leo laughed. "You will, Detective. But White Rabbit is more than a hack-and-slash scenario."

"Hack and slash?" Spencer asked.

"A game that's little more than the near endless slaughter of bad guys—and anything else in the players' paths. I find that gets boring, but some players and GMs want nothing but."

Leo glanced at his daughter. "Alice?"

She took over. "I chose a character for each of you, a job usually left to each player. The band of heroes includes Alice, of course. She's the leader. The other members of today's team are da Vinci, Nero and Angel."

She retrieved a Crown Royal bag from the floor beside her, opened it, reached inside and drew out a miniature. Made of cardboard and hand-painted, it depicted a young girl. "Alice," she said, and slid it across to Stacy. "You're the group's leader. You're intelligent and brave, with superhuman strength. Besides your physical strength, you carry a crossbow. Alice has the heart of a warrior and the spirit of an adventurer."

Alice retrieved a second figure from the bag. "Da Vinci," she said, holding up a replica of da Vinci's famous drawing "Vitruvian." She snapped it into a plastic holder and slid it across to Spencer. "Da Vinci is a genius. He's a master at spells and potions. He also possesses the ability to read minds, though he can be fooled. However, he is all brain and no brawn."

One corner of Spencer's mouth lifted. "Sexy."

Alice withdrew another figure, a male wearing black jeans and T-shirt, dark glasses. "Nero," she said.

Something in her tone piqued Stacy's curiosity. "What's his story?"

"Nero's the most unpredictable of all the characters. The most dangerous."

"Why?" Tony puffed up slightly, obviously assuming the character was his.

"He's a necromancer."

"A what?"

"A spell-wielding character who specializes in death magic. He can be hard to control and is often untrustworthy. I worried about throwing him in with an inexperienced band like yourselves."

Stacy glanced at Spencer. She suspected he was thinking the same as she— that it was creepy the way Alice described the characters as if they were real and could think for themselves.

"There's always a betrayer," Leo added. "The Judas figure."

"And I'm it?" Tony asked, not quite as puffed up now.

"No." Alice fixed the miniature in its stand and slid it to her father.

He cocked an eyebrow. "Interesting."

Tony frowned. "What about me?"

"I've reserved a very special character for you. Angel," she said, drawing the miniature from the bag. She set the figure, a representation of a dark-haired woman outfitted in a skintight superhero costume.

Tony gazed at the figure, disgusted. "I'm a chick?"

Spencer hooted in amusement. Stacy chuckled and Alice smiled, obviously enjoying her moments as "God."

"Not just any chick," the girl said. "A powerful illusionist, she uses her power to defeat her enemies."

Tony sulked. "A chick. Why me?"

"Overcome, Pasta Man," Spencer said. "Have a few more pork rinds."

"Four characters, four miniatures," Stacy murmured. "Your heroes represent real-life people, don't they?"

"Except for Alice. Lewis, who I chose not to use today, represents Lewis Carroll, Wonderland's original creator. Da Vinci is Dad, and Nero is his old partner, the co-creator of the game. Angel is Mom, Dad's nickname for her back then."

Spencer frowned. "If those are the characters, how do the Dormouse, March Hare and Cheshire Cat come into play?"

Leo stepped in. "In all RPGs, the heroes must battle foes. In D & D the foes are monsters. In our game, they are the original creatures of Wonderland. They have turned to evil and are controlled by the White Rabbit."

Stacy frowned. "But I thought this was a killer-takes-all scenario? If we're a band of heroes, that means we must betray one another."

Leo nodded. "Any of the characters can turn at any moment. Some are more susceptible, like Nero. Angel has been known to create the illusion of safety for her fellow comrades when a trap awaits."

"And some—" Alice jumped in "—have been known to sacrifice themselves for the success of the mission. Or the safety of a friend."

"Or," Leo added, "to sacrifice a fellow hero to save the world."

"So remember, only one will be left standing at the end of the game." Alice paused for effect, moving her gaze among them. "Which of you will it be?"

Stacy felt herself being drawn into the scenario. She looked at each of her fellows, wondering who would be the one to save the world. Wanting to be the one, but determined to put the safety of all before her own heroic immortality.

Alice continued. "Your success, or defeat, is determined by your choices, your skills and the roll of the dice."

"Explain," Spencer said.

"We play with a 20-sided dice. Rolling a twenty is a critical hit, a one a critical miss."

"Meaning?"

"A critical hit means your spell, move or whatever, was more effective than intended. For example, if you want to stop a monster's advance and you get a critical hit, you'll not just stop him but blow him to smithereens. A critical miss is just the opposite. The monster doesn't just hurt you, he tears you into pieces, which he then eats and burps up for the next hour."

"Lovely image," Spencer murmured.

"What about something in between?" Stacy asked. "Say an eight?"

"The GM is God, remember? He decides how successful your action is."

"Any other questions?"

There weren't, and the teenager looked at each of them, expression serious. "A last word of caution. Choose wisely. Work together. The White Rabbit is wily indeed. Are we ready to begin?"

They all looked at Stacy. "You're our leader. Are we ready?"

"Yes—it's time to begin."

The minutes passed quickly and it didn't take long for them to get the hang of it, Stacy realized. She had to admit, it was enjoyable. And powerful. The scenario sucked her in and she no longer thought of her fellow players by their real identities but as their characters. The psychological pull was great, and Stacy understood why RPGs frightened many parents. And why Billie had said they were too powerful for people with a fragile grasp on reality.

They confronted the Mad Hatter, who critically wounded da Vinci before Alice had killed him with her crossbow. Nero had been trapped in the White Rabbit's shrinking house, and they'd been forced to leave him behind.

Now they faced the most formidable foe to date: a caterpillar larger than all of them put together. He smoked a pipe; its curling green smoke a deadly poison to all it came in contact with.

Da Vinci offered an antidote potion. In his weakened state, less than a critical hit would kill him.

The game master prepared to roll. Kay appeared in the kitchen doorway. "Excuse me. Leo?"

Her voice trembled. The inventor looked up, smile dying

on his lips. Stacy turned. Kay was as pale as a ghost. She seemed to be hanging on to the door frame to keep from toppling over.

Leo got to his feet. "My God, Kay. What's wrong?"

The adults followed Leo to his feet. Stacy glanced at Alice. She sat frozen, staring at her mother.

"Come see… It's—" She brought a hand to her mouth; Stacy saw that it shook. "Your office."

"My office?" Leo said. "What—"

"Mrs. Maitlin found…she called me."

"Leo," Stacy said softly, touching his arm, "your daughter."

He looked at Alice, as if just remembering her presence. "You stay," he ordered.

"But, Dad—"

"Not a word. You stay."

Stacy frowned. She wasn't a parent, but it seemed a little more sensitivity might be in order. The teenager was obviously frightened.

They exited the kitchen. The housekeeper hovered outside Leo's office door. She looked as shaken up as Kay.

Stacy glanced toward the foyer. Word that something was happening must have spread, because Troy stood in the doorway.

He looked her way. He wore mirrored sunglasses, which she always found disconcerting. She disliked not being able to see another's eyes, but instead to see herself reflected back at her.

Freud would have had a field day with that.

"Stacy? Coming?"

That came from Leo. She tore her gaze from the driver. "Yes."

Stacy followed Spencer and his partner into the office. Leo trailed behind her.

On the gleaming wooden floor the shape of a heart had been drawn. Inside it lay two oversize playing cards, the kind magicians and kids' birthday clowns sometimes used, the Five and Seven of Spades. Both had been torn in half.

Beneath the heart, the intruder had scrawled a message.

The roses are red now.

CHAPTER
33

Spencer cleared the room. He ordered everyone to stay on the premises, including Kay and Leo.

He studied the scrawled message.

The roses are red now.

Judging by the fluid, uneven quality of the letters, Spencer judged the message to have been written with a paintbrush, dipped into paint or some other liquid.

He didn't know for certain what it meant, but he had a pretty damn good idea.

Somebody, very probably, was dead.

"That blood?" Tony asked, referring to the substance used to write the message.

Spencer squatted and touched the *W*, then brought his finger to his nose. Earthy. Distinct. Not like paint. He nodded to his partner even as he rubbed it between his fingers, checking the viscosity.

"I'm thinking. See the way the color is darkening as it dries?"

"Could be animal blood," Tony offered.

Could be. But his guess was no, it wasn't.

"Get the techs over here, ASAP. I want this tested and in evidence. And I want the place dusted for prints."

He turned. Stacy stood in the doorway. She motioned toward the message. "You saw a sketch for this, didn't you?"

"Yeah."

She frowned. "You're thinking the playing cards are dead."

"I have no proof—"

"We're not talking proof. In the story *Alice in Wonderland*, Alice happens upon two playing cards, the Five and Seven of Spades, painting white roses red. Based on the pattern set with the dormouse that would mean that whoever represents these characters is dead."

He didn't reply. They both knew he didn't need to. Of course that's what he thought.

"If our artist is the killer, why leave the playing cards instead of the real deal?"

"Obviously, the drawing didn't find its way into our perp's hands. Because we got to Pogo first."

Tony snapped his cell phone shut and crossed to Spencer. He spoke low, so only Spencer could hear. "If it is blood, the deoxidization process will help us narrow down the time this was done."

Spencer nodded. "That'll help us eliminate certain persons."

"Exactly."

"You want to question? Or should I?" Spencer asked.

"It's your show, Slick. Go for it."

They exited the office and crossed to Kay and Leo. They sat on the bottom stair, Leo's arm around his ex-wife's shoulder.

"I need to ask you a few questions. Are you up to that?"

She nodded. "I'll try."

Spencer opened his spiral notebook. "Who had access to the house today?"

"Who didn't?" She dragged a hand through her hair. "This place is like Grand Central Station, even on a Saturday."

"Could you be more specific?"

"Sure." She let out a long breath. "The family. You, your partner and Stacy. The full-time staff, Mrs. Maitlin and Troy. The yardman was here this morning as well. Barry."

"How about Clark?"

"He's off on the weekends."

"Who else?"

She rattled off a list of people who had been in and out during the course of the day. Her personal trainer and manicurist. Postman had delivered. FedEx, too.

"On Saturday?"

"It's a delivery option. Costs extra, of course."

"Could anyone have gotten in and not have been noticed?"

Kay looked at Leo, cheeks pink. "I told you we should consider a video security system. How many times?"

"No one was hurt, Kay. If you'd just calm down—"

"Calm down? They were in the house, Leo!" Kay launched to her feet, her hands clenched into fists. Spencer sensed she was not only frightened but furious at her ex-husband as well. "How am I supposed to calm down?"

The man looked flustered. "They're just trying to scare us."

"Well, they're succeeding!"

Spencer stepped in. "Take a deep breath, Mrs. Noble. We'll figure this out."

She nodded, visibly struggling to calm herself. "Go ahead."

He questioned her a bit more, then turned to Leo. "How about you, Leo? When were you last in your office?"

He thought a moment. "Two this morning."

"At 2:00 a.m.?"

"That's right."

Spencer frowned. "But not since then?"

"No. I slept late. I'm slow to wake up."

"He rarely gets to his office before noon," Kay said. "Today he didn't bother because of the game."

"And you didn't enter his office this morning?" he asked Kay.

She cocked an eyebrow. "Why would I?"

"Deliver papers. Answer the phone. I can imagine any number of reasons, Mrs. Noble."

"I'm not a secretary, Detective."

Spencer narrowed his eyes, irritated by the woman's haughty tone. He thought about pressing her, then discarded the thought, thanked them and turned his attention to the other members of the household, Mrs. Maitlin first.

"You doing okay?" She nodded. "I need you to retrace your steps this morning, leading up to you entering Mr. Noble's office. Can you do that?"

She nodded again. "I was bringing fresh flowers to the office."

"Is that something you do every Saturday?"

"No, usually on Friday. But I didn't make it to the flower market yesterday."

"So you went today?" She indicated she had. "You were out of the house how long?"

"An hour." At his expression, she darted a quick peek at her boss. "I went through the Starbucks drive-thru. The line was long."

"What time was that?"

She glanced nervously at her watch. "I don't know, between nine-thirty and ten-thirty."

"Had you entered the office at all this morning?"

"No."

He noted that her eyes didn't quite meet his. "Not even to remove the old flowers?"

"I did that yesterday." She clasped her hands together. "The blooms last a week, without fail. Mr. Noble doesn't like wilted flowers."

Who did? Lucky bastard.

"So you entered the office with the flowers?"

"Yes."

Something in her tone and body language led him to believe she wasn't being completely honest with him. "You carried the flowers to the office, then what?"

"Opened the door. Stepped inside and—" She pressed her lips together. "I saw the cards and drawing and went to get Mrs. Noble."

"And where was Mrs. Noble?"

"In her office."

"Where are they now?"

Her expression went blank. She blinked. "Pardon?"

"The flowers. They're not on the desk."

"I don't know where…the kitchen. On the counter, I think."

"We were playing White Rabbit in the kitchen. I don't re-call seeing them."

"Mrs. Noble's desk," she said, sounding relieved. "I went to get her and set the vase on her desk. They were heavy."

Spencer pictured the scenario as she'd described it. "Thank you, Mrs. Maitlin. I may need to ask you a few questions later."

She nodded, started off, then stopped. "What did it mean? Those cards, the writing?"

"We're not sure. Yet."

The evidence techs arrived. Spencer greeted them and pointed toward the office. He glanced back at the housekeeper to find her staring at the team, expression pinched, cheeks pale.

She became aware of his gaze, spun on her heel and walked away. He watched her go and frowned. She was keeping some-thing from him. But what? And why?

Spencer went in search of Troy, Leo's driver and guy Friday. He found him washing the Mercedes. He caught sight of Spencer and straightened. "Yo," he said.

"You have a minute?"

"Sure." He tossed the chamois onto the car's hood. "Needed a smoke, anyway."

Spencer waited while the man shook out a cigarette, lit it and took a drag. He flashed him a bright white smile. "Filthy habit. But I'm still young, right?"

Spencer agreed he was. "Did you notice anything out of the ordinary today?"

He sucked on the smoke, eyes narrowed in thought. "Nope."

"See anybody who didn't belong?" Again the man indicated he hadn't. "You were out front all morning?"

"Washing and waxing the Benz. Do it every Saturday. Mr. Noble likes his wheels to look sharp."

Spencer glanced toward his Camaro, parked at the curb, desperately in need of a wash.

"That your ride?" Troy asked, indicating the Camaro.

"Yeah, it is."

"Sweet." He snubbed out the cigarette. "I wasn't here all morning. Mr. Noble sent me to fetch some things for your game."

"When was that?"

"Between eight and ten-thirty. Give or take. I ran out for a sandwich around noon."

For an hour this morning both the housekeeper and driver had been off the property.

"Thanks, Troy. You going to be around all day?"

He smiled and picked up the chamois. "Gotta be here in case the boss man wants me."

"Slick?"

Spencer turned at the sound of his partner's voice. He waited as Tony ambled up the walk. "Get anything?" he asked.

"Not that matters. Old lady across the street complained about comings and goings over here at all hours. Swore the Nobles were into something illegal." He paused. "Or were aliens."

"Great. And this morning?"

"Quiet as a tomb."

"Anything else?"

"Nope." He glanced at his watch. "You done here?"

"Not quite. Need to question the yardman. Tag along?"

Tony agreed and they headed out back. The gardens were lush and well kept; the sheer volume of beds to tend, staggering. Certain times of the year, such as now, they probably required full-time attention to keep them looking the way they did.

At the moment, the yardman was on his knees in the southern- most corner of the property, planting annuals. Impatiens, Spencer saw as they reached the man.

"Barry?" Spencer asked. "Police. We need to ask you a few questions."

Not a man, Spencer saw as the kid turned. Little more than a boy.

Barry frowned at them, then removed his headphones. "Hey."

Spencer flashed his badge. "We need to ask you a few questions."

Several emotions chased across the kid's face: Suspicion. Curiosity. Fear. He nodded and stood, wiping his hands on his denim cutoffs. He was tall, gangly and thin. He'd yet to fill out his frame.

"What's up?"

"You been here all day?"

"Since nine."

"Talk to anybody?"

He hesitated a moment, then shook his head. "No."

"You don't seem so sure."

"No." His cheeks turned pink. "I'm sure."

"See anybody?"

"I was on my knees, facing the fence all day. Do you think I saw anybody?"

Touchy. "These all planted today?" Spencer indicated the border of impatiens.

"Yeah."

"Pretty."

"I think so." He smiled but the curving of his lips looked wooden.

"You go inside today, Barry?"

"No."

"What'd you do, take a piss in the bushes?"

"Pool house."

"What about water and food?"

"I bring everything I need."

"Did you see anybody you didn't recognize today?"

"Nope." He glanced toward the house, then back at them. "Mind if I get back to work? If I don't finish today, I gotta come back tomorrow."

"Go ahead, Barry. We'll be around...if you think of anything."

The kid returned to his work. Spencer and Tony started toward the house. "He was awfully defensive for somebody who'd kept his nose in the dirt all day," Tony said.

"My thoughts exactly." Spencer's cell rang; he picked up the call. "Malone here."

He listened, then asked the dispatcher to repeat what she'd said. Not because he hadn't heard, but because he wished he hadn't.

"We're on our way."

He looked at Tony, who cursed. "What now? It's friggin' Saturday."

"Walter Pogolapoulos is dead. Washed up on the banks of the Mississippi River."

"Son of a bitch."

"Oh, it gets better. The Mississippi River at the Moonwalk. A tourist from Kansas City found him. Apparently, the mayor is shitting purple bricks."

CHAPTER
34

Saturday, March 12, 2005
6:00 p.m.

By the time they reached the French Quarter Moonwalk, the scene had been entirely cordoned off. Like bees to honey, a crowd had been drawn to the crime-scene tape and police cruisers.

Spencer angled the Camaro into a spot along the railroad tracks. He popped the glove box, retrieved the jar of Vicks VapoRub he kept there and dropped it into his jacket pocket.

He looked at Tony. "Ready to do this thing?"

"Let's go."

They climbed out of the Camaro. The Moonwalk, a promenade developed atop the levee at the French Quarter, lay between Jackson Square and the Mississippi River, the Café du Monde and the Jax Brewery shopping complex.

Spencer swept his gaze over the area. Damn inconsiderate of Pogo, washing up here. In terms of visibility, few spots beat this one. In terms of unwanted heat, the spot was even worse. Anything that touched tourism, the city's biggest industry, attracted attention. The governor's. The mayor's. The media's.

The mayor would come down hard on the chief, who in turn would climb his aunt Patti's frame. Who, in turn, would put the screws to him and Tony.

Shit rolled downhill.

He and Tony were about to be hip deep in brown muck.

They crossed to one of the uniforms at the perimeter and signed in. "Fill us in."

"Tourist found him. He got good and sick." He pointed toward the cruisers. Spencer saw that the back door of one of them was open and a man was sitting sideways on the seat, head in hands. "My partner's baby-sitting him."

"Toto," Tony murmured, "I don't think we're in Kansas anymore."

The uniform snickered. "They caught the smell over at Café du Monde, thought it was somebody's garbage."

Spencer reached into his jacket pocket for the jar of Vicks. After helping himself to a smear, he held it out to Tony. He, too, smeared the goop under his nose.

They climbed the stairs to the observation area. Tony was winded when they reached the top.

He stopped to catch his breath. "I'm too old and fat for this shit."

"I'm seriously worried about you, Pasta Man. Join a gym or something."

"I'm afraid it'll kill me." They crossed the tracks, then climbed the stairs up the levee. "I'm not too far from couch-potato status. I don't want to blow it now."

"Don't want to keel over before you get that gold-toned watch and pension, right? Think about that gym—"

That's when the smell of the corpse hit them. Spencer glanced at his partner and saw the man's eyes were watering.

They descended the stairs, then picked their way to the river's edge. Spencer spotted Terry Landry, DIU from the Eighth. He'd been his brother's partner before Quentin had decided to leave the force.

Landry caught sight of them and met them halfway.

"Terror," Spencer said, greeting the man with the nickname he'd been given as a rookie. A hard-partying hothead, he was stuck with the label.

"Don't go by the 'Terror' anymore, kid. I've settled down. Mended my ways."

"Yeah, right." Tony shook his hand.

"It's true. My Thursday night AA group is my new, favorite party."

"That our vic?" Spencer asked, pointing to a misshapen form on the rocks covering the riverbank.

"Yup. Wallet was in his pocket."

Spencer tipped his face up to the purpling sky. "Going to have to get some lights over here."

"On the way."

"Did you check his pulse?" Tony asked, smirking.

"Oh, yeah," Terry answered. "I gave him mouth to mouth. Now it's your turn."

It was Homicide humor. Checking for a pulse, standard operating procedure, was unnecessary in a case like this one. Spencer and Tony picked their way toward Walter Pogo-lapoulos's remains. The artist's throat had been slit. The wound formed an obscene gaping smile. The decomposition process was well underway, sped up by the warm water.

"Sometimes I hate this job."

Tony glanced over his shoulder, toward the Café du Monde. "Either you guys want some beignets?"

"You're a sick bastard, you know that?" Spencer fitted on gloves and crossed to the corpse. He squatted beside it, ran his gaze assessingly over the body, the area around it. He had to strain to see in the gathering dusk.

The vic looked pretty beat-up, though that didn't surprise him. It was often the case when victims had been dumped in water. They were dragged by the current, scraped against the bottom, gouged by tree branches and sharp rocks and generally banged around. He'd even seen them chewed up by boat props and nibbled on by fish.

The pathologist would differentiate between pre- and postmortem wounds; a body in this state was way beyond his abilities.

From what he could see, it didn't appear the killer had made any effort to weight the body. Either he hadn't known that putrefaction gases brought a body to the surface in a matter of days   they called such vics floaters   or he hadn't cared.

Still, Pogo had popped up a bit ahead of schedule. He hadn't been dead   or submerged   long enough to have developed adipocere, a yellow, rancid smelling and waxy substance seen on most floaters. Spencer glanced at his partner. "Perp must've dumped him upriver. River currents are strong, brought him down here. What do you think? Up toward Baton Rouge? Or Vacherie?"

"Maybe. Pathologist might shed some light on it."

As if on cue, the coroner's investigator made the scene. "Where the hell is the van and the lights? What am I supposed to do with this one in the dark?"

He looked really pissed off. Spencer stepped forward, introducing himself. "Looks like your Saturday night just took a turn for the worse."

"Had theater tickets." He frowned. "How many Malones are there, anyway?"

"More than a gang, but less than a mob."

A smile touched his mouth; he looked at Tony. "Thought you retired."

"No such luck, my friend. You know Terry Landry."

"Everybody knows the Terror." The pathologist nodded in the man's direction, then scowled. "Where's that van?"

Several of the department's crime-scene vans were fitted with high-powered, alley lights for nighttime crime scenes.

"I'll check it out," Terry said.

The pathologist made his way to the body; Tony followed him. Spencer flipped open his cell and dialed Stacy.

"Hello, Killian."

"Malone."

To his ears, she sounded pleased. He smiled. "FYI, Pogo's dead."

He heard her sharply indrawn breath. "How?"

"Don't know for certain yet. He washed up on the river-bank. Throat was slit."

"When?"

"Looks like it happened a couple of days ago. Hard to tell 'cause our killer dumped him into the river. You know warm water and corpses."

Her silence said it all: they had blown it. With their best lead dead, they had nothing.

Pogo's murder was no coincidence.

The White Rabbit had silenced him, so he couldn't talk.

The area flooded with light. The van had arrived.

"Gotta go, Stacy. Just thought you'd want to know."

He flipped the phone shut and wandered over to Tony. The man grinned at him. "What?" he asked.

"The prickly Ms. Killian, I presume?"

"What about it?"

"You're going to look good with a pasta gut, Slick."

"Blow me, Sciame."

Tony's laughter echoed on the water, a strange comple-ment to Walter Pogolapoulos's decomposing form.

CHAPTER
35

Saturday, March 12, 2005
7:00 p.m.

Stacy closed her cell phone. Pogo dead. Murdered.

She took a deep breath and headed back inside the Noble mansion, to the front parlor where Leo and Kay waited for her. Even though the NOPD had done a thorough search of the house and grounds, Stacy did her own. And like them, she found nothing.

When she entered the room, Leo leaped to his feet. "Well?"

"I didn't find anything out of order," she said. "No signs of forced entry. A few unlocked windows, but I don't find that unusual this time of year. And none of the screens looked to have been tampered with."

Kay sat on the big, overstuffed parlor couch, legs curled

under her, a glass of white wine in her hand. She looked at Stacy. "You checked all the closets and cubbies?"

"Yes."

"The attics and under the beds?"

Stacy felt for the woman. "Yes," she said softly. "I promise you, there is no one hiding in this house."

Leo made a sound. Almost like a growl. She turned and watched him pace. She felt his frustration. He wasn't accustomed to being unable to control his destiny.

"You haven't been threatened," she said. "That's the good news."

He stopped. Met her eyes. "Really? I find a stranger writing a message in blood on my office floor damn threatening, thank you."

Her cheeks heated. She pictured the cat's head, strung up above her tub. "I'm sure you do," she said softly. "Your life, however, has not been overtly threatened. And that's a good thing."

Kay whimpered. "How do you know we aren't the playing cards?"

"Because I do. If you were his intended victims, he wouldn't have sent you the message. It's a game move."

In truth, it hadn't escaped her that the hypothesis might work for her as well.

The woman set her wine down so sharply some of the beverage sloshed over its rim. "I hate this."

"Let's think about the game. We played it this afternoon. Let's figure out what he's up to. Head him off at the pass."

Leo nodded. "It's the White Rabbit's game. He's in control."

"He creates the story," Stacy said. "He created this one."

"There's a band of heroes. They are on a mission to save Wonderland. And ultimately the rest of the world."

"The dormouse is dead. She was under the rabbit's control, which means that one of the heroes killed her."

"The playing cards are also in peril."

"Or already dead." She glanced at Kay. She had dropped her head into her hands. "I'm in the game. Either as the Cheshire Cat or—"

"One of the heroes." Leo snapped his fingers. "Of course! You can't be the cat because he's—"

"Under the control of the White Rabbit."

"Same with us," Kay said suddenly, lifting her head. "Thank God."

"Before you celebrate, love, remember the heroes are always in jeopardy. From the Rabbit or his minions. And sometimes—" he paused "—from each other."

Kay moaned; Stacy shook her head. "Someone is physically playing the game. A group. Like the one Cassie was a member of. It seems unlikely that Rosie Allen was a player which means this bastard chooses people to represent the characters."

"Or this could be the work of a lone sicko." Leo paused. "If it's a group, they could be e-players."

Her thoughts raced as she considered the various options, putting the pieces together, getting a feel for them. "The group could be an active part of the killing. Or—"

"Unwitting participants."

They fell silent. They needed to narrow the field. She needed to tell them about Pogo.

She turned and met her boss's eyes. "That artist, the one who created the cards, he's dead."

"Dead?" he repeated, looking confused. "But you and Detective Malone just—"

"He was murdered, Leo. His throat was slit, his body dumped in the Mississippi River."

Kay caught her breath. "Oh, my God."

"Mom?"

They turned. Alice stood in the doorway, eyes wide, cheeks pasty.

"I'm scared," she whispered.

Kay shot Leo an angry glance, even as they both rushed to the girl's side. She took the teenager into her arms, comforting her. Stroking her hair and murmuring words of comfort.

Ones that sounded authentic: promises that everything would be okay, that she had nothing to fear. Things Stacy knew the woman didn't feel. Kay was able to put aside her own fears to relieve her daughter's.

Stacy had thought Kay a cold perfectionist. Now, she would never look at the woman the same again.

On the other hand, Leo stood stiffly and silently beside them, looking like a fish out of water.

Kay looked accusingly at Leo once more. "I'm going to take her upstairs."

He nodded, visibly upset, then turned and crossed to the couch. He sat heavily. "Kay blames me."

Stacy agreed, but didn't see where saying so would help.

"I didn't make this happen. It's not my fault."

"I know," she said softly, feeling for him. "She's scared. She's not thinking clearly."

"I hate not being able to do anything. Alice is…she's the most important thing in the world to me. To see her so shaken up and being unable to—"

He bit the words off on a sound of frustration. "That artist was our best lead."

Their only real lead. "Yes."

"What are we going to do now?"

"Wait. Use caution in everything we do. And hope the police do their jobs."

"Screw the police. What are *we* going to do?"

"We know that the artist wasn't our guy. He was only the hired help."

"The White Rabbit did it."

"It could be. We don't know that for sure."

He laughed suddenly, the sound tight. "Of course it was the White Rabbit. You believe in coincidences no more than I do. When you and Detective Malone got close, he killed the artist to protect his own identity."

She didn't respond. That was her assessment as well, based not on fact, but common sense and a strong gut feeling.

"It's someone close," she said. "Within your circle. I still believe that."

"So, move in."

"Excuse me?"

"I want you to stay here. With us."

"Leo, I don't think—"

"Kay's upset. You saw Alice. They'll feel safer with you living here."

"Hire professional security. Get a dog. An electric fence. The video surveillance that Kay mentioned. Security isn't my line."

"I'd feel safer with you than with paid muscle."

"Why? And don't tell me it's because I was a cop, that doesn't wash."

"Because you wouldn't just be protecting us. You'd be protecting yourself, too."

"I'm not worried about protecting—"

"You're in the game, Stacy. You damn well better be interested in protecting yourself. Plus, the outcome of this matters to you. And if you're here, you're more likely to be a part of that outcome."

CHAPTER
36

Monday, March 14, 2005
Noon

In the end, Stacy agreed to move into the Noble mansion. Not because she thought she could protect the Nobles. And not because she felt she would be safer in the company of others.

But because the closer she was to the Nobles, the closer she was to the investigation. If she was in the middle of it, Malone couldn't shut her out.

She had insisted, however, that Leo install a video surveillance system. She had also strongly suggested that Alice and Kay move from the guest house to the main house. Although Kay had refused for herself, she'd compelled Alice to do it. That very day, they had moved Alice's daybed into the room that already served as her schoolroom.

Outfitted with a computer, high-speed Internet and cable TV, the teenager had little reason to emerge from the room. Or lair, as Stacy already thought of it.

Alice's response to the change had been typical teenage cynicism. The frightened girl Stacy had glimpsed was gone, replaced by a sullen teenager. Living with a teenager, she was discovering, was akin to living with a victim of multiple-personality disorder.

Stacy snatched up the books she needed for her evening class, then headed out, locking her door behind her.

"That's a little paranoid, don't you think?"

Stacy glanced over her shoulder. Alice stood just outside her schoolroom door. She looked bored.

Stacy smiled. "Better safe than sorry."

"Nice cliché."

"But true. How're you doing?"

"Fine and dandy." She smirked. "Speaking of clichés."

Stacy cringed at the sarcasm in the girl's tone. "I don't plan on getting in your way."

"Whatever."

"The other day you were frightened. But not anymore?"

"No." She lifted a shoulder. "I figured it out. You engineered all this, to get closer to my dad."

Stacy held back a sound of amused disbelief. "And why would I do that?"

"Star power."

Clark called the girl back to her studies then. He caught

Stacy's glance and rolled his eyes. She grinned. Obviously, he had overheard their conversation.

The rest of the day rocked by. Stacy worked on a paper due the next afternoon. Instead of working in her room, she set up in the kitchen, to keep better tabs on the comings and goings in the mansion.

Mrs. Maitlin wasn't thrilled with the arrangement.

"Can I get you something?" the woman asked as she made herself a cup of coffee.

"You don't have to wait on me." Stacy smiled. "But thanks for the offer."

The housekeeper stood at the counter with her coffee, looking uncomfortable.

"Have a seat." Stacy motioned to the chair across from hers.

"I don't want to disturb you."

"It's your kitchen." Stacy closed her laptop, stood and got herself a cup of coffee. The woman sat, but not before bringing out a tin of gourmet chocolate cookies.

Stacy helped herself to one, then returned to her seat. "How long have you worked for the Nobles?"

"A little over seventeen years."

"You must like your job."

She didn't reply, and Stacy got the impression that she'd stepped over some line. Or that the woman just didn't trust Stacy with an answer.

"I'm not a spy," she said softly. "Just making conversation."

"Yes, I do."

"You moved with them. That must have been a difficult decision to make."

She lifted a shoulder. "Not that hard. I don't have a family of my own."

Stacy thought of Jane. "Not even siblings?"

"Not even."

The Nobles were her family.

The woman gazed into her coffee for a moment, then met Stacy's eyes once more. "Why are you here? Not as a technical assistant."

"No."

"It has something to do with those cards. And that weird message."

"Yes."

"Should I be afraid?"

Stacy thought a moment. She wanted to be honest with the woman, but there was a razor's edge between educating and alarming. "Be careful. Watchful."

She nodded, expression relieved, brought a cookie to her mouth, then set it down, untasted. "It's changed around here. It's not the way—" She bit the thought back. Stacy didn't push.

"I've been with the family since before Alice was born. She was such a cute baby. A sweet child. So smart. She—"

Again, she bit her words back. Stacy sensed a deep sadness in the woman. "The house used to be filled with laughter. You wouldn't recognize Mr. and Mrs. Noble. And Alice. She—"

The housekeeper looked at her watch and stood. "I better get back to work."

Stacy reached up and touched her hand. "Alice is a teenager now. It's a difficult time. For them. And those who love them."

The woman looked startled. She shook her head. "It's not what you think. When they stopped laughing, so did Alice."

Clearly uncomfortable, she picked up her cup and carried it to the sink. She dumped the contents, rinsed it and stuck it in the dishwasher.

"Mrs. Maitlin?"

The woman glanced back. "May I call you by your first name?"

She smiled. "That'd be nice. It's Valerie."

Stacy watched her go, frowning over what she had said. What had the Nobles been like seventeen years ago? Why had they divorced? They cared deeply for each other, that was obvious. They were committed to each other and Alice, also obvious. In essence, they still lived together.

When they stopped laughing, so did Alice.

She glanced at her laptop, then stood and headed out into the bright day. The idea of working on her paper didn't appeal, and a quick spin around the property every hour or two was a good thing.

She lifted her face to the sky. Dark clouds gathered on the horizon. It looked as if the sunny afternoon would give way to a stormy evening.

At present, the security guys were installing the new system. Troy was chatting with one of them while he took a cigarette break. Previously, the driver had been sunning himself in a lawn chair. He'd hung his yellow polo shirt on the chair's back. She realized she'd only seen him fully clothed a handful of times.

She smiled to herself. As near as she could tell, Troy had pretty much the least stressful job on earth. He hung around, waiting for Leo to need him for something—run an errand, drive him someplace. He sunned, he washed the cars, he smoked.

Tough life. She wondered at the man's salary and where she could apply.

The installation tech put out his smoke and went back to work. Troy caught sight of her and smiled, his teeth almost startlingly white against his tanned face.

"Hi, Stacy," he said.

She stopped. "Hi, Troy. Keeping busy?"

"You know, typical day." He motioned to the workman. "That's a high-tech system they're putting in. The dude was trying to explain it to me." Troy shrugged, indicating he hadn't really gotten it. "Mr. Noble, if he's going to have something, it's going to be state of the art. Only the best." He scratched his chest, the movement almost absentminded. "I don't know why he's doing it, though. I'm pretty much always around. I keep an eye on things."

"Maybe it's for the times you're not?"

He nodded, drawing his eyebrows together. Something in his expression suggested that, like her, he was thinking of Saturday and the message Leo had been left.

Whoever had done it had slipped in and out during the hour he and the housekeeper had been gone.

He fell silent, as if with thought. After a moment, he looked at her. "What's going on? The new system. Alice moving into the main house. You. Has someone threatened Leo or Alice?"

"Someone's playing a sick game," she said. "Leo's just being cautious."

He stared at her a moment. They both knew she wasn't being completely truthful. But he didn't call her on it.

He shrugged and started back toward his chair. "If you need anything, I'm here."

She watched as he settled in, then glanced up at the second-floor windows.

And found Alice staring down at her.

Stacy lifted her hand to acknowledge the girl. Instead of returning the friendly gesture, Alice flounced off.

Stacy shook her head in partial amusement. It seemed she didn't have to do much of anything to offend young Ms. Noble. She was beginning to suspect that just her breathing did it.

Tough nuts, kiddo. You're stuck with me.

CHAPTER
37

Shannon's Tavern, a blue-collar bar and NOPD hangout, was located in the area of the city called the Irish Channel. Run by a mountain of a man named Shannon, the bar was a fine place to wait out a storm.

If you made it inside before the storm struck.

Spencer and Tony hadn't. They burst into the tavern, bringing the wind and rain with them. Shannon took one look at them and shook his head. "Cops."

"Blame John Jr.," Spencer said, catching the towel the barkeep tossed him. He dried his hair first, then the rest of himself, as best he could, anyway. A call from John Jr. had, indeed, gotten this particular ball rolling. Their mother and father's fiftieth wedding anniversary was only six months off; they needed to start planning immediately. That John Jr. had been the one to remember hadn't been a surprise. As oldest of the brood, John Jr. always played the role of the conscientious one.

And thank God he did. With seven of them to organize and corral, it took someone willing to own the job.

Tony had come along because Betty and Carly were shopping for a prom dress, and he was on his own for dinner.

Shannon served more than ice-cold beer; he cooked up some of the best burgers in the city—big, juicy and priced to fit a cop's wallet.

Quentin and his wife Anna arrived next. Spencer couldn't have special-ordered a better sister-in-law. He credited her with giving Quentin the confidence to follow his dreams. The rest of the family felt the same way about her as he did.

"Yo, little bro," Quentin said, slapping him on the back. "Shannon, draft and a mineral water."

"Anna." Spencer kissed his sister-in-law's cheek, then held her at arm's length. "You look wonderful."

Three months pregnant with their first child, she radiated joy.

"How's the writing biz?"

"Murder," she said, tone dry. "As usual."

Anna was a successful suspense novelist. She knew Tony through Quentin and happily took the bar stool beside the older cops.

Percy and Patrick trundled in, dripping wet. John Jr. followed moments later. His wife, Julie, a registered nurse, with him. Shauna and Mary followed.

Big, loud and good-looking, the Malone brothers always attracted attention. Mostly from females, but in New Orleans, that wasn't necessarily a given. The Malone women had learned to use their brothers' charisma to their own advantage. While all the available women in a given place vied for their brothers' attention, the Malone girls had taken their pick of everyone else.

More times than not, it worked like a charm.

Tonight, however, they had serious plans to discuss.

"Aunt Patti and Uncle Sammy are coming," Mary said, kissing each of her brothers on the cheek. "I talked to her on the way over. They're a couple minutes late."

"No problem," Percy said, signaling to Shannon, "we've never started a family powwow on time in our lives."

"I resent that," John Jr. replied, taking a long swallow of his draft.

"Represent that, you mean," Patrick, the accountant said, tone dry. "Keep in mind this is tax season. Unlike you guys, I need to pull twelve-hour days for the next month. Let's get this show going."

His siblings' responses ranged from rolled eyes to comments about the world's smallest violin. Spencer grinned. Patrick, the family's square peg.

The door burst open and Aunt Patti and Uncle Sammy sloshed in. With them came another rush of wind and rain.

"It's miserable out there," she exclaimed, closing her umbrella and dropping it in the stand by the door. "Could you have picked a worse night, John Jr.?"

Her comment was met by whistles and applause. John Jr. flushed. "Without me, this family would fall apart."

The older couple made the rounds of hugs and kisses. When his aunt reached him, she leaned close. "We have to talk. Tonight. Catch me before you go."

He frowned at her tone. "What's up?"

She shook her head slightly, indicating she couldn't discuss why now. Whatever it was, he could tell, it was about work. And serious.

Two and a half hours later, the group began breaking up. Although loud, unruly and borderline obnoxious, they'd managed to accomplish all they needed to. Plans had been made; each sibling had a job to do. John Jr. expected committee reports within the week.

Spencer looked at his aunt. She signaled he should meet her in the poolroom in back.

He found her there, back to him. When she turned, he frowned. She looked drawn. Her color off.

"Are you all right, Aunt Patti?"

"Fine." Her no-nonsense tone told him she had her captain hat firmly in place. "PID called on me today."

Public Integrity Division. The NOPD's version of Internal Affairs.

He went cold, the past crashing over him. Two years ago, when his last captain called him into the office, two PID guys had been waiting for him.

It'd been an ambush. A PID specialty.

"They were asking about you, Spencer. This case."

"This case? The White Rab- —"

"Yes."

He shook his head. "Why?"

"I don't know for sure." She rubbed her chest, almost absently. "He was fishing."

"Why's this happening?"

"You tell me."

"There's nothing." He searched his memory. "Everything's been by the book."

"There's more. Chief called me. About you. About the case."

Not good. The chief's attention always spelled trouble.

He shook his head again. "Why? I don't get it."

She curled her fingers around his forearm. "You and Tony," she said, voice suddenly strained, "watch your backs."

Spencer opened his mouth to comment, swallowing the words as her face contorted with pain. "Aunt Patti? What's wrong?"

She tried to speak but couldn't. She brought a hand to her chest. Alarmed, he shouted for his uncle and sister-in-law.

The family members came running. Julie took one look at Aunt Patti and shouted for someone to call 911.

Within twenty minutes, Aunt Patti had been sent by ambulance to Touro Infirmary, where the family learned she had suffered a heart attack.

The entire Malone clan had turned out, which explained the floor nurse's harried expression.

Spencer knew the nurse would need to get used to the crowds; cops took care of their own. His aunt was likely to have visitors 24/7. No doubt some of them would attempt to smuggle in no-no's. Things like Krispy Kreme doughnuts. And Krystal burgers.

The waiting seemed endless. They finally let Uncle Sammy in to see Patti, then Spencer's mother, who had just arrived. The rest had to wait.

When the doctor emerged, a guy who looked way too young to be trusted with the care of anyone's favorite aunt, he explained that she'd had a mild attack, brought on by a blocked artery. They'd given her a clot-busting miracle drug.

"She asked for Spencer," he said.

"Here."

The physician looked at him. "You a cop?"

"I am."

"No talking business. I don't want her worked up."

"You got it, Doc."

Spencer entered his aunt's room. For such a tough bird, she looked pretty damn vulnerable.

She smiled weakly. "I feel like I went head to head with one bad-ass perp."

"Doctor says you've got a blocked artery. Gave you some wonder drug that's supposed to solve the problem. You'll be fine."

"I'm not worried about…me. You—"

"Shh." He found her hand, squeezed it. "I can take care of myself."

"But—"

He squeezed her hand again. "I'll be careful. The investigation is on track. Tony and I will make certain it stays that way. You concentrate on getting better. That's your job right now."

She dozed off; Spencer stayed with her, watching her as she slept.

Watch your backs.

Those three little words brought back that terrible time when everywhere he turned, he faced suspicion, and everyone seemed to be gunning for him.

Why had he caught the attention of the chief and PID?

The nurse poked her head into the room. "Time's up, Mr. Malone."

He nodded, brushed a kiss across his aunt's forehead and returned to the waiting area.

Tony and several of the other guys had arrived. They had all paid their respects to Uncle Sammy and were huddled together, talking.

Spencer took Tony aside. "Tonight, Aunt Patti said we've attracted the attention of the chief. And PID."

Tony's eyes widened. "Why?"

"She didn't know. They were questioning her about the White Rabbit case."

The older man scowled. "Friggin' Pogo had to surface at the French Quarter."

Spencer nodded. "Thing is, that still doesn't explain PID's involvement. They're usually interested in improprieties."

"Let me nose around. See if anybody's heard anything."

John Jr. waved Spencer over. Spencer started for him, then looked back at his partner. "You do that. And keep me posted."

CHAPTER
38

Tuesday, March 15, 2005
9:30 a.m.

Alice popped into the kitchen. Her gaze touched on Stacy, then jumped to the housekeeper. "I'm going to run to Café Noir for a moccaccino."

Stacy searched her memory. *Alice frequented Café Noir? Had she ever seen the girl there?* A lot of kids hung out at Café Noir, mostly at night and right after school. She didn't remember having seen her.

The housekeeper, standing at the sink, looked over her shoulder at the girl. "What about your morning lessons?"

"Haven't started yet. Mr. Dunbar's pukey today. Asked if I'd mind a late start."

Clearly, Alice was delighted. The thought crossed Stacy's mind that poor Mr. Dunbar may have been poisoned.

The housekeeper sent Stacy an uneasy glance, then turned back to the teenager. "Your parents left strict orders that you're not to go out alone. If you give me a few minutes, I'll—"

The teenager flushed. "Café Noir is less than six blocks away! Surely they didn't mean—"

"I'm sorry, hon, but with everything that's happened—"

"This is so freakin' bogus!"

"I'll go with you," Stacy said, standing. "I could use the walk."

"No, thanks." Alice glared at her. "I'd rather do without."

"Your choice." She shrugged. "But I really do need the walk. Shall I bring you one back?"

The teenager stared at her a moment, eyes narrowed. "Fine. But I'm not going with you. You walk behind me."

Somebody, it seemed, did not like to be thwarted.

Stacy hid her amusement. "Whatever."

Within minutes, the two were nearing Café Noir. As promised, Stacy had stayed several paces behind Alice. She hadn't promised to keep her distance at the coffeehouse, but she planned to spring that fact on the teenager when the time came.

When Stacy entered the coffeehouse, Alice was already at the counter ordering. Billie looked up and smiled in greeting.

"Hey, girl," she called. "Long time no see. What gives?"

"Been busy." Stacy reached the counter; Alice scowled at her. "Billie, this is Alice, Leonardo Noble's daughter."

Billie smiled at the teen. "No kidding. Now I can put a name with the face."

Alice stuck a straw in her super grande frozen moccaccino. "See ya."

Stacy watched her walk away, then looked at Billie. "It's the teenage version of Dr. Jekyll and Mr. Hyde."

Billie arched an eyebrow. "More Hyde than Jekyll, apparently."

"She come in here much?"

"Sometimes."

"She and Cassie ever talk?"

"Yeah, maybe."

Stacy didn't know which surprised her more, her own uttered thought or Billie's answer. "She and Cassie knew each other?"

"They weren't friends, but I think they spoke. The usual?"

Stacy realized Billie meant her usual drink, and she shook her head. "An iced coffee. Tall."

Billie nodded, made the drink, slid it across the counter and waved away her attempt to pay for it. "On the house."

"Thanks." She frowned, thoughts still on Cassie and Alice. "When you say they talked, do you mean more than 'Hello' and 'How are you?'"

"They discussed gaming."

RPGs. Of course. After that thought came another. *Could Alice be the one who promised to introduce Cassie to White Rabbit?*

"What's going on?" Billie lowered her voice. "Where the hell have you been? And don't give that 'been busy' crap."

She glanced over her shoulder and saw that no one was within earshot. "Life's gotten a little weird since we last talked. The White Rabbit openly claimed a victim, a woman named Rosie Allen. From the calling card he left the Nobles yesterday, two more victims are on the way. And did I mention, I was welcomed to the game?"

"The game?" she repeated. "Back up, girlfriend. Way, way up."

"You remember me telling you that Leo Noble believed someone, maybe a troubled fan, had begun playing his game White Rabbit for real? That he had received disturbing cards that indicated he had been entered into the killer-takes-all scenario?"

The other woman said she did, and Stacy continued. "One of the cards depicted a mouse-like creature drowning. A woman named Rosie Allen was found drowned in her bathtub. The killer left a message at the scene. Poor little mouse drowned in a pool of her own tears. The woman had a connection to Noble. She did alteration work for the family.

"Saturday, he left another calling card at the Nobles— 'The roses are red now.' The message was written in blood."

For a long moment Billie was silent. When she finally spoke, her tone was hushed, as if to keep an employee or customer from hearing. "Stop screwing around, Stacy. You're not a cop. You don't have the support of a police force behind you."

"Too late. Apparently, I've caught the killer's fancy. Thursday night he welcomed me to the game. Left me a cat's head. The Cheshire Cat, I'm assuming. I've temporarily moved in with the Nobles to keep an eye—"

"Dammit, Stacy, you're playing with——"

"Fire? Tell me about it." She glanced toward the front porch. Alice was sitting at one of the outdoor tables. "I've got to go."

"Wait!" Billie caught her hand. "Promise me you'll be careful or I swear, I'll kick your butt."

Stacy smiled. "I care about you, too. I'll catch up with you later."

She headed out front and crossed to Alice. "Want some company?"

"No."

Stacy sat, anyway. The teenager made a sound, an exasperated huff. Stacy fought a smile. Her mother used to make a sound just like that. When she or Jane had been being particularly unreasonable.

"I saw you checking Troy out," Alice said suddenly.

"Really? When was that?"

"Yesterday. Outside."

When she had looked up to find Alice watching her.

"Don't bother to deny it, all the women do it. Even my mom."

Interesting. Could Kay have the hots for the good-looking chauffeur?

She sipped her iced coffee. "How about you, Alice? Do you check him out?"

The girl flushed. "You'd be wasting your time on him. He's gay."

Could be, Stacy acknowledged. But she didn't think so.

"Gay or not, he's easy on the eyes."

The girl frowned. "Aren't you going to ask how I know?"

"No."

"Why not?"

Truth was, she had a pretty good idea what the truth was. Alice was infatuated with the man. She had flirted with him; he'd rebuffed her. She was either labeling him gay to assuage her hurt feelings, or to discourage other women's interest in him.

"Because I don't care."

She saw by the teenager's expression that she didn't like her answer. "I know about your sister," she said. "About that boater who almost killed her."

"And?"

She was silent a moment. "Nothing. I just know, that's all."

"Would you like to ask me about it?"

She wanted to say "No," Stacy could tell. But curiosity got the better of her.

"Okay."

"We skipped school. Or I should say, Jane skipped school with me and some of my friends. It was March, and still pretty cold. We dared her to swim."

"And a boater hit her?" Alice said, her eyes wide.

"Yes. He deliberately ran her down. Or so it seemed. He was never caught." Stacy drew a deep breath. "She nearly died. It was…awful."

The teenager leaned forward. "Her face was really messed up, huh?"

"That's an understatement, actually."

"I saw a picture of her. She looks normal."

"Now. Because of many, many surgeries."

Alice sucked on her straw. "She blamed you, didn't she?"

Stacy shook her head. "No, Alice. I blamed myself."

They sipped their coffees in silence. After a moment, Alice frowned. "I always wondered what it'd be like to have a sister."

She said the words almost grudgingly. As if she knew up-front they would tell Stacy more about her than she wanted her to know. But even so, she couldn't help herself.

In that moment, Stacy realized just how lonely Alice Noble was.

"It's pretty great," Stacy offered. "Now. Though we weren't always close. In fact, for years we hardly spoke."

Alice looked fascinated. "How come?"

"Lots of misunderstandings and hurt feelings."

"Because of what happened to her?"

"There were other things that contributed as well, but yes. I'll tell you about them sometime."

Alice sucked on the straw, expression eager. "But you're close now?"

"She's my best friend. She had a baby in October. Her first. Apple Annie," Stacy smiled. "That's my pet name for her. She has the roundest, pinkest cheeks."

"A baby," Alice repeated, tone wistful. "Sweet."

Stacy glanced away, afraid the girl would see sympathy in her eyes. As often as she had wished to be an only child while growing up, she wouldn't trade her sister for anything in the world.

Alice would never know that joy.

"Do you miss them?" the teen asked.

"More than anything."

"Then why did you move here?"

Stacy was silent a moment, deciding how vague she should be. "I needed a fresh start," she said finally. "Too many bad memories."

The younger woman looked perplexed. "But your sister, her baby, they're not bad memories."

"No, they're not." Stacy shifted the conversation to Alice. "Do you have any cousins close to your age?"

She shook her head. "But I have an aunt who's really cool. My dad's sister, Aunt Grace."

"Where does she live?"

"In California. She's an anthropology professor at University of California, Irvine. We go places together."

Apparently, brains ran in the family. As did coolness.

The teenager glanced at her watch. "I better go. Clark wanted me back in an hour."

"Wait. I think you knew a friend of mine."

She narrowed her eyes, expression doubtful. "Who?"

"She was into RPGs. Came here a lot. Her name was Cassie."

Recognition flickered in her eyes. "Curly blond hair?"

"Uh-huh."

"I haven't seen her lately."

Stacy's chest tightened. "Me either."

The teenager frowned. "Is she okay?"

Stacy ignored her question, asking one of her own. "She ever talk to you about White Rabbit?"

Alice shook her head and sipped some of the frozen coffee through the straw. "Did she play it?"

"No. But she mentioned having met someone who played. I thought maybe it was you?"

"Uh-uh. Why don't you just ask her?"

The teenager's words hit Stacy hard. For a moment she couldn't breathe, let alone speak. "Maybe I'll do that," she managed when she found her voice. She stood. "Maybe we should get back?"

Alice glanced at her watch, agreed and stood. She met Stacy's eyes, expression slightly sheepish. "You don't have to walk behind me."

"You're sure?" Stacy teased. "I wouldn't want to humiliate you or anything."

"I guess I was kind of a jerk earlier. Sorry."

She didn't sound all that sorry, but Stacy gave her major points for relenting at all. She remembered what it was like to be a teenager caught in extraordinary circumstances.

When they reached the mansion, Alice went in search of Clark and Stacy returned to the kitchen. Mrs. Maitlin was unpacking groceries.

She glanced at Stacy. "Do I sense the beginning of a truce?"

"A small one, I think. Although don't get too used to it, it may be temporary."

The woman laughed. "Mr. Noble was looking for you. He's in his office, I believe."

"Thanks. I'll go see him now."

"Could you bring him his mail?" She retrieved the stack from the counter. "It'll save me a trip."

"Sure, Valerie." Stacy took the mail and headed to Leo's office. She found the door partially open. She tapped on it. It swung further open, and she stuck her head in. "Leo?"

He wasn't there. The NOPD had cleared the room for cleaning; a crew had been in two days ago. The blood had left a slight shadow on the hardwood flooring. Stacy stepped over it as she crossed to the desk with the mail and laid the stack on the top of his closed Apple laptop. She gazed at it a moment, reminded of Cassie who'd also used an Apple, though a different model. She blinked, suddenly realizing what she was looking at: a postcard from Gallery 124. Announcing an art exhibit.

Pogo's gallery.

She frowned and picked it up. The postcard had been mailed to Leo, by name. Which meant he was on their mailing list. He had visited the gallery, perhaps bought something from it.

A coincidence?

She hated coincidences. They always smelled like fish.

"Hey, Stacy. Can I help you?"

She spun around, guilty heat stinging her cheeks. "Leo. Valerie asked me to bring your mail."

"Valerie?"

"Mrs. Maitlin. You wanted to see me?"

"I did?"

"Didn't you?"

He smiled and closed the door behind him. "I suppose I did. Though I can't remember why. What's that?"

He motioned at the postcard, still in her hands. "An advertisement," she said, holding it up.

He crossed to her. Took the card. She watched him as he studied it, looking for unease, surprise or the moment he made the connection.

It didn't come. *Had she ever told him the name of Pogo's gallery?*

"I'm not so crazy about nonobjective art. It just doesn't mean anything to me."

"The gallery's name caught my attention. Not the art." At his blank expression, she added, "Gallery 124. That's where Pogo exhibited."

"Small world."

That small?

Was he a consummate actor? Or really in the dark?

"You're on their mailing list. Did you buy something there?"

"Not that I remember." He tossed the postcard on the desk. "Did you sleep well?"

"Pardon?"

He smiled, the curving of his lips boyish. And naughty. "It was your first night with us. I wanted to make sure you were comfortable."

"Fine." She took a small step backward, suddenly uncomfortable. "Everything was fine."

He caught her hands. "Don't run away."

"I'm not running. Just—"

He kissed her.

She made a sound of surprise and pushed him away. "Leo, don't."

"Sorry." He looked almost comically disappointed. "And here I've wanted to do that for a while."

"Have you?"

"You couldn't tell?"

"No."

"I'd like to do it again." His gaze dropped briefly to her mouth. "But I won't...if you object?"

She hesitated a moment too long and he kissed her again.

The office door opened. "Leo? Clark and I—"

At Kay's voice, Stacy sprang away from Leo. Mortified. So embarrassed, in fact, she wished she could crawl under the man's desk and hide.

"Sorry," Kay said stiffly, "we didn't know you were busy. We were looking for Alice."

"I was with her not thirty minutes ago," Stacy said, clearing her throat. "At Café Noir."

Kay frowned, and Stacy added, "We ran into each other. She said Clark was sick this morning. I'm glad to see you're feeling better."

The Nobles looked at him. Obviously that information had been news to them.

He laid a hand on his stomach. "I ate fish last night. I'm thinking it wasn't fresh. You have to be so careful with seafood."

"You might ask Mrs. Maitlin if she's seen her," Stacy offered.

"We will," Kay said. "Thank you."

The pair left the office, purposefully snapping the door shut behind them.

"She doesn't care, you know," he said softly. "We're not married anymore."

Stacy looked at Leo, cheeks hot. "She looked at me like I was an adulterer."

Leo laughed. "She didn't."

"It was my own guilty conscience, then."

"I told you, you have nothing to feel guilty about. I kissed you. Besides, I'm a free agent."

She thought of the way Leo and Kay acted toward each other, the affectionate way they teased, the obvious respect.

Like a married couple. A couple very much in love.

"I'm interested in you, Stacy."

She didn't respond, and he gathered her hands in his. "I get the feeling you could be interested, too. Am I right?"

He attempted to draw her back into his arms; she resisted. "Can I ask you something, Leo?"

"Ask away."

"What happened to you and Kay? It's obvious you care for each other."

He shrugged. "We're too different...we grew apart. I don't know, maybe we lost the spark that kept us working at it."

"How long were you married?"

"Thirteen years." He laughed. "Kay hung in there longer than most would have."

When they stopped laughing, so did Alice.

"Kay and I are like Wonderland. Order and chaos. The sane and insane. The insanity finally overwhelmed her."

She had wanted the divorce. He had driven *her* crazy.

He still loved his wife, Stacy realized.

She slipped her hands from his. "This isn't a good idea."

"There's no reason we can't be together."

"I think there is, Leo. I'm not ready. And I don't think you are, either."

When he opened his mouth as if to argue, she held up a hand, stopping him. "Please, Leo. Just leave it alone."

"For the moment, okay. But I won't promise to stay away forever."

Stacy backed toward the door, grasped the handle, turned and walked through.

And ran smack into Troy.

He put a hand on her elbow to steady her. "Whoa. Where are you going in such a hurry?"

"Hey, Troy." Flustered, she took a step back. "Sorry, mind's elsewhere."

"No problemo. Catch you later."

It wasn't until much later that she wondered why Troy had been right outside Leo's door. And if he had been eavesdropping.

CHAPTER
39

Stacy stood at her bedroom window. Moonlight illuminated the side garden and yard. The storm of two nights ago had left everything lush and green.

She couldn't sleep. She had tossed and turned for the last hour, then had given up. It wasn't the bed. Or the pillow.

It was a feeling of unease. Of not belonging. Here, in this house. In this city, the UNO graduate program.

In her own skin.

She frowned. How had she gotten herself to this place? She had come to New Orleans for a fresh start. To change her life for the better.

Now look at her. Embroiled in a murder investigation. A

target in a killer's twisted game. She had been attacked. Her home broken into, a cat's bloody head left as a gift. A friend had been murdered; she had found the body. She was on the verge of flunking out of graduate school.

And her boss had made a pass at her.

Which was when she thought of Spencer. She hadn't heard from him since he'd called to tell her about Pogo. At first she'd assumed him busy with the investigation. Now she wondered if he had shut her out.

She would have done the same. Back when she had been a cop.

What was keeping her here? She missed Jane. And little Apple Annie, growing and changing every day. Her life was unarguably more screwed up now than it had been in Dallas. She could resign from the graduate program, pack her stuff and head home.

Tuck tail and run? Leave Cassie's death unsolved and Leo and his family unprotected?

The last affected her like a kick to the gut. She was not the Noble family protector. It wasn't her job. It was the NOPD's and Malone's.

Damn it. Then why did she feel responsible for them? And for finding Cassie's killer? Why did she always feel like she had to take care of the whole friggin' world?

Because that day at the lake, she hadn't taken care of Jane.

The memory of that day came rushing back, as clear as if it had been yesterday instead of almost twenty years ago. The sounds of Jane's screams. Of her own. The frigid water as Stacy had launched herself in. The blood. Later the way her parents had looked at Stacy. Accusingly. Disappointed.

She had been seventeen, Jane fifteen. She should have taken better care of her. She should have been more responsible. It had been her fault it happened.

No, damn it. Stacy shook her head as if for emphasis, as if to convince herself. It wasn't her fault. She'd been a kid that day at the lake. Jane didn't blame her; why should she blame herself?

A movement in the garden below drew her gaze. A man, she realized. Heading toward the guest house.

She reached for her gun, tucked into the night table drawer. As she curled her fingers around the grip, Kay emerged from the guest house. Light spilled into the garden. She ran to the man. He took her into his arms.

Not Leo, she recognized immediately. But who? she wondered, straining to make out the man's identity. When she couldn't, as quietly as possible, she lifted her window. The couple's voices carried on the night air. Kay's husky laugh. The man's murmured endearment.

Not Leo. Clark.

Kay Noble was having an affair with Alice's tutor.

She watched the two stroll toward the guest house, then disappear inside. For a moment they were silhouetted against the window, embracing.

In the next instant, the window went black.

Stacy set the Glock carefully back in the drawer and slid it shut, thoughts racing. The pairing didn't completely surprise her. Clark was intelligent, worldly. An academic.

Anemic, she thought. Compared to Leo.

Or Malone, God help her.

But maybe that was the point. If what Leo had told her about his and Kay's relationship was true.

If? Now, why would she think that?

And why did knowing the woman and Clark were having an affair seem so wrong?

Kay and Leo were divorced. But Clark was an employee. Kay's daughter's tutor.

And Leo was so obviously still in love with the woman.

Stacy closed the window and turned away from it. Was her affair the reason Kay had refused to move into the main house? Had she carried on with Clark when Alice was there? Surely not.

The teenager was bright, intuitive. She must at least suspect the affair.

Stacy frowned as her thoughts turned to Alice. She spent an inordinate amount of time on her computer, day and night. Every so often, the sound of Alice's computer announcing an instant message awakened her.

Alice, it seemed, had inherited her father's sleep habits.

Before Stacy had finished processing that thought, a crash came from the adjoining room. Followed by a cry.

Heart lurching to her throat, Stacy retrieved the Glock and ran into the hall and across to Alice's door. She tried the door, found it locked and rapped on it.

"Alice," she called, "are you all right?"

The teenager didn't reply and she pressed her ear to the door. Silence.

"I heard you cry out. Are you all right?"

"Go away! I'm fine."

Her voice sounded funny. Shaky and high-pitched. Stacy's mouth went dry.

"Open this door, Alice. I need to see for myself that you're unhurt. If you don't I'll—"

The door opened. Alice stood before her, eyes red and face blotchy from crying. Otherwise, she appeared unhurt.

Stacy peered around her. The room looked empty. A figurine lay in pieces on the floor.

Alice had been crying. The crash the result of a fit of temper. Typical teenage drama.

Stacy felt more than a little silly. "I heard the crash and what I thought was a cry and—"

"Is that a—" Alice bit the words back, eyes widening. "Oh, my God, you've got a gun."

"It's not how it looks."

The teenager sprang backward. "Stay away from me, you psycho."

"I'm not a psycho, Alice. And there's a reasonable explanation for—"

The girl slammed the door in her face. Stacy heard the lock click into place.

Stacy stared at the closed door a moment, a bemused smile tugging at her mouth.

Having fun now, Killian?

She counted to ten, then tapped on the door. She didn't expect a response and didn't wait for one. "Alice, I have a permit for the gun. I'm an experienced shooter, and your father knows I have it."

She paused, allowing her words to sink in, then leaned closer. "I wasn't trying to interfere, just to make certain you were all right. If you need anything, anytime, I'm next door." She gave the girl a moment to digest that, then added, "Good night, Alice."

She returned to her room and listened, but the girl had either stopped crying or had become better at covering the sound. Poor kid probably felt she couldn't even cry in her own room anymore.

Stacy's gaze landed on her cell phone, charging on its cradle. Her thoughts filled with Jane. She longed to talk with her. To share everything and ask her advice.

She crossed to her laptop, opened it and turned it on. It hummed a moment before the monitor sprang to life. Stacy navigated to her mail program, to the e-mail Jane had sent today.

Pictures of Apple Annie. Wearing the denim jumper Stacy had sent, the one with the apples embroidered on the smock and pockets.

Stacy gazed at the images, throat tight with tears, wondering what the hell she was doing.

Go home, Stacy. Back to the people who love you.

To the people you love.

She wanted to, so badly she could taste it. So what was stopping her? Leaving was not running away. It was not giving up.

It'd take more than a few threats and several dead bodies to send her over the edge.

Stacy froze.

Over the edge.

Leo's partner had gone over an edge.

A cliff. To his death.

She thought of her comment to Leo that first day. That there were two Supreme White Rabbits. Leo and his former partner.

She caught her breath. Could Danson be alive?

Stacy looked at the clock. 12:35.

Leo being a night owl was proving handy; she needed to ask him a few questions about his former partner.

She grabbed her robe and headed out to the hallway, then downstairs. Sure enough, light streamed from under Leo's office door. She tapped on it.

"Leo," she called. "It's Stacy."

He opened the door and smiled that goofy, lopsided smile of his. "Someone else walking the floors at midnight," he said. "What a nice surprise."

"May I come in?"

At the formality in her tone, his smile slipped. "Sure."

She entered; he left the door open. Pointedly, she thought.

"I owe you an apology," he said. "For this afternoon."

"You've already apologized. It's over."

"Is it? I'm not so sure."

"Leo—"

"I'm attracted to you. I think you're attracted to me. What's the problem?"

Stacy looked away. Then back, meeting his eyes directly. "Even if I was interested, you're still in love with your ex-wife."

He didn't deny it, didn't try to explain or make excuses. His silence was her answer. Or rather, the damning confirmation of what she had already known was true. "This isn't why I'm here, Leo. I want you to tell me about your ex-partner."

"Dick? Why?"

"I'm not sure. I'm working on something and need more information. He died three years ago?"

"Yes. Went over a cliff in Carmel, California."

"You found out about the accident how?"

"A lawyer contacted us. Dick's death freed up some of our joint ventures, including White Rabbit."

"The lawyer tell you any more about the death?"

"No. But we didn't ask."

She digested that. "You said you guys split for personal reasons. That he wasn't the man you'd thought he was."

"Yes. But—"

"Humor me, please. Did those feelings have anything to do with Kay?"

His expression went from surprised to admiring. "How did you know?"

"A look you and Kay exchanged that first day. But that doesn't matter. Tell me what happened."

Leo let out a resigned-sounding breath. "Begin at the beginning?"

"That's usually best."

"Dick and I met at Berkeley. As you already know, we became good friends. We were both brilliant and creative, both into role-playing games."

No false modesty there. "Where does Kay fit into this?"

"I'm getting to that. I met Kay through Dick. They'd dated."

Classic motivation. A lover's triangle—which equaled jealousy and revenge.

Which equaled all sorts of nasties, including murder.

"I know what you're thinking, but it wasn't like that. They'd broken up before I ever came into the picture. And they'd remained friends."

"Until the two of you started dating."

Again, he seemed surprised. "Yes, but not at first. At first we were like the Three Musketeers. Flushed with success and excitement over White Rabbit.

"Then Dick began to change. His work became darker. Sadistic and cruel."

"How so?"

He paused, as if to gather his thoughts. "In the games, it wasn't enough to kill an enemy. He had to torture him first. And dismember him after."

"Nice."

"He insisted that was the way games were going, that we needed to stay at the forefront." He paused again and Stacy saw how unpleasant this was for him. "We constantly argued. We grew further apart...not only creatively, but personally as well. Then he—"

Leo swore, his lip curling with distaste. "He raped Kay."

Stacy wasn't surprised. She had sensed that whatever had

come between them had been bigger than a difference of opinion. The bad blood had been almost palpable.

"Kay was destroyed. She and Dick had been close. Friends, she thought. She trusted him." He made a sound that was part anger, part pain. "That night, he lured her out by telling her he wanted to talk about me. He wanted her advice on how to patch things up between us."

"I'm sorry."

"Me, too." Leo passed a hand over his face, the ebullience that made him appear so youthful, gone. "We don't speak of it."

"Ever?"

"Ever."

"Did he stand trial?"

"She didn't press charges." As if anticipating her response, he held up a hand. "She said she couldn't bear the publicity. Her personal life being scrutinized. She spoke with a lawyer. He basically said that their former relationship, though it hadn't been sexual, would blow the case. That Dick would lie, and the defense would crucify her."

Stacy wished she could argue with that. She couldn't. Too often, women were afraid of coming forward for just those reasons.

And not only did a rapist go unpunished, it left him free to hurt another woman.

"We thought if we just put it behind us, everything would be fine. That Kay would be able to forget and move on."

A popular misconception. Hiding from pain didn't help heal a wound; it simply gave it a place to fester.

But maybe Kay's experience had been different.

"Did she?"

He looked stricken. "No."

"Do you have a picture of him?"

"Probably. I could dig around—"

"Could you do it now?"

"Now?" he repeated, looking flustered.

"Yes. It might be important."

He agreed and went to work. He started rummaging through desk drawers and file cabinets. Halfway through the files, he stopped. "Wait, I know where there's a picture of Dick." He crossed to the bookcase and pulled out a yearbook.

He flipped through, found what he was looking for and handed the book to her. It was open to the section on clubs and specialty organizations. There was a picture of a very young Leo and another boy she didn't recognize. They were both smiling, holding up a certificate that bore what looked to be the university's seal. The caption read:

Leo Noble and Dick Danson, co-presidents of the university's first FPRG club.

Two gangly young men, their lives before them. Nothing in Dick Danson's smile or eyes hinted at a man capable of the violence Leo described. Brown hair, worn long and shaggy. Wire-rimmed glasses and a scruffy goatee. He'd yet to fill out his frame.

She gazed at the man's image, frustrated. Disappointed. She had hoped she would recognize him. That she would re-call having seen him.

She didn't. It had been a long shot, admittedly. But one she wasn't quite ready to give up on.

"Can I hang on to this for a while?"

"I suppose. *If* you tell me why."

She changed tack. "Do you have the legal papers that turned the game rights over to you?"

"Sure."

"Could I see them?"

"They're in a safe deposit box. At a bank downtown. I assure you, they're for real."

She looked down at the photo again. "I've got a question for you. Could Dick Danson still be alive?"

"You're joking, right?"

"Dead serious. Pardon the pun."

"Highly unlikely, don't you think?" When she simply stared at him, he laughed. "Okay, sure, it's possible. I mean, I didn't see the body."

"Maybe nobody did? Some coroners are pretty lax, especially ones who reside in quiet little hamlets. Like Carmel-by-the-Sea."

"But why play dead? Why give up the rights to projects we produced jointly? It doesn't make sense."

This time it was she who laughed, though grimly. "It makes absolute sense, Leo. What better way to seek revenge than from beyond the grave?"

CHAPTER
40

Wednesday, March 16, 2005
10:00 a.m.

Stacy waited until the Café Noir morning rush would have ended to pay Billie a visit. She couldn't let go of the idea that Cassie's death and White Rabbit were linked. And Billie never forgot a customer's face. If Danson had been in the coffee house, Billie would remember.

She entered the coffee shop, Leo's old yearbook tucked under her arm. It smelled of fresh brew and baking cookies. Her mouth watered. She'd already eaten, but it would be damn hard to turn down a cookie. Especially a chocolate chip, warm from the oven.

Billie was sure to offer one. The woman was a master at up-selling.

She'd spoken only briefly with her friend since visiting the shop with Alice. She'd called to assure her she was fine and to tell her about Pogo. Billie had sounded distracted and they had ended the call.

Billie and Paula stood at the pastry case, rearranging the goodies, showcasing those that sold best midmorning. Her friend saw her and smiled. "I knew you'd be in this morning."

"Is that so?"

"I'm psychic."

Stacy started to laugh, then stopped. Something in her friend's expression suggested she was serious. "Another of your many talents?"

"Absolutely."

Stacy crossed to the counter and ordered a cappuccino. She worked to keep herself from looking at the cookies. "You have a minute to powwow?"

"You got it. Cookie to go with that powwow? Chocolate chip?"

"No, thanks. I don't care for one."

"Yes, you do."

"And you would know this how?"

"Because I'm psychic."

She made a face. "I hate you."

Billie laughed. "Grab a table, I'll be right over."

She brought the coffee and the cookie, still warm and gooey from the oven. Stacy couldn't resist and broke off a piece. "I really do hate you, you know."

Her friend laughed and helped herself to the cookie. "Stand in line, girlfriend."

After washing down the bite with a sip of the cappuccino, Stacy opened the yearbook and slid it across the table to her friend. She tapped Danson's photo. "Ever seen this man before?"

Billie studied the photo for a few moments before shaking her head. "Sorry."

"You sure he's never been in the shop? He'd be twenty-five years older now."

Billie narrowed her eyes. "I have a great memory for faces, and I don't recall his."

Stacy frowned. "I hoped you would recognize him as a customer."

"Sorry. Who is he?"

"Leo's former business partner."

"And?"

"He's dead. Supposedly."

A slow smile curved Billie's mouth. "Now we're getting somewhere." She broke off another piece of cookie. "Explain."

Stacy leaned forward. "Most attribute the title of Supreme White Rabbit to Leo—"

"The inventor of the game."

"Right. But he didn't invent it alone. He had a co-inventor."

"This guy."

"Yes. Drove off a cliff in Carmel-by-the-Sea, California, three years ago. Leo and Kay learned about it through a lawyer. His death freed up the rights to some of their joint projects."

"Interesting. Go on."

She posed a question instead. "The person behind the letters and murders, why is he doing it?"

"Because he's a total whack job?"

"Besides that."

"Anger? Revenge?"

"Exactly. It seems there was plenty of bad blood between the Nobles and Danson, the partner."

"I get it. This Danson fakes his own death, so he can rain some seriously twisted shit down on Noble."

"Bingo." Stacy's gut told her she was onto something. The instinct that had made her solve record one of the best in the DPD. "The lawyer who visited could have been a fake, someone paid to lie. Even if the papers are legal, giving up the rights to the projects would be nothing compared to the pleasure of destroying Leo's life."

"Maybe even taking it," Billie said softly.

"Probably taking it," Stacy corrected, reaching for her coffee, hoping the hot liquid would ward off her sudden chill. "And Kay's, too. Maybe Alice's. And getting away with it. After all, he's already dead."

"An ingenious plan."

"Not that brilliant. After all, I'm onto him."

"You have your cell phone?"

She wore it in a holster, clipped to her belt—a habit acquired on the job. And one she couldn't seem to shake. "Sure. Why?"

"Hand it over."

She did, though not without asking what for. Billie held up a finger, indicating she should wait, flipped open the phone, then punched in a number.

"Connor, it's Billie." She laughed, the sound husky and sexy as hell. "Yes, *that* Billie. How are you?"

Stacy listened incredulously as her friend chatted with the man on the other end of the line, flirting and cajoling.

The woman was a professional man-eater. *How did one learn that skill? Did somebody offer a degree in it?*

"I have a friend here who needs a bit of information. Her name's Stacy. I'll put her on. Thanks, love, you're a sweetheart." Another laugh from Billie, followed by a murmured, "I will, I promise."

She held out the phone. "Chief Connor Battard."

"Chief?"

"Of police, silly. Carmel-by-the-Sea."

Stacy took the phone, doubly amazed. Did the woman know everyone? "Chief Battard, Stacy Killian. Thank you for agreeing to speak with me."

"Anything for Billie. How can I help you?"

"I'm investigating a death that occurred three years ago. Dick Danson."

"Danson's death, sure I remember it. Drove off Hurricane Point. 'Bout three and a half years ago."

"I understand the death was classified an accident."

"A suicide."

"A suicide," she repeated, surprised. "Are you certain?"

"Absolutely. He had a full propane gas tank in the trunk of his 1995 Porsche Carrerra, another in the back seat. He wanted to do the job well, and he did."

"A very big boom, I'm guessing."

"Yup. The trunk in that Porsche is in the front of the car, and there's nothing but a fire wall between it and the fuel tank. The vehicle hit nose first. The medical examiner identified Danson by his dental records."

"You didn't see the body?"

"I saw what was left of it."

"Can you remember anything unusual about the incident?"

"Other than the propane tanks and the warrant for his arrest, not a thing."

"A warrant? What for?"

"The case is closed, so I'd be happy to share the file with you. *If* you and Billie were to make a trip out."

In other words, give me what I want, I'll give you what you want. Mutual cooperation made the world go 'round.

After thanking the man, she handed the phone back to Billie. The two spoke another moment or two, then Billie ended the call.

"And how do you know Chief Battard?" Stacy asked, reholstering the phone.

"I lived there for a few years. Connor's a sweetie." She sighed. "He was in love with me."

Stacy cocked an eyebrow. *Weren't they all? And judging by the man's response to the call, there was nothing past tense about his feelings for the woman.*

"Does he know you're married?"

Billie lifted a shoulder. "Suspects, I'm sure. I almost always am."

"Would you like to see him again?"

Her eyes sparkled. "Road trip?"

"I'd like to see that file. He offered it." Stacy smiled. "Though, he made it clear I wouldn't be welcome without you."

"Rocky's being such a pain in the ass right now, a road trip would be the perfect attitude adjuster."

CHAPTER
41

Thursday, March 17, 2005
9:00 a.m.

Stacy and Billie quickly put together a travel itinerary. They found nonstop flights to San Francisco for the next day. Billie insisted that they should rent a car there and drive to the Monterey Coast. Waiting for a connection to the tiny regional airport would have taken longer than the two-hour drive. And besides, to miss such a beautiful drive would be a sin.

Especially made in a convertible. Something sleek and European. Or, so said Billie.

Billie believed in traveling in style.

Stacy had decided to make the trip, with or without Leo's blessing. However, when she'd presented him with her plan, he had not only given her his blessing, he had agreed to pay for the trip.

A good thing, since booking at the last minute had sent the airfare from exorbitant to utterly ridiculous.

Which Billie could easily afford. And Stacy could not.

An exploding credit card was not a pretty sight.

Stacy zipped her carry-on, into which she had stuffed enough for a two-day stay. She quickly scanned the bedroom, then bath to make certain she hadn't forgotten anything.

That done, she hoisted her bag. As she stepped into the hallway, Stacy glanced left, toward Alice's room. She thought of her crying the night before. The girl was most likely in class. Acting on instinct, she crossed to the closed door and tapped on it. Clark answered.

"I'm sorry for interrupting," she said, "but could I speak with Alice? It'll just take a moment."

He lowered his eyes to her bag, then returned them to hers. "Sure."

A moment later Alice appeared. "Hey," she said, not quite meeting Stacy's eyes.

"I have to go out of town for a couple days. If you need me for anything, call me." She scrawled her cell phone number on a piece of paper and handed it to her. "If you need *anything,* Alice. I mean that."

The girl stared at the paper and its scrawled number, throat working. When she lifted her gaze to Stacy's, her eyes were bright with tears. Without a word, she turned and went back into the schoolroom. As the door swung shut, Clark looked at Stacy.

She met his eyes just before the door closed.

She stood rooted to the spot as the hair on the back of her neck prickled.

The doorbell sounded.

Billie. Stacy paused a moment more, then readjusted the bag and headed down to meet her friend.

Traffic proved to be on their side, and the trip to Louis Armstrong International Airport took just under twenty minutes. A good thing, because unlike her single carry-on, Billie had two bags to check. Big bags.

"What," Stacy asked, "could you possibly have in there that you'll need in the next forty-eight hours?"

"My essentials," the woman answered breezily, smiling at the skycap. The man, ignoring several people in line in front of them, asked if he could help her.

Amazingly, no one complained.

Not so amazingly, the skycap totally ignored Stacy, leaving her to schlep her own bag.

As they proceeded to the gate, her cell phone rang. Stacy saw from the display that it was Malone.

"You going to answer that?" Billie asked.

Was she? If she told him what she was up to, he could skewer her meeting with Chief Battard, Billie or no Billie. All he had to do was claim she was interfering with an active investigation, and the file the chief had offered would be sealed shut.

Besides, this was the first time she had heard from Spencer since Saturday. Clearly, he had cut her out. She was cutting him out, as well.

She smiled to herself. "Nope," she said, hitting the device's power button.

CHAPTER
42

Thursday, March 17, 2005
10:25 a.m.

"You filed your taxes yet, Slick?" Tony said as they slammed the car doors and stepped onto the sidewalk.

Crime-scene tape stretched across the front of the ironwork-laced French Quarter apartment building. Located just down the block from two of New Orleans' most popular gay bars, Oz and the Bourbon Pub and Parade, clusters of men stood around the scene, some crying, some comforting and others stony-faced with fury or shock.

"Nope. Got a month still. I like to wait to the last minute. It's an act of defiance," Spencer answered.

"Death and taxes, man. Can't get around 'em."

Death would be the reason for this particular tête-à-tête.

Double homicide. Called in by a friend who discovered the bodies.

That would be him, Spencer thought as he caught sight of a man huddled on a bench in the building's lush courtyard.

Spencer and Tony crossed to the first officer and signed in. The kid looked a bit green.

The two detectives exchanged glances. *Not a good sign.*

"What've we got?"

"Two males." His voice shook slightly. "One black. One Hispanic. In the bathroom. Been dead awhile."

"Great," Tony muttered, digging a bottle of Vicks from his jacket pocket. "Another stinker."

"How long?" Spencer asked. "Your best guess."

"A couple of days. But I'm no pathologist."

"Names?"

"August Wright and Roberto Zapeda. Interior designers. Nobody had seen them for a couple of days, their friend over there was concerned. Came to check on them."

Spencer scanned the sign-in. Techs hadn't made it yet; neither had the coroner's office.

"Going up," he said, then motioned toward the bench and the two men. "Keep your eyes on our friends there. We'll be back to question them."

The kid nodded. "Will do."

They made their way to the second-floor apartment. Another officer stood outside the door. Guy named Logan. Spent a lot of time at Shannon's.

Spencer nodded at him as they passed. He looked hungover. No surprises there.

Just beyond the apartment, Tony handed Spencer the open jar of Vicks. Spencer smeared some under his nose and handed it back.

They stepped into the apartment. The smell rushed over Spencer in a stomach-churning wave. He forced himself to breathe deeply through his nose and counted to ten, then twenty. Between the Vicks and his fatiguing olfactory glands, the smell became tolerable.

The front room appeared undisturbed. Elegantly appointed with a combination of new and antique pieces, richly patterned art and stunning floral arrangements.

"Classy," Tony said, moving his gaze over the room. "Those gay boys got the gift, you know?"

Spencer angled him a glance. "They were interior designers, Pasta Man. What did you expect?"

"Ever see that show? *Queer Eye for the Straight Guy?*" Spencer indicated he hadn't. "They take a regular guy like me and transform him into a *GQ* dude. It's something."

"A guy like you?"

The older man arched his eyebrows, indignant. "You don't think they could spiff me up?"

"I think they'd take one look at you and kill themselves."

Before his partner could comment, the techs arrived. "Hey," Tony called. "You guys ever see that *Queer Eye* show?"

"Sure," Frank, the photographer, answered. "Hasn't everybody?"

"Junior here says they'd take one look at me and kill themselves. Think that's true?"

"Pretty much," one of the other guys answered, smirking. "If I was your wife, I'd kill myself."

"We're burning daylight, boys," Spencer interrupted. "Do you mind?"

They all turned their attention to the scene, a few of them grumbling. Not a magazine or bric-a-brac out of place. He always found it bizarre that there could be such calm only feet from horrendous violence.

And horrendous it was, he discovered moments later. The victims had been tied together and herded into the bathroom. Obviously instructed, or enticed, to climb into the claw-footed tub and kneel.

There, they had been killed.

But that wasn't the part that was out of the ordinary. It was the blood.

Everywhere. The walls, the fixtures. The floor.

As if it had been painted on, with a house paintbrush. Or a roller.

"Holy shit," Tony muttered.

"At least." Spencer made his way to the tub, conscious of the sound his rubber-soled shoes made on the blood-streaked floor. Cursing any evidence that might be destroyed, but acknowledging no other option.

The victims faced each other, arms tied behind their backs. They appeared to have been in their thirties. In good shape. One wore only his skivvies, the other drawstring pajama bottoms.

They had both been shot in the back.

He frowned. But it didn't appear either had put up a struggle. Why?

"What're you thinking, Slick?"

He glanced at his partner. "Wondering why they didn't put up a fight."

"Probably thought not struggling would save their lives."

Spencer nodded. "Guy had a gun. Herded them in here. Probably thought they were being robbed."

"Why not shoot them out front? Why this elaborate stage?"

"Wanted the blood." Spencer pointed to the tub. The killer had put the stopper in, to catch the blood. Some pooled in the bottom of the tub. "Part of a ritual maybe?"

"Detectives?"

They turned. Frank stood in the bathroom doorway. "Miss something?"

A plastic bag had been taped to the back of the door. Spencer looked at Tony. "You thinking what I'm thinking?"

"That this is a bit too familiar?"

"Uh-huh." Spencer fitted on his gloves, crossed to the door. "Got your shot?" When the photographer nodded, Spencer carefully peeled the bag off.

With a sense of déjà vu, he removed the note inside. It read simply: *The roses are red now.*

CHAPTER
43

Thursday, March 17, 2005
Monterey Coast, California
3:15 p.m.

Billie hadn't lied; after they'd gotten out of the city, the drive had been lovely. When they turned off Carmel Way and onto the famous Seventeen Mile Drive, Stacy caught her breath. The curving road, densely forested on both sides, wound its way through the breathtakingly beautiful hilly terrain. That stretch proved short-lived, transforming into a sinuous roadway, lined on both sides by fabulous estates and glimpses of the Pacific Ocean.

Billie's friend had booked them into the Lodge at Pebble Beach—the Pebble Beach of golf fame—which even Stacy had heard of, though she'd never played golf. Excluding the goofy variety, of course. She'd been pretty damn good at that, championship material, if she said so herself.

Somehow, she didn't think that'd hold much sway here.

She leaned toward Billie. "What? The local no-tell-motel couldn't fit us in?"

"Hush," Billie said as a man hurried toward them. Tall, beautifully dressed and handsome, with silvering temples. The hotel manager, Stacy decided.

"Max, my love," Billie said as he caught her hands, "thank you so much for making room at the inn."

"How could I not?" He kissed her cheeks. "You've been away too long."

"And I've been despondent every moment of that time." She smiled. "My dear friend, Stacy Killian. It's her first visit to the Lodge."

He greeted her, motioned to the bellman, then turned his attention back to Billie. "Are you planning to golf?"

"Regrettably, no."

"The pro will be devastated." The bellman appeared; Max handed Billie over to his care—after he had coaxed her to promise to call if anything didn't meet her expectations. Anything at all. No matter how small.

After they had been seated in a golf cart modified for passengers and were on their way to their rooms, Stacy looked at Billie. "I'm surprised they didn't ask me to walk behind the cart."

Billie laughed. "Just relax and enjoy yourself."

"I can't. Your friend Max, he knows I'm a fraud."

"A fraud?"

"I don't belong here."

"Don't be silly. If you can pay your bill, you belong."

"But I can't."

"Leo's paying for you. Same thing."

She frowned, unconvinced. "You golf?"

"Quite well, actually."

"I got that impression." The cart stopped in front of an alcove shielded by a camellia tree covered with pink blossoms. "How well, by the way?"

"I was the U.S. Junior Amateur champion three years running. Gave up the game for love. Eduardo."

Eduardo. Jeez.

They climbed out of the cart and followed the bellman. They had side-by-side rooms, both accessible from the alcove. The bellman opened Billie's first—no surprises there—and they stepped inside.

"My God," Stacy said. The room was large, complete with a sitting area and big stone fireplace. Sliding glass doors led to a shady patio. The pillows on the king-size bed had the look of down.

Billie brought her hands together in girlish delight. "I knew you'd love it!"

How could she not? She might be uncomfortable with wealth and luxury, but she was human, after all.

The bellman opened Stacy's room, accepted Billie's exorbitant tip and left them alone.

Stacy took in the room, stopping on the set fireplace, then

glanced back at Billie, standing in her doorway, expression pleased. "I don't want to know what this place costs a night."

"No, you don't. But Leo can afford it."

"This just seems all so...extravagant. And unnecessary. Cops don't live like this."

"First off, sweetie, you're not a cop anymore. Second, extravagance is never unnecessary. I know this. Trust me."

Before Stacy could argue, she added, "I promised I'd call Connor the minute we'd checked in. Do you mind?"

She didn't and used the opportunity to go to the bathroom. While there, she checked her cell and found that Malone had tried her again. He hadn't left a message either time.

When she emerged, she found Billie waiting by the door, expression that of a cat presented with a saucer of cream.

"Good news. He's free now."

No surprise there either—the carrot was Billie, for heaven's sake.

The trip from the Lodge to downtown Carmel-by-the-Sea took less than fifteen minutes, including parking the Jaguar at a meter on Ocean Avenue.

Carmel-by-the-Sea was as picturesque as Stacy had imagined it would be. More so, actually. Like a town out of a fairy tale, but inhabited by humans instead of fairies, elves and hobbits.

As she and Billie strolled up Ocean Avenue, her friend filled her in on all things uniquely Carmel. Billie explained that there were no street addresses in Carmel. Everyone had a post office box that served not only as a place to receive mail, but also as a social hub. Many a piece of news had been shared—then disseminated—from the post office.

"What about ambulances?" Stacy asked, disbelievingly. "Or FedEx deliveries?"

"All done by direction, description or association. For example—" she pointed to Junipero Avenue "—the third house from the corner of Ocean and Junipero." She pointed toward another. "Or, the house across the street from the East-wood place on Junipero."

Stacy shook her head. In today's high-tech world, it seemed impossible that any community still operated this way.

Stacy glanced at her friend. "By the way, when you say East-wood, you don't mean—"

"Clint? Of course I do. He's a great guy. Very down-to-earth."

A great guy. Very down-to-earth. Billie said this as if they were personal acquaintances. Buddies, even.

She wasn't even going to ask.

They reached police headquarters; the officer at the information desk called the chief, who directed them to his office.

Chief Connor Battard was waiting. A big, handsome man with a head of dark silvering hair, he held his hand out when Billie made the introductions.

Stacy took it. "Thank you for agreeing to see us, Chief Battard."

"Happy to help."

Although his words were directed to her, he could hardly take his eyes off Billie.

"As I explained on the phone, I'm looking into Dick Danson's death."

"I have the file here. You're welcome to it." He slid it across the desk to her. "I'm sorry, but it can't leave the building."

Of course. Standard operating procedure. Stacy didn't move to pick it up. She preferred to ask questions first. "On the phone, you mentioned a warrant for his arrest. What for?"

"Embezzlement. From a company he was doing game designs for."

"Think the charge would have stuck?"

"Point's moot now, don't you think?"

"Maybe. Maybe not."

The chief frowned. "What are you thinking?"

She shook her head, not ready to share her theory. Yet. She wasn't in the mood to be laughed out of the room.

"How certain are you that it was a suicide?"

"Pretty damn certain. We had a warrant for his arrest. A search of his property turned up, considering the circumstances, the notable lack of an outdoor grill. Or any other device requiring portable propane. Those canisters were in his car for one reason only—to cause a really big explosion.

"He drove off Hurricane Point. Again, in terms of getting things done, he picked the right spot. And most damning, he left a note saying he had nothing to live for."

"Did your investigation back that up? Did he have financial or emotional problems?"

The chief narrowed his eyes, obviously growing annoyed with her questions. She supposed she didn't blame him.

"Frankly," he said, "the case was open and shut. We had a positive ID. A suicide note. And a pending arrest. Danson was seeing a shrink. Let's just say the man wasn't shocked by the news. I didn't see a need to dig deeper. It's all in the file."

"Thanks," she said, disappointed. She'd been so certain she was onto something, now she felt like an idiot. And one who had blown a lot of time and money on an unsound hunch.

Her instincts *had* turned to shit. She picked up the file. "Why don't you and Billie go catch up. Get dinner. I'll review the file."

"Great." He rubbed his hands together in what Stacy was certain was anticipation of being alone with Billie.

"I'll get you set up in one of the interrogation rooms."

Stacy spent the next couple of hours alone with the file, a Coke and bag of corn chips from the vending machine. Long after the chips and a soft drink were history, she was still reading.

And learning little new. Sure, details. Times. But nothing that promoted her hunch.

Dick Danson was dead.

And she'd left Leo and his family alone with a killer.

She called Billie to let her know she was finished. She heard music in the background, people laughing. Connor offered to have one of his officers drive her back to the Lodge.

Apparently, the night was still young.

The officer, a nice young man barely out of his teens, dropped her off at the hotel. She lit the fire, ordered room service and slipped into her robe.

Her cell rang. She saw that it was Malone. Again. This time she answered, ready to grovel if need be. Admit to being a hunch-happy, burned-out, instincts-shot has-been.

She needed to hear his voice.

"Malone."

"Where are you?"

He sounded tense. He wasn't going to like her answer. "In California. The Lodge at Pebble Beach."

A long silence followed. "You're playing golf?"

She smiled at his obvious confusion. "No. Checking out a hunch. With Billie."

"Man-eater Billie?"

Funny, she had thought of her that way, too. "The very one."

"Can-do Killian. Girl Wonder. The hunch?"

"I've learned my lesson, actually. My hunches suck."

He laughed, but the sound was tight. Humorless. "The playing cards are dead—August Wright and Roberto Zapeda. Partners. Professionally and personally."

"Any connection to Leo?"

"His interior designers."

"Shit."

"I'd say. Your boss is knee-deep in it right now."

"Leo? What—"

"Got to go."

"No, wait—"

He ended the call. She flipped her cell shut and looked at the crackling fire. All this luxury was wasted on her.

Time to go home.

CHAPTER
44

Friday, March 18, 2005
Carmel-by-the-Sea, California
6:30 a.m.

"I'm not ready to go home," Billie said, sliding into the Jaguar's passenger side seat. "I love that room. I love being waited on. I love the coast."

"Stop whining. You have a business to watch over. Not to mention a husband."

She made a face. "Rocky's attitude won't be changed yet. I need another couple of days for him to really appreciate me."

From what she'd heard about Rocky St. Martin, *really* appreciating Billie would take more energy than the man had left. Even on a good day.

"Face it," Stacy said, "the trip was a bust. Not only that,

while I was here, living in the lap of luxury, the playing cards turned up dead."

"Now who's whining?"

Stacy scowled at her. "Stay if you'd like, I'm going home."

Billie sighed dramatically, slipped on her sunglasses and leaned her head back against the rest. "Connor will be despondent."

Stacy angled her a glance as she started the car. "And you?"

"I love my husband."

She said it as if she meant it, and Stacy felt her mouth drop in surprise.

"What?"

"Nothing, it's just...I—"

"Thought I'd married him for his money? Because he's so much older than I am? Why would I do that? I have money of my own."

"Sorry," Stacy murmured, easing away from the curb, "I didn't mean to offend."

"You didn't. But if I'm going to be monogamous, which I am, at least give me credit for it."

"You've got it."

"Thank you." She sighed again. "Damn, I'm going to miss the coast."

Shaking her head, Stacy opened her cell, punched in Malone's number.

He answered right away. "Malone here."

"I'm on my way to the airport."

"Miss me that much, do you?"

"What did you mean about Leo being hip deep in—"

"That was knee-deep. As in looking guilty as hell."

"Leo guilty? That's not right."

"Whatever you need to tell yourself."

"What does *that* mean?"

"Nothing." His voice took on an edge. "I've got to go."

"Wait! How good's the evidence?"

"Let's put it this way, doll. By the time you touch down in Louisiana, you may be unemployed."

He ended the call, and she frowned. "That's wrong."

"What?" Billie asked.

"Malone says they've got evidence that Leo's guilty."

"Of what? Really bad hair?"

"I like his hair."

"You do not!" Billie faced her, aghast. "He looks like he stuck a finger in an electrical socket."

"Does not. It's all crazy and windblown. Like a surfer's."

"Or a deranged killer's—"

Billie bit the word back, realizing how inappropriate it was in light of the situation. "Bad hair or not, the man seems pretty harmless to me."

"Me, too."

Stacy fell silent. She glanced at the clock on the Jag's dash and swore. She needed to speak to Chief Battard, ASAP. "You don't happen to know Connor's home number?"

"Sure I do. Have it right here in my cell."

"Could you call him? I need to ask one last question. I think it's important."

Billie did as she asked; several moments later Stacy greeted the sleepy-sounding police chief. "I apologize for calling so early, but I have one last question. I didn't see the answer in the file."

"Shoot," he said, yawning.

"What was Danson's dentist's name? Do you remember?"

"Sure," he said. "Dr. Mark Carlson. Great guy."

She glanced at the Jag's dashboard clock. They had plenty of time until their flight; even with the drive and returning the rental car. Enough, anyway, for a quick call on a dentist. "Do you think there's any way I could speak with him before I leave?"

"It'd be damn difficult, Ms. Killian. Dr. Mark's dead. He was killed during a robbery."

"When?"

"Last year." He paused. "It was Carmel's only murder in 2004. We never solved it."

A moment later, Stacy ended the call. "Gotcha, asshole," she said, pulling off the road to turn around.

"What?"

"Remember when you told me you'd always wanted to be a spy?"

Billie turned to her, eyebrows raised. "You bet I do."

"How would you feel about spending a few more days in paradise?"

CHAPTER
45

Friday, March 18, 2005
New Orleans
9:10 a.m.

Spencer tapped on his aunt's hospital room door. He heard her inside, giving her doctor a tongue-lashing. He bit back a smile. She was insisting the man release her. Demanding to speak to someone with more authority. Someone who had actually earned a medical degree.

To the physician's credit, he kept his cool. In fact, he actually sounded pleased.

Spencer stepped into the room. "'Morning, Aunt Patti," he said. "Am I interrupting something?"

"Yes," she snapped. "I'm telling this quack—"

"Dr. Fontaine," the man said, stepping forward, hand out.

They shook hands. "Detective Spencer Malone. Patient's nephew, godson and ISD whipping boy."

She glared at him. She looked good, he thought. Healthy and strong. He told her so.

"Of course I'm healthy. As fit as a fiddle."

"You want me to bust you out of here?" he asked her.

"God, yes."

The physician shook his head, amused. "Soon, Patti, I promise." He gave her shoulder a squeeze.

The moment the doctor had left the room, she ordered Spencer to pull up a chair and sit. She wanted news.

"Remember Bobby Gautreaux, the suspect in the Finch homicide?"

"Sure, kid was a worm."

"The very one." A smile tugged at Spencer's mouth. "DNA came back this morning. The hair we found on Finch's T-shirt was his."

"Excellent."

"There's more. Cross-referenced the results against blood taken from the attack on Stacy Killian at the UNO library and got ourselves a solid match."

She opened her mouth as if to question him more; he held up a hand, stopping her. "It gets better. They ran the results against the semen samples taken from the three UNO rape victims. Solid matches all."

She looked pleased. "Good work."

He thought so, too. "Stacy Killian was convinced the guy

who attacked her was warning her away from poking her nose into the Finch investigation. That works now."

"You didn't buy it then."

"We didn't have the DNA link to Gautreaux then."

She nodded. "You said she nailed him pretty good with the pen. He should still have the wound."

"He does. Which we photographed, of course. In terms of the Finch and Wagner homicides, throw in his print from the scene, the strand of Finch's hair we collected from his clothing and the threats he had made against the woman, we've got ourselves a compelling case."

Mr. Gautreaux was going to spend the remainder of his youth behind bars.

"I agree. But you're holding on the murder charge and moving forward on the rapes."

He smiled. "You got it. Because of the serial nature of his crimes, the judge will deny bail, and we can take our sweet time amassing the evidence to put him away for murder one."

She murmured her agreement. "No sense setting the judicial clock ticking until we have to. Is he in custody yet?"

"Being processed as we speak."

"Good. What about the White Rabbit case?"

"The playing cards are dead."

"I heard. Leads?"

"Working on one. The game inventor."

"Keep me posted." She sighed and glanced at the wall clock. "Damn, I'm ready to get out of here."

"It won't be much longer. How's Uncle Sammy doing without you?"

"Eating pizza every night, the idiot. He'll be in here with a clogged artery next."

Chuckling, Spencer stood, bent and pressed a kiss to her forehead. "I'll stop by later."

"Wait." She caught his hand. "Any trouble for you? Personally?"

He knew what she meant—had he heard from PID?

He shook his head. "No. Tony's asked around, nobody's heard anything. But I have this sensation at the back of my neck, like hot breath."

She nodded, understanding. "By the book, Malone. Not one finger out of line."

He saluted and headed out. As he stepped off the elevator on the first floor, his cell rang. He checked the display, saw that it was Tony.

"Pasta Man."

"Where are you?"

"Just left Aunt Patti. Heading downtown now."

"Don't bother. Head for the Noble place instead."

He stopped. The sensation at the back of his neck grew stronger. "What's up?"

"Kay Noble's missing."

CHAPTER
46

Friday, March 18, 2005
11:10 a.m.

When Spencer arrived at the Noble mansion, the first officer directed him to the guest house. He found Tony inside.

"Hey, Slick. Made good time."

"A land speed record." He looked over the tidy room, noting how tasteful it was. Like something out of *Southern Living* magazine. He wondered if the now-deceased designers, Wright and Zapeda, had done the decorating. "Fill me in."

"Apparently, Kay didn't show for breakfast this morning. The housekeeper didn't think too much about it. Although the woman's typically an early bird, once in a while she sleeps in. Suffers with migraines, too. Again, occasionally."

He glanced at his notes. "Complained of one coming on the afternoon before."

"Who finally sounded the alarm?"

"The kid."

"Alice?"

"Yes. When Kay didn't show by ten-thirty, Leo sent Alice over to check on her mom."

"Door was unlocked?"

"Yup."

"Why'd they call us? She could be taking a walk or out with friends."

"Not likely. Take a look at this."

His partner led him to the bedroom. Unlike the front room, which had been pin neat, this one showed signs of a violent struggle. Lamp toppled. Paintings askew. Bed torn apart.

Spencer's gaze landed on the jumbled bedding. The periwinkle-blue-and-bone silk spread was marred by dark stains.

Blood. He crossed to the bed. There wasn't a tremendous amount, but more than could have been caused by a scratch or other small wound. More blood on the floor led to an arched doorway at the back of the room. At the archway, a bloody handprint stood in stark contrast to the light-hued wall.

Spencer crossed to it. He studied the print a moment, then looked at the other man. "Size is consistent with a woman's."

Tony nodded. "We should test it against the hands of other members of the household. See if the glass slipper fits."

Might be the perp's print, not the vic's. It didn't feel that way, but that didn't necessarily mean squat.

Spencer motioned to the doorway.

"A study," Tony said. "Patio beyond."

Spencer nodded. Mindful not to destroy evidence, he picked his way around the trail of blood. Every drop would be collected and tested. Only testing would prove whether or not all of it was from the same person.

The study also showed signs of a struggle. Furniture at odd angles. Knickknacks toppled, broken. As if Kay had been struggling, grabbing onto furniture, putting up a fight.

A good thing. It meant Kay had still been alive.

The sliding glass doors that led to the patio stood open. More blood, on the door frame and glass panel.

He crossed to them and peered out. The patio was surrounded by shrubs, making it private, like a courtyard. The perp had known the guest house layout, had chosen this route to be away from prying eyes. He had wanted to keep the alarm from sounding as long as possible.

"Crime-scene techs on their way?" Spencer asked.

"Called 'em myself."

"You talk to anybody yet?"

"Nope. Got it all from Jackson."

DIU, Third District. "So Noble called 911?"

"Yup. Communications contacted DIU first. The guys at the Third realized the connection to our case, called me."

"Wonder why Noble didn't call us directly?" Spencer murmured more to himself than Tony.

Maybe to delay that alarm.

"I want to interview everybody on the property. Let's start with the big man himself."

"You want us to stick together or split up?" Tony asked.

"Split up, we'll cover ground more quickly. Start with the housekeeper, then move on from there. We'll compare notes later."

Tony agreed and headed for the kitchen. Spencer found Leo in his office. He sat at his desk, staring into space, expression flat. His daughter, on the other hand, huddled in the corner of the couch, knees to her chest. Unlike her dad, she looked devastated.

"I need to ask you a few questions, Mr. Noble."

"Leo," he corrected. "Go ahead."

"When did you last see your wife?"

"Ex-wife. Last night. About seven o'clock."

"Working late?"

"We all had dinner together. Right, pumpkin?"

The teenager looked up, like a deer caught in headlights, and nodded. "We went for sushi."

Her voice cracked and she pressed her forehead to her knees. Spencer motioned toward the doorway. "Perhaps we should talk in the hall?"

"Sure. Of course." He crossed to his daughter. "Pumpkin?" She looked up. "The detective and I will be in the hall. Will you be okay alone?"

She nodded, looking terrified.

"Call me if you need me. Okay?"

She indicated she would, and the two men left the room, quietly shutting the door behind them.

"I thought it'd be better if she didn't overhear us," Spencer said softly. Which was true—just not for the reason Noble thought. He didn't want the father's answers to influence the daughter's.

"I should have thought of that," Leo said. "I sent her to get Kay. It's my fault she saw—" His voice cracked. "Why didn't I go myself?"

He sounded genuinely guilty. But over what? Inadvertently exposing his daughter to what very well may have been the scene of her mother's death? Or for having involved her in his crime?

"Let's go back to the previous evening," Spencer said. "The name of the sushi restaurant?"

"Japanese Garden. Just up the street."

Spencer made a note. "Do you do that often, have dinner together?"

"Several times a week. After all, we're a family."

"But not the typical family."

"It's a world filled with variation, Detective."

"And you didn't see her again after dinner?"

"No. I was out on the back porch around midnight—"

"Midnight?"

"Smoking a cigar. Her light was on."

He said it as if it was the most logical thing in the world. "At dinner, she say anything about a headache?"

"A headache? Not that I recall. Why?"

Spencer ignored the question, sending another of his own. "Typically, she a night owl?"

"No. That's my role."

"She ever leave her door unlocked?"

"Never. I used to tease her, call her anal retentive about such things. She was always a detail person."

Spencer jumped on his use of the past tense. "Was? Do you know something we don't, Mr. Noble?"

The man flushed. "Of course not. I was referring to the years we were married. And her business abilities."

"In terms of your business, what role does Kay play?"

"Basically, she's my business manager. She works with the accountants and lawyers, reviews the contracts, stays on top of the employees…and generally leaves me to be creative."

"To be creative," Spencer repeated. "If you'll pardon me, that sounds pretty self-indulgent."

"To you, I suppose it does. Most people don't understand the creative process."

"Why don't you explain it to me?"

"The brain has two sides, the left and right. The left side controls organization and logic. It also controls language and speech, critical thinking and so forth."

"So you had Kay to take care of all those left-brain details. Could you have hired someone else to do the job?"

He looked perplexed by the question. "Sure. But why would I?"

Spencer shrugged. "I suspect you would have to pay less. As your ex-wife, she probably feels entitled to half of everything you have."

Leo flushed. "She is entitled. I've never made a secret of

that. Without Kay, I wouldn't have gotten where I am. She kept me focused, harnessed my enthusiasm and creativity in a way that allowed me to make money using my imagination."

"You say she's entitled to half. That's what you give her?"

"Yes. Half."

"Of everything?"

His expression altered, as with understanding. "You think I had something to do with this?"

"Answer the question, please."

"Of everything." He flexed his fingers. "I'm not that kind of man, Detective."

"What kind is that?"

"The kind who puts money before people. Money doesn't mean that much to me."

"I can tell."

At Spencer's sarcasm, color flooded Leo's face. "I know who did this, and you should, too!"

"And who would that be, Mr. Noble?"

"The White Rabbit."

CHAPTER
47

Friday, March 18, 2005
3:30 p.m.

Spencer dropped the receiver back onto the cradle and smiled. Kay Noble's disappearance had convinced a judge to give them a search warrant for Leo's home, office, vehicles, business and financial records.

He stood, stretched and started toward Tony's desk. Between the two of them, they'd questioned everyone in the Noble household. Everyone's answers pretty well mirrored Leo's—with one exception. Only the housekeeper recalled Kay having a headache.

"Yo, Pasta Man." His partner sat at his desk, staring at a small logbook. "What's up?"

Instead of answering, he made a growling noise.

Spencer frowned and indicated the logbook. "What's that?"

"Points keeper."

"Excuse me?"

"Weight Watchers. Wife signed me up." He sighed. "Every food has an assigned point value. You log everything you eat and subtract it from your daily points limit."

"So, what's the problem?"

"I've already used up all my points."

"For the day and night?"

"Yeah. And some of my weekly flex points."

"Flex poin—" He bit the question back. "Forget about it. Let's take a drive."

"Where?"

"Noble's. By way of the Criminal Courts Building."

Tony grinned. "Judge granted a search warrant?"

"Bingo, baby."

In the end, they picked up the warrant, and since they were downtown, paid a visit to Noble's lawyer. Winston Coppola was a partner in Smith, Grooms, Macke and Coppola, located in the Place St. Charles building.

They parked in a tow zone—legal spots were few and far between in the Central Business District, and flipped down the visor to display their police ID. As they crossed the sidewalk to the building's main entrance, the St. Charles Avenue streetcar rumbled past.

They found the law firm on the building's directory, caught an elevator and headed for the tenth floor.

The pretty young woman at reception smiled when the two men approached her desk. "Spencer Malone, what a surprise."

He returned the smile, not having a clue who she was. Luckily, he'd noted her name on the desk placard. "Trish? Is that you?"

"It is."

"Gee, look at you. How long's it been?"

"Too long. I changed my hair."

"I see that. I like it."

"Thanks." She pouted. "You never called. We had so much fun that night at Shannon's, I was certain you would."

Shannon's. No wonder.

Must have been back in his big drinking days.

"I thought I'd never see you again," he said with what he hoped was just the right note of sincerity. He imagined Tony beside him, rolling his eyes. "I lost your number."

"I can remedy that."

She caught his hand and turned it palm up. She wrote the number across his palm, then closed his fingers around it. "Call me."

Tony cleared his throat. "We're here to see Winston Coppola. Is he in?"

"Mr. Coppola? Do you have an appointment?"

"This is official business."

"Oh...I see," she said, obviously flustered. "I'll buzz him."

She did, and a moment later, she replaced the receiver and directed them to the man's office. As they made their way back, Tony leaned toward him, "Good save, Slick."

"Thanks."

"What a knockout. Are you going to call her?"

Truth was, calling the pretty Trish was the furthest thing from his mind at the moment. Well, maybe not the furthest, but the need wasn't pressing. "I'd be crazy not to. Right?"

Tony didn't answer, because they had reached the attorney's office; he was waiting at the door for them. Handsome, well-dressed, impeccably groomed, but with a slightly freaky George Hamilton tan, he appeared to be a smooth operator.

Spencer greeted him. "Detectives Malone and Sciame. We need to ask you a few questions about Kay Noble."

"Kay?" He frowned. "You have IDs, Detectives?"

After inspecting them, the man ushered them into his office. None of them sat.

Spencer noted the framed diplomas; the photographs on the desk, credenza and walls. One, he saw, depicted the lawyer skiing, another at the beach. No wonder the guy was so brown.

Tony looked around, openly admiring the office. "Nice place."

"Thanks."

"You have an interesting name, Mr. Coppola."

"English mother, Italian father. I'm a bit of a mutt, actually."

"Any relationship to Francis Ford?"

"Sadly, no. Now, about Noble?"

"She's missing. We have reason to believe she's in harm's way."

"My God. When——"

"Last night."

"How can I help?"

"When did you see her last?"

"Early this week."

"May I ask what the meeting was about?"

"A licensing agreement."

"How's business? Their business?"

"Very good." He slipped his hands into his trouser pockets. "I'm sure you understand I can't share confidential information."

"Actually, you can. We have a warrant." Spencer produced the document; the attorney looked it over, then handed it back.

"First off, this document does not release me from attorney-client privilege. It allows you access to Leonardo Noble's home and vehicle, and financial and business records you might find there.

"Second, as a lawyer, I understand the significance of the warrant and your underlying reasons for obtaining it." He leaned toward them. "You're barking up the wrong tree. If something's happened to Kay, Leo had nothing to do with it."

"You're certain?"

"Absolutely."

"Why?"

"They're devoted to each other."

"They divorced, Mr. Coppola."

"Let go of all your notions about what that means. They'd worked all that out. They are friends. Partners in raising their daughter and in their business ventures."

"And how is their business?" Spencer asked, repeating his earlier question.

"Very good, actually. Leo and Kay just signed several big licensing agreements."

"For really big money?" Tony asked.

He hesitated, then nodded. "Yes."

"How big?" Spencer pressed. "Are we talking millions?"

"Yes, millions."

"Who pays your bill, Mr. Coppola?"

"Excuse me?"

"Your bill, who pays it? Leo or Kay?"

Red stained his cheeks. "That question offends me, Detective."

"But I'm certain the money doesn't."

"Noble's not just a client, but also a friend. Billable hours have nothing to do with that. Or with how I answered your questions. I'm sorry, but I'm out of time."

Spencer stuck out his hand. "Thanks for speaking with us. We'll be in touch."

Tony handed him a card. "If you think of anything, give us a call."

The attorney showed them out. Trish sat at her desk but was too busy to do more than look up and smile as they passed. The moment the door of the elevator whooshed shut, Tony looked at Spencer. "Interesting how rich people always claim money's not important. If it's not important, why do they work so hard to hang on to it?"

Spencer nodded, recalling how Leo Noble had claimed money didn't mean that much to him. "I'm thinking that Coppola believes Leo's the power behind the empire. Did you get that?"

"Yeah, I got that. You think that influenced his answers?"

"Maybe. He's a lawyer, after all."

For the most part, cops didn't think highly of lawyers. Except for prosecutors, like Spencer's brother Quentin.

The elevator reached the first floor; the doors opened and they stepped off. "You're married, Pasta Man, give me some perspective."

"Shoot."

"I'm a little muddy about this whole 'they still love and respect each other' thing. This 'I owe it all to her, so I'm giving her half' thing. Let's say the missus divorces you. How are you going to feel about that?"

They reached the car. Spencer unlocked it and they climbed in. Tony buckled his safety belt and looked at Spencer. "I've been married thirty-two years and I don't get it, either. We love and respect each other, fight and disagree, but we stay together. It's the fact that we made a commitment to each other that keeps us together, working at it. If she divorced me, I'd be pretty pissed off."

"And if, after she divorced you, she got half of everything you made—past and future. How would you feel about that? Could you still be friends?"

"It wouldn't happen, dude."

"Why not?"

"After you sleep with a woman, you can't be friends."

"Neanderthal."

"And how many of those friends do you have?"

Spencer drew his eyebrows together in thought. *Exactly . . . none.*

He glanced at Tony, then pulled away from the curb. "Everybody who knows them is singing the same song. Friends. Employees. Daughter."

"And you think it's an act."

It wasn't a question; instead of answering, he asked one of his own. "Who stands to gain the most by Kay Noble dying?"

"Leo Noble."

"Damn right, he does. Call for a couple uniforms to meet us at Leo's. It's time for the games to begin."

CHAPTER
48

Friday, March 18, 2005
4:45 p.m.

Stacy's plane landed in New Orleans exactly on schedule. As it taxied toward the gate, she reviewed the events of the day. After learning the dentist who had identified Dick Danson had been murdered, she had U-turned and headed back to the Lodge. Billie had reregistered, getting her room back before it had even been cleaned. From there, they had called Chief Battard—to inform him that Billie was staying and to ask if Stacy could meet with him quickly to explain why.

And to ask for his help.

On their way, Stacy had filled Billie in on what she wanted her to do: look into any missing-persons cases in the area at the time of Danson's suicide, and if one appeared, to somehow uncover if he had been a patient of Dr. Mark Carlson's. She also wanted her to find a way to gain access to the dentist's records and cross-reference them against the ones used to ID Danson's corpse.

Chief Battard would be instrumental in making that happen. Medical records were damn near impossible to access without official authorization.

They'd met Chief Battard in his office at headquarters. Stacy had run her theory by him and asked for his help. To his credit, he hadn't laughed.

And he'd agreed to help.

Stacy suspected the prospect of a few more days with the sultry Billie had something to do with his equanimity.

Stacy exited the plane. She was right about one thing—she was certain of it.

Dick Danson was alive. He was the White Rabbit.

And he was a killer.

As soon as she had cleared the terminal, she turned on her phone. She had three messages waiting. Judging by the callback numbers, all three were from Leo.

She'd spoken with him first thing that morning, had told him the trip had been a bust and that she was flying home.

A lot had happened since she'd made that call.

More, apparently, than she'd even realized.

While she made her way to the parking garage, she checked the messages. The first call was, indeed, from Leo. He was upset. His voice shaking.

Kay's...gone. She's...someone...the White Rabbit...she may be dead. Call me as soon as you touch down.

The second was from Alice, not her father. She was crying, so hard Stacy could barely make out what she was saying. Her message, in essence, mirrored her father's. She was scared.

Grimly, Stacy quickened her pace. The third was again from Leo. According to her cell's time stamp, it had come in just before she touched down. Malone had gotten a search warrant and was at the house now. He didn't know what to do.

A search warrant.

The ball was in motion now.

She stepped outside the terminal and the humid New Orleans air caught her in a bear hug. Crossing the traffic lanes to the parking garage, she found her vehicle, unlocked it and tossed her bag inside.

Minutes later, Stacy was on the airport access road, heading toward I-10 East. She anticipated the trip taking about fifteen minutes, barring accidents, construction or a game in the Superdome.

Stacy tried Leo, got his recording and left a message. She rang Malone, also with no luck. She used the rest of the drive to review what she knew of the recent events and to prepare herself for what awaited.

The playing cards were dead. Now Kay had gone missing. Malone and his partner had gotten a search warrant—which meant they had evidence enough to convince a judge they had just cause.

What did they have on Leo?

She meant to find out.

Stacy reached Leo's mansion in what she suspected was

record time. Judging by the number of cars parked out front, one of them a NOPD cruiser, Malone and company were still there.

She angled her own vehicle into a narrow spot, hopped out and hurried to the front door.

Mrs. Maitlin, looking pale and shaken, answered. "Valerie," Stacy said, holding out a hand. "I heard. What's happening?"

The woman grasped it and glanced over her shoulder, then looked back at Stacy. "They're tearing the place apart. As if Mr. Leo could have done a thing to Mrs. Noble. And poor Alice, she's the one who…the blood—"

"Stacy!" Leo rushed across the foyer. "Thank God." He reached the door and drew her inside. "This is unreal. Insane. First, Kay disappearing. Then this search—"

"Did you call your lawyer?"

"Yes. They had already visited him, shown him the warrant. Said it looked legal. That there was nothing I could do but cooperate."

"If you're innocent, you have nothing to—"

He cut her off, looking hurt. "If I'm innocent? You doubt me, Stacy?"

"That's not what I meant. Focus, Leo. They won't find any-thing—it will force them to look elsewhere."

From the corner of her eye she saw Alice, huddled on the parlor couch. She looked lost.

Even though her heart went out to the teenager, she kept her attention on Leo. "Was there any kind of message left at the scene?"

"No, not that I saw."

"It sounds as if they suspect foul play. Why?"

He looked at her blankly. "The scene," she said softly. "There were signs of a struggle? Blood?"

He nodded, understanding. "Yes. And I...I sent Alice to look for her." His voice broke. "She saw   It's my fault."

"How'd he get in, Leo?"

"I don't know." He rubbed his hands over his face. "They asked me if she ever left her door unlocked."

Which meant there had been no evidence of a break-in.

"What did you tell them?"

"I told them she did not."

She laid a reassuring hand on his arm. "Where are they?"

"Upstairs."

"I'll be back. Hold tight."

Stacy headed upstairs, then followed the sound of voices. She saw that the place had been torn apart. Typical cops, she thought, as she found them in her room. Going through her skivvies drawer.

"Having fun, Detective?"

He looked over his shoulder. "Killian."

"They're a size five. Not so sexy, but comfortable."

Tony laughed out loud, Malone shut the drawer, looking a bit flushed. "Warrant covered the entire property. You know the drill."

"Yeah, I know. Could I have a word with you?"

He glanced at his partner, who motioned for him to go, then joined her in the hall.

"Clock's ticking."

"So I'll get right to the point. You're wrong about Leo."

"That so? And what makes you so certain?"

"Dick Danson's alive. He—"

"Who?"

"Leo's former partner. He and Leo parted acrimoniously. Supposedly, he committed suicide last year."

"Ran off a cliff in Carmel, California. It's all coming back to me. That's why you were out there. Your hunch."

"Yes."

"I thought that hunch had turned out to be gas."

Quickly, she explained about the suicide and the fact that Danson was identified by his dental records.

"Proof enough for me," he said, glancing pointedly at his watch.

"Me, too. Until this morning when I found out the dentist who provided those records was murdered not that long after." She paused. "His killer was never caught."

For the space of a heartbeat, she thought she had him. Then taking her by the elbow, he led her farther from the other officer. "Ran a little financial check on your buddy Leo Noble. Seems business is good. Very good. Recently did a couple licensing deals. Worth millions, Stacy. *Millions.*"

"So? What does that have to do with—"

"Kay gets half. Of everything. Past. Present. And future."

She stared at him, understanding. *Greed. One of the oldest motives for murder.*

She shook her head. "He loves her. She's the mother of his

child and his best friend." Even as she said the words, she acknowledged how naive she sounded.

She pressed on, anyway. "There wasn't a message from the White Rabbit on this one, was there?" She could tell by his expression that there wasn't. "No message. No body. Doesn't fit the White Rabbit MO."

"All the victims had ties to Leo. He was the recipient of the first three notes and the last was found in his office. And, he knows the game better than anyone else alive."

"Clark Dunbar is having an affair with Kay. Did you know that?"

She saw by his expression that he didn't.

"I saw them together. Late one night." She motioned toward her bedroom. "My window faces the guest house entrance."

He took out his notebook. "When was this?"

"The night before I left for California. Wednesday."

He noted the fact. "You're certain it was Dunbar?"

"Absolutely. I couldn't make out who it was, so I opened my window. I heard his voice."

Spencer cocked an eyebrow. "Opened the window?"

"My curiosity got the better of me. Have you talked to Dunbar?"

"He's out of town. Had a long weekend off."

"And the woman he's having an affair with disappears, leaving a scene that suggests foul play. Convenient."

Spencer closed the spiral notebook and tucked it into his breast pocket. "We'll check it out."

This time it was she who caught his elbow. "Danson's alive," she said. "He's the White Rabbit. And he's exacting revenge on Leo and his family."

"Get a clue, Killian. Noble created this whole White Rabbit thing to get away with killing his wife."

"That doesn't make sense."

"Of course it does. It's genius. A big, elaborate smoke screen. Even *you're* part of the plan, Stacy." He shook off her hand and walked down the hall.

CHAPTER
49

Friday, March 18, 2005
6:30 p.m.

Stacy watched him walk away, a knot in the pit of her stomach. The past rushed up, so thick and bitter it nearly choked her. This wouldn't be the first time her judgment had proved faulty. Wouldn't be the first time she had been deceived. Her good intentions used.

She struggled to breathe evenly. To get a grip on her emotions.

The past was *not* repeating itself. She wasn't that woman anymore.

"Stacy?"

She turned. Alice stood just inside her bedroom door. Everything about her body language suggested she might bolt at any moment.

The teenager brought a finger to her lips, pointed to the room where the officers were conducting their search, then motioned her over.

Stacy glanced toward the officers, then strolled past the open doorway, before ducking into Alice's room.

Alice drew her across the room. Her hands were trembling, clammy. She stopped at the desk and turned on the computer. The device came to life and quickly began loading.

Stacy looked questioningly at Alice and saw that the teenager was near tears.

"I know what the police think. I heard them talking. It's not true. Dad didn't do anything to Mom. Or anyone else. I know he didn't."

"How, Alice? How do you know?"

She nodded and turned back to the computer terminal. With a few keystrokes, she called up a screen with dated entries. She clicked on the most recent, dated today at 3:00 p.m. It was an e-mail message.

The Mouse, Five and Seven have been eliminated. The Queen is compromised. The Cheshire Cat is making her move; her claws are long, her teeth sharp.

What's your response?

Stacy knew what she was looking at; a game of White Rabbit in progress.

Not any game, either.

The game.

"I thought I'd better…I wanted you to see this first. Because of Mom. And Dad."

Her Mom. The Queen of Hearts.

Stacy quelled her excitement, her urge to shake information out of the teenager. "Who's the White Rabbit, Alice?"

"I don't know. I met him in an RPG chat room. But he's my friend, he wouldn't hurt me or anyone else."

"Your friend?" Stacy worked to keep her voice low, her tone measured. "People are dying, Alice."

"I know how it looks, but it can't—" She clasped her hands together. "It's just a game. Right?"

The teenager longed to be convinced, reassured. Unfortunately, Stacy couldn't do that. "Rosie Allen is dead. Her killer left a message by her body—poor little mouse, drowned in a pool of tears. August Wright and Roberto Zapeda are also dead. The killer left a message by their bodies as well—the roses are red now. Judging by the cards and message left in your dad's office, the pair represented the Five and Seven of Spades."

She paused to let her words sink in. "Now your mother is missing. And coincidentally, in your game the Queen of Hearts is 'compromised.' Is it simply a game, Alice? You tell me."

The girl broke down. "I di...didn't know," she managed to say around sobs. "Until...Mom...then I...then I knew the White Rabbit was using me to...decide—"

"Let's figure this out," Stacy said softly. "We'll do it together. Figure out who he is and stop him."

Alice wiped her tears and met Stacy's eyes. "How? Tell me what to do."

Stacy nodded, proud of the teenager. "First, the Queen is compromised. What does that mean?"

"It's a game strategy. Incapacitate one of the players, then move on to another. Return later for the…for the kill."

Return for the kill. Of course.

Kay was still alive.

"You know what this means, Alice. Your mother's alive."

The young woman's eyes widened, filling once more with tears. This time with relief, Stacy suspected.

"Who is he?" Stacy asked again. "You must have some idea."

"I don't. Honestly." She wrung her hands. "We met in an RPG chat room. We became…friends. He asked if I wanted to play."

"How long ago did you meet?"

"Eight months ago. Maybe a year."

"Did he ever suggest a meeting?"

"No." She tilted her chin up. "But I wouldn't have gone. I'm not that stupid."

She flushed as if realizing that maybe she was, considering the turn of events.

"I know he's really smart. We discussed everything from anthropology, to psychology, to art. He was knowledgeable about them all."

A real Renaissance man.

Stacy glanced up, to the bookshelf above the computer. She took in the eclectic hodgepodge of titles, everything from fiction to law texts and gaming manuals. She even had a copy of the *DSM-IV*, the clinician's guide to mental illness. The DPD shrink kept a copy in his office.

"How about his age?" Stacy asked.

Alice screwed up her face in thought. "Older than me, I'm pretty sure. He seemed mature."

Seemed mature. Which illustrated one of the dangers of meeting people online, Stacy thought. Being unable to accurately gauge a person's age or character. Having to depend on their version of the truth.

"Older? As old as your father?"

"Not *old*." She shook her head. "We liked the same music and stuff. When I talked about my parents, he understood. Totally."

"About your parents," she repeated. "What did you tell him about them?"

Alice looked embarrassed, upset. "I complained about how they treated me like a baby. How they wouldn't let me go to university, stuff like that." Her eyes welled with tears. "Considering the circumstances now, I wish I could take it all back."

Stacy pressed on. "Playing online, how does it work?"

"It's a one-on-one. I'm battling the monsters of Wonderland."

"The mouse, the Five and Seven of Spades and so forth."

"Exactly. The narrative is the same, but I'm the future's only hope."

"It's up to you to kill the evil White Rabbit and all his Wonderland henchmen, thus saving the world."

She nodded. "The White Rabbit controls the game, absolutely. He creates the traps, the monsters, everything. Before beginning the game, I'm notified of every monster I'll face. But not when or where the confrontation will take place.

"I'm also informed of their particular strengths, powers and weapons. It helps level the playing field. And eliminates the temptation to improvise as you go, creating just the power or weapon necessary to defeat the player."

"Is play determined by the roll of dice, as in the live version?"

"Yes. Electronic dice. I receive the result of all moves against me from the White Rabbit. And the result of my moves against the others from him as well."

"How do you know he's telling the truth? He's got the dice."

"What would be the point of lying?"

In a regular game, with a sane game master, sure.

But with an obvious whack job like this guy?

"My friend Cassie, could she have been part of this game?"

"I don't know for sure, but I don't think so."

"Did you and she discuss White Rabbit or this game at Café Noir?"

"No."

"You're telling me the truth, right? It's really important."

"I didn't, I swear. We talked about gaming in general, but not White Rabbit. It's not really done, and certainly not with a stranger."

Stacy believed her. "Who knew you were playing?"

"No one."

That she found hard to believe. She told her so.

"It's true! White Rabbit's that way. Dad suspected, I suppose. He knows I game. It's not unusual for an online gamer to have several scenarios going at once."

"Do you know what monsters lay ahead?"

Alice typed in a code, accessing the game. She read them aloud. "The Mad Hatter and March Hare. The King of Hearts. The Cheshire Cat. And the White Rabbit."

"When do you have to make your move?"

"Soon."

"Can you put him off? Delay your move?"

"No more than twenty-four hours. If I fail to act, I'm automatically eliminated."

And in this game, being eliminated was fatal.

"I think I know who he is, Alice."

"Who? Not Dad."

"No, not your dad. Dick Danson."

"Dad's old partner? But he's——"

"Dead? Maybe not." Stacy explained about her trip to California and what she had learned. "I don't have any proof yet, but I will."

"Soon?"

"I'm going to try. The first thing we need to do is get Detectives Malone and Sciame in here. Show them what you've just shown me."

A look of panic crossed her features. "What if they don't believe me? What if they think——"

"They won't," she said, gently squeezing her hand. "I'll be right here."

"Promise?"

Stacy did, then went to the door and called Spencer and Tony. Malone poked his head out the door of the bedroom on the other side of hers.

"I think you might want to take a look at this," she said, motioning them over.

They crossed to the computer. Stacy swiveled the monitor toward them, watching Spencer's face as he scanned the documents, seeing the moment he understood what he was looking at.

He faced Alice. "You have some explaining to do, Ms. Noble."

Stacy stepped in, filling them in on what Alice had told her: how she had become involved in the game, where she had met the White Rabbit, how the game was played online. And that, if they were right, Kay was still alive. "It wasn't until her mother disappeared that she realized she was involved," she finished. "Then she did the right thing and came forward."

Spencer sent her a look that clearly communicated that *he'd* be the judge of that. "You have no idea who the White Rabbit is?"

"None." She looked at Stacy as if for confirmation. She saw that the girl's lips trembled.

"We'll have to confiscate your computer," he said. "We can trace—"

Stacy cut him off. "Can I see you in the hall? Now?"

He nodded, though he looked irritated. He followed her to the hall and faced her, hands on hips. "What?"

"You can't take her computer."

He arched his eyebrows in question. "That so? Why?"

"Alice has to respond to the White Rabbit in twenty-four hours or her character is eliminated. And in this game, being eliminated really is the end of the line."

"Shit." He looked away, then back. "You have a suggestion, Killian?"

"Copy all her files. I bet she's got a built-in CD burner, so it shouldn't take too long. Plug them in downtown."

"Just leave the door between her and that bastard open?"

"Closing it might be more dangerous for her. It'd also tip him that we're onto him. In the meantime, get a court subpoena to force her e-mail provider to release the name and address on the White Rabbit's e-mail account."

He gazed at her a moment, eyes narrowed, then nodded tersely.

Several moments later, Tony was on his cell, setting their plan in motion. Alice sat slumped on the edge of the bed, arms curled around her middle. Stacy sat beside her, listening to Tony.

"What's going on in here, Stacy?"

Before she could respond, Alice caught sight of him. "Dad!" she cried.

She ran to her father and threw herself into his arms. "I didn't mean for this to happen! I didn't know, I promise I didn't!"

"Baby, what—"

"Mr. Noble," Spencer interrupted, "I need to take you down to headquarters for further questioning."

"No!" That came from Alice. She spun toward Spencer. "He didn't do anything! Don't you see—"

"It's okay, Pumpkin." Leo separated himself from her. "They're just going to ask me some questions. I'll be back in an hour."

CHAPTER
50

Friday, March 18, 2005
8:10 p.m.

Stacy stayed with Alice, and while the minutes ticked past, she did her best to reassure the girl. Reminded her that her father had done nothing wrong and that as an innocent man, he had nothing to fear.

After a while, it seemed the girl wasn't even listening. It was as if she had drifted off to a place where she couldn't be touched. If she had noticed that more than an hour had passed since the detectives had left with her father, she didn't mention it.

Stacy fell silent as well. She made sure they ate the meal Mrs. Maitlin had left, then straightened the kitchen. All the while, she went over the facts as she knew them, conscious of the ticking clock.

The e-mail from the White Rabbit had come in at 3:00 p.m. Which meant they had until the same time tomorrow to catch him.

Why was Malone wasting time questioning Leo? Danson was behind this. Her gut told her he was.

Now she needed proof.

She glanced at her watch for what she knew was the dozenth time in the space of as many minutes. Why hadn't Billie called? She had hoped her friend would unearth something quickly.

She called the other woman's cell phone, left a message, then began to pace.

"I've figured it out," Alice said suddenly.

Stacy stopped pacing and looked at her. Alice sat at the kitchen table, a pen in her hands, staring at what appeared to be doodles she'd made on her napkin. "Figured out what?"

"What the White Rabbit's up to." She motioned to the napkin. "Wonderland is a maze, fashioned in a sort of spiral."

Stacy crossed to her and saw that her doodles were actually a sort of diagram. "Go on," she said.

"I was playing the game, working my way through Wonderland. Each victim has been a step closer to the epicenter of Wonderland. The Queen and King of Hearts." She paused. "Mom and Dad. And me."

Stacy was amazed at the girl's calm. "But you've already gotten to the Queen. If she's at the epicenter—"

"The Rabbit left me an opening. I jumped the gothic forest and got to her. I disabled her and vaulted back because the forest was a dead end. No road to the King."

"What about the Cheshire Cat? The e-mail indicated she was making her move."

"It makes perfect sense. The Cheshire Cat is a shape-shifter. And a ferocious fighter."

"With long claws and sharp teeth."

She nodded. "I put myself in Dad's former partner's head. If it's him, he wants revenge. He wants to punish Dad. And Mom. And what better way to do so than by using the game Dad stole as a means to kill him?"

"Stole? That's not the way I heard it went down."

"I'm in his head. Trying to think like him. He's angry. Resentful. His life went nowhere. Dad's a huge success."

"So he's not crazy," Stacy murmured. "Just wants to look like he is."

"Not crazy," Leo said from behind them. "He's brilliant."

"Dad!" Alice cried, running toward him. "Are you okay?"

He took her in his arms and hugged her tightly. "Fine, Pumpkin."

But he wasn't, Stacy thought. He looked as if he had aged ten years in the past ten hours. The lines around his eyes and mouth appeared more deeply etched than before, the light in his eyes seemed to have been extinguished.

The detectives had put him through his paces.

"How'd it go?" she asked quietly.

"I'm home." His simple answer spoke volumes.

Alice curled her hand around his. "Are you hungry?"

When he shook his head, she pursed her lips. "I'm making

you a sandwich. Or there's some of Mrs. Maitlin's chicken gumbo left."

"Sandwich."

She didn't ask what kind. Stacy watched as she fixed her dad a big peanut butter, honey and banana sandwich. She also poured him a glass of milk.

Watching the two interact brought a lump to her throat. It was an oddly sweet dynamic, the child caring for the parent. For all her adolescent bluster, Alice adored her father.

Alice looked at Stacy. "Dad and I used to eat these every Saturday morning for breakfast."

"While we watched cartoons." He took a bite, then washed it down with milk.

"Roadrunner was his favorite."

"Because of Wile E. Coyote," he said.

"What was your favorite?" Stacy asked the teenager.

"I don't remember. Maybe the same." Her eyes became glassy with tears. "Any news about Mom?"

"Not that they told me." He set the remainder of the sandwich on the plate. "I'm sure they're looking, Alice."

Bright color spotted her cheeks. "No, they're not! They're wasting time questioning you."

Stacy had to agree. She kept her mouth shut.

"They asked lots of questions," he murmured. "About my relationship with Kay. Our financial agreement, my recent licensing deals. What I did last night."

"The search turn up anything?"

"Of course not."

"Sometimes nothing looks like something. It happens, Leo."

He shifted uncomfortably, his gaze moving to a point somewhere behind her.

She narrowed her eyes slightly. *Was there something he didn't want to say?*

He looked at her then, giving his head the smallest of shakes. As if to say "Not now, not here."

She understood. Besides, he and his daughter needed some time alone.

And she needed to talk to Malone. She intended to convince him she was right.

She excused herself, grabbed her purse and car keys and headed outside. As she climbed into her car, she called Malone from her cell.

"Where are you?" she asked.

"Home." He sounded as tired as Leo had looked.

"Where's home?"

"Why?"

"We need to talk."

For a long moment he was silent. "I'm talked out, Killian."

"Alice told me more about the game." A tiny exaggeration, but one she could live with. "And my short-term memory's not so great."

He rattled off his address and hung up.

CHAPTER
51

Friday, March 18, 2005
10:30 p.m.

Stacy made Malone's Irish Channel address in no time at all. He lived in an in-the-process-of-being-renovated Creole cottage, which made her wonder if he was doing the work himself. And if he was, when he found the time.

The front door opened just before she knocked. Malone leaned against the doorjamb, arms folded across his chest. His soft, worn T-shirt pulled across his shoulders.

"Going to ask me in?"

"Do I have to?"

"Asshole."

He laughed and stepped aside.

She entered his house and he shut the door behind her. He'd

been eating a pizza, she saw. Out of the box. In front of the TV. ESPN.

Typical guy.

"Beer?" he asked.

"Thanks."

He got one for both of them, handed her hers, then turned off the television. Facing her, he asked, "The kid had information?"

"Insight, really."

He cocked an eyebrow; she suspected he was onto her already—that she was not here with information, but to plead her case. Again.

She set the stage, anyway, explaining how Alice had described Wonderland being a spiral and about the King and Queen being at its epicenter. "Each death brought the killer, through Alice, a step closer to them."

"So?"

"So, it makes sense that Danson—"

"The ex-partner thing again?"

"What can I say, I'm a one-note song."

"Right." One corner of his mouth lifted in wry amusement. "Shoot."

"Alice is playing the game, but none of the deaths has been by chance. The drawings you recovered from Pogo's studio prove that all the deaths are predestined. The White Rabbit is executing his very well-thought-out plan in an effort to terrorize."

"Or create a smoke screen."

She ignored that. "Obviously, to be able to control the game the way he has required someone with superior knowledge of the game. A master player."

He opened his mouth to comment; she stopped him. "He also has to be someone who had no hesitation about involving Alice in murder."

"And her father wouldn't?"

"Think about it, Spencer. A father involving his daughter in the murder not just of others, but of her mother, as well. That'd make him—"

"A monster?"

"Yes."

"If not a monster, how do you describe someone who's willing to kill for nothing more than financial gain? Where do you draw the line?"

"Hear me out. Danson's the game's co-inventor. He and Leo parted acrimoniously. Leo went on to wealth and celebrity and Danson—"

"Killed himself."

"Or not. He's brilliant. He concocts a plan to punish Leo—"

"You're beautiful when you're determined."

"Don't try to distract me."

"Why not? It worked."

She made a sound of frustration.

"You always have to be right, Killian? You always have to be in the driver's seat?"

"Don't make this personal."

He set his beer bottle on the kitchen counter. "All right, the facts. Leo's also co-inventor. He's the one who received the first messages from the White Rabbit. He had personal knowledge of each of the victims. He's the one with the most to gain from Kay's death."

"Says you."

"Consider this, Stacy. The drawings we recovered from Pogo's, there were drawings of all the major characters, except the King of Hearts. What do you think that means?"

That he was a better cop than she had given him credit for.

She decided to defy logic, anyway. "Perhaps the artist simply hadn't started that drawing."

"That's bullshit. And you know it. No drawing means the King of Hearts' death wasn't predestined. Because he's the killer."

It all made sense. Perfect sense. Why couldn't she buy into it?

"Leo's on Gallery 124's mailing list," he added. "Put on about the time of Pogo's show."

No wonder they had been closing in on Leo, even before Kay disappeared. "What about Cassie? What's the connection there?"

"There's not," he said flatly. "We arrested Bobby Gautreaux this morning. We charged him with the three UNO rapes. And plan to charge him with Cassie Finch's and Beth Wagner's murders soon."

She caught her breath. "On what evidence?"

"DNA. He left a hair at the scene. We swabbed him and got a match. I checked it against the blood your attacker left in the library—"

"And got a match," she finished for him.

"Yup. From the blood left there…and the semen from the rapes."

He took a swallow of his beer. "In addition, he left a print at the Finch and Wagner scene. He threatened and stalked Cassie. We found her hair on his clothing. And he warned you to keep your nose out of the investigation."

She couldn't quite believe what she was hearing. Bobby Gautreaux had been the one who attacked her. He was a serial rapist. And he'd left solid physical evidence tying himself to the murder scene. It was shaping up to be a strong case.

She was glad. Relieved.

Her goal had been to ensure Cassie's killer would be caught. *But it didn't feel right. Why?*

"What's he saying?" she asked.

"That he's innocent. That he was there that night, but he didn't kill her. What he whispered in your ear, you were correct about it. He was warning you to keep your nose out of the investigation. Because he'd been there. But he claims he didn't kill either of the women."

Same thing they all said. "Why'd he go to Cassie's that night?"

"Wanted to talk to her. About their relationship."

"They had no relationship. They hadn't in nearly a year."

"Of course they didn't. He's lying. That's what snakes like Bobby Gautreaux do. What was he supposed to tell me, he went there to murder her?"

"You think he went there intending to kill her?"

"I like it. With intent means the state can go for murder one."

"Find the weapon?"

He frowned slightly. "No."

She took a long drink of her warming beer. "Why didn't you tell me before now?"

"I've been a little busy."

"This doesn't change my thoughts on Leo's inno—"

"Maybe this will." He took a step toward her. "Remember how I accused Leo of creating an elaborate smoke screen to get away with killing his wife? That after meeting you, he handpicked you to help him?"

"How could I forget?"

He took another step closer. "He's writing a screenplay, Stacy. About a game inventor who receives threatening cards depicting the deaths of characters from his most famous creation."

She felt as if Spencer had punched her.

"You're in the story, Stacy," he said softly, crossing to stand behind her. "The emotionally wounded ex-cop who's running from her past."

Leo had manipulated her from the get-go.

The past was repeating itself.

She turned away from him, crossed to the window, stared out at the darkness. What? Did she have a sign on her forehead proclaiming *Easy Mark. Stupid, Gullible Fool?*

"And ultimately," he continued, "she can't resist the inventor's charms and falls willingly into his arms—"

"Stop it, Spencer." She whirled to face him. "Just shut up."

She held his gaze, even as she struggled to keep what he was saying in perspective. To fit all the pieces of the puzzle together, including this one.

Struggling to separate herself from the feeling of betrayal threatening to strangle her.

Leo had been writing a screenplay. The whole time. He'd planned this, used her.

"You uncovered it in today's search."

It wasn't a question; he answered, anyway. "Yes. Locked in his desk."

"You questioned him about it?"

"Yes. Claimed he just started it. That he recognized its 'narrative potential.'"

That's what Leo's guilty expression had been about tonight. The reason why he had avoided meeting her eyes and shifted uncomfortably.

"Narrative potential," she repeated, hearing the bitter edge in her own voice. "People are dying."

"For a brilliant man," Spencer said softly, "he sure is stupid."

"Leaving such potentially damning evidence hardly seems the work of a supergenius, does it?"

"Stupid to cross such a smart, beautiful woman," he corrected.

She made a sound of pain. "I surely don't feel either of those things right now. Try gullible idiot."

Several moments passed. He swore, then cupped her face in his palms. "Strong. Smart. Determined."

As she gazed at him, something inside her turned over. Or opened up. Without pausing to think it through, she kissed him. After a moment, she broke the contact. "I thought you wouldn't make a pass at me because I'd kick your ass?"

"You made the pass. All ass-kicking is off."

Stacy smiled. "I can live with that."

CHAPTER
52

Saturday, March 19, 2005
7:15 a.m.

Stacy awakened early. She moaned, stretched and realized in a galvanizing jolt where she was. And what she had done.

Shit. Shit. Damn. Damn.

What was wrong with her?

She cracked open her eyes. Spencer lay next to her——sleeping. He'd half kicked off the blanket and she saw that he was naked. Gloriously, fabulously naked.

She squeezed her eyes shut. He hadn't been exaggerating about his bedroom abilities. The man was so hot, he could melt butter on his backside.

What had he thought about her?

No. She didn't care what he thought. Last night had been a big, stupid mistake. Another to add to her fast-growing list of screwups.

Once upon a time, she had been so smart. So capable.

She could barely remember what that had been like.

Carefully, so as not to wake him, she slid toward the edge of the bed. She figured she could slide off it, gather up her stuff and get out before he woke up.

That'd give her time to prepare her "let's forget this ever happened" speech.

She eased toward the edge. The angle at which she lay facilitated a head-and-hands-first escape. Her hands found the floor; her torso eased over the side.

As she prepared to make her final descent, his hand clamped around her ankle, trapping her.

Shit. Shit. Damn. Damn.

He was awake. And here she was, hanging half off the bed. Naked. Backside up.

"Could you let me go, please?" she managed to say.

"Do I have to?" She heard the amusement in his voice and grimaced. "The view's spectacular."

"Thanks. But yes, you do."

"Pretty please?"

She groaned and he let her go. She slid off the bed, landing in an inelegant heap.

He leaned over the side of the bed and smirked at her. "Moving mighty quietly this morning, Killian. Tired? Too sore to stand?"

Her face heated. "I was just heading…going to—"

"The bathroom."

"Home."

"Sneaking out without so much as a goodbye? Or a thanks for the good time? Tacky, Killian. Extremely."

She yanked the sheet free, wrapped it around her and stood. "Don't make this more difficult than it already is."

He propped himself up on an elbow. "This is difficult?"

"You know what I mean. Awkward. Embarrassing."

"Oh, sure." He threw back the bit of blanket still covering him and climbed out of bed. And stood buck naked in front of her. "I know just what you mean. Totally embarrassing."

The man deserved to die, she decided. Unfortunately, she'd left her Glock back at the Noble place.

She went for the next best thing, a bed pillow. She flung it at him as he made his way to the bathroom. She missed and it hit the bathroom door casing, then dropped to the floor.

His laughter ringing in her ears, she snatched up her panties and tugged them on, careful to hold on to the sheet. She found her bra, made certain the bathroom door was still shut, then dropped the sheet. From there, she went for her trousers.

She retrieved them from where they hung half on and half off the dresser, her cheeks heating as she remembered shimmying out of them, then flinging them over her shoulder.

Her cell phone, clipped to the waistband of her pants, buzzed. She'd set it to mute, she remembered. Unclipping it, Stacy saw that she had a new text message waiting.

The game's exciting, isn't it? It will be more so for you.
Soon, Stacy. Very soon.

She reread the message, blood humming in her ears. From the White Rabbit, she acknowledged. A warning.

She was next.

Stacy glanced at her watch. It read 7:20 a.m. The game's clock was still ticking. In slightly more than seven hours Alice had to make her move. Against the Cheshire Cat.

Who had sent the message? Leo? Danson?

Or neither?

The bathroom door opened; Spencer stepped out. He'd wrapped a bath towel around his waist. It did little to cover him, but she appreciated the effort.

"Nice getup," he said, referring to her panties and bra.

"We have contact."

"Excuse me?"

"A text message on my phone. Take a look."

He crossed to stand behind her, then read the message over her shoulder. When he'd finished, he shifted his gaze to hers. "Want to give him a call back?"

"I'd love to."

She punched in the number. It rang once, then clicked over to voice mail. She angled the phone so Spencer could hear it as well.

"Hi. You've reached Kay Noble of Wonderland Creations. Leave a message and I'll get back to you."

Stacy ended the call. "Not a good turn of events."

"No shit." He strode across to the bed, snatched up his own cell phone and punched in a number. "Rise and shine, Pasta Man. We've got mail."

While he spoke to his partner, Stacy scooped up the rest of her clothing and headed to the bathroom to finish dressing. When she returned to the bedroom, Spencer was fully dressed and strapping on his shoulder holster.

She remembered when she'd had a shoulder holster. Remembered the weight of it, the way it had hugged her side. The way wearing it had made her feel.

"Tony's working on getting the location that call came from. At the least, the cell company will be able to triangulate a position. At best, with GPS technology, they'll pinpoint the exact location. I'm predicting the latter. I seriously doubt Kay Noble was carrying anything but the most up-to-the-moment cell technology."

"You think she's dead, don't you?"

He stilled, looked at her. "I hope to hell she's not."

But it didn't look good. Not for Kay Noble.

And not for her.

Six hours, forty-five minutes. And counting.

"I need a favor," she said.

He cocked an eyebrow in question.

"I want to talk to Bobby."

"That's going to be tough, he's in the Old Parish Prison. I doubt he'd put you on his visitor list."

"You could get me in."

"And why would I do that?"

"Because you owe me?"

"After last night, I would have thought it the other way around."

He had a point, she thought, a smile tugging at her mouth. She held her ground, anyway. "If I hadn't injured young Mr. Gautreaux, you wouldn't have had the blood to link him to me, then to the three coeds."

Spencer folded his arms across his chest. "True."

"Look, I just want to talk to him. I want to hear it from his own lips. That he didn't kill Cassie and Beth."

He paused, then sighed. "Okay, I'll see what I can do. But you have until two o'clock this afternoon to do your thing."

"Then what? I turn into a pumpkin?"

"I put about a dozen men trailing you. If this guy makes a move on you, we'll be there."

CHAPTER
53

Saturday, March 19, 2005
8:10 a.m.

Malone made a couple of calls and managed to get her on the prison admit list. But before she paid Bobby a visit, she needed to check on Alice.

"How're things there?" Stacy asked when Mrs. Maitlin answered the phone.

"I've never seen Mr. Leo so subdued."

"How about Alice?"

"Quiet."

"May I speak with her?"

The woman agreed and went in search of the teenager. Moments later the girl greeted her. "Stacy? Where are you?" she asked.

"Checking out a lead. Are you all right?"

"Fine. The police sent someone over. He's out front, guarding the place."

Probably shooting the shit with Troy. "Good."

"You didn't come home last night."

"I stayed with a friend. How's your dad?"

"He's getting ready for a meeting downtown. You want to talk to him?"

She thought of his screenplay. "No, I don't think so."

For a long moment, Alice was silent. When she finally spoke, her tone was hushed. "Dad's scared. He won't admit it, but I can tell."

Scared of getting killed? Or caught? "It's going to be okay, Alice. I'm not going to let anything happen to you."

"When are you coming back?"

"Not long. Don't do anything until I get there. Understand? No messages to the Rabbit."

"Yes, ma'am."

She used the title to tease and Stacy smiled. What had happened to the surly teenager who had once warned Stacy to stay out of her way?

Stacy ended the call by reminding Alice she was no farther than a phone call away.

Spencer had arranged her admit pass to the prison through his cousin, who happened to be on staff there. He'd told Stacy to ask for Connie O'Shay; she was being admitted as a court-appointed therapist.

"Thanks for doing this," Stacy told the redhead.

"Always happy to help a fellow clinician."

Stacy didn't correct her, and within minutes she was facing Bobby through unbreakable Plexiglas.

She picked up the phone. He did the same. "Hi, Bobby."

He sneered at her. "What do *you* want?"

"To talk."

"Not interested."

He started to hang up, but she stopped him. "What if I tell you I don't believe you killed Cassie and Beth?"

Her words surprised her as much as they appeared to surprise him. He returned to his seat.

"Is this a joke?"

"No. You may be a rapist, Bobby, but I don't think you're a killer."

"Why?"

Just a hunch, slimeball. "Let me ask the questions."

"Whatever." He slouched in his seat.

"Why'd you go to Cassie's that night?"

"I wanted to talk to her."

"About?"

"Getting back together."

"Right."

He lifted a shoulder. "Call me a romantic."

"So, you didn't go there to kill her?"

"No."

"Then why? To rape her?"

"No."

"I see why the police arrested you, Bobby. You have no credibility."

"Fuck you."

"No, thanks." She stood. "Have a nice stay."

"Wait! Sit down." He waved her toward the seat. "I saw her leaving Luigi's, out by campus. So I followed her home."

"Just because?"

"Yeah. Like a fuckin' idiot."

"And?"

"I sat out front. For a long time."

She could imagine the young man, staring at Cassie's house, getting angrier by the moment. Hating her. Wanting to punish her. To make her pay for hurting him. His ego.

For rejecting him.

"And?"

"I decided to force the issue."

Force. Bad word for a serial rapist to use.

"What happened?"

"She answered the door. Let me in. We talked."

"That credibility thing's happening again." He didn't respond; she pressed the issue. "She wouldn't have willingly let you in, Bobby."

"No?"

"No. So, you pushed your way in. You're angry. You want to let her have it for rejecting you. Embarrassing you."

She leaned slightly forward. "What stopped you?"

"Someone came to the door."

She experienced a tickle of excitement. "Who?"

"Don't know. It was some guy. Never saw him before."

"Could you pick him out of a photo lineup?"

"Maybe." At her disbelieving look, he became defensive. "I was angry. Jealous. Figured she was screwing him. I left."

"Did she greet him by name? Think, Bobby. It's important. The sentencing difference between a rape and murder conviction is the rest of your life."

"She didn't."

"You're certain?"

"Yes, damn it!"

"You told the police this?"

"Yeah." He shrugged. "They figured I was lying."

So they weren't bothering to look. They had their guy. "Was he tall? Short? Medium height?"

"Medium to tall."

"Dark-haired or—"

"He had a cap on."

"A cap?"

"Yeah, a stocking cap. The kind that hip-hop dude, Eminem, wears. Black."

"He carrying anything?"

Bobby screwed up his face, as with thought. "Nope."

"You see Caesar?"

"Her mutt?" He nodded. "Little shit tried to piss on my shoes."

Caesar was out when he was there. Cassie had locked him up after Bobby left. "You have any idea what kind of car the guy was driving?"

He shook his head and she silently swore. *Great.* "Why'd you attack me in the library?"

"Because you were there," he said simply. "And because I was pissed at you. I wanted to scare you."

"Hope I didn't disappoint you too much."

He looked down at his hands, cuffed together, then lifted his face to hers. They smoldered with rage. "Better hope I don't get out of here."

"I'm not too worried."

"You think you're so cool, don't you? So tough." He leaned toward her. "If I had wanted to hurt you, I could have. If I'd wanted, I could have fucked you silly."

Stacy stood. She calmly hitched her purse strap across her shoulder. She knew the more unaffected she was by his tirade of filth, the more agitated it would make him.

She reached the door and glanced back. "If you'd tried, Bobby, that ballpoint would have been in your eye. Or straight up your ass."

She exited the Parish Prison. Sunlight spilled over her and she breathed deeply, feeling as if she needed to be cleansed from the inside out.

Bobby Gautreaux was a dirty little snake.

But had he killed Cassie?

He may have. But quite possibly he was telling the truth.

She crossed the parking lot, unlocked her SUV and climbed inside. She hadn't visited her apartment in a week and she supposed she'd better stop by and check on things.

* * *

The first thing she noticed was the overflowing mailbox at her apartment. The second, that her calls had not been forwarding to her cell number.

Her message light was blinking. She hit Play and listened to several hang-ups, and then messages from her sister and her graduate adviser.

"Stacy. Professor McDougal. I'm concerned about you. Please call me."

Professor McDougal. Great. Just frigging wonderful.

She stared at the answering machine, even as she acknowledged that she could stare at it until Christmas and it wouldn't alter the fact that she was screwed. When was the last time she had actually attended class? She had a paper due Monday. She'd barely even started it. What, she wondered, was the last day to withdraw from classes without a grade penalty? She'd bet she'd already missed it.

Suddenly crushingly tired, Stacy rubbed her eyes. She crossed to her couch and sank onto it. She laid her head against the back and closed her eyes. She wasn't going to pass her first semester of graduate school, and if she didn't pass, she wouldn't be welcomed back. Even if her professors were willing to let her try to bring her standing to current, she didn't have the time to devote. Finding the White Rabbit took precedence. Protecting Alice, saving Kay. Living to see the next semester.

Or maybe the truth was, she didn't have the heart for school.

Her cell buzzed. Though a part of her wanted to ignore the call, she unclipped the device. "Killian here."

"Billie Bellini, super spy."

Stacy sat forward, instantly focused, all thoughts of grad school falling away. "What have you uncovered?"

"No missing persons, but I think you'll find this interesting. Dr. Carlson donated his time and professional abilities to the homeless. One day a week, he saw people referred to him from the local shelters and missions."

Stacy knew where Billie was going with this: indigents weren't likely to be reported missing. No employer to sound the alarm, no family or friends looking for them.

The dentist could have chosen someone with a similar build to Danson's and switched their dental records. Then Danson did the rest.

Danson plans it all carefully. He leaves a suicide note. Packs his trunk with propane. Offers the bum a ride. Or incapacitates him. The charred body is positively identified by his dental records.

"Did the chief have any comments on your discovery?"

"He's going to take a look at the dentist's patient files and financial records. He'll officially reopen the case if he finds anything suspicious." She sounded proud. "He contacted Malone at NOPD and promised to keep in touch with us as well. If Charles Richard Danson is alive, we're going to nail him."

Stacy stopped on the name. She frowned. "What did you call him?"

"Charles Richard Danson. That was his full name, though everyone called him Dick."

Charles Richard Danson.

Stacy froze, remembering a conversation she'd had with Alice's tutor about his name. He'd joked about his parents giving him decidedly unsexy names.

Clark Randolf Dunbar.

Initials, C. R. D.

"Holy shit," Stacy said. "I know who he is."

"What?"

"I've got to go."

"Don't you dare until you tell me—"

"Danson made a fatal mistake. The same one many people who try to drop out, or create a new identity, make. He chose a name with the same initials as his previous one. It's human weakness. A desire to hold on to the very past they're trying to leave behind."

"So who is he?" Billie asked, tone hushed, admiring.

"Clark Dunbar," she said. "Alice's tutor."

CHAPTER
54

Saturday, March 19, 2005
9:30 a.m.

Stacy flipped her phone shut and ran for the front door. She darted through, locked it and jogged to her car, parked on the street. She stopped and swore when she saw it. She was wedged in. Both the car in front and behind her had squeezed into too-small spots, leaving her about three inches to maneuver with.

Not enough.

Leo's place wasn't much more than a half a mile away. She could make it on foot in six or seven minutes— without denting any fenders.

She started off, urgency pushing her. She dialed Malone. He picked up right away. "Malone."

"Run a background check on Alice's tutor, Clark Dunbar," she said.

"Hello to you, too, Killian. A little intense this morning, aren't we?"

"Just do it."

He became all business. "Ran him through the NCIC already. No priors."

"Take it a step further."

"What's going on?"

"Clark Dunbar's the White Rabbit." A car sped by, windows open, hip-hop blaring. "I can't go into it now, just trust me."

"Where are you?"

"On my way to Leo's. On foot." She paused at a crosswalk, looked both ways, then darted across—earning the scream of a horn. "Don't ask. Let me know what you find out."

She hung up before he responded and dialed Leo's cell number. "Leo, Stacy. I think Clark's the White Rabbit. If you see him, stay away. Call me when you get this."

She called the mansion next. Mrs. Maitlin answered.

"Valerie, have you heard anything from Clark?"

"Stacy? Are you all right? You sound—"

"I'm fine. Have you? Heard from Clark?"

"He's here."

Stacy's heart dropped. "He's there? I thought he was out of town for the weekend."

"He was. I was so surprised to see him. Something about a reservation mixup, he said. Hold on a second."

Stacy heard a male voice in the background, then the housekeeper's reply. In the next instant, the woman returned. "So sorry. Where were—"

Stacy cut her off. "Just now, was that Clark?"

"No. Troy."

"Valerie, this is important. Where's Clark now?"

"Outside. With Alice."

God, no. The crossing light changed and Stacy darted across the City Park Avenue and Wisner Boulevard intersection, cutting over to Esplanade. To her left stood City Park with its tennis and golf complexes, lagoons and the New Orleans Museum of Art.

"What about the police officer?" she asked. "Is he still there?"

"Out front."

"Good. I want you to get Alice," she said, working to keep her voice even. "Call her to the phone. Do not mention my name to Clark. Understand?"

"Yes, of course."

"When Alice is inside and safe, get the officer. Have him stay by Alice's side until I get there."

"What's going on?" The woman sounded rattled. "Should I call—"

"Just get Alice. Now, Valerie."

Stacy heard the woman lay down the phone as she went after the teenager. She counted the seconds as they ticked past, heart thundering in her ears, praying the man didn't catch wind that they were onto him and hurt Alice.

Just as she began to sweat, Alice came on the line. "Stacy, what—"

"Clark's the one, Alice. The White Rabbit. Mrs. Maitlin is getting the police officer, and I'm just two blocks away."

"Clark? That can't—"

"It is." Alice sounded terrified. "Stay put, do you understand? Until the officer comes inside, pretend you're still on the phone."

Alice agreed; Stacy reholstered her cell and broke into a run. It made perfect sense. Clark, with unfettered access to the household. To everyone in it, their schedules and routines. As Alice's tutor, access to her thoughts and feelings. Her computer. As Kay's lover, he had been privy to the woman's most intimate thoughts.

The night she disappeared, Kay had welcomed him into the guest house. That's why there'd been no sign of forced entry.

Until the bedroom, where he'd attacked her. Until the point she realized he wasn't who he professed to be.

He had played them all. Expertly.

But that's what a game master did.

Spencer and Tony arrived at the Nobles only a moment behind her. She waited for them at the front gate.

"Clark's here," she said, without greeting the two men. She filled them in on her call to the mansion.

"Good work," Tony said.

"Thanks." She glanced at Spencer. "You ran a background check on Dunbar?"

"Clark Dunbar doesn't exist. Bogus social. Not registered at the DMV. How much you want to bet the Nobles never checked even one of his references?"

It never ceased to amaze Stacy how trusting people were. Even ones with as much to lose as Leo Noble.

"How did you know?"

"Billie. She learned that Danson's real name wasn't Dick. It was Charles Richard Danson. Guess what Clark's middle name begins with?"

"An R."

"Bingo. Billie also learned that the murdered dentist who identified Danson by his dental records volunteered his services to the poor and disenfranchised."

"The 'poor and disenfranchised,'" he repeated. "The kind of folks who can go missing without anyone sounding an alarm."

"Give the man a gold star."

"So, he faked his own death, changed his appearance with plastic surgery—"

"And headed down to New Orleans to rain a little bizarre justice down on his former partner and ex-girlfriend."

They reached the front door, which, as usual, was opened by Mrs. Maitlin. Alice stood with her, clinging to the woman's arm. "He's gone," Mrs. Maitlin cried. "When I called Alice inside, he walked to his car, climbed in and drove off. I realized what had happened and got Officer Nolan, but it was too late."

"Where is Nolan?"

"He went after Clark."

Spencer swung to Tony. "Get him on the radio!"

The other man sprang to action. Stacy wouldn't have guessed Tony could move so fast. She indicated to Spencer that she would take care of Alice and Mrs. Maitlin. He nodded and she herded them inside.

They waited in the kitchen. Mrs. Maitlin made herself busy baking cookies, distracting Alice by enlisting her help. Just as the delicious aroma from the first batch began to fill the room, Spencer appeared at the doorway. He motioned to her.

"Don't eat them all while I'm gone," Stacy teased, forcing lightness into her tone.

Spencer led her out to the foyer. "Nolan lost him. We put out a broadcast for Danson and his car. A search warrant for his quarters is on the way."

Her cell buzzed. She saw it was Leo. She mouthed the man's name to Spencer, then picked up the call. "Leo, where are you?"

"Downtown." The connection crackled. "I got your message. Clark's the White Rabbit? My God, how did you—"

"There's more, Leo. Clark is Danson."

"Dick? You can't mean—"

"I do. He faked his own death. Must have changed his appearance with plastic surgery, intent on punishing you for how he imagined you cheated him."

Leo went silent, so silent Stacy thought the call had been dropped. "Leo? Are you still—"

"Yes, I'm here. Just digesting. It's hard to believe—" His words broke on a sound of surprise. "What the...my God, you're—"

Stacy heard a loud *pop*.

A gunshot.

"Leo!" she shouted. "Shit, Leo—"

Spencer grabbed the phone. "Mr. Noble? This is Detective Malone. Are you all right? Mr. Noble?"

Stacy watched Spencer, hoping, knowing her hope was futile.

He looked at her, expression grim. "I don't want the kid to be alone," he said, handing her the phone.

She looked at its display.

Call ended.

9:57 a.m.

Stacy swallowed hard, hurting for the teenager. "I'll stay with her."

"Better yet, I'll send her over to Tony's. She'll be safer there."

CHAPTER
55

New Orleans' central business district at 5:00 p.m. on Saturday resembled a movie set more than a bustling commercial district. Dusk had begun to settle over the tops of the skyscrapers, although calling them skyscrapers was a little like calling a donut a beignet. The two had elements in common, but the donut lacked the *Ahh* quality of a beignet.

Spencer stood on the sidewalk just beyond the established perimeter, a narrow alley across the street from the International House Hotel. Tony pulled up, parking his Ford behind the Camaro.

They'd located Leo. He and Tony had gotten the call just as they finished the search of Danson's quarters and storage locker. The preliminary search had uncovered little, besides proof that Clark really was Dick Danson. Spencer hoped they had better luck here.

Leo had been shot once. Right between the eyes.

"How's the kid?" Spencer asked, referring to Alice.

"Scared," Tony answered. "Carly's taken her under her wing."

"Did you hear from the aunt?"

"Not yet. Left a message."

Alice hadn't been told about her dad—yet. Spencer prayed her mother was alive to comfort her, but he didn't hold out much hope.

They crossed to the first officer, signed in, then ducked under the crime scene tape. The crime-scene guys and the photographer were doing their thing; they spared little more than a glance and nod in acknowledgment of Spencer and Tony's arrival.

They crossed to the body, located not twenty-five feet from the entrance of the alley.

Noble lay flat on his back, eyes open, staring blankly up. Judging by the wound, he'd been shot at close range, probably with a small caliber pistol. Cell phone and briefcase beside the body.

Tony squatted beside Noble. "Still wearing his Rolex. Briefcase looks intact."

Spencer snapped on latex gloves and checked for the man's wallet. He found it; eased it out and flipped it open. "Three hundred bucks. Credit cards. Motive certainly wasn't robbery."

"You surprised by that?"

Spencer smiled grimly. "I look surprised, right?"

"Oh, yeah. Brazen son-of-a-bitch. Did it in broad daylight. Downtown, just off Camp Street."

Spencer visually inspected the contour of the body, then moved his gaze outward. "Where's his calling card?"

As if on cue, one of the techs called, "Yo fellas, you might want to take a look at this."

They crossed to the man. He had his flashlight beam pointed at a doorway, at several pieces of debris the wind had pushed into the corner.

Spencer saw immediately what had caught the tech's attention: a Ziploc plastic bag.

Spencer bent and carefully retrieved the bag. The killer had drawn a smiley face on it. Inside he'd placed a single item. The King of Hearts card.

Tony absently rubbed his five o'clock shadow. "I like a psycho who clearly tells us it's his crime. Takes the guesswork out of the job."

"Let's bag it and tag it," Spencer said to the tech.

"If it's Dunbar, he knows we're onto him. He wants to get the job done, even if it means getting nailed."

"Figures he's made already." Spencer narrowed his eyes. "I'm glad the kid's squared away. Until this asshole's in custody, she's a mark."

"Maybe our guy just wanted to take out the big kahunas?"

"Uh-uh. Remember Pogo's drawing of Alice hanging by the neck, quite obviously dead."

"Right. But no King of Hearts, and he got whacked."

Spencer glanced up at the rapidly darkening sky, then back at his partner. "Stacy had a theory on that. The artist simply hadn't gotten to that illustration. I wasn't buying that then. Am now."

"Smart lady. Maybe you should let her know what's going on?"

"That wouldn't exactly be by the book."

"Screw the book. She's one of the good guys." Tony motioned to the first officer. "I'll get a canvas of the area started. Maybe somebody in one of these businesses saw something."

Spencer nodded and watched his partner walk away. Stacy *was* one of the good guys.

But that wasn't why he wanted to call her.

He unclipped his cell and dialed Stacy. "Hey," he said when she answered. "Are you okay?"

"I'm fine. Is Leo—"

"Yes. Dead—shot between the eyes."

"The White Rabbit?"

"If a certain playing card here at the scene is any indication."

"Shit. Poor Alice. You've got to find Kay."

"We're doing our best." He glanced over his shoulder; the coroner's investigator and his driver had arrived. "Got to go, Killian. Call you later."

CHAPTER
56

Spencer did one better than calling Stacy. He went to see her.

He rang the bell.

Stacy answered the door after a couple of rings. He couldn't be certain, but he suspected she had been crying.

"Haven't you heard? Game's over. Leo's dead."

He held up a takeout sack. "I brought Subway. Have you eaten?"

"I'm not hungry."

"How about some company?"

"Why not?" She turned and headed into the double. He followed her, shutting the door behind them.

They ended up in the kitchen. He saw a bottle of beer on the table, her Glock beside it.

She crossed to the fridge, got another beer and handed it to him.

"Thanks." He twisted off the cap and took a long swallow, watching as she returned to her table and took another drink.

"None of this is your fault," he said softly.

"No? You're sure?" Her voice vibrated with a combination of grief and fury. "Leo's dead. Kay's most probably dead. They hired me to keep them safe. And if so, Alice—" her voice broke "—is an orphan now. I did a great job, didn't I?"

"You did the best job you could."

"Is that supposed to make me feel better?" She balled her hands into fists. "He was right under my nose. This whole time, he—"

Spencer crossed to her, drew her to her feet and cupped her face in his hands. "He was under all our noses the whole time. You're the only one who had a clue what was really going on."

Tears welled in her eyes. "A lot of bloody good it did anybody."

She was trying so hard to be tough. To focus on her anger. To pretend she didn't hurt. Didn't feel helpless.

He trailed his thumbs across her cheeks. "I'm sorry."

"Stop it. Stop looking at me that way."

"Sorry, Killian. No can do."

He bent and kissed her. Her lips trembled beneath his. He tasted the saltiness of her tears.

She flattened her hands against his chest. "Stop it," she said again. "Stop making me feel weak."

"Because you have to be strong."

She tilted up her chin. "Yes."

"So you can stand up to the bad guys. Kick their asses, maybe even save the world."

She stepped away from him. "I think you should go."

"So it can be just you and Mr. Glock?"

"Yes."

"Your choice, Stacy. If you change your mind, you have my number."

He drained his beer, collected the take-out and left her. He crossed to the NOPD cruiser parked in front of the duplex. He bent and greeted the officers inside. "Keep a close eye on the place. I'm going to catch a few hours' shut-eye, then I'll be back."

CHAPTER
57

Sunday, March 20, 2005
2:00 a.m.

Stacy awakened with a start. She realized she was uncomfortably hot. That she was sweating. She moved her gaze over the dark room, focused on the illuminated dial of her bedside clock.

As she registered the hour, a floorboard creaked.

She wasn't alone.

Stacy rolled, reaching for her gun.

It wasn't there.

"Hello, Stacy." Clark stepped out of the shadows, her Glock in his hand. Pointed at her. "Surprised to see me?"

She scrambled into a sitting position, heart thundering. "You could say that. Someone as smart as you, I thought you'd be long gone by now."

"Really? And where would I go?" He sucked in an angry sounding breath. "Everything was going so well until you stuck your nose into it. My business. Mine!"

She worked to keep her head, keep the panic at bay. To maintain regular breathing and heartbeat. She did a mental inventory of her position, the situation. No one to hear her scream. No weapon.

Only her wits.

She couldn't lose them.

He crossed to stand beside the bed, gun trained on the point directly between her eyes.

Between the eyes. That's where Spencer said he'd put the bullet that killed Leo.

"Why'd you do it?" she asked. "Why throw your whole life away?"

"What life?" He all but spit the words at her. "I was in debt up to my eyeballs. The cops circling like vultures to pick at my carcass. And Leo, living like royalty. I deserved to live like that. He stole my ideas! He refused to give me my due!"

"And Kay, did he steal her, too?"

He laughed. "You can't imagine the satisfaction it gave me, knowing I was screwing his wife, right under his nose."

She stared at him a moment, looking for some resemblance to the young man pictured in Leo's yearbook. She found none. "Ex-wife," she corrected. "I think that would have dimmed your satisfaction a bit."

Color flooded his face. *He meant to make his move.*

She rolled to the right, reaching for the bedside clock, intent on smashing it into his face. She didn't move fast enough. His hand closed over hers, wrenching the device away.

He flung it aside; it hit the wall and shattered. In the next instant, he was on top of her, the gun's barrel pressed to her temple. He brought his free hand to her throat. "I could kill you now. So easily. Hand to your throat, gun to your head. So many choices."

"What's stopping you?"

She asked, though she knew. He wanted to brag. Wanted to relive his actions through her reactions to them.

He didn't let her down. "It was fun. Watching them squirm. Poisoning Alice's mind. Turning her, little by little, away from her parents. They treated her like a baby. I pointed that out constantly. I reminded her that she was smarter than both of them. That they only thought of themselves, their needs."

She watched his face, the light in his eyes as he spoke. The man was a maniac.

She told him so.

He laughed. "That day, when Kay and I walked in on you and Leo," he said, "we laughed about it later. Leo still loved Kay. In his own perverse way. But he thought of her as his property. He'd have had a fit if he'd known about us. She told me. She told me everything."

"When exactly was that? Before you killed her? Or while you were doing it?"

"You think you're so smart. But you don't know shit." He smirked at her. "Maybe I should show you what a real man can do? Kay told me I was better in bed than Leo. That he never satisfied her the way I did." His weight pressed her into the soft mattress. Trapping her. Smothering her. "I could do the same for you."

She struggled for a breath and against the urge to fight. Fighting would do nothing but force him to act. She silently counted each breath to ten, then tried another tack.

"You were angry," she said quietly, tone nonjudgmental. "Furious with Leo. And Kay. You decided to use the very game Leo stole as a way to make him pay. A way to get away with killing him."

He laughed, the sound derisive. "Stupid, stupid bitch. I'm not the White Rabbit."

Considering the circumstances, his declaration took her by surprise. He saw that and leered at her. "Your precious Leo is. He came up with the whole White Rabbit thing to get away with killing Kay. Because she gets half of everything. The half that should have been mine. Greedy bastard wanted more, so he decided to get rid of her.

"She told me she was afraid of him," he continued. "She told me she feared he was behind the notes. That he might do something to hurt her. Because of the money."

"That'd be a neat explanation, Mr. Danson. Except for one small problem. Leo's dead. You killed him this afternoon."

For an instant, his expression went slack. With surprise. Disbelief. His hand shook. She felt the gun tremble against her temple.

He intended to pull the trigger.

Stacy thought of her sister, Jane, her baby; she thought of all the things she had never done.

She didn't want to die.

"You're going to jail for a long time," she said, hearing the desperation in her voice. "Killing me isn't going to change that. They know who you are. You have nowhere to go. If you think—"

"If you think I'm going to jail, think again, bitch."

Before she could react, he turned the weapon on himself and pulled the trigger.

Her scream mingled with the sound of the blast.

His brains decorated the delicate floral wallpaper with gore.

CHAPTER
58

Sunday, March 20, 2005
3:12 a.m.

"We have to stop meeting like this."

Stacy lifted her head and looked at Spencer, standing in the doorway to the kitchen. He wore soft-looking blue jeans, a House of Blues T-shirt and the windbreaker from the night at the library. She wondered if he had a Snickers bar tucked into the pocket.

"Are you okay?" he asked.

"Define *okay.*"

He crossed to her, bent and dropped a kiss on the top of her head. The gesture brought tears to her eyes. She fought them.

She hadn't cried earlier. She wouldn't now.

He pulled a chair out, turned it to face her and sat. "Can you talk about it?"

She nodded and ran a trembling hand through her hair, still damp from the shower. After the officers stationed out front had found her and helped her get out from under Danson's dead weight, she'd run to the bathroom to wash—to try to cleanse herself of the experience.

She explained about waking, about Danson confronting her with her own gun.

"He hated Leo. Blamed him for everything that had gone wrong with his life. He admitted his affair with Kay. Claimed he was poisoning Alice's mind against her parents. Getting sick kicks out of it."

She looked away, then back. "He wasn't the White Rabbit."

"Come again?"

"He claimed Leo was. That Leo had created an elaborate plan to get rid of Kay. For financial gain. He claimed Kay was afraid of Leo. That she believed he might hurt her, because of their financial agreement."

"As I'm sure you're aware, there's a big problem with that theory."

"No joke. He realized it, too, when he learned Leo was dead." She pressed her point. "He didn't know Leo was dead. When I told him...he got this look. He knew he was screwed. That he was going to jail. So he blew his brains out."

He frowned. "I don't know, Stacy. Maybe you should sleep on this."

"You still think Danson's our guy?"

"Sorry."

She supposed she didn't blame him—he hadn't been there, he hadn't seen Danson's face when he learned about Leo.

Stacy stood, shocked to realize her legs shook. More shocked to realize she had no idea what to do. Of her next move. She felt numb and uncertain.

Numbness she was familiar with. Cops turned off their emotions a lot, some with alcohol or drugs. It was one of the reasons the divorce rate for cops far outpaced that of the civilian population.

Uncertainty was another matter. She'd always been a woman prone to action, even when that action proved rash.

To not know what move to make next, terrified her.

He crossed to her, took her hands in his. "They're cold."

"I'm cold."

He folded her in his arms and rubbed her back. "Better?"

"Yes." He made a move, as if to ease away from her, and she tightened her arms. "Don't go. Hold me."

He complied and gradually his body warmed hers. She stepped regretfully away from him. The broken contact brought a sense of loss. A thread of panic. "It's really late, isn't it?"

"Yes. You should sleep."

"Lovely thought. Problem is, when I close my eyes—" She pressed her trembling lips together, hating the show of weakness.

"I could stay?"

She met his direct gaze, held out a hand.

He took it. And led her to the guest bedroom.

Fully dressed, they slid under the covers and lay facing each other.

He had known, without asking, without having to be told, that wanting him to stay had been about comfort. And company. Not sex or sexual desire.

"Warmer now?"

"Much." She curled her fingers into his soft T-shirt. "Would you believe that once upon a time, I was in control of my life? I hardly ever made mistakes. Now...I'm a total screwup."

He laughed softly and trailed his fingers through her hair, brushing it away from her face. "You, Stacy Killian, are the antithesis of a screwup."

"*Antithesis* is a mighty big word."

"I learned that one just to impress you. Did it work?"

She'd already been impressed. She smiled weakly. "Absolutely."

"Glad to hear that. I'll learn another one for tomorrow." He rested his forehead on hers. "It's true, you know. You are the most capable, self-assured, kick-ass woman I've ever known. Excluding my aunt Patti, of course."

"Your aunt Patti?"

"My mother's sister. My godmother. And my direct superior at ISD."

"She a captain?"

"Yup. Captain Patti O'Shay. One of only three female captains in the NOPD."

"Bet she didn't flunk out of grad school. Or have everyone she was supposed to be protecting get whacked, practically right under her nose?"

"If you want to go and talk about screwup, I'm your man. The one who only worked enough to get by. Who never considered the consequences. The one who thought it was all one big drunken frat party."

"You? That's not the man I know."

"You've brought out the best in me, Stacy Killian. Made me see what I wanted to be. The kind of cop I wanted to be."

"I'm not a cop anymore."

"We both know you're a cop in every way but one."

She opened her mouth to argue; he stopped her. "You want to know the humiliating truth?" he asked softly. "I'm not ISD. I didn't earn it. It was given to me."

"For being such a screwup?"

"I'm baring my soul here, Killian. This is serious."

Stacy fought a smile. "Sorry."

"It was payola," he continued. "To keep me from suing the department."

She caught his hand, curved her fingers around his in silent support.

"I'd finally made detective. Way behind my brothers. And in all truth, partly because of them. My DIU superior set me up. Lifted a kitty of snitch money and made me the fall guy. Everybody bought into it because of my reputation."

"Not everybody, I'll bet. Not Tony. Not your family."

"No, not them." A smile touched his mouth. "Thank God."

"What happened then?"

"Because of the few who stood behind me and wouldn't give up, Lieutenant Moran was caught. I was reinstated. And given ISD so I wouldn't make trouble for the department. I jumped at it."

She was quiet for a long moment, thinking of the man he described himself as being and the one she had come to know. "Are you sorry?"

"That I was given ISD?"

"That it happened? If you could make it all go away, go back to who and what you were before, would you?"

He stared at her a moment, expression a curious combination of surprise and introspection. Then a slow smile curved his lips. "You know, I don't believe I would."

"Good." She returned his smile. "Because I'm liking the man I'm looking at right now."

He moved to kiss her, then stopped and swore. "I'm buzzing." He drew away, unclipped the device and brought it to his ear. "Malone here. It'd better be good.

"Gone? When?" His expression tightened. "Dammit, Tony, how the hell did you——"

Concerned, Stacy sat up. Spencer held up a hand to hold off her questions. He paused to listen; when he spoke again, Stacy knew she hadn't been mistaken about what she'd heard.

"This is worse news than you know, Pasta Man. Dunbar's dead. And he-may not have been the one."

A moment later, he hung up. Stacy was already out of bed, straightening her clothes. "Alice is missing, isn't she?"

"Yes."

"How did that happen? What, did she just walk out?"

"Basically." He climbed out of bed. "Earlier in the evening, Betty thought she heard Alice's phone ring and the girl answer. She didn't think anything about it. A while later, she decided to take a peek at the girl, make certain she was okay. She wasn't there."

"How long ago was this? She couldn't have gotten far on foot."

"A couple hours."

"Damn. This is bad."

Spencer frowned. "By the way, where do you think you're going?"

"To find Alice."

"I don't think so."

"The hell I'm no—"

"The game could still be in play. I want you to stay put. Understand?"

"But Alice—"

"Tony and I will find her. You stay. She may come here looking for you."

Stacy opened her mouth to argue; he stopped her with a kiss. After a moment, he drew away. "I don't want anything to happen to you. Promise me you won't do anything stupid?"

She did, though as he left her apartment she acknowledged that her promise depended on his definition of *stupid*.

CHAPTER
59

Sunday, March 20, 2005
7:30 a.m.

Stacy awakened. She'd had strange dreams, ones populated with characters out of *Alice in Wonderland*. Ones that had disturbed her sleep and left her feeling fatigued and edgy.

Spencer hadn't called. Which meant they hadn't found Alice.

She'd given them their chance.

Today she joined the hunt.

Resolve set, Stacy climbed out of bed and headed straight for the bathroom. After starting the coffee she showered and dressed.

The coffee had brewed. She filled a travel mug, added sweetener and cream, grabbed a granola bar and headed out.

Stacy intended to search the mansion and guest house. Check in at Café Noir. City Park. Gaming stores. Any place Alice might be hiding out.

As she neared her car, Stacy saw that someone had left a flyer under her windshield wiper.

No, she realized when she retrieved it, not an advertisement.

A zip-style storage bag. With a note card inside.

Carefully extracting the bag from under the wiper, she opened it and slid out the card.

Her knees went weak; her hands began to shake.

A drawing. Like the ones Leo had received. This one of Alice.

Hanging from the neck. Face engorged and bloated with death.

She swallowed hard, forced herself to open the card.

Game in play. Clock ticking.

She stared at the message, mouth dry. Danson had been telling the truth. He wasn't the White Rabbit.

Think, Killian. Take a deep breath. Slow down. Put it together.

If the White Rabbit held to history, the card meant Alice was still alive. That the White Rabbit either had her in his sights—or worse, in his grasp.

Clock ticking. He was giving her the chance to save Alice's life. Game was in play and it was her move.

Her cell phone sounded and she jumped. She unclipped the device and answered the call. "Killian here."

"Hello, Killian."

A man. Voice deliberately masked.

The White Rabbit.

"Where is she?" Stacy demanded. "Where's Alice?"

"That's for me to know and you to find out."

"Cute. Let me speak to her."

He laughed and she tightened her grip on the phone. Whoever he was, he was enjoying this immensely. Sick bastard.

"If you want to see Alice alive, you'll do what I say. No cops. Understand?"

"Yes."

"Take Carrollton Avenue uptown to River Road. There's a bar at the corner of River Road and Carrollton Avenue. Cooter Brown's. Go in. The bartender has an envelope for Florence Nightingale."

"Let's just cut to the chase here, shall we? What do you want?"

"To win the game, of course. Be the last man standing."

"You think you're good enough?"

"I know I am. You have thirty-five minutes. One minute late and it's goodbye, baby."

Esplanade to Carrollton Avenue at the river would take a good twenty-five minutes. Maybe more with traffic.

Which left her damn little leeway. She darted back into her apartment, retrieved her Glock and left the White Rabbit's message on the kitchen counter for Spencer to find. Just in case.

Back outside, she grabbed her travel mug off the car's hood, unlocked the door and slid inside. She started the vehicle, checked the side mirror and pulled into traffic.

The dash clock read 8:55.

Traffic heading uptown alternately sucked and sailed. She wheeled into Cooter Brown's parking area in twenty-eight minutes. A mural on the side of the building boasted the bar was home to 450 different kinds of bottled beer. She slammed the SUV into Park and darted inside.

The interior was dark and smelled of cigarettes. A couple of biker types stood by the pool table, cues in hand. They stopped playing and watched her cross to the bar.

The bartender looked tough. Big, muscular, with a bald head and a full beard.

"You have something for Florence Nightingale?" she asked. "An envelope?"

He didn't reply, simply crossed to the register, opened it and extracted an envelope. He handed it to her.

She glanced at it, then back up at him. "What can you tell me about the person who left this for me?"

"Nada."

"What if I tell you I'm a cop?"

He laughed and walked away. She glanced at her watch. *Thirty-two minutes.* She tore open the envelope.

Inside was a phone number. Nothing else.

She unclipped her cell and punched in the number. He answered right away.

"You like to live dangerously, don't you, Killian? You're just under the wire."

"I want to talk to Alice."

"I'm sure you do." She heard the amusement in his voice.

"Patience is a virtue. But you never had any of that, did you? Your sister, Jane, on the other hand, she's the patient one. And by the way, I love the name Jane and Ian picked for their baby. Annie. So sweet. Uncomplicated."

Stacy went cold. "If you harm anyone I love, I swear I'll——"

"What? I hold all the cards. You can do nothing but follow my directions."

She bit back what she wanted to say and he laughed. "Take River Road toward Vacherie. Stop at Walton's River Road Café. Cool your heels until I call you. One hour, Killian."

"Wait! But I don't know where I'm going! One hour might not be——"

He hung up before she finished. Swearing softly, she hurried outside and to her car, squinting as the sun stung her eyes. Moments later she was on her way.

Called River Road because it followed the contour of the Mississippi River, the winding road was alternately scenic and industrial. If what she remembered was correct, it wound its way to Baton Rouge, then up to St. Francisville, Natchez and beyond.

She wondered how far the White Rabbit intended for her to go.

She caught site of Walton's River Road Café up ahead, a charming Creole cottage nestled in the curve of the road. A magnificent oak tree graced the front of the property, so large it shaded most of the structure and half the side parking area.

Her cell phone rang. Startled, she nearly swerved into oncoming traffic. She got to her phone, flipped it open. "Killian here."

"Hello, there. You sound a little tense."

"Can I call you back?"

Spencer's pregnant pause said it all. "I'm in the bathroom," she lied. "Talk to you in five."

She ended the call and swung into the café's shady parking lot. It'd been a small lie, she told herself, because in a minute she would be using the restaurant's facilities. And from there, in case she was being watched, she would return Spencer's call.

"Please say you called to tell me you have Alice," she said when he answered.

"Sorry."

"Any leads?"

"No. But every cop in the city has a picture of her. We're canvassing the neighborhood around Tony's. So far, no one's seen anything."

"You searched the mansion?"

"Last night and again today. No luck. We have someone stationed there, just in case."

Damn it. She hadn't expected better. But she had hoped, anyway.

"What are you doing?" he asked.

"Cooling my heels."

"I'm glad to hear that."

Behind the counter, a busboy dropped a pan of dirty dishes. She jumped.

"What the hell was that?"

"Dropped some dishes. Trying to keep busy, multitasking here."

"Multitasking?"

She forced a laugh. "You didn't know I could do that, did you? I have many talents."

"Yeah, you do." She heard Tony say something, though she couldn't make out what. "Got to go. I'll keep you posted."

"Call my cell. I'll have it on."

He paused. "You're going somewhere?"

"I might have to run out. You know how it is."

"I know how you are. Stay put."

He hung up, and she exited the ladies' room. No one paid her any undue attention. She chose a table by a window that looked out at the parking lot. Being able to watch her vehicle made her feel less vulnerable.

The waitress, a girl not yet out of her teens, stopped at her table. Stacy realized that she was starving. "What's wonderful on the menu?"

The girl shrugged. "Everything's pretty good. People like our soup. It's homemade."

"What's today's?"

"Chicken noodle."

Comfort food. A good thing, considering the circumstances.

Stacy ordered a cup and, continuing with the comfort theme, a grilled cheese sandwich.

That done, she sat back in her seat. She glanced at her watch, thinking of the White Rabbit and when he would call. Thinking of Alice. Worrying.

And acknowledging that he had her just where he wanted her.

Alone and unable to make a move until he was ready.

CHAPTER
60

Sunday, March 20, 2005
6:20 p.m.

The White Rabbit called just as evening began to fall. And just as she had begun to believe she'd been duped.

"Comfy?" he asked, obviously amused.

"Very," she replied. "I've been sitting here so long my ass's numb."

"It could have been worse," he murmured. "I could have had you wait in a place with no bathroom. With no food or drink."

Chill bumps moved up her spine. Had he been watching her this whole time? Did he know she had used the bathroom and had eaten? That she'd spoken to Spencer? She moved her gaze over the restaurant, the other patrons. Looking for one talking on a cell phone.

Or was he assuming? Anticipating how his words would affect her?

One thing was certain, he was playing her like a drum.

"Can the dramatics. What do you want me to do next?"

"Head up the road six miles. Turn toward the river. From there, turn left onto the first unmarked drive you come to. Leave the car. Follow the oak alley. You'll know what to do. You have twenty minutes."

He hung up, and Stacy reholstered her phone, grabbed her check and got to her feet. After leaving the waitress a generous tip for tying up her table for so long, she hurried to the door.

"Everything okay, sweetie?" the woman at the register asked as she totaled the bill.

"Great, thank you." She glanced at the woman's name tag. Miz Lainie. "Can I ask you a question?"

"Sure, sweetie. Shoot."

"Up the road, toward the river, what's up there?"

The woman frowned. "Nothing. Just what's left of Belle Chere."

Stacy handed the woman a twenty-dollar bill. "Belle Chere, what's that?"

"You're not from down here, are you?" The bell above the door jangled. Miz Lainie looked up and scowled at a tall young man coming through the door. "Steve Johnson, you're late! Fifteen minutes. Do it again and I'm callin' your mama."

"Yes, ma'am."

He winked at Stacy and she bit back a smile. Obviously, he wasn't buying Miz Lainie's tough act.

"And hike up those pants."

He sauntered past, hitching up his trousers.

"I'm sorry," Stacy said, "but I have to go."

The woman returned her attention to Stacy. "Belle Chere's an antebellum plantation. In its heyday, it's said to have been one of the finest in Louisiana."

That was it. That was where the White Rabbit was holding Alice.

The woman made a sound of disgust. "They've just let it go to ruin. Me and the mister, we always thought the state or somebody'd step in and—"

"I apologize," Stacy said, cutting her off, "but I really do have to go."

She exited the café, jogged to her car. No doubt the woman thought her rude to cut and run, especially after loitering for the past several hours, but there was nothing she could do about that.

Fifteen minutes and counting.

She started the car, backed out of her parking space, then roared out of the lot, kicking up gravel as she did. She flipped open her phone and dialed Malone. An automated message announced the subscriber was unavailable, then dumped her into his voice mail.

"The White Rabbit has Alice. He said he'd kill her if I didn't come alone. Don't worry, I'm not alone. Mr. Glock's with me. Belle Chere Plantation. Six miles up from Walton's River Road Café in Vacherie."

She snapped the phone shut, knowing he'd be furious with her.

She didn't blame him. If it'd been her case, she'd be furious, too.

Stacy followed the Rabbit's directions and soon came upon the plantation. A chain barred access to the drive—a sweeping pathway lined by a double row of towering oaks, their branches creating a magnificent, arched canopy. A No Trespassing—Private Property sign was posted on either end of the chain barricade.

Stacy parked her car as best she could, then climbed out. She started up the oak alley.

Her first look at Belle Chere took her breath. It stood in ruins, a ghostly, crumbling hulk. It looked as if much of the roof had caved in. Two of the columns had toppled, their ornate Corinthian capitals lay abandoned, fallen soldiers in the army of time.

Yet it was still beautiful. A magnificent specter, glowing in the twilight.

Beyond what was left of the big house stood a small, ramshackle structure. It didn't look like one of the original buildings. A caretaker's cottage? she wondered. By the looks of it, also abandoned.

Stacy started toward the main house, then picked her way up the rotting stairs to the front gallery. The doors had long since disappeared, either to decay or scavengers, and she made her way into the structure, Glock gripped firmly in both hands. As it was considerably darker inside than out, she wished she'd brought a flashlight.

The interior smelled of moisture and mold. Of decay. "Alice!" she called. "It's Stacy."

Silence answered. One that shouted the absence of human life. All life here buzzed, hummed or silently crept, devouring walls, floors and anything else in its path.

She wasn't here.

The caretaker's cottage.

Stacy carefully backed out. When she'd cleared the stairs, she made her way to the back of the property. Toward the cottage.

No light shone from the interior of the building. She touched the door; it creaked open. She slipped inside, weapon out. Stacy saw a small living area, empty save for beer cans, a couple milk crates and a smattering of cigarette butts. She wrinkled her nose. It stank of urine. Ahead lay two doorways, one to the right, the other to the left.

She moved toward the left first. The door had no handle. She saw that it stood slightly ajar. Gun gripped in both hands, she eased the door open with her foot.

In the dim light spilling through the adjacent window, she saw Kay and Alice huddled together in the corner. Their hands and feet were tied, their mouths secured with duct tape. The side of Kay's head was caked with what looked to be dried blood. From what she could see, Alice was unhurt.

Kay looked her way, eyes wide with alarm. Not for her own fate, for Stacy's.

A trap. RPGs were known for them.

He was either behind her. Or in the closet directly across from the women.

Stacy didn't enter the room. She mouthed the question to Kay. The woman's eyes flickered toward the closet.

Made sense. He expected her to race across to the pair to free them. Which would put her directly in his line of fire.

Alice straightened suddenly, as if becoming aware of something going on. She looked Stacy's way.

Which tipped the White Rabbit.

The closet door burst open; Stacy swung, aimed and fired. Once, then again and again, emptying her magazine into him.

He went down without getting off one shot.

Troy, Stacy saw. She gazed at him with a sense of relief. That it was over. The White Rabbit was dead, Alice and Kay had been saved.

And of disbelief that Troy, the handsome bimbo, "Mr. The-Living-is-Easy," was the White Rabbit? He was the last person she would have attributed enough smarts—or ambition—to have orchestrated this thing.

She'd been fooled before. By a man who'd been just as handsome. And just as heartless.

Stacy turned away from the fallen man and hurried across to the two women. She untied Kay first, then Alice, freezing at the distinctive click of a revolver's hammer being cocked.

"Turn around slowly."

Troy. Still alive.

He'd come prepared.

Stacy did as he ordered, cursing that she'd emptied her magazine. She met his eyes. "Back from the dead so soon?"

"Did you think I wouldn't expect you to be armed? Or that I didn't know you were an expert shot?" He thumped his chest. "A Kevlar vest, available from any number of gun dealers."

She forced a cocky smile. "Stings like hell, though, doesn't it?"

"Worth the sting, because now you're empty, another predictable move, by the way." He lifted his weapon, aiming directly at her head. "So, what are you going to do, hero?"

She stared at the gun's barrel, realizing she had come to the end of the road. She was flat out of both ideas and options.

"Game over, Killian."

He laughed. She heard Alice's scream, the roar of blood in her head. The shot's blast drowned out both. But the moment of shattering pain didn't come. Instead, Troy's head seemed to explode. He stumbled backward, then fell.

Stacy turned. Malone stood in the doorway, gun trained on Troy's still form.

CHAPTER
61

Sunday, March 20, 2005
7:35 p.m.

The next minutes passed in a blur. Malone called for an ambulance and a crime-scene unit. Informed dispatch of a fatality. Tony and Stacy led the two women outside to a car.

Moments later, Spencer joined them. "Everyone's on their way. Including an EMT unit." He turned to Kay. "Do you feel strong enough to answer some questions, Mrs. Noble?"

She nodded, though Stacy saw her clasp her hands in her lap—as if to keep them from shaking. Or keep her strong.

"He was crazy," Kay began softly. "Obsessed with White Rabbit. He bragged about how smart he was, how he was playing us all. Even Leo, the Supreme White Rabbit."

"Start at the beginning," Spencer said softly. "The night he abducted you."

"All right." She glanced at Alice with concern, then began. "He came to my door. Asked if he could speak with me. I let him in. I never thou   I never—"

Her voice cracked; she brought a hand to her mouth, visibly fighting for control. "I fought him. Kicked and clawed. He hit me. I don't know what with. Next thing I remember, I was in a car trunk. Tied up. We were moving."

"What happened then, Mrs. Noble?"

"He brought me here." She swallowed hard. "He came and went. He told me about…about killing—"

Alice began to cry. Kay put an arm around her shoulders and drew her daughter closer.

"He bragged about how he had taken out the King of Hearts."

"Leo?"

She nodded, eyes welling with tears. "Sometimes he just rambled."

"About?"

"The game. Characters." She wiped at the tears on her cheeks. "Killing Alice was his goal," Kay said. "He set it up to watch her character kill one player after another. Then when they were all eliminated, he'd kill her."

The woman looked at Stacy. "You eluded him. He couldn't kill Alice until you were out of the way."

And Alice was the bait to get her out here.

"There were other Alices," the girl said quietly. "I wasn't the first."

Spencer's mouth tightened. "Where? Did he say?"

They both shook their heads. Kay caught her daughter's hand and squeezed it tightly. "But she was the ultimate. *The* Alice. He found us through news stories and online interviews."

The EMTs arrived. Tony helped Kay and Alice to the ambulance.

Stacy watched them a moment, then turned to Spencer. "How'd you get here in time? We're two hours from your stomping grounds."

"You're not as good a liar as you think you are."

"The busboy dropping the pan of dishes?"

"Nope. Your promise not to do anything stupid. Got the okay to install a GPS tracking device to your SUV."

"How'd you get a judge to okay that?"

"Fudged the facts."

"I suppose I should be pissed."

He cocked an eyebrow. "Funny, I'm thinking I'm the one who should be pissed." He leaned toward her, lowered his voice. "That was a pretty dumb stunt. You know that, right?"

She could be dead. She would be, if not for him. "Yeah, I know that. Thanks, Malone. I owe you."

CHAPTER
62

Tuesday, April 12, 2005
1:15 p.m.

March became April. Much had happened in the two weeks since that night at Belle Chere. Stacy had given her statement no less than four times. It was discovered that Troy had been a drifter, an underachiever who had used his looks to prey on women—leaving them both broke and brokenhearted.

But very much alive. Without priors, his turn as the White Rabbit didn't fit a profile. But did prove that anything was possible when it came to criminal behavior.

The police were contacting the various places he'd lived, looking for any unsolved murders of girls named Alice.

So far they hadn't found any, but their search had just begun.

The White Rabbit case had been officially closed. Leo had

been buried. Spencer and Chief Battard in Carmel-by-the-Sea, California, had been in touch.

The accident the Carmel police had originally classified as Dick Danson's suicide had been changed to a homicide perpetrated by Danson. The victim: John Doe. Chief Battard hoped to change that before long.

Bobby Gautreaux had been officially charged with the murders of Cassie Finch and Beth Wagner. Stacy didn't know if she bought it, but she had reached the end of the road. Her leads had dried up, and the police and D.A. believed they had enough for a conviction.

Who was she to say otherwise? She wasn't a cop anymore. At least that's what she kept telling herself.

Of course, nor was she a grad student. Stacy pulled up in front of her apartment, parked and climbed out of her Bronco. She'd officially flunked out. The head of the English Department had acknowledged there'd been extenuating circumstances and agreed to allow her back in the fall. After all, up until Cassie's murder, she had been performing well.

She appreciated his understanding and offer, but had told him she wasn't certain what she wanted to do.

She was burned out.

Nothing moving back to Dallas wouldn't cure. Or so her sister said. They'd spoken that morning. Jane had done her best to convince Stacy to come home, at least until she knew for certain what she wanted to do. She'd filled her in on all Annie's firsts: she had begun to crawl, she was sleeping through the night, laughed at herself in the mirror.

Stacy missed her, too. She longed to be a part of Annie's life.

Then there was Spencer. She'd spoken with him that morning, as well. They'd hardly seen each other since that night at Belle Chere Plantation. Not that she wasn't interested in him.

But she had to take charge of her life, do what was best for her, long term.

A cocky homicide detective wasn't it.

At least, she didn't think so. Damn, but she was turning into a wishy-washy pain in the ass.

She climbed her porch steps and crossed to her door. Her new neighbor, a perky, rail-thin blonde, popped her head out her door.

"Hi, Stacy."

"Hey, Julie." The girl wore a spandex shorts set. From her apartment came the sound of an aerobic workout video. "What's up?"

"I've got a package for you."

She ducked back inside, then a moment later returned with a FedEx box. "They dropped this just after you left. Told 'em I'd make certain you got it."

Stacy took the box. For its size, it was fairly heavy. She rocked it, and the contents thumped against the sides of the box.

"Thanks."

"No problem. Have a great day!"

The girl disappeared inside. Stacy crossed to her own door, unlocked it and entered the house. She kicked the door shut behind her, dumped her purse and keys on the entryway table, then turned her attention to the package. She quickly realized there wasn't a shipping label affixed to the box and frowned.

She headed back over to her neighbor's and knocked.

Julie appeared at the door. "Hi, Stacy."

"Got a question. The package doesn't have a shipping label. Did they hand you one?"

"Nope. I gave you just what they gave me."

"You signed for it?"

The blonde looked confused. "No. I assumed I didn't need to. 'Cause they left a form or something at your door."

"They didn't."

"I don't know what to tell you, Stacy." By her tone, her confusion had become irritation.

"No probl— Wait! One last question."

The blonde stopped in her doorway, expression exasperated.

"The FedEx guy, was he in uniform?"

"She," Julie corrected, drawing her eyebrows together, as if trying to recall. "Don't remember."

"What about the truck? Did you see it?"

"Sorry." When Stacy opened her mouth to ask another question, the girl cut her off. "I'm missing the best part of the workout. Do you mind?"

Stacy said she didn't and headed back into her own apartment. She crossed to the box, grabbed the pull tab, tore it open and eased its contents out. The item had been secured in bubble wrap. A note card was taped to the wrap.

She freed the card and flipped it open. It read, simply:

The game's not over yet.

Stacy's hands began to shake. *The White Rabbit.*

It couldn't be.

Carefully, Stacy loosened the tape. Pulled away the bubble wrap.

Her breath caught. A laptop computer. An Apple, twelve-inch. Pretty white case.

One she recognized.

Cassie's computer.

Even as she told herself it could be any Apple laptop, she opened it, hit the "on" button. The device sprang to life.

She forced herself to breathe as the programs loaded; then the finder filled the screen. She scanned the files, stopping on one titled *My Pics*.

Stacy opened it. The preferences had been set for a slide show. Rows of thumbnail-size photos popped up. She clicked on the first. A photo filled the screen. Cassie and Magda, wearing New Year's Eve's hats and blowing horns. Next appeared one of the rest of the game group, doing a cancan. Then a photo of Cassie's mom and sister.

The next caused her heart to lurch to her throat.

She and Cassie. At Café Noir. Mugging for the camera.

A cry slipped past Stacy's lips. She jumped to her feet and strode to the front window. She pressed the heels of her hands to her eyes, struggling against the pain. The sense of loss.

She remembered the day that picture had been taken. Billie had taken it. With her camera phone. It seemed like just yesterday.

Cassie had been alive. And now she was gone.

Stacy balled her hands into fists. She had to focus. Not on the past. Not on the pain. But on what was happening. Why it was happening.

Bobby Gautreaux hadn't killed Cassie and Beth.

But who had? And why had they sent her the computer?

She dropped her hands and turned toward the device. They'd wanted her to know that Cassie's death and White Rabbit were linked. That Troy's death hadn't ended the game.

The White Rabbit was still at large.

Stacy sucked in a sharp breath, turned and went back to the computer. She closed the photo file and scrolled down the Finder menu, stopping on a file labeled *White Rabbit*.

Bingo.

She clicked on the item. It opened to a menu with only one item listed.

The Game.

Judging by the date, the document had been created Sunday, February 27, at 10:15 p.m.

The night Cassie had been killed.

Stacy opened it and began to read. A play-by-play game strategy, she realized. The game as she, Malone and the others had played that day. The White Rabbit had assembled all the characters. Da Vinci and Angel. The Professor. Nero. Alice.

And just as in the game they had played, the Dormouse, the two playing cards and the Cheshire Cat weren't characters.

They were the obstacles. The monsters sent by the White Rabbit to weaken or kill players.

The players.

Of course. They were all dead now. Even the White Rabbit.

All except Angel and Alice.

Stacy leaped to her feet. That was it! Of course. Sure, Leo got everything if Kay was out of the picture.

But that scenario worked in reverse, as well. None of them had considered it.

With Leo gone, Kay got everything.

Stacy began to pace. Excited. Kay had been the one who had known Pogo, who had put Leo's name on Gallery 124's mailing list. She'd been in cahoots with Troy. Somehow their plans had gone awry.

Because of her. It had to be.

So, who had sent her the computer?

Alice.

Alice had figured it out. Alice knew her mother was guilty. That she had killed Leo.

Killer Takes All. All the spoils. Leo's entire estate. The profits from the recent, lucrative licensing deals.

Stacy would bet Troy had become an employee of Wonderland Creations sometime after those deals had been made.

But what of Dunbar? Stacy rubbed her temples. Had Kay recognized him right off? Is that what had gotten her going? Had she realized Danson made a perfect fall guy and enlisted Troy's help?

The woman was brilliant. The plan had been brilliant.

I'm smarter than both of them. Did he tell you that?

Alice. She'd figured it out.

Of course, Stacy realized. Two characters still stood. The game wouldn't be over until all players were dead but one.

Killer Takes All.

Alice needed help.

Stacy brought a hand to her mouth. Did Kay intend to kill Alice, as well? Down the line, in a way that wouldn't arouse suspicion?

How did Leo's will read? Was Kay the sole recipient of Leo's wealth? Or was she merely a trustee?

Stacy snatched up her cell phone, punched in Malone's number, then hung up when she got the message service. Next she dialed ISD. The woman who answered informed her that Detective Malone was in a meeting and asked if she could direct her to another detective.

"Is Detective Tony Sciame available?"

He was, and several moments later, he came on the line. "Stacy, what's up?"

"I'm trying to reach Spencer. It's important."

"He's in with the captain and a couple of the guys from PID."

Public Integrity Division. Internal Affairs. The division that justified its existence by the number of cops they busted. A meeting with those guys always boded ill. She should know—just before she'd left the Dallas force, they'd raked her over the coals.

She frowned, concerned. "What's going on?"

"Don't know for sure. It's the captain's first half day back, and those jokers come bustin' in. Next thing we know, Malone's getting drilled."

"You're his partner, Tony. You've got to have a sense of what it's about."

He was quiet a moment. When he spoke, she sensed how carefully he chose his words. "He's been under the microscope and there've been a few irregularities recently."

A judge approved that trace?

I fudged the facts.

"It's because of me, isn't it, Tony? Because he kept me in the loop?"

"Not just that."

She swore. "What else?"

"I can't say."

"I'd be dead if not for Spencer. So would Alice."

But not Kay. How had the woman planned to explain it all away? By killing Troy? By managing to escape?

"Stacy? You there?"

"Yeah, I'm here. How long do you think Malone will be?"

"No guess. But they've been in there awhile already."

"Tell him to call me on my cell. It's about White Rabbit and Cassie."

"White Rabbit? But that's—"

"It's not over. Don't forget, okay? It's important."

"Stacy, wait—"

She hung up on him. She didn't have a plan for confronting Kay Noble, only a sense of urgency pressing her to action. Alice needed her. She doubted Kay would make a move so close to Leo's death, but she wasn't taking chances with the girl's life.

Or with her own.

With that in mind, she tucked her Glock into her handbag.

CHAPTER
63

Tuesday, April 12, 2005
3:00 p.m.

Stacy pulled up in front of the Noble mansion. She saw that Kay Noble had wasted no time: A For Sale sign hung from the property's iron fence; a minivan emblazoned with a moving company's logo sat in the drive.

Stacy parked, climbed out of her vehicle and started for the house. As she reached the front porch, Kay emerged from the house with a man Stacy didn't recognize. From the way he was dressed and the clipboard he was carrying, she assumed he was from the moving company.

The two shook hands; he told her he would be in touch, then walked away.

"Stacy," the other woman said warmly, turning toward her. "What a nice surprise."

"I wanted to check on you and Alice. See how you're both doing."

"Carrying on. Moving on."

"I see that."

"Too many memories." She released a sad-sounding breath. "It's been especially hard on Alice. She's been so quiet."

I'll just bet. Probably too terrified to speak.

Stacy made a clucking noise she hoped sounded genuine. "It's to be expected, I would think. She lost her father in a shocking way. She was exposed to a horror beyond the comprehension of most girls her age."

"I'm getting her counseling. Her doctor said to expect healing to take time."

The woman was the picture of love and concern. An award-winning performance, Stacy thought. Oscar-worthy.

"I just hope one day she can forget."

"May I see her?"

"Of course. Come in."

Stacy followed the other woman into the home. She saw that they had already begun consolidating their things for packing. She glanced around. "Is Valerie here? I'd like to tell her hello, as long as I'm here."

"Valerie's gone. She's moved on."

"Really? I'm surprised."

"She was Leo's hire, and now that he's gone... I guess she didn't feel comfortable."

Mrs. Maitlin had thought of herself as so much more than a "hire." She had considered herself one of the family. That had been obvious.

Stacy felt a moment of compassion for the woman. But only a moment: considering the circumstances, she was better off this way.

Kay crossed to the bottom of the stairs. "Alice!" she called. "Stacy's here to see you." She waited a moment, then called her daughter again.

When she still got no answer, she looked at Stacy. "That's the other thing, she's hardly come out of her room."

Again, probably afraid to. Probably couldn't bear to look at her mother.

The woman started up the stairs. "We owe you our lives, Stacy. And I want you to know how much I appreciate what you did for us. The chances you took."

Her dark eyes welled with tears and Stacy once again silently congratulated her on her performance.

"If you hadn't happened into our lives...I don't even want to think about it. We'll never forget you."

"I'll never forget you, either, Kay."

They reached Alice's room; Kay tapped on the closed door. "Alice? Stacy's here to see you."

The girl came to the door. When she saw Stacy, her lips lifted in a weak smile. "Hi, Stacy."

"Hey," she said softly. "How are you?"

The girl looked at her mother. "Okay, I guess."

"Kay," Stacy said, "go do what you have to do. I'll visit with Alice awhile."

The woman hesitated, then nodded. "I'll be downstairs."

Stacy watched her exit the room, then led Alice to the window seat. She wished she could close the door, but she didn't want to arouse Kay's suspicions.

Once seated, Stacy didn't waste time. Tone hushed, she began, "I received a very interesting package today." The girl didn't comment and Stacy went on. "A laptop computer. An Apple. You know anything about it?"

Alice glanced toward the open doorway, obviously terrified. Her throat worked, as if she was trying to speak but couldn't.

Stacy covered her hand. "I'll take care of you. I promise. Did you send me the computer?"

She nodded, eyes welling with tears.

"Where did you get it?"

"Found it," she whispered. "In a box of things Mom set out for trash pickup."

Trash pickup. Stacy flexed her fingers, fighting the anger that surged through her. That computer had been Cassie's, her most prized possession. The way Kay had discarded it was a metaphor for the way she had trashed Cassie's life.

"What made you go through the box?" she asked.

"I saw her put some of Dad's things in it. Things I wanted. She's been doing a lot of that. She——"

Her throat seemed to close over the words and she cleared it. "I knew she'd argue with me, call everything I wanted junk, so when she went for a massage, I went through the box."

"And that's when you found it?"

"Yes. In a black plastic garbage bag. I don't know why I looked in the bag, but the minute I saw it, I knew something was wrong. Mom never used an Apple. None of us did."

"What happened next?"

"I...I opened it. And turned it on."

She choked up then, tears spilling over. "I recognized your friend. And I knew."

The house phone rang. Stacy heard the jangle from the hall. Once, then twice. It stopped, followed by the faint murmur of Kay answering.

"Why didn't you call the police?"

"Because I...I trust you. I knew you wouldn't let her get away with it." She looked down at her hands, clasped tightly in her lap. "I've been so afraid she'd somehow...find out what I did. What I found. I think she means to...to—"

"What, Alice?"

"I think she means to kill me, too."

Stacy thought she did, too.

"I'm going to call Malone," she said softly, reaching for her holstered phone, finding the holster empty.

She'd left it in her car.

"What?" Alice asked.

"My cell's in the car. You stay put, I'll be right back."

She grabbed her hand, squeezing tightly. "Don't leave me!"

"I'm just running to the car. I promise I'll—"

"Use the house phone."

She shook her head. "Too risky."

"I'm coming, too."

Stacy freed her hand. "Stay put. We don't want to arouse your mother's suspicions."

"Please, Stacy." Her voice quivered. "I'm scared."

And no wonder, poor kid. Her mother was a cold-blooded killer.

Stacy glanced out Alice's window. Her car sat parked at the curb. She could retrieve the phone and be back in five minutes. Or less.

"My Glock's in my purse. You know how to shoot?"

She shook her head. "No."

"Aim and pull the trigger. Think you can do that?" The girl nodded. "I'll leave the gun with you. But don't touch it unless you have no other option. Understand?"

She said she did and Stacy opened the window. "Call me if you need me. I can be back up here in seconds."

She took one glance back at the teenager before she exited the room. The child was huddled on the window seat, Stacy's purse hugged to her chest.

Poor kid. How was she going to get beyond this?

Stacy descended the stairs, forcing herself to move at an un-hurried pace, just in case Kay appeared.

She made her car, retrieved her cell phone and called Malone.

He picked up. He sounded tense. "I can't talk."

PID. "Then just listen. Get over to the Noble place. Bring Tony and a couple uniforms with you."

"I don't have time for games just now—"

"Actually, the game's why I'm calling. It's still in play."

"Are you—"

"Certain? Absolutely."

"Stacy! Help!"

She looked up; the two women were silhouetted in the window. They were struggling. It looked as if Kay was trying to overwhelm her daughter.

"Get off of me! I hate you!"

Stacy swore. "I've got to go! Get over here—"

"What's going—"

"Just get over here. Now!"

She hung up and ran toward the house.

"Murderer!" Alice screamed. "You killed Dad!"

Stacy reached the front steps and launched herself up them, across the porch. The gun's blast came as she cleared the door. A high-pitched scream followed.

God, no. Please let the girl be safe.

Stacy took the stairs two at a time, making the top landing in seconds. She reached the girl's room. Alice faced the window. It stood open; Stacy saw that the screen had been pushed out.

"Alice?"

The girl turned. The gun slipped from her fingers. "I killed her."

"Where—"

Then she knew. She ran to the window and peered out. Kay lay faceup in the garden bed, her eyes open. Vacant.

Alice began to cry, the wail of sirens mingled with her sobs. "Come on," she said softly, wrapping her arm around the girl and leading her to the bedroom door. "They're going to need to ask you some questions. It'll be okay. I promise."

CHAPTER
64

Tuesday, April 12, 2005
4:10 p.m.

Malone, Tony and two cruisers arrived. Stacy met them at the front door, briefly explained what had occurred and let them get to work.

She stayed by Alice's side, all the while imagining the various teams processing the scene. She knew what to expect. For one thing, her Glock was now evidence in a murder case. She would not be getting it back for some time. In addition, they would need a detailed statement from both her and Alice.

And they would have to call *ChildWelfare Services* to come for Alice.

It was going to be damn difficult to let her go. She didn't know if she would be able to.

After what seemed an eternity, but was in reality about an hour, Spencer sought them out. He squatted in front of Alice. "You think you're up to answering a few questions?"

The girl looked at Stacy, eyes wide and terrified.

"May I stay with her?" Stacy asked.

When Spencer agreed that she could, the teenager breathed an audible sigh of relief. She began with how she had found the computer, how she realized the truth and about sending it to Stacy and why.

Her voice quivered when she reached the most recent part of the story. "She must have overheard us talking. Stacy left, and she appeared in the doorway. She was so…angry. She called me a…an ungrateful little bitch."

She clutched Stacy's hand. "She flew into the room. Going after me like a crazy person. I didn't know what to do," she whispered, voice small and shaky. "She had a…had a hold of me. She was dragging me toward the window…I had the gun. Stacy's gun. I took it in my hands and I…I—"

She broke down then. Sobbing. No doubt over her mother's betrayal. The loss of her father. And despair for her life, which had been forever altered.

It broke Stacy's heart. She held the girl while she cried, giving Malone her statement in pieces.

Tony ambled over to where they sat. "Good news," he said.

They all looked up at him. The words felt odd. Inappropriate and out of place. Could there be anything good about this day?

"I just talked to your aunt Grace, Alice," Tony said. "She was able to book a flight leaving tonight and will be in around midnight. I figured I'd meet her plane."

"Aunt Grace," the girl repeated, a tremor in her voice. As if she had forgotten she still had family. As if being reminded now that she did was the greatest gift she could have been given.

Spencer met Stacy's eyes briefly. "You go home, Tony. We'll meet that flight. The three of us."

Midnight at the New Orleans airport was a little creepy. A market the size of the Big Easy received very few flights this time of night. Their footsteps echoed in the cavernous terminal, all the kiosks and vendors had closed, and only a handful of weary agents manned the terminal desks.

Alice said little but hung close to Stacy as they waited at the end of the terminal. Thankfully, the woman's flight arrived on time. The pair held each other for a long time, clinging to one another and crying. As gently as she could, Stacy nudged them along, first to Baggage Claim for the woman's luggage, then the parking garage.

"We took the liberty of making a hotel reservation," Stacy said. "If you made other arrangements—"

"Thank you," Grace said. "No…I didn't even think…I always stay with…"

Her words trailed off. They all knew what she had been about to say.

She had always stayed with her brother. Leo.

Within thirty minutes, they had dropped Grace and Alice

at the hotel. Stacy accompanied the pair inside, made certain there wasn't a problem with the reservation, then returned to the car.

She buckled up. Spencer looked at her. "Where am I taking you, Stacy?"

She held his gaze. "I don't want to be alone, Spencer."

He nodded and pulled away from the curb.

CHAPTER
65

Wednesday, April 13, 2005
3:30 a.m.

Stacy sat bolt upright in bed, awakened by the truth. "Oh, my God," she said, bringing a hand to her mouth. "She lied."

"Go back to sleep," Spencer mumbled.

"You don't understand." She shook him. "She lied about everything."

He cracked open his eyes. "Who?"

"Alice."

He frowned. "What are you talking about?"

Her head filled with the memory of the day she had carried Leo's mail to his office. Valerie had asked her to do it; she'd set it on the top of his laptop computer. Her focus had been on the mail itself, on the Gallery124 invitation.

Not on the computer.

No longer. With her mind's eye, she could see it clearly. Titanium case, a distinctive apple-shaped logo at its center.

"Alice told me she found Cassie's computer and knew it was wrong because no one in their family used an Apple. But Leo did. It was on his desk."

"You're certain about this?"

"Yes, positive."

"It'd be really easy to verify."

Stacy struggled to come to grips with what she was thinking. *Could it have been Alice all along?*

"The law books," Stacy said. "The *DSM-IV.* She was studying, covering her ass. Just in case."

He sat up. "You realize what you're suggesting, right? That the teenager was an integral part of the plan."

"I'm not suggesting that at all. I think the plan was hers alone."

She had his full attention now, she saw. All traces of sleep had fled his features. "Alice planned every move, by herself?"

"Yes."

"She brought Troy in."

"Yes."

Stacy shook her head. *It hurt. She didn't want it to be true. Didn't want Alice to be that person.*

He was silent a moment. "Do you really think a sixteen-year-old could have pulled this off?"

"She's not an ordinary teenager. She's a genius. An experienced gamer. I imagine a brilliant strategist."

I'm smarter than both of them. Did he tell you that?

"She made a point of telling me how smart she was. She was very proud of her IQ. Arrogant about it, really."

He rubbed a hand along his jaw. "But why'd she do it, Stacy? The money? We're talking about both her parents, for God's sake."

"The money was secondary. She wanted her freedom. She felt she deserved it. They were holding her back. Overprotective. She said so. They kept her from going to university, insisted on having her home-tutored."

"You overheard her and Kay fighting, saw Kay trying to kill her."

Stacy shook her head. "No, I saw them struggling. Heard Alice's shouted accusations."

"Which confirmed what you already believed."

"Yes." Stacy dragged a hand through her tangled hair. "Kay was most likely trying to figure out what the hell was going on. Trying to calm Alice, bring her to her senses. Why didn't I see it until now?"

"*If* what you're thinking is true."

Stacy met his gaze, determined. "It is."

"You're going to need proof. More than catching her in a lie that's based on a memory you recalled while asleep."

She laughed, the sound tight. Angry. "I'm not going to let her get away with this."

"So, what are you going to do, hero?"

CHAPTER
66

Friday, April 15, 2005
10:30 a.m.

Alice and her aunt were staying in a suite at the Hilton Hotel at the Riverwalk. Stacy had been in contact with the pair, had told the woman she planned to visit, so Grace wasn't surprised when she saw her.

Smiling, the woman swung the door open. "Stacy, how nice of you to come by."

"With one of her favorites." She held up the frozen moccaccino. "Super-size."

"She'll like that," Grace murmured. "She's hardly left the suite. Just for meals and when the maids come." The woman's eyes filled with tears. "It's horrible. She must feel so alone. And so betrayed."

Stacy would describe her emotion more as self-satisfied and elated, but she kept it to herself. For now.

"I hate leaving her," Grace said, "but I'm trying to get all of Leo's things packed up and—"

Her throat closed over the words. Stacy felt pity for the woman: she had lost her only sibling.

And was about to learn that his daughter was the one who had killed him.

"She's having a bad morning," Grace added. "I don't know how to make it better."

Stacy squeezed the woman's hand, fighting the anger that surged through her. It was all one big game to Alice. People, their emotions. Their very lives. One big competition to be won.

The woman went to Alice's bedroom door and tapped on it. "Alice, sweetheart, Stacy Killian is here to see you."

After a moment, the girl emerged from her room. She looked like she had been to hell and back, her face so ravaged Stacy experienced a moment of doubt.

Could she be wrong about this? Could Leo's laptop have been new? Could Alice simply have not known, made a mistake?

No. She wasn't wrong. Alice had orchestrated this, had cold-bloodedly planned her parents' deaths.

Stacy forced a concerned smile. "How are you?"

"Hanging in there."

"I brought you a moccaccino."

"Thanks."

"Alice, honey, I'm going to meet the movers. Will you be okay for an hour or two?"

"I'll stay with her, Grace," Stacy said. "Don't you worry about a thing."

The woman waited for confirmation from Alice, who nodded.

Grace exited and Stacy kept things chatty for several moments, until she felt confident Grace wouldn't unexpectedly return.

Then she faced Alice. "Let's cut the shit, shall we? It's just you and me now."

The teenager's eyes widened. "What are you talking about, Stacy?"

She leaned forward. "*I know, Alice.* It was your plan. You're the one."

She started to deny it; Stacy cut her off. "You're brilliant. They were holding you back. Treating you like a baby. You must have thought 'How dare they?' After all, you were smarter than both of them. Weren't you? Or did you just make that up?"

"Yeah," she said softly, "I'm smarter than they both were. Too smart to be fooled by this."

"By what?"

"Your pathetic attempt to trap me. Toss me your cell phone."

"My cell. But why?" she asked, though Stacy knew she'd used an open cell call to trap the man who'd tried to kill Jane.

"Because I know everything about you, that's why. Everything you've ever done. I do my homework."

Stacy tossed the girl the phone.

She caught the device, looked at it and met Stacy's gaze. "Smart. But not smart enough."

She hit the end button and tossed it back. "Who was on the other end of that open call? Spencer Malone and his chubby partner?"

Stacy kept up the facade. "How did you know?"

"You've used that little trick before. When your partner tried to kill your sister. Like I said, I did my homework."

"Fine by me. It really is just you and me now."

Alice smiled. "You've asked me, now it's my turn. What gave me away?"

"You lied. About your dad's computer. He had an Apple laptop."

She nodded. "I regretted that lie the moment it passed my lips. I wondered if you'd catch it."

"And now I have."

She shrugged. "Big deal. It's not going to do you any good. Wouldn't it have been better to go on thinking you saved the day?"

"Truth is always better than a lie."

Alice laughed, her expression transforming. "Mom was supposed to die that night at Belle Chere. As were you. Your buddy Malone screwed that up."

"Lucky me."

"I tried to get rid of him several times, but he was either too stupid, or too lucky, to back off."

"Get rid of him? How?"

"Anonymous calls to the NOPD. About his involving a civilian in an official investigation."

"Aren't you just the smart little cookie. All brain, no heart or soul. Just like a character from White Rabbit."

She bristled. "I needed my freedom. I deserved it. It was ridiculous the way they tried to control me. I should have controlled them."

"And why's that? They were the adults, you their child."

"But they weren't my equal. I could think rings around both of them."

"So you formulated a plan, carefully piecing it together into a flawless scenario."

"Thank you." She gave a small bow. "You see? I should have been at university three years ago. But *he* wouldn't let me go. And *she* sided with him. She always did, even after they divorced. So they stuck me with these lame tutors."

"Like Clark."

She laughed. "Clark was the first piece of the puzzle. I discovered who he was not long after he was hired."

"How?"

"Searched his room. Found a receipt for a local storage locker. Lifted the key one afternoon and ta-da, the real Clark Dunbar was revealed."

She was resourceful, Stacy'd give her that. Evil but resourceful.

"He'd kept all sorts of stuff from his past. Pictures. Letters. Diplomas and papers. Interesting that he'd been unable to let those things go. I could have."

"No doubt. After all, you were able to murder your parents without so much as a sniffle."

"Except for Mom, I didn't actually kill anybody."

"Troy did."

"The second piece of the plan."

"Where'd you find him?"

"Online. An RPG chat room."

Stacy glanced toward the painting on the far wall, a non-descript landscape. "How'd you get him to join up with you?"

"Easy. Troy liked his women young. And he liked money. A lot."

The girl's words sickened her. She continued. "Troy was lazy and stupid. But useful. He was good at following orders, at keeping his eyes on the prize. He wanted that carrot."

"What'd you promise him?"

"A million bucks."

A million dollars. The cost of all those lives. Enough to entice a man such as Troy to murder.

Alice curled up on the couch, like a satisfied cat. She sipped her coffee drink. "Would you believe Mom let me do *the* background check on Troy? It was all I needed to see. I knew he was perfect."

"When did you get the idea to create a White Rabbit scenario?"

"When I knew who Clark really was. He was the perfect fall guy."

Stacy nodded. "You could plant clues to lead the police to his real identity. Once they uncovered it, they would look no further."

"The way you did," she said, expression smug. "I thought of everything."

"And once your mom and dad were dead, you'd be free."

"And rich. Very, very rich."

"And all those people in between? Their deaths were just a means to an end?"

She shrugged. "Basically. Their deaths served a higher purpose."

"But I came along and mucked it up."

"Don't give yourself too much credit. A kink, that's all. I like thinking on my feet. Keeps me sharp."

Stacy longed to wipe the smug expression from the teenager's face. "And Cassie?" she asked.

"Wrong place, wrong time. I was in Café Noir, she looked over my shoulder and saw the game. Asked me about it. She became a loose end. Sorry."

She didn't sound sorry, not at all. Stacy balled her hands into fists.

"So, you told her you'd hook her up with a Supreme White Rabbit."

"Yes."

"Troy?"

"Yes, again."

"You're not going to get away with this."

"You're too average to outthink me. That's a fact."

"It doesn't bother you that I know the whole truth?"

"Should it?" She sucked more of the frozen beverage through the straw. "Go to the police, they won't believe you. You don't have any proof. No evidence, no case."

"Define *evidence*."

"Please. We both know what evidence is. And how much you'd need to try a case like this one."

"Okay." Stacy smiled. "Don't define *evidence*. How about a word you used earlier. *Kink?* As in the one I put in your plan."

The girl stared at her. For the first time, an emotion other than self-satisfaction passed over her features. "I don't know what you're talking about."

"See that painting?"

Alice glanced at it. "Yeah."

"Like it?"

"Not particularly."

"Too bad. Because you're going to spend the rest of your days thinking about it. Cursing it."

The teenager made a sound of impatience. "And why would that be?"

"Because the police are on the other side of the wall, behind that painting. Because this morning, when you left for breakfast, the NOPD techs installed an audio-surveillance device. They've caught your entire confession on tape."

Her face went slack with surprise and disbelief. Then with a howl of rage, she sprang from the couch and lunged at Stacy. She clawed and kicked. Stacy subdued her with relative ease, got her pinned, arms behind her back.

"You have the right to remain silent—"

The police burst though the door. Stacy continued reciting the Miranda rights, anyway, from memory. "Anything you say can and will be used against you in a court of law.

"You have the right to an attorney. Now and during all future questioning. If you cannot afford an attorney, one will be appointed to you, free of charge. Do you understand these rights as I have recited them to you?"

"Go to hell."

"No," Stacy murmured, "that would be *your* final destination."

Only then did she look up. The entire group, including Spencer, Tony and the techs stood in the doorway.

"Killian," Spencer murmured, "you're not a cop anymore."

She stood. "True. But I'm thinking I need to remedy that."

The two uniforms crossed to Alice, helping her up though she cursed them.

"I see you still have a job?"

He opened his jacket, revealing his shoulder holster. "I live to serve another day."

"And PID?"

"Rapped my knuckles pretty good over the way I handled the case. Asked lots of questions about you. Now we know from whom they got their suspicions."

"Yo, Slick. What now?"

"Take care of the suspect. I'll take Ms. Killian's statement."

Tony chuckled. Spencer held out his hand. "That okay with you, hero?"

She took his hand, lifted her face to his. "Did I tell you you're not nearly as annoying as I first thought?"

"You didn't have to, Killian. I got that."

* * * * *

Please turn the page for an exclusive preview of
COPYCAT
A chilling new thriller from New York Times *Bestselling Author*
ERICA SPINDLER
Available in hardcover June 2006

Rockford, Illinois
Tuesday, March 5, 2001
1:00 a.m.

The girl's hair looked silky. He longed to feel it against his fingers and cursed the latex gloves, the necessity that he wear them. The strands were the color of corn silk. Unusual in a child of ten. Too often, as the years passed, the blond darkened until settling on a murky, dishwater color that only bleach could resuscitate.

He cocked his head, pleased with his choice. She was even more beautiful than the last girl. More perfect.

He bent closer, stroked her hair. Her blue eyes gazed lifelessly up at him. Breathing deeply, he let her sweet, little-girl scent fill his head.

Careful...careful...

Mustn't leave anything for them.

The Other One insisted on perfection. Always pushing him. Demanding more. And more.

Always watching. Every time he looked over his shoulder, the Other One was there.

He felt himself frown and worked to smooth the telltale emotion from his face.

My pretty baby. Most beautiful creation.

Sleeping Angel.

The woman detective, Kitt Lundgren, had coined the name Sleeping Angel Killer. The media had jumped on it.

The name pleased him.

But not the Other One. Nothing, it seemed, pleased him.

Quickly, he finished arranging the scene. Her hair. The nightgown he had chosen just for her, with its pink satin bows. Everything had to be just so.

Perfect.

And now for the finishing touch. He took the tube of pale pink lip gloss from his pocket. Using the wand, he applied a coat of the gloss to the girl's lips. Carefully, smoothing, making certain the color was even.

That done, he smiled at his handiwork.

Good night, my little angel. Sleep tight.

Rockford, Illinois
Tuesday March 7, 2006
8:10 a.m.

The shrill scream of the phone awakened Kitt from a deep, pharmaceutically induced sleep. She fumbled for the phone, nearly dropping it twice before she got it to her ear. "H'lo."

"Kitt. It's Brian. Get your ass up."

She cracked open her eyes. The sunlight streaming through the blinds stung. She shifted her gaze to the clock, saw the time and dragged herself to a sitting position.

She must have killed the alarm.

She glanced at Joe's side of the bed, wondering why he hadn't awakened her, then caught herself. Even after three years, she expected him to be there.

No husband. No child.

All alone now.

Kitt coughed and sat up, working to shake out the cobwebs. "Calling so early, Lieutenant Spillare? Must be something pretty damn earth-shattering."

"The bastard's back. Shattering enough?"

She knew instinctively "the bastard" he referred to— The Sleeping Angel Killer. The case she never solved, though her obsession with it nearly destroyed both her life and career.

"How—"

"A dead little girl. I'm at the scene now."

Her worst nightmare.

After a five-year hiatus, the SAK had killed again.

"Who's working it?"

"Riggio and White."

"Where?"

He gave a west Rockford address, a blue-collar neighborhood that had seen better days.

"Kitt?"

She was already out of the bed, scrambling for clothes. "Yeah?"

"Tread carefully. Riggio's—"

"A little intense."

"Territorial."

"Noted, my friend. And...thanks."

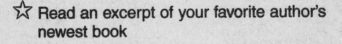

ERICA SPINDLER

32169	SEE JANE DIE	___ $7.50 U.S.	___ $8.99 CAN.
32037	IN SILENCE	___ $6.99 U.S.	___ $8.50 CAN.
66963	CAUSE FOR ALARM	___ $6.50 U.S.	___ $7.99 CAN.
66962	SHOCKING PINK	___ $6.50 U.S.	___ $7.99 CAN.
66961	FORTUNE	___ $6.50 U.S.	___ $7.99 CAN.
66960	ALL FALL DOWN	___ $6.50 U.S.	___ $7.99 CAN.
66794	BONE COLD	___ $6.99 U.S.	___ $8.50 CAN.
66751	FORBIDDEN FRUIT	___ $6.50 U.S.	___ $7.99 CAN.
66683	DEAD RUN	___ $6.99 U.S.	___ $8.50 CAN.

(limited quantities available)

TOTAL AMOUNT	$ _____
POSTAGE & HANDLING	$ _____
($1.00 FOR 1 BOOK, 50¢ for each additional)	
APPLICABLE TAXES*	$ _____
TOTAL PAYABLE	$ _____

(check or money order—please do not send cash)

To order, complete this form and send it, along with a check or money order for the total above, payable to MIRA Books, to: **In the U.S.:** 3010 Walden Avenue, P.O. Box 9077, Buffalo, NY 14269-9077; **In Canada:** P.O. Box 636, Fort Erie, Ontario, L2A 5X3.

Name: _____

Address: _____ City: _____

State/Prov.: _____ Zip/Postal Code: _____

Account Number (if applicable): _____

075 CSAS

*New York residents remit applicable sales taxes.
*Canadian residents remit applicable GST and provincial taxes.

MIRA®

www.MIRABooks.com

MES0506BL